The Lyre Thief

WAR OF THE GODS TRILOGY: BOOK ONE

The Lyre Thief

Jennifer Fallon

TOR

A TOM DOHERTY ASSOCIATES BOOK · NEW YORK

THE LYRE THIEF

Copyright © 2016 by Jennifer Fallon

All rights reserved.

Map by Ellisa Mitchell

A Tor Book
Published by Tom Doherty Associates, LLC
175 Fifth Avenue
New York, NY 10010

www.tor-forge.com

Tor® is a registered trademark of Tom Doherty Associates, LLC.

The Library of Congress Cataloging-in-Publication Data
is available upon request.

ISBN 978-0-7653-8079-1 (hardcover)
ISBN 978-1-4668-7556-2 (e-book)

Our books may be purchased in bulk for promotional, educational, or business use. Please contact your local bookseller or the Macmillan Corporate and Premium Sales Department at 1-800-221-7945, extension 5442, or by e-mail at MacmillanSpecialMarkets@macmillan.com.

First Edition: March 2016

Printed in the United States of America

0 9 8 7 6 5 4 3 2 1

For the Champions and those I trust . . .

Acknowledgments

I'd like to thank Claire Eddy from Tor and Rochelle Fernandez from HarperCollins Australia for believing in this series enough to allow it to continue. I would also like to thank my many fans for the thousands of e-mails I have received over the years, begging me to continue the story of the characters who populate Medalon, Hythria, and Fardohnya.

I would also like to thank my beta readers, who offered such valuable advice and epic proofreading.

Most of all, I would like to thank my family, TJ (plot-hole finder extraordinaire!), Dace, and David, for their unwavering support and belief. Without their support, this series would have remained in my head. They have inspired me to bring these people back to life and find new characters to love and follow in this world.

I hope you enjoy them as much as I do.

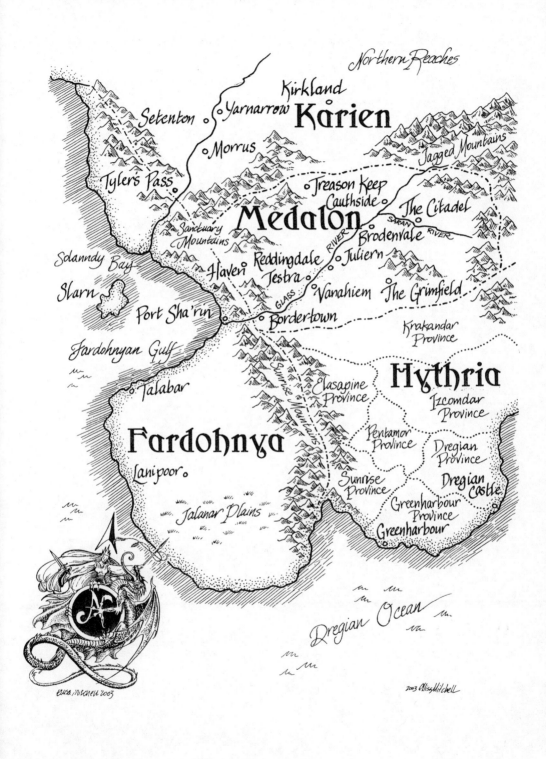

The Lyre Thief

Prologue

WERE IT NOT for the voices in his head, Mica would have been incredibly lonely.

They kept him entertained. They often kept him company.

And lately, they'd been urging him to do something more than wander the halls of the God of Music's palace, humming to himself, occasionally breaking into song, while contemplating the relative merits of suicide as opposed to a lifetime of aching loneliness and boredom.

He didn't see Gimlorie much. The God of Music had little interest in his captive. He cared for Mica insofar as the young man had never starved all the time he had been a prisoner here, never wanted for sustenance, shelter, or material comfort, but the god felt no need to interact with his charge.

Mica's only companions since he was ten years old were the demons who owed their allegiance to the Lord of Song. And the voices.

Always, the voices.

Mica blinked and looked down. Below the ledge of the tall window where he balanced, bracing against the crisp breeze that blew around the tower, was a drop so perilous the ground was hidden beneath a layer of fog, making it seem as if Gimlorie's palace were built on a cloud.

It wasn't—Mica had been outside several times and knew the ground beneath the tower was firm—but it looked that way from up here.

Mica couldn't remember how he came to be standing on this ledge, looking down.

Or why.

It's your only escape.

Ah, that was why. This particular voice had been talking to him a lot lately, reminding him with seductive frequency that he was trapped here. Reminding him that his life stretched before him endlessly; he was a lost soul wandering these hollow, empty halls, singing a song nobody but the demons would ever hear.

The voice was compelling. And it was right.

He was trapped here.

Maybe death is my only escape.

Mica wondered for a moment why nobody had ever come for him. He'd had family. A brother, he recalled. Where was he? Where was the heroic rescue attempt?

Why had nobody in the real world noticed he was missing?

He remembered snatches of his life before coming here, but nothing much. Just a hollow emptiness inside in the place where he thought love and family should dwell. Mica knew of love. He'd heard plenty of songs about it here and occasionally Kalianah came to visit. When the Goddess of Love spoke of love, she seemed sad for him. But she had never intervened.

He was a prisoner of Gimlorie, the God of Music, and that was enough for Kalianah.

Perhaps I should jump, this time. Perhaps this really is the only way I'll ever escape this place.

Are you sure it's the only way to escape?

The voice was taunting him, tantalizing him with possibilities.

Do you know of another?

The voice didn't answer straight away. The chill breeze tugged at Mica's ragged shirt, one he'd long outgrown. He looked down again. All he had to do was step off the ledge and his loneliness would be over. He lifted his foot. One small step . . .

What if I told you there was a way out of here? Even better, a way to even the score with those who trapped you here.

Mica pulled his foot back, skeptical but intrigued. He thought the voice was lying, but if he wasn't . . .

I cannot escape this place. Gimlorie is too vigilant. And the demon child sent me here.

The voice didn't seem particularly concerned. *Gimlorie can be . . . rendered ineffectual. And the demon child should be punished for what she did to you. You were a child and she was the one who made you Gimlorie's puppet in the first place.*

He shook his head. Although the voice's words tugged at a long hidden memory, it didn't seem to understand.

She is the demon child. R'shiel has all the power of the gods at her disposal. I am one small boy with nothing more than a magical song.

That song turned back an army once, the voice reminded him. *And you are no longer a small boy.*

One step, and it wouldn't matter. One step and he would fall silently through the clouds to his death on the rocks below the tower.

Jump, then, the voice said, full of contempt.

The sudden change of tone surprised Mica.

Now you want *me to kill myself?*

Every day you come up here, stand on that ledge, and consider ending it all. So do it. Die. Or do something to change your life.

Mica looked down. The voice was right. Every day he came up here and considered jumping off. And every day he discovered he lacked the courage.

Die. Or do something to change your life.

It seemed such a simple choice. He closed his eyes for a moment and let the chill wind caress his face, wishing the answer would come to him on the breeze.

Die. Or do something to change your life.

Perhaps that was the answer. *Vengeance will taste good*, he thought. *As clean and sharp as the cold wind swirling around the tower.*

Filled with an unfamiliar sense of purpose, Mica opened his eyes and stepped back off the ledge. He turned his back to the window and looked around the empty tower room.

It certainly couldn't be any worse than this place.

"Very well, then," he said aloud to the voice inside his head. "Talk to me about vengeance."

You will find it a salve for your wounded soul.

"I won't find it at all unless I can get out of this place," Mica informed the voice, impatient, now, to get on with it. This was the first decision he'd made in years that gave him any sense of control over his own destiny. "So let's start with how you think we can render the God of Music ineffectual."

Mica was ready and he had a long list of scores to settle.

Well, the voice told him. *First, there is something you have to steal . . .*

Part One

Chapter

1

Naveen Raveve, chamberlain to King Hablet of Fardohnya, examined the marriage proposal from Frederak Branador, Lord of Highcastle, who controlled one of only two navigable passes between Hythria and Fardohnya, and then looked up to meet the gaze of his visitor, who was finding his silence unsettling.

"Well?" she asked. "Will you do it?"

Naveen bit back a smile. He was a slave, after all, and yet here he was, with a princess of the realm standing before him, begging him for a favor.

Not just begging. He suspected she was willing to pay handsomely for it.

The women of the royal harem had so much to learn about how different he was from his predecessor.

"You ask this favor as if you expect to be able to purchase it, your highness. I am not Lecter Turon. I am not for sale."

"Lecter made himself a wealthy man being for sale."

"He used coin to compensate for the fact he wasn't a full man, your highness. That is quite a different thing." The old eunuch used to sweat like a pig, too, something Naveen was much better at controlling. The humidity in Talabar was dire at this time of year, and Lecter's rich robes—while impressive—just made the problem worse. Naveen had no need to dress in brocade to impress others. He was tall and handsome and a *loronged court'esa*. He had years of specialized training behind him. He had survived being poisoned with the foul sterilizer, *loronge*, and survived more than a decade as a harem *court'esa*. He had presence and knew how to use it to his advantage. He'd entertained half the women in the Fardohnyan royal harem before managing to convince Lecter his talents lay elsewhere.

The old fool wouldn't have taken him on as his protégé, Naveen supposed, if the old eunuch had known the first thing his apprentice would do, once Lecter considered him trained, was kill him and take his place as the king's most trusted aide.

"Even if I were prepared to do this for you, my lady, what you ask will be difficult to arrange." He leaned back in his seat, savoring her discomfort. He'd never lain with Sophany, something that left him at a disadvantage. He knew the quirks and peculiarities of many of the royal wives, but not this one. She didn't know that, though. "Your daughter is neither the only nor the most worthy contender."

"Who else is my husband considering?"

Princess Sophany was trying too hard to sound commanding, but there was an edge of desperation to her words that intrigued Naveen. Sophany of Lanipoor was usually much more circumspect. In fact, she'd gone out of her way to keep her head down in all the years Naveen had been in the king's harem. Carrying the double stain of giving him yet another daughter, and being the younger half-sister of Hablet's first wife, who'd been beheaded for attempting to murder a rival, she'd done all she could not to draw attention to herself for more than twenty years.

And yet here she was, willing to sell her soul for a boon that would surely bring her to the king's attention.

There was a mystery here. Naveen knew it would niggle at him until he solved it.

"I am not at liberty to say, your highness. But you can be sure there are several other wives in the harem just as anxious as you to see their daughters elevated." And then he added with a hint of malice: "*Younger* daughters."

"My daughter is barely twenty-one."

"That is quite old in some circles."

"Has this Hythrun warlord demanded a child bride to seal the deal?"

Naveen shook his head. "He has requested a royal bride of childbearing age. And the king is determined to see he is accommodated. Highcastle is strategically the second most important place on the border, and once this deal is struck it could well become the most important. He will not risk offending Lord Branador by offering him anything less than the best. At twenty-one, her serene highness barely qualifies as being of childbearing age."

"That is ludicrous, Naveen, and you know it. Adrina married at twenty-eight. She's given Damin Wolfblade four healthy children."

"And incurred the king's eternal suspicion and enmity in the process," he reminded her. "Is that what you want for *your* daughter, your highness?"

Sophany shook her head. "Any suspicion or enmity Hablet holds toward his eldest daughter is a direct result of her running away from the husband he chose for her and marrying the Hythrun high prince without his permission. It has nothing to do with any children she's produced since then."

Sophany was desperate, but she wasn't stupid. Another reason to be suspicious. She was too clever to take a risk like this for no good reason.

"Lord Frederak is eighty-one years old, and he doesn't carry his age well. How does your barely twenty-one-year-old daughter feel about being given to a scabby old man? And a foreign one at that?"

"Probably the same way I felt when I was given to King Hablet at seventeen and he was already over forty. I was not consulted about my feelings on the matter then. I don't expect my daughter to be treated any differently now."

Ah, Naveen thought. *She hates the king.* He wasn't surprised. Hablet would be hard pressed to find a single wife in his vast harem who actually loved him. Still, her resentment was not usually so palpable. And it didn't explain why she was so anxious to remove her daughter from the harem.

"I will consider your request, your highness," he said, deciding he needed time to investigate this. It was puzzling. It reeked of something going on that he knew nothing about. Lecter Turon had kept his position at the king's side all these years by knowing everything that was going on in the harem. Naveen would only survive his new position if he did the same.

He needed time to look her daughter over, too. He remembered little about the girl, other than she was pretty—nothing special there. All of Hablet's wives were stunning beauties, so it was no surprise his scores of offspring were universally attractive. There was some nonsense a few years ago, he recalled, involving the child. It was hard to recall the details. He'd been working in the harem as a *court'esa* back then and had his own problems with Hablet's wives and older daughters to worry about. Still, he needed to find out what he could about the girl from his harem spies. And he needed to find out why Sophany was so anxious to foist her daughter onto someone as unpleasant as Lord Branador of Highcastle.

"What do you want, Naveen?"

"Excuse me?"

"What is your currency? What bribe do I have to offer you? What is your price to ensure my daughter is the next baroness of Highcastle?"

Naveen was rather taken aback by her bluntness. "The decision is the king's, your highness, not mine."

"Hablet doesn't belch without consulting his chamberlain first," she said. "He never did with Lecter Turon when he held the post and I don't imagine you're any different. If I know my husband, he will hand over whichever of his daughters you recommend, and probably not even ask the reason. I want your recommendation to be my daughter, and I am far more desperate than any other mother in the harem. So let us not play games, Naveen. Tell me your price."

"Tell me your reason."

Sophany didn't hesitate, which meant she was telling the truth or had practiced her story enough to conceal her lie. "I don't want my daughter in the harem when Alaric takes the throne."

"Alaric is not even twelve years old, your highness, and the king is alive and well."

"Alaric is a spoiled and indulged little monster and Hablet is over seventy. I know what happens when a new king takes the throne in Fardohnya, Naveen, and I don't intend that fate to be my daughter's." She stared him down defiantly, and then added, "I would not be surprised if you have not considered your own fate, should our beloved king join the gods before you have ingratiated yourself with his heir."

For the first time since Sophany requested this meeting, Naveen felt he might be in danger of losing control. "I don't know what you're talking about."

"Really? You were a slave in this harem not so long ago, Naveen, waiting on the whim of every woman there. You know things about many of them they would prefer you didn't, and they mightily resent the way you managed to get yourself promoted out of the harem and into a position of such trust at the king's right hand. Every wife and daughter in the harem with a grudge against you is already whispering in Alaric's ear about how the first thing he should do when his father dies is get rid of you."

Naveen truly hadn't thought about it, but now that he did, the scenario was frighteningly plausible. He'd spent the past twenty years playing with the wives of his king, often for his own entertainment rather than theirs. The idea that rather than retaliate directly the women he had been toying with were poisoning the mind of the king's only son to get their revenge was something he had never contemplated. Worse, Alaric would not leave the harem and the care of his mother, Sybill of Tarkent, until he was fourteen years old. That was still years away. More than enough time to seal his fate.

And the crown prince *was* a spoiled little monster. Right now, one of his father's most trusted generals was languishing in a cell, being tortured on a daily basis, because he'd had the temerity to scold the heir to the throne about not keeping his heels down as he rode. That wasn't the official reason the general was arrested, of course. Alaric had concocted some ridiculous story about overhearing the man plotting against the king, but everyone knew the true reason Meyrick Kabar currently resided in a dungeon was because he would tolerate no nonsense from the young crown prince of Fardohnya.

What will he do, Naveen wondered, *if the little horror ever decides he doesn't like me?*

"What are you offering?" he inquired, feigning disinterest.

"A safe haven," Sophany said, sounding much more certain of herself now she had managed to rattle him a little. "I can arrange my brother, Liance, the Prince of Lanipoor, to provide an estate where you can retire after the king dies. Somewhere safe in our province. And I can arrange for you to get there in one piece. *Before* Alaric decides to put you to the sword along with the rest of the harem."

Naveen didn't answer immediately, although he should have. He should have scoffed at her offer and sent her packing, lest he betray how much her prediction of his fate once Hablet died had affected him.

"Well?"

"I will give the matter my serious consideration, your highness."

"Then I will return to the harem," Sophany said, "where I shall approach my sister-wife, Princess Sybill, the mother of our heir, and volunteer to aid in the care of our most precious Prince Alaric, only son to our beloved husband. It will be an honor to be in a position to influence his . . . opinions."

If threats were a substance that could be bottled and sold, Naveen could have gotten rich just off what was dripping from Sophany's words. He didn't resent her for it. Naveen admired a worthy adversary, particularly one who might be in a position to save his life someday.

How many more politically savvy vipers like Sophany are there, lurking unseen and unsuspected in Hablet's harem?

"The king will announce his decision at the banquet in honor of our Hythrun guest tomorrow evening, your highness."

"I will expect to be invited," she said. "Along with my daughter."

"I'll do what I can," he promised. "For both of us."

She studied him for a moment, as if trying to determine his sincerity, and then she nodded. "Very well. I will await your . . . I mean, my *king's* decision, before I write my brother about any arrangements he may need to make for your future."

He rose and treated her to a respectful bow. "Good morning, your highness."

Sophany didn't respond. She simply turned on her heel and strode toward the door, leaving Naveen watching after her, wondering if she would return to the harem to praise him to the future king of Fardohnya or condemn him to an unfair and undoubtedly painful death.

Probably the latter. She was right about that much. Alaric was a spoiled little monster.

Naveen sighed and picked up his quill. There really wasn't any decision to make. Princess Lani had offered him gold to promote her daughter, but money didn't interest him. He'd spent a lifetime as a *court'esa*, so no offer of women or any other sexual perversion could entice him, as Princess Palina had found out when she suggested he put forward her daughter.

No, none of the offers he'd received, until Sophany walked into his office, held any real attraction for him.

Alarmingly, she had known his currency. That bothered him almost as much as her reasons for doing this. Her story about protecting her daughter from the bloodbath that would inevitably follow Hablet's death was reasonable enough, but there had to be something more.

He would not rest until he discovered what it was.

Then, when the time came and Sophany betrayed him—as he was sure she was planning to do—he would have his own currency to use against her.

Naveen picked up his pen, dipped the quill into the ink pot, tapped it on the side to shed the excess drops, and then carefully wrote the name *Her Serene Highness, Rakaia of Fardohnya*, into the blank space reserved for the name of the daughter Hablet was trading for unfettered access to the mountain pass at Highcastle.

He sighed again when he realized that not only did he have to sort out a bride for Lord Branador, but, thanks to Alaric's tantrum, he needed to find a new general somewhere, too. He'd have to put some feelers out. There were plenty of men who had the coin to buy the position. After years of dealing with Lecter Turon, word had got about that everything the king owned was for sale, one way or another.

It was time Fardohnya learned that Naveen Raveve was in charge now. Things were going to change.

2

PEOPLE WOULD NOT think the life of an assassin so exciting, Kiam Miar thought as he shifted his weight from one foot to another to ease the stiffness, if they realized how much of the job involved sitting around, bored witless, waiting, chewing on a strip of venison jerky to stop a betraying stomach rumble from giving his presence away.

He glanced up at the moon, hoping it would slip behind the clouds again before he had to move. Up here on the Burglars' Bypass, as the roofs of Greenharbour were known, it paid to stay in the shadows. There was a truce of sorts between the assassins and the thieves of the city, but they didn't like the idea of assassins knowing their business, any more than the assassins liked the idea of thieves knowing theirs.

Kiam's target was late. His instructions regarding this kill were explicit and detailed, and came—he suspected—from the target's long-suffering wife. That was another sad fact those who romanticized the life of an assassin would be horrified to learn: by far the majority of clients who hired the guild were disgruntled wives who had come to realize life as a widow in Hythria was far more comfortable than life as a divorcée.

This errant and soon-to-be-dead husband was a tailor named Shilton Rik. He would be at the Fullers' Rest, as usual, by midnight, his informant had assured him, where he would drink himself into some courage before amusing himself with the house entertainment, which was, Kiam knew, a diverse selection of amateur *court'esa*. Far from the accomplished professionals a man like Shilton Rik could probably afford, these amateurs were usually poor country girls and boys, scratching to make a living in a large hungry city. They arrived from the provinces looking for work every spring, full of expectation and hope, expecting Greenharbour's fabled streets to be paved with gold.

A few months later, by the time they found their way to places like the Fullers' Rest, those hopes and dreams were long turned to dust and they were trading their bodies for a roof over their heads and enough sustenance to keep themselves alive.

A cloud drifted across the face of the moon, plunging Kiam into darkness once more. Down in the street a couple of drunks staggered through a puddle left over from an earlier rainstorm. The Fullers' Rest was doing a roaring trade, all the windows but the one Kiam was watching ablaze with warm yellow light. That window lighting up was his signal. But it should have happened before now. His informant—who Kiam was quite certain was the man's wife—seemed to know his routine intimately. It made sense that Shilton's wife had arranged this hit. Even with the reforms the High Prince had made this past decade, divorce still favored a man in Hythria, particularly when there were children involved. And being a widow was still more socially acceptable than being a spurned wife.

Rik was a tailor with a small but profitable business he ran with his wife in one of the better parts of the city. They weren't rich, but they were comfortable enough for Shilton to afford whores and Madam Rik to afford an assassin. He couldn't imagine who else would want the man dead. It was unlikely the tailoring business was so cutthroat that a competitor would use the Assassins' Guild to have him removed, and a disgruntled customer would surely just take his business elsewhere.

Not that it mattered. Kiam was not privy to the name of his employer. No assassin was ever told who had contracted them for a kill.

And he didn't have time to dwell on the identity of his employer in any case. In the upstairs window across the street, the room was slowly filling with warm yellow light, as someone carrying a lamp moved farther into the room.

Kiam rose to his feet. Hours ago, he'd established the best route across the rooftops to the Fullers' Rest, and the easiest way to access the room where his unsuspecting victim was getting ready to have his way with some poor, disillusioned country girl. There was a narrow balcony outside the room—or at least a poor man's version of one. The balcony—and the three others like it facing the street—had a wrought-iron balustrade and a landing barely wide enough to stand on. But they gave the building an air of grandeur it truly didn't deserve—not to mention a convenient place for an assassin to land when he lowered himself down from the roof.

It took him more than a quarter of an hour to work his way silently across to the other side of the street. It narrowed to a slender laneway closer to the wharves, making it a simple jump across the shingled rooftops from one side of the street to the other. Shouldering his knotted rope and grappling hook, Kiam ran noiselessly along the tiles, jumped across to the roof of the Fullers' Rest, and then counted the steps he'd estimated would place him directly above the small balcony opening into the room where Shilton Rik was enjoying his last few moments of happiness.

Once the rope was secured around the chimney, he lowered himself down, hand over hand, onto the balcony. The lock on the diamond-paned glass doors was the decorative type designed to keep only honest people out. It took only seconds before Kiam heard the faint snick as it clicked open. He pushed the door open in time to find a middle-aged, portly, and stark naked man push a terrified girl onto her back on a large four-poster bed.

The girl saw him. Her eyes widened in terror at the sight of the black-hooded apparition coming through the window.

That's torn it, Kiam thought.

He wasn't here to fight Shilton Rik to the death. This was supposed to be a quiet assassination. He would have to move fast. Before the girl warned her client of his approach.

Pulling out his long dagger with its raven-etched blade from his belt, he braced for a struggle as he crossed the room in three strides, mentally kicking himself for not taking measures to silence the girl first, or at least waiting until Rik was done with her before he burst in here like a rank amateur.

But the girl did nothing to alert her customer that his death was approaching. She lay there as he pushed himself on top of her, head turned to the side, and watched Kiam as the man tore at her clothes. She said nothing, did nothing, to warn him. Her face was etched with terror and disgust, and yet she did nothing to stop what was about to happen.

Even as Kiam grabbed Shilton Rik from behind, pulled back his head and sliced his throat open in a spray of warm blood, the girl didn't make a sound. No scream. Not even a whimper.

Just that wide-eyed look of terror and disgust.

Kiam lowered Rik to the floor as the last breath gurgled out of him. Pulling off the glove of his right hand, he dipped his Assassins' ring into the blood puddling on the threadbare rug and then pressed it into Shilton Rik's forehead, leaving the impression of a bloody raven behind. With that taken care of, he stood up and turned to look at the witness he now had to deal with.

"Are you going to kill me, too?" she asked in a hoarse whisper. Covered in blood and not much else, she had scrabbled back to the far corner of the bed, pulling her knees up to make herself as small a target as possible.

Kiam took a step closer to look at her. He'd thought her a young woman when he came through the window, but on closer inspection, she didn't appear to be much more than a child. She was caramel-skinned, making her part-Denikan or perhaps from somewhere like the Trinity Isles where the various races of this world had interbred so much that they had almost become a different race in their own right. The girl certainly wasn't from around these parts.

"Gods, how old are you?"

"Twelve."

He shook his head in wonder. It wasn't his place to judge. Or to remedy the many ills in this world. "Well, lucky for you the person who wanted this man dead couldn't afford to make it look like an accident. You just tell them an assassin came through the window." Kiam pointed to the bloody raven on Shilton Rik's forehead. "I've already told them the same thing."

She said nothing, still curled in a ball of terror in the corner of the bed. Kiam turned for the window as someone out in the hall bashed impatiently on the door. "Half-hour's nearly up, Rik! It's another ten rivets if you plan to stay longer."

Kiam didn't have time to hang about. The Assassins' Guild was tolerated as a necessary evil in Greenharbour, but being caught red-handed was an entirely different matter.

"Please . . . take me with you."

He turned to find the girl standing behind him, dressed in her torn and blood-soaked shift. Her eyes were still terrified, but she wore a determined look.

"I can't take you with me."

"If you leave me here, I'll die."

"You don't know me, girl. For all you know, I'd take you with me, rape you, and kill you as soon as we're outside."

She shook her head. "Assassins don't kill innocent bystanders," she said. "And you would have killed me already if you were going to."

"Not killing you out of hand does not equate to being willing to let you run away with me," he told her, stepping onto the balcony. This discussion had gone on long enough. He wasn't responsible for this child.

"My name is Tritinka Berin," she told him, managing a remarkable amount of dignity, given the state she was in. "I arrived in Greenharbour two days ago on my brother's ship, the *Sarchlo*."

"Well, I'm sorry you ran away and wound up here, but it's not my—"

"I didn't run away. I was shopping in the markets. Someone threw a hood over my head and dragged me here against my will to punish my brother. They told me if I didn't want to earn my keep entertaining the guests, they'd kill me."

"Don't make me come in there!" the innkeeper yelled, bashing on the door again with his fist. "You want more time, you pay more money."

Tritinka's dark eyes filled with tears. "If you won't help me, sir, will you at least get a message to my brother? He'll pay you, if that's what you're worried about. But you'll have to find him tonight," she said, brushing away her tears. "The *Sarchlo* sails on tomorrow's tide."

Kiam cursed, and grabbed her by the wrist. He pulled her toward the tiny balcony as he tried not to count how many types of a fool he was for buying into this. The door handle began to turn. He lifted her slight frame bodily onto the roof and then swung himself up after her, pulling the rope up in the nick of time. Below them the innkeeper bellowed in horror when he realized his customer was lying on the floor with his throat slit and there was no sign of the girl he had paid to deflower.

Pushing Tritinka flat against the roof, he held her there as the innkeeper ran out onto the balcony, looking for the girl or his customer's killer, obviously convinced they were one and the same. Kiam lay against the warm tiles of the roof waiting with his arm around Tritinka, still as a cat, for the man to retreat inside. He could feel her trembling, but she didn't make a sound.

Once he was satisfied the innkeep was no longer on the balcony, he lifted his arm from the child, placing his finger on his lips to warn her to silence. She nodded, let him help her up, and then followed him carefully up the steep slope to the narrow ridge capping at the peak of the roof. The building below was alive with shouts and people running back and forth. Someone was yelling to summon the City Watch. Kiam knew they only had moments before somebody inside the inn ran into the street and thought to look up. He glanced up at the sky. The moon still lingered behind the clouds, but the wind had picked up and their cover was starting to break up.

Still holding Tritinka by the hand, he motioned her to stay down, as much to lower her center of gravity as to remain unseen, and ran along the ridge cap with her small hand tightly gripping his until they reached the end of the building. He stepped across the small gap to the chandler's shop next door. Barely hesitating, Tritinka jumped across after him and followed him trustingly to the end of the next building.

The sounds of chaos and alarm at the inn faded with the distance. Another three rooftops and Kiam unfurled the rope, hooking it around the chimney, and then turned to tie the other end around the girl. She held her arms out to give him room. Kiam could smell the blood on her as he secured the rope under her armpits, although in the darkness he could only make out a dark stain on what was left of her shift. He would need to find her something else to wear before walking her through the streets of Greenharbour. He'd certainly never get near the *Sarchlo* and Tritinka's brother with her covered in all that blood. At least, he was certain he knew what he would do in her brother's place if he spied a strange man roaming the docks with his missing sister looking like that.

Once they were down at street level, Kiam retrieved the rope and took Tritinka by the hand, a little daunted by the trust she was showing him by letting him take her anywhere. He led her behind the row of narrow terrace houses, clinging to the shadows as they walked. He glanced over the fences for a washing line that might provide something more respectable—and less bloody—for the child to wear. Most of the lines were empty, but there was one, almost at the end of the lane, that was still laden with washing. It looked as if it might have been there for a few days, which meant it was probably hung out by a slovenly bachelor rather than a house-proud wife, liable to chase them down if she caught them stealing anything.

"Stay here," he whispered as he reached over the gate to unlatch it.

"Is this your house?"

He smiled. "No. I'm going to find you something else to wear."

"Will you take me home then?"

He supposed she meant the boat she'd arrived on. Kiam nodded. "Yes. Now stay down. I'll only be a minute."

The latch proved to be tied up with twine, making it impossible to open it from the other side. He gave up after a couple of futile attempts and grabbed the gate with both hands. Lifting himself up, he balanced on the top for a moment before dropping into the yard—straight into the path of a large, reddish brown dog about the size of a small pony with a low, threatening growl coming from his throat.

Staying crouched and low, Kiam immediately lowered his eyes and slowly turned his back to the beast, figuring the quickest way to become dinner was to challenge the brute. The massive dog continued to growl but didn't attack. They stayed like that for an interminable length of time—Kiam not moving and the dog growling his warning. After a time, when Kiam didn't react to the threat, or, indeed, make a move to run away, he felt a hot nose nudge against his hand. He let the dog push his palm for a moment, before he reacted, gently scratching the beast under its chin. With his other hand, he reached into his pocket and withdrew the strip of jerky he'd been chewing on while he waited on the roof opposite the inn.

He turned slightly and offered the dog the jerky. The beast snatched at it, but he jerked it out of reach before he lost a few fingers. "Ah! Gently, my friend, or not at all."

Although he was speaking at little more than a whisper, the dog accepted his authority and sat down, looking at him expectantly. This time, when Kiam offered him the jerky, he took it from Kiam's hand with much more decorum and then gobbled it down like he hadn't seen food for a month.

Satisfied he was no longer on the menu, Kiam rose to his feet and headed for the clothesline. The small yard reeked of dog shit. He had to treat carefully to reach the line, where he pulled off a gray shirt and a pair of linen trousers. As he turned to leave, the moon peeked out from behind the clouds, revealing the filthy squalor of the yard. The dog was bone thin, tied to a stake by the wall of the house. There was an empty clay water dish on the stoop leading to the back door, and a grimy scrap of rag by the wall that apparently served as the dog's bed. It looked as if nobody had been in the yard for days, but the dog was too thin to be suffering only a few days of neglect.

Kiam squatted down again, and the dog came straight to him, looking at him with hopeful eyes. "When was the last time anybody checked on you?"

The dog licked his face in reply and sat down.

"I have to go," he explained, wondering why he was explaining anything to a dog.

The beast reached up and placed a saucer-sized paw on Kiam's knee.

He glanced around, wondering if the dog would simply be left to starve or, worse, die of dehydration. It wasn't his problem, but no creature deserved to be treated like this. He patted the massive head, rose to his feet, and pulled out the wickedly sharp blade he'd used to slit Shilton Rik's throat.

"I am a sentimental idiot," he announced softly to the night, and then reached down and cut the rope securing the dog to the wall. He turned and cut the twine holding the latch shut and pulled open the gate in a startlingly loud screech of hinges. The dog was out through the gap before Kiam could warn Tritinka, but the beast wasn't interested in the girl. He charged down the lane and stopped at the first puddle he found, lapping at it thirstily.

"Did you find something?"

Kiam handed her the clothes and turned to watch the dog guzzling from the puddle. Who knew how long it had been since the poor thing had been offered water. Once he'd drunk his fill, the dog wandered down the lane, sniffing at every interesting smell he encountered, which seemed to be every few feet. Kiam supposed someone would find him and take him in. Even if they didn't and the dog ended up a stray roaming the city streets, the brute was still better off than locked in that squalid yard, tormented by thirst as he slowly starved to death.

"I'm ready."

He turned to find Tritinka had changed into the too-large shirt. She hadn't bothered with the trousers; the shirt reached almost to her ankles.

"Let's get you to the docks, then."

"What about the dog?"

"He'll find his own way."

The child smiled, her teeth white against her caramel skin. "I think he's chosen his way."

Kiam turned to find the dog had returned and was sitting behind him, as if waiting for them. "Shoo!"

The dog didn't move. He just looked up at Kiam with trusting liquid brown eyes. Kiam turned back to Tritinka. "Don't worry about him. He'll be off the first time he sees a cat. Let's get you home, eh?"

Tritinka placed her hand in Kiam's and smiled up at him. "You are a good person, Master Assassin. My brother won't forget this kindness."

Kiam turned in the direction of the docks, her small hand in his, muttering to himself as they headed back down the moonlit lane, "Actually, I'd rather he did forget. In fact, it might be better for everyone concerned if he forgets all about my kindness the moment he sails out of Greenharbour."

3

"My mother is up to something, Chari."

Rakaia had her arms folded over her horse's back while she talked. When she got no immediate reaction to her news, she glanced over her shoulder to make sure nobody else in the stables could overhear them before turning back to her half-sister, adding, "She went to see Naveen Raveve this morning."

Charisee kept up her long strokes on Snow Blaze's withers with the currycomb and said nothing.

"What do you suppose she's up to?"

"I have no idea."

"Aren't you curious?"

"Curiosity in this place gets you disappeared," Charisee said without looking up. "If you had any brains you'd shut up about it, too."

Sometimes, Rakaia mused, Charisee forgot who was the princess and who was the slave in this relationship. "If you had any brains you'd shut up about it, *your highness.*"

Charisee looked up. She wasn't smiling. "I'm already grooming your horse for you, *your highness*. Don't push it."

"You're mad at me."

"What gave it away?"

"Why are you mad at me?"

"Because you're a fool and you're going to get us both in trouble if you don't keep that big mouth of yours shut."

Before Rakaia could scold Charisee for her rudeness—or her tactless honesty—she heard footsteps approaching. Firm, booted footsteps. It was probably one of the eunuch grooms who served the harem stables. She waited until they passed the stall and faded into the distance before she turned back to Charisee.

"What are you talking about?"

"What am I—Gods, Rakaia! Where have you been this past month?

Father is trading one of his legitimate daughters for unfettered access to Highcastle."

"So?"

"So . . . who do you think he's considering?"

"Not me. I'm way too old."

"You *hope* you're way too old, you mean."

A chill gripped Rakaia despite Talabar's notoriously hot and humid spring. "Do you think that's why mother went to see Naveen? To stop my name being put forward?"

"Can you think of another reason? I've heard stories about Frederak Branador. They say he's old and diseased and a lecher. His last wife died of syphilis, they say. And she caught it from him."

"How do you know that?"

"Slaves talk."

"Slaves gossip, you mean."

"Either way, he's looking for a new wife and your father has far too many daughters to choose from."

"Then I have nothing to worry about," she said. "You missed a spot."

"Charisee shouldn't be grooming your horse at all, Rakaia. You should be doing it yourself."

She spun around in alarm to find her mother standing at the entrance to the stall. The princess was dressed far too formally for the stables. Her skirt was a diaphanous cloud of blue silk, her jeweled bodice displaying her ample bosom and her surprisingly well-toned midriff. Her soft leather slippers were encrusted in crystals and were the reason she'd been able to sneak up on the girls without them hearing her approach. It was the sort of outfit one wore for a special occasion. It was striking and more than a little seductive—something completely wasted on a man like Naveen Raveve.

"Is that what you wore to visit a *slave*?" Rakaia hated Naveen and the power he held over them all, even more than she'd hated his predecessor, Lecter Turon. He had always been a snake. Naveen had pretended to be their friend. It annoyed her to see her mother pandering to him, even if it was on her behalf.

"Charisee, please go back to the palace and ensure your mistress's lavender gown is clean and ready to be worn tomorrow at dinner."

Charisee handed Rakaia the currycomb over Snow Blaze's back with a serves-you-right sort of look, and then ducked under his head to stand beside her. Her base-born half-sister curtsied to Princess Sophany. "Will that be all, your highness?"

"For now, dear," Sophany said. "Run along. I wish to talk to my daughter in private."

Charisee curtsied again and hurried off, leaving Rakaia alone in the stall with her mother.

"I don't know why you sent her away, Mama. You know I'm going to tell her everything we talk about later."

"Not this time," Sophany said, straining to listen. Once Charisee's footsteps had faded to nothing, she pointed to the comb. "The horse can wait for his rubdown. Let's walk so we can't be overheard."

Rakaia had lived in the king's harem all her life and knew well the only place one could guarantee a private conversation was walking along the many graveled paths that crisscrossed the harem gardens. Curious, but unworried, she placed the comb on the ledge and followed her mother out into the corridor between the stalls, making sure she secured the door behind her as they left. Neither of them said a word until Snow Blaze and the stables were well behind them.

Once she judged it safe, Sophany slipped her arm through Rakaia's and smiled at her as they walked. "No matter what I tell you, darling, I want you to smile and nod and laugh like a giddy girl as if we are sharing a bit of idle gossip."

Rakaia smiled. Her mother was being quite melodramatic. "You're worried someone is watching us?"

"I am certain of it. Even if they weren't watching us before today, after my visit to Naveen this morning, you can be certain his spies are every-where now."

Rakaia glanced up at the high wall surrounding the harem, patrolled by her father's guards, and then around the riotously fabulous gardens. Full of nooks and crannies and flowers of every imaginable color and type, the spring air was heavy with their perfume and the buzzing of frantic bees, quite drunk on the endless bounty. Their low humming was hardly no-ticeable unless you listened for it. Other than that, they appeared to be alone. It was almost lunchtime. There was nobody in sight, but in the dis-tance Rakaia could hear the sounds of her younger sisters playing. She thought her mother was being overly cautious. But she'd seen women escorted out of the harem for no apparent reason, never to be seen again, so she wasn't prepared to completely dismiss her paranoia.

"What did you say to Naveen?" Rakaia asked, a little alarmed Sophany might have done something foolish. "That he would set his spies on us?"

"Have you ever wondered why you have blue eyes, Rakaia?"

Despite instructions to seem giddy and unconcerned, she looked at her mother in surprise. "What?"

"You have blue eyes," she repeated. "Now laugh as if I've said something hysterical."

Rakaia let out a fake laugh for the benefit of anybody who might be watching and then leaned in closer to her mother's ear. "So does Charisee," she hissed. "And half the slaves in the harem. It's probably because we have, you know, the same *father*."

"Charisee is the daughter of your father and a whore of who-knows-what ancestry," Sophany reminded her without malice, a fixed and entirely false smile on her face. She wasn't being mean. It was the truth, after all. "You, on the other hand, are a daughter of the Royal House of Talabar and the Royal House of Lanipoor. We come in many shades of green and brown, my dear, but until now, nobody ever produced a blue-eyed beauty like you."

"You're trying to hide whatever bad news you have for me with flattery," Rakaia accused through an insincere smile.

"I'm trying to help you understand what I've done for you, Rakaia. You need to appreciate that no matter how distasteful, what has been done has been done to protect you."

Rakaia would have stopped her mother right there to demand an explanation, but Sophany had her by the arm and continued to drag her ever so subtly along the graveled path. "What are you talking about, Mama? What have you done?"

"I have bribed Naveen Raveve to put your name, and only your name, forward to the king as a bride for Frederak Branador."

Rakaia laughed and this time it was quite genuine. "Don't be ridiculous."

"I am serious, Rakaia. You will be gone from the Talabar harem within a week. I believe the plan is to send you to Greenharbour to stay with your sister Adrina until the wedding. The ceremony will take place in the Temple of the Gods at the Sorcerers' Collective at the end of summer. Lord Branador is very devout, it seems."

"Why would you do this to me?"

Sophany didn't answer.

Rakaia studied her mother closely, looking for some hint she was joking, but underneath the false air of cheerfulness she wore for the benefit of Naveen Raveve's spies, her mother's eyes were filled with pain. "What's really going on, Mama? Why does it matter that I have blue eyes?"

"They are proof of my crimes, Rakaia."

"Crimes? What crimes? Stop being ridiculous. If you have a problem, you shouldn't go to that worm Naveen Raveve to fix it. You should go straight to the king. My father—"

"Is not who you think he is," Sophany said softly. "And you need to be gone from the harem before the king learns the truth."

Rakaia was stunned into silence.

"Smile!" Sophany ordered. "We are supposed to be talking about something trivial!"

"Triv—" Rakaia began. She didn't know what to say. Didn't know where to begin. The implications of her mother's news were only just beginning to sink in. "He'll kill me," she said after a moment, certain of that one thing. "If he finds out about this, the king will kill me, and you, and whoever . . . Who *is* my father, by the way, if not the king? And how did you even manage such a thing here in the harem surrounded by eunuchs and *loronged court'esa?*"

Sophany looked around, still fearful of being overheard, before she answered in a low voice. "Even in here, the Captain of the Guard is traditionally an entire male."

Rakaia took a moment to realize what her mother was telling her. It felt as if the very ground upon which she stood was crumbling to dust beneath her. She managed to force out a loud and entirely false laugh for the benefit of any spies watching, then hissed out of the corner of her mouth, "Gods preserve us, Mama! Are you telling me you had an affair with the Captain of the Guard?"

Sophany's eyes filled with pain. "Don't make it sound so sordid, Rakaia. It wasn't just an affair. We were in love."

"Which is all very romantic of you, Mama. But it doesn't alter the fact I'm a bastard and not a princess. Does he know about me?"

Sophany nodded. "Of course. I told him as soon as I knew I was pregnant." Her mother's eyes softened with the memory for a moment and she smiled a genuine smile. "I had this ludicrous idea in my head that we'd run away together and live . . . I don't know . . . just live. To be honest, even back then, my fantasy didn't really reach much beyond getting out of this gilded prison."

"I gather your heroic captain thought otherwise?" Rakaia said, wondering if that made her true father a cad or a realist.

"Even attempting such a thing would have gotten us both killed. In the end we agreed to say nothing. He asked for a posting to Bordertown and left a few days after I realized I was pregnant, and sanity prevailed. For my part, to protect us both, I made certain I caught the eye of the king as soon as I could, so there would be no question about my child's paternity."

Rakaia didn't know what to say. Everything she knew about herself was a lie. Everything she'd ever thought about her mother was wrong. And the man she loved as a father would likely kill her if he ever learned the truth.

"Why now?" she asked eventually, forcing herself to think this through rationally. As if that were possible. "Why are you telling me this now? Gods, why are you telling me at *all*?"

"Because Meyrick has been arrested."

Rakaia frowned, wondering what difference the arrest of some general who'd offended her little brother made, until it dawned on her what Sophany was getting at. "Meyrick Kabar? *General* Kabar? Dear gods, *he* was the Captain of the Guard back then?"

"Lower your voice!" Sophany ordered looking around fearfully.

"Has he betrayed you?"

"Not yet," her mother said. "But they are torturing him to learn of some plot that undoubtedly exists only in Alaric's head. I fear he'll say something, eventually . . . no man can resist torture forever."

"And you think this Hythrun brute can save me?"

"I think a betrothal to any Hythrun, brute or otherwise, will get you over the border and out of the king's reach," Sophany said. "Once you reach Hythria, you can disappear, but without this betrothal, you'll never get out of the harem alive."

Her mother was right about that much, but her plan only took care of Rakaia; Sophany would be in more danger than her daughter if Meyrick Kabar betrayed them. "What about you, Mama?"

"I have a plan to take care of myself."

Rakaia knew she was lying, but was too stunned, too confused, to call her mother out. She couldn't think. Could barely comprehend the change in her fortunes these last few minutes had wrought. "What . . . what do I tell Charisee?"

Sophany smiled for the benefit of anyone watching. At close quarters, it wasn't a happy smile. It was sad and filled with genuine remorse. "I have a plan for that, too."

"I'm almost afraid to ask what your *plan* involves," Rakaia said, still too bewildered by her sudden change from privileged princess to potential fugitive to really take all of this in.

"You need to trust me, Rakaia," her mother said.

"Easy for you to say."

"It will all work out for the best, Rakaia, I promise. All you need tell your base-born sister, my dear, is that she's finally going to have a chance to be a real princess."

4

CHARISEE WAS CERTAIN Princess Sophany didn't give a rat's behind about Rakaia's gown. She'd wanted to get rid of her because something was going to happen to Rakaia and the princess wanted to break the news to her daughter in private. Whatever that news was, it undoubtedly impacted Charisee.

Rakaia's fate was her fate to a large degree. It was in her best interests to discover what that fate was.

Finding out would not be easy. Unlike the king's bastard sons, Charisee was a slave. Her mother had been a slave too, although the king acknowledged her paternity, and even let her call him "Papa." But while her base-born brothers were free and honored with positions of trust, she was a servant and would remain so for life, because she was female. The king had far too many daughters to deal with and didn't need his bastard daughters adding to his burden. What to do with her had been decided when she was six years old. Charisee was only a year younger than the legitimate Princess Rakaia. As a king's bastard, she was considered a suitable companion. The two of them had been inseparable ever since.

But there was something afoot, something that might change everything. Charisee was determined to find out what it was. The logical person to ask was the man who knew everything, Naveen Raveve.

Doing anything of the kind, of course, was completely out of the question.

Like everyone in the harem, Charisee made it a policy to stay out of Naveen's way. The *court'esa* was a treacherous friend, an even more perilous enemy.

Today, however, as Charisee hurried along the wide hall that led from her mistress's apartments to the common areas of the harem, Naveen found her.

"Charisee?"

She froze at the sound of his voice behind her. Slowly, she turned to face the most powerful slave in all of Fardohnya, curtseying as respectfully as she knew how as he approached.

"My lord."

He smiled down at her. "You've no need to address me so formally, Charisee. We are both slaves here."

And yet you love it when you're addressed like that. "I'm sorry, sir, it's just, well . . ."

Naveen smiled. "I understand. Where are you off to in such a hurry?"

"Princess Sophany wants me to check on Princess Rakaia's dress for dinner tomorrow." The truth was always the safest thing to tell Naveen Raveve.

"How forward thinking of her," Naveen said. "Is there a special occasion?"

Charisee shrugged. There really was no answer to a question like that. If anyone knew of a special occasion, it would be the king's closest aide, not a lowly slave like her. "She didn't say, my . . . sir."

"Has your mistress spoken of her plans for the future?"

"Nobody plans anything for the future in this place," Charisee said before she could stop herself. When she realized how she must sound, she added apologetically, "I mean . . . we all . . . well, we serve at the king's pleasure, of course. It's not my mistress's role to anticipate the king's wishes by making her own plans."

Naveen seemed amused by her excuses. Or perhaps her discomfort. "You're a sharp little thing, aren't you?"

"Sir?"

"If you hear of anyone making plans that might interest the king, you would come to me about it, wouldn't you, Charisee?"

"Of course."

"And if you heard anything about your mistress, or her mother, that you feared might alarm her father, you would tell me also, so that we may stop her doing something foolish?"

Charisee nodded. "I would not hesitate, sir."

Naveen smiled even wider, but it was a skeptical smile. He clearly didn't believe a word she was saying. "I'm glad to hear it," he said. "I'd like to think I can rely on you in the future for . . . help."

Charisee was too afraid to ask exactly what Naveen Raveve meant by help.

And too afraid to deny him.

"Of course."

He smiled at her indulgently. "Well, off you go, then, and see to your mistress's wardrobe. It might pay you to start packing for her, too."

She doubted Naveen would let anything slip by accident. "Is she going somewhere, my lor—sir?"

"Somewhere cold," he told her, smiling at her barely concealed curiosity. "If you're unlucky enough, she may wish to take you with her."

"I live to serve my lady," Charisee said, lowering her eyes, not so much out of respect but so he wouldn't read her expression.

"I've no doubt you do," he agreed. "Now run along. I have some princesses to disappoint."

Charisee curtsied—even though she didn't need to—and scurried past Naveen, certain he had just confirmed what she had always feared.

A chill gripped her as she hurried along the wide tiled hall. Rakaia had been chosen to marry the lord of Highcastle—and that meant her handmaiden was going to be made redundant. Nobody took their slaves with them to their husband's house, particularly not slaves from Hablet's harem, as everyone assumed that meant—not unjustly—they were Hablet's spies.

Charisee knew this day might come, but it seemed unfair it had come so soon. She had even begun to hope of late that Hablet would simply run out of suitable husbands for his daughters and Rakaia would remain in the harem, unwed. She was nearly twenty-one, after all, and almost too old for consideration by a man hoping for a litter of healthy sons.

Charisee wiped away a tear and slowed her steps, afraid someone might realize how upset she was if her unseemly pace was noticed.

She didn't know what would happen to her once Rakaia left. There were no vacancies in the harem—all the princesses had their handmaidens assigned as small children. Hers had never been a position that offered any chance of promotion. The sad irony, of course, was that had her mother been a princess instead of a whore, she would have had her own handmaiden to torment and eventually abandon. She and Rakaia had the same father, after all . . .

Charisee forced herself to push aside that dangerous line of thought. Dwelling on the unfairness of her lot in life just made her stomach burn and served no useful purpose.

Her job was to prepare Rakaia for her wedding and if it happened to be to a scabby old Hythrun with syphilis . . . well, maybe there was some justice in this world after all.

5

CADEN FLETCHER WAS watching the Lord Defender of Medalon sign his death warrant at the moment the music was stolen.

Of course, he didn't know it was stolen at the time. Not then. And strictly speaking, the death warrant was his only insofar as it was his job to prepare it for the Lord Defender's seal.

But he remembered the moment the music changed from the sweet harmonies rising up from the traveling minstrel chorus in the Citadel's distant amphitheater to a discordant, sour cacophony that stopped abruptly as every musician, every singer, every soul in the Citadel simply humming to himself as he went about his business momentarily lost the ability to make music.

Any kind of music. Cade had tried it himself. Although the effect wore off within a few hours, at that moment, he couldn't even whistle.

But when the music stopped the Lord Defender was reading over the warrant before he signed it with a flourish and was pressing his seal into the wax.

"That's one miscreant the world will be better off without," Lord Tenragan was saying as he ordered the execution of a man who'd beaten his wife to death with the handle of an axe. "Sometimes I wonder what sort of man would . . ." He looked up. "Did you hear that?"

Cade nodded and turned toward the window. It was a windy evening and suddenly silent. The Citadel was strangely hushed as the sun set over the huge white city, its luminescent walls fading with the sun into darkness. The encroaching Dimming seemed ominous tonight for some reason.

"What happened to the music?"

AN HOUR LATER they still didn't have an answer.

The Temple of the Gods was shrouded in shadows as the fading rays of light stole the color from the murals. The white luminescent walls were just beginning to fade for the night. Cade glanced up, wondering, as he did every time he entered this temple, how they'd managed to paint it so beautifully with such a detailed frieze depicting all the Primal Gods on a ceiling so perilously high. When he'd asked the Lord Defender once, he told him it had taken the Harshini nearly half a century to complete it.

Cade suspected that if you stared at it for a lifetime you'd never find everything there was to see. Along the gallery above them was another mural dedicated to the Incidental Gods. Their followers came in every day to add to the mural as part of their acknowledgment of their gods' existence. Parts of it were magnificent, particularly the panels devoted to the God of Artists. There were sonnets covering the section of the wall devoted to the God of Poets, too, although Cade had read a few and decided worshiping the God of Poets apparently required more enthusiasm for the art form than talent.

The most worrying thing tonight, though, was the marble balustrade circling the upper gallery. If you looked closely, you could see each pillar was drilled with holes. With the windows open on either end of the temple, on a windy evening like this one, the whole hall should be singing in honor of the God of Music.

But it was silent. There was no music. Just the haunting, ill-omened sighing of the wind.

The sound was eerie and unsettling. Cade shivered inexplicably and wondered if it was more than the sudden and complete loss of music that made the world feel so poised on the brink of something unpleasant.

Shananara, the queen of the Harshini, could feel it too. In fact, she was beside herself. The Harshini were incapable of experiencing extremes of emotion, but the queen was pacing the Temple of the Gods in front of the massive Seeing Stone like a caged leopard. The cupola above her was tiled in an intricate pattern, resting on a curved wall painted with a glorious fresco, although from where Cade was standing he could not make out the detail. The stone itself—which had been hidden behind a plaster wall when he was a child—was taller than a man and mounted on a block of polished black marble. But it was the queen and not the Seeing Stone he couldn't take his eyes off. He'd never seen her like this before.

Neither had the Lord Defender, if the frown on his face was anything to go by, and he'd known her much longer than Cade.

"I don't understand what you mean, your highness," the Lord Defender was saying. "Are you suggesting the God of Music is dead?"

"Of course not, Tarja," she replied, turning to face them. Her black-on-black eyes made it almost impossible to guess what she was thinking. Harshini eyes didn't offer a window into their souls. They were more like pools of darkness into which you had to stop yourself from falling. "Gimlorie is a Primal God. He's not even immortal in the way you understand it. He can't die. He just . . . *is*."

"Then what happened just now?"

"I don't know."

"Is it just the Citadel?" Cade asked, mostly to stop himself staring at Shananara.

Tarja glanced at him. "What do you mean?"

"Well, I'm no expert on the gods, sir . . . hell, I don't even believe in them . . . but . . ."

Shananara stopped her pacing long enough to look at him. "You *don't*?"

"I don't *worship* them," Cade corrected. It was hard to deny the existence of the gods or real magic now the Harshini were back in charge of Medalon, and you couldn't walk down the street without someone wielding magic or a god appearing anytime Shananara chose to summon one of them. But a man didn't have to worship them if he didn't want to. The Sisters of the Blade may have been corrupt, and like most Medalonians, Cade welcomed the coup a decade ago led by Tarja Tenragan and his half-Harshini sister, R'shiel, which restored the Harshini to power, but two hundred years of the Sisterhood's doctrine of atheism ran deep. So deep that Cade still thought of himself as an atheist, even though he'd met more than one god in person since being appointed the Lord Defender's personal aide. "My point is, your majesty, if there is only one Gimlorie, and something has happened to him, then surely the music is gone everywhere, not just here in the Citadel."

Shananara nodded in agreement. "Of course. You're absolutely right. I don't know why that didn't occur to me sooner. I'll contact the Sorcerers' Collectives in Yarnarrow, Talabar, and Greenharbour and maybe even Calavandra to see if they're having the same problem."

"Surely if even one city other than ours has suffered the same fate, that would answer the question," Tarja suggested.

Shananara nodded distractedly. "I will call the High Arrion in Greenharbour first. She will know if Hythria suffers the same problem."

That was their cue to leave, Cade knew. Shananara rarely used the Seeing Stone when there were humans about. He and the Lord Defender turned to leave. As they did, Cade frowned, thinking something amiss. There were twenty pillars spaced evenly around the temple supporting the gallery. Each pillar was a shrine to one of the Primal Gods, and contained a small representation of the god it honored, although only a true believer understood the significance of the artifacts. Zegarnald, the God of War, was easy to spot. His shrine held a tiny golden sword. Kalianah's shrine, on the other hand, made no sense at all to Cade. It held nothing but a small white feather. As he glanced around, he realized every shrine held its tiny representation of its god, except one. The shrine about halfway down the line of columns on the left was empty.

"Is that supposed to be empty?" he asked, pointing to the alcove set about shoulder height into the pillar.

Tarja and Shananara both turned in the direction he was pointing.

"That is . . . was . . . the shrine to Gimlorie," Shananara said, shaking her head with a slight quiver in her voice.

"What was in it?"

"A lyre," the queen told him, unable to take her eyes off the empty shrine. "A tiny golden lyre."

"Is it just a coincidence that it's missing or does it have something to do with the music?"

"It has everything to do with it," Shananara said softly. "Each representation of the gods is their Covenant seal."

"Their what?" Tarja asked, which surprised Cade because he thought the Lord Defender and the queen of the Harshini were fairly tight and there weren't too many secrets between them.

"The Covenant," she repeated. "It is the Covenant which gives the gods the ability to walk among us. It is the Covenant that brought the Harshini into being."

"So it's important then?"

"More than you could possibly imagine."

"Then the God of Music isn't dead," the Lord Defender said. "Someone has stolen him."

6

THERE WERE CERTAIN qualities one looked for when recruiting an assassin, but they were not immediately obvious in a child of twelve.

Elin Bane cast his eye over the small group of hopefuls gathered in the tiled courtyard below and wondered if he would choose any new apprentices this year or turn the applicants away again, as he had the last three times the guild had conducted a recruiting drive.

"A likely looking bunch this time?"

Elin glanced over his shoulder and smiled at the woman who posed the question. The princess was sitting on a straight-backed chair in his office, her hands balanced on the cane she required to help her get about these days. Although she wasn't particularly old, a fall from a spirited sorcerer-bred stallion last spring was still healing. She could have sought a magical cure, but even after all this time, she was still distrustful of letting the Harshini inside her head. Given some of the things Marla Wolfblade must have done over the years, as she fought to keep Hythria safe from its enemies, both inside and outside the country, Elin was quite certain he knew why she was reluctant to submit herself to any kind of close scrutiny by the Harshini. Unfortunately, neither of the two sorcerers she did trust to heal her had been in Greenharbour when it happened and by the time they returned, the injury—so she claimed—was beyond an easy magical fix. So Marla suffered in silence and hobbled about on her cane, carrying it almost as a badge of honor.

"I won't know until we've properly tested them, your highness."

"And how *do* you test for cold-blooded killers?" Marla asked with a raised brow. "Galon would never tell me."

"I don't know," Elin told her, turning back to look down at the new batch of candidates. "We don't accept cold-blooded killers."

"Really?"

He didn't need to turn around to imagine the skepticism on Princess Marla's face. "The Assassins' Guild takes on contract killings, your highness," he reminded her. Not that she needed reminding. She'd hired his guild often enough to know exactly how it worked, and been married to his predecessor for a time. "Contract killing—as opposed to random thuggery—requires thoughtful judgment and a surprisingly strong sense of right and wrong. There's a reason we guarantee no harm will come to innocent bystanders."

"It never ceases to amaze me that the two most principled men I know are the heads of the Assassins' Guild and the Thieves' Guild."

"That's because you're a princess, your highness. There are more scoundrels in politics than in all the Assassins' and the Thieves' guilds put together."

"I fear you may be right about that," Marla chuckled.

The door opened and a man entered carrying the tray of refreshments he'd ordered when Marla first arrived. Elin turned to discover it wasn't a slave bringing the tray in but Marla's stepson, and the son of the previous Raven, Galon Miar. Trained assassin though he was, Kiam didn't seem to mind acting as a servant on this occasion. It was a mark of his fondness for Marla, Elin supposed.

Kiam placed the tray on the low table in front of Marla and then leaned forward to kiss her on the cheek. "To what do we owe this rare honor, your highness? You don't visit the Assassins' Guild often these days. At least not in broad daylight."

She smiled up at him fondly. "Still not ready to call me mother, are you?"

Kiam look a little uncomfortable at the question. "Well, since my father is dead, and you're not really my stepmother any longer, I'm not sure it's appropriate. I'm always amazed and touched that you continue to ask me to call you that, though."

"She likes causing trouble," Elin told Kiam, moving away from the window. "It amuses her royal highness to remind her enemies that her last husband was the Raven of the Assassins' Guild and her son, the High Prince, has an assassin for a stepbrother."

"You make me sound a terrible person, Elin."

"You are a terrible person, your highness," he told her. "And you're far too unprincipled to make the grade as an assassin." He turned to Kiam. "Speaking of making the grade, have you looked over the latest crop?"

Kiam shook his head. "I've been at the palace with the High Princess Adrina."

Marla sighed, which made Elin smile. The dowager princess shared an uncomfortable relationship with her Fardohnyan daughter-in-law. "Who is Adrina arranging to have assassinated now?" Marla asked. "Me, I suppose?"

"You know he can't answer that."

"Actually, your highness, she wasn't arranging to assassinate anybody. She wanted to hire me as an escort."

"Why does she need an escort?"

"It's not for her. It's for her sister, Rakaia."

Marla rolled her eyes. "Dear gods, are we to be inflicted with more of Hablet's unwanted horde of daughters?"

The Fardohnyan king had scores of them, Elin knew, and only one legitimate son. Marrying his daughters off to suitable husbands was proving to be something of a chore for the Fardohnyan king, his sources in Talabar informed him. It wasn't just that Hablet wanted to marry his daughters off; he needed to make sure none of them found a suitor rich or powerful enough to threaten his throne someday, something he'd failed at spectacularly with his eldest daughter. Every single daughter he had managed to dispose of had been so comprehensively removed from the line of succession their husbands had no hope of pushing one of their sons to challenge Alaric for the throne in the future.

It was a wise precaution. King Hablet's plan to ally with his vast resource-rich northern neighbor, Karien, by marrying Adrina to their crown prince more than a decade ago, resulted in her eventually becoming the wife of his sworn enemy and High Princess of Hythria. It was only the Wolfblade family's willingness to relinquish any similar claim on the Fardohnyan throne that placated Hablet and allowed peace to settle over the previously warring nations.

Kiam nodded. "Hablet has done a deal with Frederak Branador, according to Adrina. It's quite a coup, from what Adrina was saying. Hablet gets access to the pass, but our trade delegates have been able to squeeze quite a bit out of Hablet in return. I have to say, though, the High Princess didn't seem any more thrilled about the idea of her sister coming here to Hythria than you are, your highness."

"That's because Adrina knows her wretched father only sends the troublesome ones away from his harem." Marla sniffed, adding, "Like his eldest daughter, for instance."

"I'm curious, your highness," Elin said, taking a seat on the low cushions opposite Marla. "Are you ever going to admit defeat?"

"What are you talking about?"

"Are you ever going to concede that Adrina loves your son, that Damin adores her even more, that she has given you four beautiful grandchildren and she has never done anything to warrant your low opinion of her, other than being unfortunate enough to be the eldest daughter of the Fardohnyan king?"

Marla pretended to consider the question for a moment and then shrugged. "No."

"You see. You are a terrible person."

"I'm a cautious person, Elin," she corrected, and then turned to her stepson. "When did Adrina say we are to be inflicted with the curse of yet another entitled, spoiled, obnoxious Fardohnyan princess?"

"She wants me to leave for Winternest within a few days. I'm to meet Rakaia's entourage at the border with a century of Greenharbour Raiders and escort them back here."

"You see," Marla pointed out to Elin. "She's coming with an entourage, every one of whom will be sponging off us for months, if not years, while spying for Hablet."

"Would you like me to kill them all before they get here?"

Marla smiled. "Ah, if only I thought for a moment that you weren't joking, Ky."

"I'm sure she's a lovely girl," Elin said.

"I wish I shared your optimism, Master Raven." Marla held out her hand to Kiam. "Help me up, Kiam. I really need to be getting back to the palace. If the Fardohnyans are coming, I need to lock away the silverware."

Kiam helped Marla to her feet. Once she was balanced on her cane, the princess turned to Elin. "Don't bother getting up. Enjoy your lunch. I know you have a busy day ahead of you. Ky can see me out."

He smiled at her. "It was good to see you again, your highness. You should visit us more often."

"I should, Master Raven. And I will."

He returned to the window as Marla limped from the room on Kiam's arm. Below him, the Master of Assassins was putting the candidates through their paces around an obstacle course set up to test their fitness, among other things. He watched the boys struggling to scale the wooden barrier, some of them trying to climb, others thinking it better to take a run up and hope their momentum would carry them over.

A little while later the door opened and closed behind him. Kiam came to stand beside him at the window. Down in the courtyard, one of the boys trying to climb the barricade fell, landing heavily on the tiles. Another boy running toward the barricade stopped to help him up, before continuing on his way.

"Find out who that is," Elin told him.

"The boy who fell?"

"No, the one who helped him up." He glanced at Kiam. "Did the princess get away safely?"

"Still bitching about the Fardohnyans, but yes."

He smiled. "There's some history there, I suspect, which explains why she feels that way about Hablet. But she is right about one thing, and you need to be very wary if you take on this job as escort to Adrina's sister."

"I know. Adrina did warn me."

"I hope she warned you enough. Because whether you trade on the relationship or not, your stepbrother is still the High Prince of Hythria, Kiam, and there is nothing more dangerous in this world than a Fardohnyan princess let out of the harem for the first time." He turned from the window and indicated the buffet he'd had sent up for the princess. "Care to join me for lunch? That curry is blue-finned arlen."

"That's a fairly exotic dish for a lunch menu," Kiam remarked, lifting the silver lid on the tureen to take a sniff. "Even with Marla coming for lunch."

"The arlen was a gift," Elin said, watching the assassin closely. "From a particularly grateful Trinity Isles sea captain."

Kiam froze for only a fraction a second. The Raven would not have noticed his flinch, had he not been looking for it.

"Apparently, the Assassins' Guild did him a favor recently."

"What favor?" Kiam inquired with a perfectly straight face.

Elin folded his arms and studied Kiam, looking for his reaction. "His sister had some fanciful tale about being rescued from a whorehouse by one of our number and escorted safely back to her ship."

Kiam turned to look at the Raven. He didn't seem the least bit contrite. "Oh. That favor."

"You came back with a dog, too, Ky."

"He followed me home."

"You forgot to mention the girl."

"It was a busy night."

"Stop to adopt any orphans along the way?"

"It was help her or kill her," Kiam pointed out with a shrug. "What was I supposed to do?"

That was the dilemma, Elin supposed. The Guild insisted they didn't harm innocent bystanders, but the truth wasn't nearly so noble or so cut and dried. "Word of this is going to get about," he warned.

"Is that such a bad thing?" Kiam asked, replacing the lid on the tureen. "She doesn't know my name, just that I'm from the Guild. The rumor will spread. People will whisper about the child who was saved by the Assassins' Guild. Should buy us quite a bit of good will against the next time we accidentally slaughter a few innocents in the line of duty, don't you think?"

"You're turning into a cynic, Ky."

The assassin smiled at that. "I achieved cynic years ago."

"You'll be careful with Adrina's sister, won't you? You'll not stop along the way to set up a home for stray cats?"

Kiam laughed. "Don't start giving me ideas."

Elin leaned forward to lift the lid off the tureen. He placed it on the cart beside the dish and took a deep, appreciative breath. He wasn't going to let this meal go to waste. "Well, take that damned beast with you when you leave," he instructed as he spooned some of the thick, aromatic curry into a bowl. "He's eating the Guild out of house and home."

"I will." Kiam turned for the door, stopping when he reached it. He turned back to look at the Raven with a frown. "I just had a thought. Isn't Frederak Branador one of Marla's cousins?"

"I believe so. Why?"

"That makes him . . . what? In his eighties?"

"So?"

"Adrina's sister is not even twenty-one."

Elin put down the serving spoon and glared at the man everyone assumed he was grooming to be his successor. "Dear gods, Kiam Miar, I swear by every Primal God there is, if you even *think* about trying to rescue her from this marriage, I will kill you myself."

Kiam opened the door, grinning. Elin realized—or at least hoped—that he was just trying to get a rise out of his boss. "Never fear, my Lord Raven. I promise to restrict my heroics to small children, puppies, and kittens. I really do like that idea about a stray cat home, by the way."

"Get out of here, you idiot."

Kiam shut the door behind him. Shaking his head at the young man's folly, Elin sat down, settling back against the cushions to enjoy his stew, unable to completely push aside the uncomfortable notion that Kiam Miar's absurdly noble nature, and unfortunate tendency of doing the right thing, even if it wasn't what he'd been contracted to do, would eventually be the undoing of them all.

Chapter

7

IN THE WHIRLWIND of their departure, Rakaia barely saw her mother. It was only on the eve of her departure that Sophany was finally able to steal a moment alone with her daughter.

Once again, they took a turn around the gardens, only this time it was dark, the sun long set, so there was no need for false frivolity to fool any spies who might be watching. The night was hot and humid and seemed uncomfortably close. Rakaia doubted it was the weather unsettling her so.

More likely it was her mother's insane plan to save her from Hablet's wrath. She suspected agreeing to be a party to it made her certifiably insane, too.

"You must give no hint of what you're planning," she warned her daughter as they made their way along the secluded path. "Not to anyone. Especially not to Charisee."

"She'll know something is wrong, Mama. She can read me like a book."

"You must let her. More importantly, you will have to convince her your nervousness is due to your upcoming wedding and not something more sinister."

"I'm a terrible liar."

"Then behave in such a way that you have no need to lie."

Easier said than done, Rakaia thought, but there was no arguing with her mother on this. Sophany's insane—and not terribly well thought out—plan was too far along now for it to be abandoned without serious consequences for both of them.

"Everything is in place," Sophany told her. For someone plotting against the kings, she seemed remarkably collected. "I have been able to get a letter to my brother, your uncle Liance. He will protect you once you reach Lanipoor."

"Assuming I can get to him." Rakaia was far from confident her mother's plan for her escape was going to work. "How did you manage to get a letter out of the harem detailing your plan, anyway?"

"I would never be so foolish as to commit this plan to paper, Rakaia."

"Then he doesn't know I'm coming."

"Get to Lanipoor," Sophany insisted, refusing to acknowledge the shaky foundation on which her plan was built. "Your uncle will look after you."

"What about you, Mama?"

"I'll be fine."

"How will you get away?"

"I won't need to. Meyrick has held his tongue. The king knows nothing."

"Then why do I need to leave?"

"Because that may change."

"Then what happens to you?" she asked again. Sophany was avoiding answering her question quite determinedly.

Sophany glanced sideways and smiled at her with eyes full of unspoken fears. "You need not worry about me, darling. I can look after myself."

Rakaia didn't believe her for a moment, but her plans were too far along to back out now. "What happens when they find out I'm missing?"

"They mustn't," Sophany told her. "Whatever you have to do, whatever you have to tell her to make her play along, you must convince Charisee not to betray you. Even if she can't keep up the charade for more than a few days, you need to be long gone from Winternest before she breaks down and confesses the truth. If not, we'll all be in serious trouble."

"No pressure, then."

Sophany stopped and turned to look at her daughter. "You can do this, Rakaia."

"I don't know anything about surviving in the outside world, Mama."

"Then you need to learn. Quickly."

"What about my entourage? How am I supposed to convince them to keep quiet about what I've done?"

Sophany was silent for a moment. Apparently she hadn't thought of that.

"Mama?"

"Send them home."

"What?"

"Send them home. When you get to Winternest, send your entourage home."

"What possible reason would I have for doing that?"

"I don't know," Sophany snapped, a little impatiently. "Tell them you're worried they'll be homesick or something. Use your wits, Rakaia. You'll not survive in the outside world without them."

Rakaia fell silent, a little hurt her last words with her mother might be spoken in anger. "It doesn't seem fair to Charisee."

"It's fairer than the lot in life she was destined for."

"I wonder if she'll see it like that."

"Make her see, darling, or we will all suffer the consequences."

Sophany slipped her arm through Rakaia's and they continued to walk, treasuring this last moment of solitude together. As they walked, Sophany talked low and urgently, trying to tell Rakaia everything she could think of that might help her before her sheltered and woefully unprepared daughter had to fend for herself in a cruel and unsympathetic world beyond the walls of the Fardohnyan Royal Harem.

Chapter

8

"There! You look beautiful! Just like a real princess."

"You're going to get me killed, Rakaia."

Rakaia smiled as she adjusted Charisee's borrowed veil. Red looked so much better on her half-sister than it did on her. "Don't be so melodramatic. Now hold still."

Charisee pushed Rakaia's hand away and turned from the polished bronze mirror to face her sister. She put her hands on her hips and frowned. "Nobody in Hythria is going to believe I'm you for a moment. Quite the opposite. And when they realize what we've done, they'll whip you, kill me, and then probably go to war with Fardohnya over the insult."

Rakaia shrugged, trying to appear nonchalant and not desperate, wishing she could tell Charisee the truth. "Well, then, we'd better not get caught then, had we?"

Charisee pulled the veil from her head and began to remove her borrowed finery and toss it on the bed. It was chilly in their guest room here at Winternest. The thick stone walls seemed to suck all the warmth from the air, even though the fire in the fireplace was blazing and it was—despite the three feet of snow outside—supposed to be almost summer. Her sister's skin prickled with gooseflesh as she got down to her undergarments. Charisee wasn't smiling. She wasn't having fun any longer.

Perhaps guessing what her half-sister was thinking, Charisee glared at her. "This is not funny, Rakaia."

"Oh, come on, of course it is."

Stepping out of her borrowed petticoat, Charisee picked up her own woolen dress. It was much less grand—simple gray with a red band on the bottom denoting the wearer's status as an indentured servant. The garment of a slave, not a princess.

Rakaia snatched it from her. "We've only got one chance at this, Chari. If we don't do it, you'll be a slave for the rest of your life, and six months from now I'll be married to a disgusting, ill-educated Hythrun brute who wants nothing more from me than babies and a bed warmer, being raped every night for that very purpose."

Annoyed, Charisee reached for the slave dress. "You don't mind if that happens to me, though, I notice."

Rakaia realized how that must sound and smiled winningly, all the while backing up to keep the slave dress out of reach. "You get to *not* be a slave, Chari. And you never know, Lord Branador might drop dead from the pox and Adrina might even find you another husband who's halfway decent."

"She might find *you* another halfway decent husband. Not me. You're her royal half-sister. I'm the *court'esa's* bastard, remember? Adrina probably won't even acknowledge we're related."

"Which is why you don't want to arrive in Hythria with everyone thinking you're a slave. When we get to Greenharbour, you can be the princess and I'll be your servant. Free servant, of course, not a slave. That way, I can leave whenever I want."

"To do *what*, Rakaia?"

She shrugged. That part of the plan she wasn't able to share with Charisee. It was so hard not to say something. Not to tell her the truth. She and her sister had never had secrets before. "I don't know. Have an adventure. Have some fun. Not die of an unfortunate accident before I reach my majority because I'm one of Hablet's wretched unwanted daughters."

Charisee shook her head. "If you'd ever been a slave, you'd know being one of Hablet's daughters—even an unwanted one—isn't such a bad thing."

"And that's why it's my gift to you, Charisee. You're as much Hablet's daughter as I am. Just because you were born on the wrong side of the blanket doesn't mean you should have to suffer for it. *You* should be the princess. You're prettier than me. You're better mannered than me. You speak more languages than me. You're not nearly as mean, or selfish or shallow . . ."

Having left an opening for her half-sister, she waited expectantly, but Charisee did not apparently feel the need to fill the silence with a similar compliment or disagree about her sister's less than desirable personality traits.

But then, Charisee was nobody's fool. She must know that however much Rakaia insisted otherwise, she might well be setting up her half-sister to die in her place.

Charisee sighed in resignation and stopped trying to reach for the slave dress. "Look, I know we used to do this for fun, Rakaia, but nobody here is going to think it's funny if I pass myself off as you. It might even be treason."

"Then we won't tell them."

"What happens when you want to go back to being you?" Charisee asked. "You think it's hilarious now, but what happens when you're cold and hungry and homeless and decide it wasn't so bad being a princess? *You'll* be welcomed back into the fold and told off for being troublesome. *I'll* be put to death for impersonating you."

Rakaia shook her head. "It won't happen."

"You say that now . . ."

"And I mean it," Rakaia said, never more certain of anything in her life. Her smile faded. "I've seen what happens to Hablet's daughters when he has no further use for them, Chari, and so have you. When Papa dies and our brother takes the throne, he's going to kill every one of his legitimate sisters still left in the harem, and you know it." She didn't mention the other reason—the one about Hablet killing her and almost certainly her mother when he learned the truth about who had actually fathered her.

Charisee remained silent. She knew nothing about Sophany's infidelity, but she knew how the succession went. The first thing every new Fardohnyan king did was eliminate all potential challengers, brother and sister alike, who might threaten his claim or one day have children with a claim to his throne. Hablet had more than forty children between his legitimate daughters, his one legitimate son, and the score of bastards like Charisee he'd sired on numerous slaves and *court'esa*. Unless his other children managed to do something like his eldest daughter had done—make a marriage so powerful he could not risk touching her without causing a war—Rakaia was living on borrowed time. Hablet was not a well man, and her brother was nearly twelve now. Any day, Hablet's life of excess might catch up with him.

And four of Rakaia's older legitimate sisters were already dead. They were accidental deaths, supposedly, but they were all sisters who might inherit the throne if her father died and something happened to Alaric.

Charisee would have no trouble believing Rakaia had no intention of waiting around for an "accident" to happen to her.

"If I follow your logic, Rakaia, and everybody believes I'm you, *I'll* be the one killed when Alaric takes the throne. How is that supposed to win me over to this ridiculous plan of yours?"

Rakaia had thought of that. "Simple. The fact that you're base-born is what will save you. When Alaric takes the throne, all you need do is go straight to Adrina and confess who you really are. She will protect you."

Charisee rolled her eyes, unconvinced. "You haven't seen Adrina since you were ten years old. You have no idea what she'll do. For all you know, she's just as likely to have me killed for deceiving her."

Rakaia shook her head. Sophany had thought this through. "She can't, even if she wants to. By then, everybody will be so convinced *you* are Rakaia that Adrina will have to protect you to protect herself. She's the High Princess of Hythria now. She can't afford to be seen as part of a plot to pass off an imposter as her sister. She'll *have* to keep quiet about the truth, just to save herself."

Still skeptical, Charisee shook her head again. She really was being quite annoyingly intransigent about this.

"What if Adrina hates me?"

"Nobody hates you, Chari," Rakaia assured her, a little impatiently, putting her arm around her half-sister's shoulder. "That's what makes you a better princess than me. I'm a holy terror. You just ask Papa."

Truth be known, her father had been glad to see the end of both of them. Charisee was right about that much. This wasn't the first time they'd pulled this switching identities prank, either. Perhaps just the most dangerous.

Sophany had been preparing for her daughter's escape ever since she bribed Naveen Raveve to put her forward as a bride for Frederak Brana-dor. And the first and most important part of her plan was to ensure nobody realized Rakaia was missing, so she'd been adamant her daughter wouldn't leave Talabar without her slave, best friend, and closest companion, Charisee.

Poor Charisee didn't know what Sophany was planning until they'd crossed the border into Hythria.

It was only here, at Winternest—the border fort where Rakaia could dispense with her entourage and continue her journey with the escort her sister, Adrina, would send to meet her—that Rakaia had been ready to reveal Sophany's plan for both her and her beloved base-born sister to escape the destinies their accidents of birth had laid out for them.

She would wear Charisee down eventually. They still had a few days before their Hythrun escort arrived.

By then Charisee would be Rakaia, and Rakaia would be an unnoticed nobody who could slip away to find a new life where she had some hope, even in a dangerous unknown world, of surviving the king of Fardohnya learning that his wife had cheated on him and his beloved Rakaia was just as much a whore's bastard as Charisee.

9

WINTERNEST LOOMED MAJESTICALLY ahead of Kiam and his escort of Greenharbour Raiders, its massive walls rising out of the mountainside as if it had been grown from the very rock of the mountain rather than been constructed in the traditional way by men. It had been built by the Harshini more than a thousand years ago, its tall spires and elegant lines reminiscent of the magical race.

The castle guarded the Hythrun end of the Widowmaker Pass, named for the number of widows created during the numerous battles that had taken place on the border between Fardohnya and Hythria before the treaty hammered out by the current High Prince. It was one of only two navigable passes across the Sunrise Mountains between the two countries. The other pass was much farther south, near Highcastle.

Winternest was actually two castles in one, built on either side of the road leading through the pass into Fardohnya, joined by an arched and heavily fortified bridge high above the road, which linked the northern wing where most of the commerce of the border post was carried out, to the southern wing, which remained the private domain of the ruling Lions-claw family when they were in residence. There was a similar fortress on the Fardohnyan side of the border at the other end of the pass, Kiam knew, about ten miles west of here. Kiam thought it not nearly so grand nor impressive as Winternest.

The keep served as a garrison, customs house, inn, and fortress. It catered to the steady stream of traffic moving between the two countries. Commerce was the lifeblood of Fardohnya, hence the true reason he was here.

The king of Fardohnya was horse trading again, although the filly in question this time was one of his own daughters, and undoubtedly one of the troublesome ones because they were the only daughters, according to his eldest child, Adrina, that he ever bothered to rid himself of.

Adrina hadn't been able to tell him much about Rakaia. She hadn't seen her younger sister since she was a child, and even then Rakaia was just one face among many in a harem full of younger sisters. Adrina had been too busy planning her own escape, she told Kiam, to worry about the countless offspring of her father's many junior wives. So Rakaia was a mystery. The only thing of which Kiam was certain was that she was going to be trouble.

The gates were open when they arrived, although they had to wait as a caravan pulled out, loaded with bales of wool. The lead wagon was huge—a veritable house on wheels. Sitting on the front seat next to the driver was a plump woman with a baby at her breast and two more leaning out of the wagon, waving to the soldiers as they rode out of the keep.

Kiam smiled and waved back while they waited. The trader was a successful one, Kiam guessed. There were more than ten fully loaded freight wagons in his caravan, along with the other wagons carrying their supplies. Between the trader, his family, the wagon drivers—and some of them had families too, by the look of them—and the guards protecting them all, the caravan was almost as large as Kiam's military escort.

As he waited for the road to clear, he spied a figure coming from the keep, cutting between the wagons to greet the newcomers. Broos sat patiently beside his horse, waiting for his master to give the command to move on. Whether the dog was just pathetically grateful to have been rescued, or whether Kiam had some heretofore undiscovered talent with animals, he'd never encountered a creature so anxious to be trained. He'd spent every evening on the road to Winternest sitting around the campfire teaching the dog to sit, lie down, fetch, and even hold his mare's reins while he relieved himself. A few weeks on real meat and plenty of exercise running beside Kiam all day had transformed the skeletal beast into a sleek, handsome dog. Kiam didn't know what breed he was, but his head was as high as Kiam's hip and when he stood on his hind legs, he was taller than a grown man.

"Easy, Broos," Kiam commanded as he dismounted, not sure of the reception he would get, or what the dog would do if he thought this man was hostile. He wasn't expecting trouble. Kiam was stepbrother to the High Prince. At least, he had been for the eight years his father was married to Princess Marla. Now that Galon was dead, his position was harder to define. Sometimes he was treated like he was still a member of Damin Wolfblade's large extended family.

Other times, strangers—never Damin or his family—treated him like a pariah because he was "the assassin."

He didn't know Valorian Lionsclaw well enough to know into which camp the heir to Sunrise Province, and the commander of Winternest, fell.

Valorian approached, hand on the hilt of his sword. He was a middle-aged man with a trim beard and the athletic body of one who lived by the sword. Kiam eyed him warily until he realized Valorian was simply holding the blade in place to stop it banging against his leg while he darted between the wagons, and wasn't preparing for an attack. In fact, the commandant smiled as he approached and offered Kiam his hand without hesitation.

"Welcome to Winternest," he said. "I'm Valorian Lionsclaw."

"Kiam Miar," he replied, accepting the handshake. Adrina had sent word by pigeon so Valorian knew in advance who was leading the escort to collect Princess Rakaia and her entourage. Valorian either had no problem with it or had had sufficient time to adjust to the idea. "You look fairly busy. Sorry to inflict another hundred hungry souls on you."

Valorian shrugged and glanced over at the noisy departing wagons. "We're not as busy as we look. I got rid of a traveling carnival last night, two rather shady-looking ore merchants this morning, and once the Farman brothers and their caravan are through to the pass, we'll have plenty of room."

Kiam was surprised. "Aren't you full of Fardohnyans? Or isn't Princess Rakaia here yet?"

"She's here," the commander assured him. "But she sent her entourage home as soon as she arrived. Something about not wanting to take all those poor people so far from their families by making them travel to a foreign country."

Kiam stared at Valorian. "Are you serious?"

The commander shrugged. "There'll just be the princess and her handmaiden heading back to Greenharbour with you."

Kiam didn't know what to say. All the way to Winternest he'd been mentally bracing himself for their return journey full of obnoxious Fardohnyan courtiers, and a bratty Fardohnyan princess.

"Um . . . that's good. I think. What's she like?"

"Haven't seen her yet," Valorian said. "I was out chasing bandits in the mountains when she arrived, and her Serene Highness hasn't deigned to grace us with her royal presence since she let her entourage go. I'm hoping now that her escort has arrived she'll come out of her room and be on her way."

"Has your wife met her?"

"Bayla's visiting her brother, Tav, in Dregian Province for the summer," he said, not sounding terribly upset by the absence of his wife. "She misses the lad terribly and her mother has not been well of late. It's probably a good thing she's not here. My wife is not particularly fond of Fardohnyans."

Kiam nodded in understanding. "Are the children with her?" he asked, knowing he would be surprised to learn Valorian had allowed his two sons to travel that far from Sunrise Province. Although there were no rumors abroad about trouble in Valorian's marriage, Bayla was an Eaglespike and her family had a long and bitter history with the Wolfblades, and the Lionsclaw family into which she had married.

Sure enough, the Lord of Winternest shook his head. "Gods, no! They are in Cabradel, at present, being spoiled rotten by my mother. We're all going to meet up in Greenharbour at the end of summer for the royal wedding."

Everyone who was anyone was going to be in Greenharbour at the end of summer for the royal wedding. It was shaping up as the social event of the decade.

"How is Lady Lionsclaw?"

He smiled. "She will outlive us all, I swear. I kind of wish she was here, actually. She'd know exactly what to do with a snotty Fardohnyan princess."

"She sounds like a right royal pain." Kiam glanced over his shoulder at the Greenharbour Raiders he'd brought to escort Adrina's sister back to the capital. Hardened, common-born warriors, every one of them. Adrina had sent him here with an honor guard, not an entourage. There wasn't a serving girl, masseuse, or a *court'esa* among them. "Gods, she's not expecting us to look after her all the way to Greenharbour, is she?"

Valorian smiled as the last of the caravan wagons trundled past, two collared *court'esa* waving and calling out cheerful, if rather optimistic, offers to the Raiders waiting patiently to enter the fort. Their departure left the way open for Kiam's troop to enter Winternest. The commander wasn't trying to hide his delight at the knowledge that in a very short time, this unpredictable Fardohnyan guest wasn't going to be his problem. "Cheer up, Master Miar. Aren't you assassin types supposed to be trained to withstand pain and torture?"

Kiam decided, at that moment, that he really liked Valorian Lionsclaw. The Sunrise heir knew who and what Kiam was and he wasn't trying to pretend otherwise. Kiam had met his mother, the Warlord, Tejay Lionsclaw, on a number of occasions when she was in Greenharbour for the annual Convocation of the Warlords. She was a no-nonsense woman with a very clear idea of what she wanted out of life and a great sense of humor to go with it. Valorian, it seemed, was very much his mother's son.

"There are limits to the amount of torture even a trained assassin can stand, you know," Kiam agreed. "This has the potential to exceed that limit, very quickly."

Valorian slapped his shoulder and laughed. "I'm heading back into the Widowmaker tomorrow to hunt down some murdering bandits who robbed a caravan in the pass a few days ago, cut their victims' throats, and left them to bleed to death. Care to join the hunt? It might be safer."

Kiam pretended to give the matter his serious consideration for a moment. "Murdering bandits, you say?"

"I know . . . it's a hard decision."

He sighed with regret. "Tempting, my lord, but I did promise the High Princess I'd deliver her little sister safely back to Greenharbour."

Valorian nodded and glanced over at the waiting Raiders. "Let's get your men settled, then. They deserve at least one night of peace before you head back. Meanwhile, I'll see what I can do to coax her Serene Highness out of her room so you can be on your way tomorrow."

Kiam nodded. Grabbing hold of Broos's collar to stop him darting underfoot, he turned to wave the Raiders forward, thinking he'd felt less apprehension about this favor he was doing his former stepsister-in-law-by-marriage than the last time he'd been commissioned to carry out a hired kill and rid the world of Shilton Rik.

HER SERENE HIGHNESS agreed to grace them with her august presence for dinner later that evening. She refused to mingle with peasants in the working part of the keep, so Valorian arranged their meal to be served in the hall of the southern wing where his family kept their residence and visitors of noble station were usually accommodated. Kiam stood in front of the fireplace warming his hands with his back to the fire while he waited for her to arrive. Broos was curled up on the rug at his feet, snoring contentedly. Valorian had suggested he be accommodated in the stables, but the dog would have none of it when one of the keep's stable boys tried to lead him away. Rather than risk the poor lad being mauled by a dog so large Kiam was tempted to measure him in hands like a horse, he vouched for Broos's good behavior indoors and the dog had followed him inside like he owned the place.

The dining room was lit with scores of candles, the table set with a snowy white tablecloth and more eating implements than one person could use in a dozen meals. Kiam would have bet all his former step-brother's vast wealth that the cutlery was entirely for Rakaia's benefit. Valorian didn't strike him as a man who stood on ceremony too much when his wife was away and he wasn't entertaining royal visitors.

He looked up as the door at the end of the hall opened, expecting Valorian, however the small figure that pushed the heavy, banded-oak door open wore a diaphanous lavender skirt with a matching bodice. As she neared him, the jewel in her exposed navel caught the light, although he couldn't tell what she looked like, as a sheer veil covered most of her face. It was a Fardohnyan fancy, this idea that if a woman covered her mouth in public, nobody would think it the least immodest if she exposed every inch of her flesh from just below her breast to just below her navel.

She was alone as she stepped into the room. The princess looked about uncertainly for a moment, not noticing Kiam by the fire at the other end of the hall. When she spied him, she squared her shoulders, almost as if she were bracing herself to meet him, and began to walk forward.

Broos lifted his head and growled softly in the back of his throat. "Down, boy," Kiam ordered in a low voice. "Not going to help either of us if you eat one of the king of Fardohnya's daughters."

The dog sat up, looking up at him expectantly. Kiam turned his attention to the princess, figuring the only polite thing to do was meet her halfway. Kiam stepped forward, but she held up her hand to halt his approach.

What? Am I not permitted to grubby her royal presence with my proximity?

"Please, don't leave the fire," the princess said as she approached in almost perfect Hythrun. "It's freezing in here. I'd not have anybody turned into an icicle on my account."

Kiam wasn't expecting that. He bowed as she approached and accepted her hand, kissing her palm in the traditional Fardohnyan manner. Her hand was small and calloused, as if she had ridden too often without gloves, the skin was rough and her nails unmanicured—something else he did not expect in a Fardohnyan princess.

"Your highness. Welcome to Hythria."

Rakaia lowered her veil and smiled at him. She was quite gorgeous. Not unexpectedly—all Hablet's wives were great beauties. This daughter was stunning; a dusky beauty with kohl-lined eyes the color of sapphires, long dark lashes, and lips so full and ripe Kiam could imagine himself gladly selling his soul to get a taste of them. *Oh, you are going to cause a riot when you make your first appearance in Greenharbour.*

Adrina was right to be worried.

"You are too young to be Lord Lionsclaw," she said as she took his measure. She spoke Hythrun flawlessly, but with just enough of an accent to make it endearing. "Which makes you one of his younger brothers, I'm guessing?"

"Actually, I'm not a Lionsclaw at all, your highness. My name is Kiam Miar. Your sister, the High Princess Adrina, sent me to escort you to Greenharbour."

She seemed a little puzzled for a moment and then recognition dawned on her and she snatched her hand from his, glancing at the silver raven ring he wore on his left hand. "Oh . . . you're the assassin."

Stuck-up little bitch. Apparently his common-born status wasn't good enough to escort someone as exalted as a princess. Or maybe it was his occupation. He forgot, sometimes, that people assumed his profession as an assassin made him a heartless, cold-blooded killer. "I am the High Prince's stepbrother, your highness."

The princess seemed unaccountably relieved. "I'm sorry . . . It's just . . . we hear stories in Talabar about Adrina and how she's become so . . . Hythrun . . . these days. I just wondered . . . Is that your dog? He's gorgeous!"

Broos seemed to have a change of heart about this newcomer. He padded over to her, wagging his tail. His head came up to her waist, but she seemed unafraid. In fact, she appeared quite enchanted by him. "Can I pat him?"

"If you're prepared to risk being his dinner."

"Oh, he wouldn't hurt me. Would you, gorgeous?" She took off her veil and tossed it over the nearest chair, as if she knew it might confuse and frighten the dog, and then held out her hand.

Rather than take her arm off at the elbow, Broos surprised Kiam by licking the princess's hand gently and then sidling up to her for a pat. With the veil off and her attention on the dog, he had a chance to study her more closely. She looked nothing like Adrina, who—with her green eyes and dark hair—embodied the ideal of exotic Fardohnyan beauty. Her younger sister was much smaller boned and finer featured, with sapphire blue eyes—unusual in a Fardohnyan—and luscious, light, honey brown hair. With her attention on Broos, Rakaia had momentarily dropped all pretense of arrogance or aloofness. This, Kiam guessed, was a rare glimpse of the girl behind the princess.

"What's his name?"

"Broos."

She rubbed his head, and Broos lapped it up like a harem lap dog. "Hello, Broos. You're just the friendliest old thing in the world, aren't you?"

"I doubt the stable boy who tried to convince him he should sleep in the stables would agree with you," Kiam said with a laugh. "You have a real way with animals."

"Comes from a lifetime of—" She stopped abruptly, as if she'd changed her mind about what she wanted to say. Then the sweet girl was gone and the princess was back, suddenly unsure of herself. "I mean . . . it's just . . . well, Adrina didn't send you here to kill me, did she?"

"No."

"I didn't mean to imply . . ."

"You have nothing to fear from your sister, your highness," he assured her. "Quite the contrary. The High Princess is looking forward to your visit. She so rarely gets to see any of her sisters. She gave me very specific instructions about delivering you safely to Greenharbour."

Actually, Adrina had told him: *Get her here in one piece, Ky, as fast as you can. Don't let her distract you, flirt with you, or flirt with anybody else along the way. Truth is, I'm sending you to fetch her because you occupy a unique position here—you're a member of the Wolfblade family but you're not high-born, so she's less likely to consider you a prospect. I'm pretty sure she won't be too thrilled about the man she has to marry, and I don't want her trying to make alternative arrangements. Make sure the Raiders you take are all common-born too, so she doesn't get any ideas about one of them.*

Adrina had turned to him then, looking deeply anxious. *And for the gods' sake, get to Winternest before she has a chance to spend any time alone with Valorian Lionsclaw. I don't want to be the one to break it to the Warlord of Sunrise Province that her son and heir has been amusing himself with a Fardohnyan.*

Adrina's concerns were not unfounded, Kiam decided. This girl could probably melt the stoutest heart if she set her mind to it.

"That's a relief to hear, my lor—What do I call you?"

"Master Miar is the acceptable form of address in Hythria for commoners, your highness." Then he added, before he could stop himself. "Or you could call me Ky."

Rakaia smiled at him. *Oh, this is going to be an interesting trip.*

"Do we know each other well enough yet for first names, Master Miar?"

He bowed formally. She'd been here less than five minutes and he was already falling under her spell. "Of course, you're right, your highness. Forgive me for being so forward."

"Ah! There you are!" Valorian announced as he strode through the door at the other end of the hall. "I've just ordered our meal brought up. Welcome to Hythria, your highness."

Rakaia turned to Valorian with a winning smile, but not before she winked at him and whispered out of the corner of her mouth, "You're forgiven."

After that, Rakaia focused her attention on Valorian Lionsclaw, and for the rest of the evening Kiam was able to watch and listen while they shared a meal and decide that nothing about Her Serene Highness, the Princess Rakaia of Fardohnya, made any sense at all.

Chapter

10

THE FIRST THING Her Serene Highness, the Princess Rakaia of Fardohnya did when she returned to her room after dinner was throw up.

It wasn't the rich food she'd eaten at dinner that caused her upset
stomach.

It was fear. It was anxiety.

It was dread anticipation, waiting for someone to look at her and realize immediately she wasn't who she claimed to be.

It was the certainty that she couldn't carry this off.

It was the positive expectation that any minute somebody would turn
and point at her and yell: *Imposter!*

How could you do this to me, Rakaia?

Truth was, Rakaia had done nothing to her. Charisee had done it to
herself. There was nothing stopping her going downstairs right now and
admitting to Lord Lionsclaw that she wasn't Rakaia but the princess's
base-born half-sister and servant, Charisee.

She would be in trouble, of course, and so would Rakaia when they
found her and brought her back. But Rakaia would get a telling off. Her own
fate was far less certain, particularly because she hadn't raised the alarm
the moment she learned Rakaia had run away. Adrina might just have
her whipped for her temerity or she might send her back to Talabar, where
Charisee had no doubt her father, King Hablet, would have his base-born
daughter put to the sword for embarrassing him so.

Charisee wiped her mouth and sat on the bed in her borrowed finery.
She closed her eyes, relieved her stomach had settled somewhat. She supposed it was because there was nothing left to expel. For a moment she
just sat there, a frozen mass of indecision and panic. And then she turned
and reached under the pillow for the only real evidence of her deceit.

Charisee unfolded the letter carefully, although she'd read it so many
times since she'd woken this morning to find Rakaia missing she already
knew its contents by heart.

Dearest Chari, the letter began. *Please don't be mad at me.*

I know you think this is a crazy idea and I know you swore you wouldn't have a bar of it, so I've decided to make the decision for both of us.

I cannot, will not, follow the path Papa has laid out for me, while I wait for Alaric to ascend to the throne. When you calm down and have time to reflect on this, you'll understand why I believe everything will turn out for the best. You deserve more than life as a slave, even a well-positioned one, while I cannot abide the future laid out for me. We have this one chance to change our fortunes. I'm going to grab it with both hands.

I pray to all the Primal Gods and Goddesses there are that you'll do the same.

I've arranged passage with a caravan heading west, which will get me safely out of Winternest. I'll just tell them I'm you. Nobody has seen my face in Winternest, and with my entourage sent home nobody in Hythria will deny you when you claim to be me. We both have blue eyes and Adrina hasn't laid eyes on either of us since we were children. She has no reason to suspect you are not Rakaia, while ever you conduct yourself like a princess.

I know you can. The gods know you're always telling me how it should be done.

Please don't worry about me. I've taken my bridal jewelry to sell along the way, so I will be well catered to, and I've left enough for you so it won't look too suspicious. I can't wait to start my new life. Maybe, some day in the future, when I think it's safe, we'll get together again and I'll tell you all about the grand adventures I've had. You can tell me about the wonderful life you can now have, as a princess of Fardohnya.

Anyway, it is done. I am gone, and any day now Adrina's escort will arrive. What you tell them is entirely up to you. If you must admit the truth, then so be it. I'll understand. And if they do manage to find me and drag me back, I'll try not to be too upset with you.

Or you could do the smart thing. You could put on my dress, hold your head up high, and announce you are Her Serene Highness, Rakaia, Princess of Fardohnya, marry Lord Branador, wait until he dies a few years from now (sooner if you feed him up until he's too fat to walk), and have the life you would have had if your mother had been a noblewoman instead of a whore.

I love you, Charisee. You have been my best and truest friend all my life. I will miss you desperately and think of you often. But I won't turn back, and if they find me I'll just run away again, as soon as I get the opportunity. Please save all of us the trouble and take this gift I'm giving you.

Once you've read this letter, burn it. Few people outside the harem know what Rakaia of Fardohnya looks like. Even Papa used to forget which of us was his legitimate child. Once this letter is destroyed, nobody can deny your claim.

You can do this.

I have done it.

Be well, little sister. Have a happy life.

Love, Rakaia

Charisee folded the letter and glanced over at the fire, wondering why she hadn't burned the letter yet. Rakaia was right about so many things. They would never in their lives have an opportunity like this again. This was her chance to have what her accident of birth had always denied her—a position of wealth and privilege as one of the king of Fardohnya's royal daughters. And Rakaia didn't want it.

Since she was a small child, Rakaia had dreamed of wild adventures, sailing the world to visit exotic ports, and making her mark in the world like Adrina had done. It was Rakaia's admiration of her eldest sister that had lulled Charisee into thinking she wasn't serious when she first suggested they swap identities once they reached Winternest. She thought Rakaia was dying to meet Adrina and find out how she'd managed to defy their father and end up married for love rather than political gain.

She hadn't counted on Rakaia wanting a different life so badly she was prepared to forfeit that opportunity for the chance to escape.

Charisee turned the letter over and over in her hands. If she confessed now, would Rakaia hate her? Was it selfish to deny her sister this rare chance, just because she was afraid of what they might do to her accomplice?

And it's not as if I'd be lying if I present myself to Adrina as her half-sister. I am still Hablet's daughter.

Just not the daughter she's expecting.

Charisee realized she'd made her decision and started to feel nauseous again wondering how she could pull it off. She'd almost ruined everything, she knew, when she let Kiam Miar kiss her palm. He was so handsome and he'd been so charming and pleasant and then he'd noticed the calluses on her hands and her slave's work-worn fingernails. She could see him wondering about them. She was careful not to let Valorian greet her in the same manner after that, and realized she would need to wear gloves until her nails grew longer, the calluses faded, and her hands looked more like those belonging to a princess. That wouldn't be hard as they rode down from the mountains, but she would need to be careful when they reached Greenharbour.

But even if Kiam Miar thought it odd, Rakaia was right in her claim that few people outside the harem knew what Princess Rakaia looked like.

Her missing sister was wrong about one thing, however. There was no way Charisee was going to burn this letter. It was the evidence she might need someday to prove this madness had been Rakaia's idea. If she were ever caught, if Rakaia was ever caught, perhaps if—as Rakaia suggested—Charisee needed to throw herself on Adrina's mercy someday when Alaric became king and started eliminating his siblings, then she needed proof Rakaia had instigated this deception. Otherwise they might simply think she had just killed her sister and taken her place for her own advancement.

"Dear gods, what am I thinking?" she said aloud. And then she closed her eyes.

Jakerlon, she prayed silently. *Hear me, please. If I take on my sister's identity, I will be honoring the God of Liars for the rest of my life. Please watch over me, Jakerlon, God of Liars. Please keep me safe and I will not let you down.*

The God of Liars did not answer her, of course, but it made it a little easier to think she was honoring the gods while helping her sister.

Charisee tucked the letter back under her pillow. She would have to find somewhere safe to store it tomorrow, and she needed to get some sleep because they were leaving for Greenharbour at first light. She didn't want to be late for her escort.

And then it occurred to Charisee that it didn't matter. She was a princess now, and if she wandered down to breakfast mid-morning, while they all waited shivering in the snow for hours for her to appear, well, then, so be it.

They were here to escort her, not the other way around.

Being Rakaia is going to be harder than I thought, Charisee realized, which was depressing in the extreme because until this morning when she woke to discover Rakaia had run away, she'd thought it almost impossible.

"IF YOU'RE NOT looking for work, how much are you willing to pay for passage?"

Lose yourself at Winternest. That's what Sophany had instructed her daughter to do. *Under no circumstances can you leave Winternest with Adrina's escort.*

Once that happened, there was no escape. The Princess Rakaia would be guarded like the precious commodity she was, and she would never again have a chance to escape her eventual assassination when King Hablet learned his wife had betrayed him.

As the bearded, impatient merchant stared her down, waiting for her answer, she quivered, unable to answer his question. She had no idea what passage in a trade caravan cost. She hadn't even asked where they were headed. All she knew is that the customs man said this fur-cloaked, hairy brute might be willing to take passengers. There were two other girls already seated in the wagon. That might mean safety or trouble. Rakaia had no way of telling which.

"Are you deaf as well as stupid?" the trader bellowed.

Rakaia looked around the courtyard of the Winternest keep, certain everyone must be staring at them. It was barely dawn and the caravans were anxious to be on their way. Several fires lit in metal braziers had clusters of caravan guards huddled around them, drinking mulled wine and warming their hands. It was spring, but there were still piles of dirty snow shoveled against the walls and the air stung with a stiff, icy breeze. Shivering in her half-sister's borrowed cloak—not nearly as grand or warm as her own—Rakaia feared that any moment now someone was going to point at her and yell, "That's her! The princess! Don't let her leave!"

But nobody said a word. The yard was filled with people and wagons, livestock, chickens, and soldiers stationed here at the keep, wearing the red and gold livery of Sunrise Province emblazoned with the lion's head escutcheon of the Lionsclaw family, in addition to the scores of mercenaries who guarded the caravans. There were several whores relaxing on the steps of the main hall after their night's labors and a number of harried customs men running back and forth, trying to make sure no revenue slipped past them and into the greedy hands of their Fardohnyan counterparts on the other side of the Widowmaker Pass.

"Um . . . what would *you* consider a fair price?" she asked, hoping he'd give her some idea. Rakaia had never had to buy so much as a jug of wine in her entire life before today.

The man laughed. It was a big, hearty bellow that made her feel like a small child. "Ha, you think you're cleverer than me, don't you?"

"I guess we'll find that out when we've agreed on a price," she replied, not sure how much longer she could hedge like this without naming a figure. It wasn't that she didn't want to pay. Her mother had equipped her with a handful of gold coins and she carried a king's ransom in jewelry tucked into the belt of Charisee's borrowed dress. What she lacked, she was discovering very quickly, were the basic life skills one needed to survive outside a harem.

"Very well. One hundred rivets!"

The only thing Rakaia knew about haggling was something she'd overheard her father say once when he was negotiating a trade deal with some Denikan princes who'd driven a hard bargain, by all accounts, for their precious sulfur and saltpeter—*he who mentions a price first, loses.*

And by the way the guards walking past them were laughing, she figured his price was ridiculous.

"Five rivets," she countered.

"That's insulting!"

"So is your offer."

"Eighty, then, and if you don't like it, you can walk."

She guessed he was bluffing. She hoped he was bluffing. "Twenty."

The trader studied her for a moment and then he nodded. "Twenty it is."

It seemed a little quick, but at least now Rakaia had her way out of Winternest. She turned her back to the man as she fished the coins from her purse, and then turned back and placed them in his outstretched hand.

He laughed again as his meaty, grimy fingers closed over the coins. "Ha! Who is so clever now! I would have taken you for five rivets."

You're not so clever, Rakaia thought. *I'd have been happy to pay eighty.* But she kept her thoughts to herself as she followed the man to the covered wagon he owned. Let him have his minor victory.

She glanced up at the sky. It would be full daylight soon and Charisee would wake. "How long before we leave?"

"Soon." The trader then wrapped his big, meaty hands around her waist and lifted her bodily into the wagon. "In the meantime you can keep Aja and Barlia company."

She supposed he meant the two young women already seated in the wagon, who were watching her curiously. She smiled at them warily and turned to the trader. "Are they your wives?"

That set the man off again, laughing hilariously. "Wives? Oh, you are too much, girl . . . Wives." He headed off toward the front of the wagon and his horses, still guffawing. As she took her seat on the wooden bench that lined each side of the wagon, she could hear him saying, "Hey, Kirko, did you hear that? Aja and Barlia are my wives!"

The girls seemed to find it amusing, too. Rakaia didn't get what was so funny or why they were laughing at her. One of the girls noticed her irritation. "Marten is our . . . employer," she explained. "He's flattered you think him respectable enough to own two young wives. Or maybe that you think he has two wives at all."

Only then did Rakaia notice the jeweled *court'esa* collars the women wore. She cursed her foolishness. They weren't "fine ladies"; they were whores, albeit well-trained and very valuable whores. Even if they hadn't been, she should have remembered Hythrun men only took one wife at a time. She was demonstrating nothing but her breathtaking ignorance of the wider world by not acknowledging that. "He's not offended, is he?"

The older girl shook her head. "You've probably made his day. Are you riding all the way to Tarkent with us?"

Is that where we're headed? Tarkent was the largest seaport in southern Fardohnya. She had a chance to find a way to her uncle's province overland as well as by sea, from Tarkent. Rakaia glanced out of the wagon. Surely they would be leaving soon? Charisee might wake any moment, find that letter, and then do what she invariably did and blurt out the truth. "I hope so."

That was the fatal flaw in her mother's plan, Rakaia had always thought. Charisee was a terrible liar. Neither did Rakaia share her mother's view that her slave-born half-sister would jump at the chance to become a princess. More likely she would come clean about her true identity and where her sister had gone the first time someone looked at her sideways.

Rakaia looked out of the caravan again, wondering what was taking so long. Although she knew Charisee would not deliberately betray her, she also knew the younger girl was honest to the point of being exasperating. Even if she'd wanted to help Rakaia escape, even if Rakaia had confessed the true reason for fleeing the harem, Charisee might not be able to help herself and accidentally give the game away.

Either way, Rakaia had no intention of being in Winternest when her half-sister's conscience got the better of her.

It had been much easier than she'd feared to get away. While the huge Fardohnyan caravan filled the courtyard of Winternest and drew everyone's attention from the Fardohnyan princess in residence, Rakaia had taken Charisee's plain, homespun servant's dress and cloak, and most of the bridal jewelry her father had gifted to her, while her sister slept in her bed, made her way across the bridge connecting the two halves of the fortress, then headed downstairs to the main yard to negotiate her passage.

She had chosen well. Tarkent. From there Rakaia could make her way to Lanipoor and her uncle's palace. Her mother promised he would protect her. She just had to find a way to Lanipoor.

Find a way . . . Gods, a month ago I was a princess. I never in my life thought I'd need to worry about finding my way anywhere.

The caravan finally moved off, trundling slowly out of the massive studded gates of Winternest in the early morning, and not a moment too soon. As they made their way out of the keep and onto the road to the Widowmaker Pass, a century of Greenharbour Raiders waited patiently for them to pass on the southern side of the road. Rakaia hunkered down in the back of the canvas-covered wagon while Aja and Barlia waved and flirted with the Raiders as the troop rode by. She heard Marten exchange a greeting with the soldiers, but couldn't hear exactly what they were saying. She didn't need to. This was the escort, she didn't doubt for a moment, sent to bring Princess Rakaia to Greenharbour.

"Did you see her?"

Rakaia looked up as Aja—the younger of the *court'esa*—tired of watching the Raiders, returned to her seat in the back of the wagon. They traveled in an unremarkable vehicle, with no obvious signs of wealth, not even a guard. Marten thought the caravan protection enough, apparently. Perhaps he worried an extra guard only served to advertise that he had something worth protecting. The Widowmaker Pass and the mountains surrounding Winternest were riddled with bandits. Marten carried a large quarterstaff across his knees as he drove to deter trouble, and kept his *court'esa* out of sight, in case the thought of taking slaves or the chance for a bit of recreational rape and pillage overcame the mountain bandits' natural caution.

"Did I see who?" Rakaia asked.

Aja was a pretty girl of about seventeen with thick curly hair and skin the color of rich dark chocolate. Her companion, Barlia, was a little older and well on her way to becoming jaded. Her hair was braided into hundreds of thin strands with various charms and beads plaited into the ends, making her clink softly whenever she moved her head. Aja still teetered on the brink of childhood—all gangly legs and tactless curiosity.

"The princess."

"What princess?"

"The Fardohnyan one that was supposed to be at Winternest when we were there."

"How do you know about her?"

"We passed her retinue in the Widowmaker," Aja said. "They were heading back to Talabar. Do you suppose she's very pretty?"

"It won't matter," Barlia said, pushing aside the canvas wagon cover to take a seat on top of one of their trunks as the rattle of tack and clop of the Raiders' horses faded into the distance. "She'll be a spoiled, stuck-up little bitch, whatever she looks like."

"How do you know that?"

"All Hablet's daughters are. She could be the most beautiful creature in all creation, but I'll bet you anything you name she's as ugly as sin on the inside."

Rakaia was shocked. And more than a little wounded by Barlia's harsh and completely unwarranted assessment of her character.

"She might be nice," Rakaia suggested.

Barlia shook her head. "I know you probably feel the need to defend your countrymen, but really . . . even in Fardohnya, have you *ever* heard anybody with anything good to say about a single one of Hablet's daughters?"

Rakaia was shocked. *Is that true? Do people hate us?*

And why do I care—I'm not one of Hablet's daughters.

"Do you despise the High Princess of Hythria as much as you despise her sisters?" Rakaia asked. Even if she dismissed Barlia's words as simple Trinity Isle prejudice against Fardohnyans, surely they didn't think that about the Fardohnyan-born High Princess of Hythria. Besides, Rakaia thought everybody in Hythria loved Adrina. Her mother had assured her the Hythrun would welcome their high princess's younger sister with open arms when she expressed concern for Charisee's eventual fate. It never occurred to Rakaia people might hate her just because of who she was.

Barlia shrugged. "Adrina seems a cut above your average Fardohnyan princess, I suppose, from what I hear. They say the High Prince is besotted by her."

"I heard she bewitched him."

"That's ridiculous, Aja," Barlia said, settling herself more comfortably on her makeshift seat. "She did no such thing."

"Maybe the Harshini bewitched him, then," Aja insisted. She liked the idea of somebody being bewitched, apparently.

"Why would they do that?" Rakaia asked. She didn't believe such nonsense for a moment, but this was proving to be a very strange new world she was entering. She needed to find out everything she could about it, while she had the opportunity. Once they reached Tarkent, she would be on her own.

"Well, for peace, of course," Aja said, rolling her eyes at the obviousness of the answer. "There hasn't been a proper war on this continent since Damin of Hythria married Adrina of Fardohnya."

"What about the war in Medalon?" Rakaia asked, wishing she'd paid more attention to her lessons in government and history. "Didn't someone lay siege to the Citadel in Medalon, or something, after they got married?"

"That was right after. And Hythria didn't lay the siege. Prince Damin *broke* the Karien siege of the Citadel and then the demon child saved the Harshini by killing the Karien god, Xaphista," Barlia said. "That's what Aja means. Since then, the Harshini have returned to the Citadel, the Sisters of the Blade are done, Karien has embraced all the gods again, and King Drendik's sworn to stay on his side of the border. The High Prince of Hythria and the Lord Defender of Medalon are apparently best friends. And Hythria and Fardohnya can't go to war any longer, because the Hythrun High Prince is married to your king's eldest daughter, so even if he wanted to, Hablet's not permitted to declare war. Hythria even has a treaty with our people now."

Aja nodded in agreement. "Marten says that's why there's so many bandits about these days in the Sunrise Mountains. All that's left for fighting men to do is be a bandit or be employed chasing them down."

"But isn't being at peace a good thing?" Rakaia asked, not sure she understood what these girls were complaining about.

"Not if you're the God of War," Aja chuckled.

"We used to pray to him all the time when I was little," Barlia told her with a sigh. "Now we pray to the God of Thieves to protect us on the road from his followers. Who do you pray to . . . ? What is your name, anyway?"

"Ra . . . Raka," she stammered. "And I used to worship Jelanna. My papa wanted lots of babies."

"He must be a very rich man!" Marten called from the seat of the wagon outside. Their employer must have been listening to their conversation. Then he added with a chuckle, "No pauper wishes for more mouths to feed."

"Well, he wasn't a wise man," Rakaia called back, forcing a laugh to cover up the fact that she had almost let something about her true identity slip. "I can promise you that!"

"He taught you to speak Denikan well," Barlia remarked, looking at her with a hint of suspicion.

"He made sure we all spoke as many languages as possible," she said, silently cursing her mother for not coming up with a plausible reason for that. It wasn't common to be multilingual, particularly not a girl, unless she was of noble birth. Hablet's reason for educating his daughters was simple. They were easier to marry off to foreigners in far distant lands where they would no longer bother him if they spoke the language.

"Well, it's a good thing, I say," Aja said, smiling at Rakaia. "It's a long way to Tarkent. This way you can practice your Denikan and we can practice our Fardohnyan."

"You'd all be better served practicing not saying anything at all," Marten called back to them from the front of the wagon, but his *court'esa* laughed and ignored his comments. As the sound of Rakaia's escort faded into the distance, and the caravan moved westward into the narrow mountain pass, Rakaia spent the rest of the morning naming items in the wagon for her traveling companions while they taught her the correct pronunciation in their language.

Running away, it seemed, had proved not only remarkably easy, but it turned out to be kind of, well, fun.

12

CHARISEE FOUND IT difficult to sleep. By the time dawn broke over the edge of the Sunrise Mountains the following morning, she knew what she needed to do.

She couldn't do this.

The only thing to do was to march downstairs and announce she was Charisee, Rakaia's base-born sister, that the Princess Rakaia had run away yesterday, and she had bought herself passage in that big caravan heading back to Fardohnya.

She rehearsed her speech over and over. In her head, it sounded reasonable. All she could do, really, was throw herself on the mercy of Lord Lionsclaw. She wished she could rehearse what would happen after that.

Charisee did wonder, for a fleeting moment, if she would be better off not mentioning anything to Valorian Lionsclaw, but waiting until she was alone with Kiam Miar. Lord Lionsclaw was a nobleman, and although he seemed reasonable enough, that was probably because he thought he was dealing with a genuine Fardohnyan princess. She didn't know what he would do when he discovered one of Hablet's daughters had been able to run away while in his care.

Kiam, on the other hand, was an assassin. He'd seemed really . . . well, nice. And he, at least, she could trust not to kill her out of hand. The Assassins' Guild had rules about who they could and couldn't kill. The irony of knowing she might actually have a better chance of making it to Greenharbour alive if she waited until she was on the road with an assassin before she broke the news about her true identity was not lost on Charisee for a moment.

Bent low into the wind, Charisee pulled her cloak tight against the spring sleet battering the fortress as she ran across the high arched bridge. She ignored the bows and salutes of the guards patrolling the bridge joining the two halves of Winternest castle. By default, she supposed it made her look even more regal—a princess refusing to even acknowledge the greetings of lesser mortals. It couldn't be helped. Besides the biting wind driving the sleet obscuring her vision which cut through her like a blade made of jagged ice, she wasn't sure if her courage had enough conviction in it to survive any sort of delay—particularly not a delay that reinforced the notion she might actually get away with posing as Rakaia if she just kept her big mouth shut.

She hurried through the heavily studded, reinforced door the shivering guard opened for her and took the worn stone steps down to the main hall as fast as she dared, grateful to be out of the blizzard. The circular stairwell was dark, lit only by the occasional west-facing arrow slit and a sputtering torch every few score steps, which struggled to burn in the chilly air. Outside she could hear the wind howling around the fortress, making her doubt that even with the best of intentions they'd be traveling anywhere today—at least not until the weather settled down.

Lord Lionsclaw, I have a confession to make . . .

That's how she would start. Charisee repeated the phrase over and over to herself as she ran down the stairs, each step taking her closer to the end of her brief, glorious moment as a real princess.

I wonder what the dungeons are like here?

She opened the door at the foot of the stairwell, expecting to find Lord Lionsclaw and Kiam Miar waiting for her by the customs table, tapping their feet impatiently.

Instead, she stepped into chaos.

Despite the bitter weather outside, the main hall—the beating heart of Winternest—was filled with Raiders, obviously preparing to ride out. There must have been more than two hundred men checking weapons and equipment, sharpening swords, and piling on extra furs to protect them from the cold. At first, Charisee couldn't even pick out Valorian Lionsclaw or Kiam Miar, and then she spied them by the huge fireplace on the hall's eastern wall near where the barkeep stored his barrels.

Lord Lionsclaw, I have a confession to make . . .

Whatever these fighting men were up to, she had her own mission. Charisee braced herself for what she must do, striding purposefully across the hall through the melee until she reached her goal. Valorian Lionsclaw looked up as she approached, closed his eyes for the briefest of moments as if he'd forgotten about her, and then he forced a smile.

Lord Lionsclaw, I have a confession to make . . .

Before she could get the words out, Valorian shook his head apologetically and bowed to her. "Your highness, I am *so* sorry you weren't advised. But your journey to Greenharbour won't be happening today."

"Why not?" she asked, which was not what she'd intended to say at all. *Lord Lionsclaw, I have a confession to make . . .* That's what she should have said. And it was a stupid question anyway.

"The Farman Brothers' caravan was hit by bandits in the Widowmaker last night," Kiam explained, surprising Charisee with the reason, because anybody with eyes could see the weather was unfit for travel, and she'd assumed that was the only reason their journey would be delayed.

She must have been staring at them like an idiot, prompting Valorian to add, "The large caravan that left here yesterday morning, your highness. Do you remember?"

Charisee felt the blood drain from her face. "Oh . . . gods . . . no . . ."

"Your highness?"

I've arranged passage with a caravan, which will get me safely out of Winternest . . . Rakaia was in that caravan. Charisee was certain of it. She glanced around the hall at the Raiders getting ready to ride out in the storm. "They're . . . they're going to rescue the survivors, yes?"

Lord Lionsclaw shook his head. "No. They're going out to hunt down the bandits before the trail grows cold—no pun intended. There are no survivors."

Charisee's world suddenly shuddered out of alignment. She felt ill with the force of the jolt.

"*What* . . . ?" She didn't have the breath or the strength to finish the question.

Valorian didn't answer her. Someone was hailing him from across the hall. Too distracted to notice her distress, he apologized for his rudeness, bowed briefly, and hurried off, leaving Kiam Miar to answer her questions.

Kiam watched him leave and then turned to Charisee. "Best they can tell, the bandits hit the caravan just on dusk yesterday. They were sitting ducks, actually. The lead wagon broke an axle—which may or may not have been an accident—blocking the whole caravan in the pass about three miles our side of the border. The bandits hit them just before the storm did. Do you need to sit down, your highness?"

This can't be happening. It can't be true. She felt her knees give way. Kiam caught her before she could fall, his arms the only real thing she had to cling to in a world suddenly spinning out of control. "But there were guards . . . lots of them. And . . . all those people . . ."

"Oh . . . they put up a decent fight by all accounts," Kiam agreed, leading her to a bench so she could sit down. "Lord Lionsclaw thinks they were pretty badly outnumbered. Apparently, the bandits around the Widowmaker have been getting more and more aggressive these past few years." Kiam studied her with concern for a moment. "Pity they tried to fight. They might have been better off just handing over the goods. I'm not sure a few wagonloads of wool and some barrels of ale are worth more than fifty lives."

"No . . . but . . . but . . . there must have been *some* survivors. What about the women? The children?"

"Raped and put to the sword, according to the patrol who found them. Those who didn't die in the fighting were left to perish in the blizzard. I'm sorry, is this distressing you, your highness? You've gone very pale."

Raped and put to the sword.

Oh, Rakaia, what did you do? Did you fight them off? Did you die in terrible agony because you resisted or did you perish afterward in the cold, broken and battered and alone?

"Your highness?"

Charisee had to force herself to concentrate. "What?"

Kiam was looking at her with real concern. "Did you want some mulled wine? You really shouldn't have braved that wretched bridge in this weather."

Charisee shook her head. The last thing she needed was alcohol dulling her senses. "Are you going out with your men to hunt the bandits too?"

"My job is to escort you to Greenharbour, your highness."

That surprised her. Surely the last thing on the minds of anybody here was escorting a lone woman to Greenharbour, even one as important as the imposter posing as the high princess's sister.

"But doesn't Lord Lionsclaw need the Raiders you brought with you? I mean . . . if there were enough bandits to overwhelm a caravan so large . . . ?"

"Those Raiders are here to escort *you*, your highness."

"But one princess doesn't need a hundred-man honor guard," she said before she could stop herself. "She's just one person . . ."

I have a confession to make. I'm not even the person you think I am.

"Excuse me if I misunderstand you, your highness, but are you suggesting you'd be happy traveling to Greenharbour with a reduced guard so the remainder can stay here and help hunt down these bandits?" He spoke as if he couldn't believe such a circumstance were possible.

Had Charisee been a real daughter of Hablet, it probably wouldn't have been possible. But she was a fraud. *And the only person in Hythria who knows it is dead.*

I love you, Charisee . . . take this gift I'm giving you.

"Um . . . yes . . . I believe that's exactly what I'm suggesting." *Oh, dear gods and little demons, what am I doing?*

The assassin was silent for a long moment and then he nodded. "Very well, I'll speak to Lord Lionsclaw and tell him he has reinforcements, news I'm quite sure he'll welcome. Would a guard of, say . . . ten . . . be considered suitable to escort someone of your rank to the capital, do you think?"

Charisee nodded slowly as the enormity of what she was doing began to dawn on her. She gulped and then waved her hand to cover her nervousness. "My dear sister, the High Princess Adrina, clearly trusts your judgment in these matters, Master Miar," she said, trying to answer the way Rakaia might have done, "or she would not have sent you to escort me. Whatever number you think is appropriate will be acceptable to me."

There. That wasn't so hard.

Still staring at her as if he couldn't believe what he was hearing, Kiam nodded, and then called over one of his Raiders, ordered him to arrange wine for the princess and to see she wasn't disturbed. The Raider—a young ginger-haired lad with dark freckles scattered across his nose—ordered her wine from the barkeep who catered to Winternest's travelers and residents alike, and then took up post to guard her from the riffraff.

Charisee accepted the wine a few moments later with a grateful nod to the barkeep, sat with her back to the rest of the hall, and buried her face in the goblet to hide her guilt, a puddle of nervous self-loathing and grief.

I love you, Charisee . . . take this gift I'm giving you.

Charisee drained the wine in a gulp as her eyes filled with grief-stricken tears. As soon as she got back to her room, she was going to burn that wretched letter. There was no point keeping it now.

I love you too, Rakaia. And I will.

Chapter

13

RIDING IN A wagon with no suspension on a wooden box covered with a sheepskin that had seen better days proved a very uncomfortable way to travel, even with a couple of talkative *court'esa* for company. By mid-afternoon, Rakaia was quite certain she would be permanently twisted out of shape, and when the caravan ground to a halt when the lead wagon broke its axle, she was relieved beyond words for the chance to get out, stretch her legs, and, most of all, relieve herself.

She wasn't the only one who took the opportunity, despite the cold wind howling though the Widowmaker, funneled by the steep cliff walls lining the road still covered with snow. The trees at the top of the jagged cliffs had shed most of their winter white, but down here in the pass, where the ground was shadowed for much of the day, it was cold, unpleasant, and nerve-wracking.

Bandits were a problem in the pass. Even in Talabar they knew that, hence the reason her father . . . or rather, the king of Fardohnya, had been so anxious to broker a deal with Highcastle farther to the south, where attacks on trading caravans were much less frequent. Stopping was never a good idea in the Widowmaker. The rule, so Marten had explained as they entered the pass this morning, was no stopping. Not for anything.

"If you want to pee, you hop out of the moving wagon, do your business, then run to catch up," he instructed them all as they trundled into the pass at the end of the caravan. "Hope you don't need a crap, because we'll not be waiting for anybody's shit." He'd laughed uproariously at his own joke and clucked the horses forward.

It hadn't seemed such a problem first thing this morning. As the day wore on, however, Rakaia could feel her bladder filling until it was painful. Her two companions had done exactly as Marten instructed, some time ago, laughing as they ran to catch the slow-moving wagon and clamber onboard. If they guessed how much pain Rakaia was in, they said nothing, although when Rakaia grunted after they'd hit a particularly nasty pothole, they exchanged a look she just knew was laden with amusement at her expense.

Once they were out of the wagon, Rakaia discovered most of the passengers, and quite a few of the traders and their guards, had the same idea. Within moments there was a long line of men unlacing their trousers and more than a few women lifting their skirts to irrigate the icy cliff wall, accompanied by jokes about the size of their equipment and the lousy aim of quite a few of the men. Shivering in cold wind, Rakaia knew she should join them. She was supposed to be a commoner. Relieving herself in full sight of everyone should have meant nothing to her. She just couldn't bring herself to do it.

"Look at Lady Prim-and-Proper," Aja laughed as she lifted her skirts and squatted on the side of the road, not caring in the slightest that she had an audience. "You waiting for a private privy?"

Rakaia forced a smile and glanced around. There was a scraggly bush forcing its way between the rocks some twenty paces from their wagon, which was the last one in the caravan. "Looking for somewhere *upwind*," she said. "This wind is brutal and I don't fancy a golden shower."

Barlia laughed. "I could introduce you to a few men who'd pay handsomely for a golden shower!"

Rakaia laughed too, or at least she pretended to, and made her way toward the bush. There was one lone guard standing at post, hand on his sword, watching the pass behind them. He nodded to her as she passed, but seemed more concerned about what might be coming up the road than what she was up to. The pass curved slightly behind the bush, giving her the illusion of privacy. Anxious to relieve her pain she raised her skirts, squatted down, and sighed with relief as her bladder emptied.

She closed her eyes for a moment, wondering how she was going to get from Tarkent to Lanipoor, where her mother promised her uncle—whom she had never met—would provide her with a safe place to hide from Hablet's wrath. Rakaia still thought the plan was just a little bit crazy. Surely, if anybody tried to look for her, the first place would be with the only family she owned outside of the harem.

But then, the plan was that nobody would realize she was missing. That's what Charisee was for . . .

"Talk about being caught with y'pants down."

At the sound of the whispered comment, Rakaia's eyes flew open.

Infuriated, she silently cursed whoever had followed her and ruined her momentary illusion of privacy. Ready to give this rude miscreant a piece of her mind, Rakaia stood up, pulled down her skirts, and then she hesitated.

The voices were not coming from the caravan, out of sight around the slight bend in the road, but from above her on the cliff.

Bandits, she thought, her anger dissolving into fear.

A bird whistle echoed across the steep cliff walls, remarkable mostly because there were no other bird sounds. She studied the opposite wall, searching for movement. If this were an ambush, surely there would be bandits on both sides of the pass. A moment later she caught a glimpse of someone moving. It was then she realized the sheer steepness of the cliff was an illusion. It looked sheer from the ground, but it was actually quite stepped and weathered, offering endless places of concealment.

"There's the signal," the whispered voice above her hissed. She was too afraid to look up to see how close the bandits were, or indeed, make any movement that might attract their attention.

Despite the cold, Rakaia could feel herself breaking into a sweat. Marten and his *court'esa* had claimed their caravan too large to be a target. Too many guards, he said, and they weren't stopping for anything.

But they had stopped . . .

A scream split the air. Rakaia flattened herself against the cold, jagged cliff face. Within moments the air was full of shouting, more screams, and the clang of metal on metal, the icy wind whipping away the sounds of the battle, leaving her with only a vague idea of what was happening just around the curve of the cliff wall, and too afraid to move so she could see what was happening for herself.

Run, she told herself, firmly, as if that would force her fear-frozen muscles into action. *Run before they find you.*

Run to where? Behind her were miles of icy road through the Widowmaker Pass and it was almost dark. She would not survive a night out here wearing a slave's dress. Her woolen cloak was back in Marten's wagon and she had nothing with which to make fire, assuming she could find the fuel to burn or had the faintest idea how to make fire in the first place. And even if she somehow managed to get back to Winternest, what would she tell them? If Charisee was posing as her, either they wouldn't believe she was Rakaia or Charisee would be in peril for impersonating her.

But ahead of her was a pitched battle. Rakaia closed her eyes as if that could block out the sounds. There were more screams. One of them sounded like Barlia. She wanted to be sick. There was only one reason a woman screamed like that.

Her indecision cost her dear. While she was still internally debating what to do, Aja ran past, heading back toward Winternest, a bandit right on her heels. The man was bearded and dressed in a coat that was almost the same light caramel color of the cliff walls. He was panting heavily, his short blade dripping blood as he charged after his quarry. He caught Aja not three paces from where Rakaia was standing, pressed against the cliff.

Aja screamed, fighting like a trapped wild cat. But the bandit was stronger and clearly annoyed this *court'esa* would not provide willingly the service she was trained to provide. He threw her down onto the road. From where she was standing, Rakaia clearly heard her head crack as she hit the rocky ground. Stunned by the fall, Aja lay there, limp and unresisting as the bandit dropped to his knees, groping at the laces on the front of his trousers.

Rakaia wanted to run. She wanted to help. She wanted to look away. She wanted to live.

But she was too afraid. Tears filled her eyes as she watched, as much at her own cowardice as what was happening to Aja.

But if she moved, the bandit would see her and she would be next.

For the briefest of moments she considered stepping forward and announcing who she was. That might distract the bandit and stop this abomination. She might not suffer the same fate if she told them she was a daughter of the Fardohnyan king. Prisoners of rank were always treated better than ordinary folk because they were worth more unharmed.

Surely, even the savage bandits of the Sunrise Mountains would hesitate before raping a Fardohnyan princess to death.

Assuming they believed she was a princess.

Rakaia didn't look anything like a princess. She'd run away from Winternest with everything Charisee owned, rather than her own possessions, mostly to stop her far-too-honest-for-her-own-good half-sister from refusing to take part in Sophany's clever escape plan.

It didn't seem so clever now.

Aja lay still as death while the bandit took his pleasure with her. Rakaia couldn't tell if she was unconscious, dead, or merely giving in to the inevitable.

She held her breath, wishing for it to be over. Wishing this beast would be done with his conquest and go back to the real fight—assuming there was anybody left to fight.

Wishing she was not such a craven coward that she would stand here and watch Aja being raped, and do nothing to stop it, just because she was afraid of the same thing happening to her.

And then with a grunt of satisfaction he was done. He lay on top of Aja for a short time, savoring the moment, and then pushed himself up onto his knees and looked around. Aja lay motionless, eyes wide open, staring sightlessly at Rakaia. She was dead, skirts up around her waist, her lower body exposed to the elements, a small trickle of blood coming from her ear. Rakaia tried to melt into the rocks.

But he saw her. Smiling slowly, Aja's rapist, her murderer, climbed to his feet, and fixed his gaze on Rakaia. "Waiting your turn, eh, little one?"

She ran. There was no point in doing anything else. No other thought than to get away filled her mind; no other thought than to not be laying there like Aja, raped and dead, and probably not in that order. The same fear that had paralyzed Rakaia a moment ago suddenly gave her strength. She bolted east, back toward Winternest, as if she could somehow outrun her fate.

The road was icy and after only a few steps she slipped, coming down hard on her knees. Scrambling to her feet, the bandit only a step behind her, she tried to run again, but this time was beaten down by a powerful gust of wind from above.

Looking up, Rakaia forgot all about the bandit pursuing her. She gaped and turned, open mouthed, as another powerful beat of wings rent the air. The world fell silent, all the sounds of the battle stopping abruptly, as if someone had ordered it to end.

She looked up, her eyes fixed on the sky, as the dragon let out a screech, its rider guiding it gently to the ground.

Then she glanced at the bandit, expecting him to be staring at the dragon too, but he was staring at her, frozen mid-step in his pursuit.

There was clearly magic at work here. The pass was eerily silent, the bandit frozen in an impossible pose. Rakaia ventured a step toward him and came up against an invisible wall between her and the bandit.

But it was the dragon and its rider that drew her attention. She couldn't approach any closer. The beast was huge and had landed just near Aja's body. The dragon rider dismounted and looked around and then turned toward Rakaia.

It was a woman. A Harshini dragon rider.

The tall young woman had long red hair and wore the fabled dragon-rider leathers like they'd been painted on her skin. She spotted Rakaia, studied her for a moment, but made no other acknowledgment of her presence, and then turned and raised her face to the sky.

"Death," the Harshini woman cried. "We need to talk!"

14

DEATH WAS AN elusive creature when he didn't want to be found.

R'shiel té Ortyn didn't know for certain Death didn't want to be found, but she did know that no matter how hard to she'd tried to find him these past ten years, he was always one step ahead of her.

She'd been sure she would find Death in Calavandra when plague decimated the island city, but as soon as she arrived, things started to improve—no doubt helped by the city elders calling on the experience of their new Hythrun allies in dealing with a similar situation—and he slipped away before she could locate him.

R'shiel was certain she would find Death on the battlefield when the Denikans invaded the Principality of Ronstinelle, after their prince murdered his royal Denikan wife for not giving him a son. But by the time R'shiel reached the western border of Denika, King Shadow Lunar Kraig had accepted Prince Barshell's surrender and then executed him for murder of his sister, so there was nothing left to die for.

And so it was for a decade. Wherever the demon child went, Death departed just ahead of her. She began to worry someone might recognize her, or worse. If they knew who she was, people might start to think that somehow the arrival of the demon child meant she could drive Death away.

Ironically, R'shiel was quite certain she *was* driving Death away, but not for the reason most ordinary souls might imagine.

Death was avoiding her, because he knew she wanted something he was not prepared to grant her.

She was just as certain she could negotiate what she wanted from him, if only she could pin him down.

The gods were little or no help in her quest. With Medalon, Hythria, Karien, and Fardohnya at peace since she'd killed the One God, Xaphista, the God of War's power was significantly reduced. Zegarnald had turned his attention to Denika and the Trinity Isles since then, but the southern nations didn't have the vast populations of the northern continent, so any skirmishes he managed to instigate in the south were necessarily limited.

She'd hoped Dacendaran might help. R'shiel even tried pitching the idea of stealing something from Death, hoping it would entice the God of Thieves to aid her, but he was no more help than Zegarnald.

Kalianah, the Goddess of Love, was even less cooperative. Apparently, the goddess was still annoyed with R'shiel for being in love with the wrong person in the first place. Especially when she'd gone to all the trouble of putting a geas on Tarja to make him love her. Breaking the geas—while it had been unintentional and saved Tarja's life—offended the goddess. She rarely, if ever, came when R'shiel called these days, and on the odd occasion Kalianah did deign to appear, she was anything but the adorable child goddess her worshippers imagined. She appeared to R'shiel in adult form and she was begrudging at best.

The Goddess of Love was less than lovable, it seemed, when you had the temerity to love someone other than her choice for you.

The hardest part of R'shiel's quest was more than the effort involved. It was taking so long.

Almost ten years, in fact.

And R'shiel still hadn't managed to pin Death down.

She understood that what she wanted of him was against the rules. She also knew that, rules or no rules, Death had the power to grant her wish.

She just needed the right currency.

Which had brought her here to the Widowmaker Pass.

With a wave of her arm, R'shiel had frozen time to stop anybody in this bloodbath dying. There were plenty of souls here waiting for Death to harvest them. He would notice if they suddenly stopped coming. She'd waited weeks for a caravan large enough to entice Death to deal with the harvest personally.

It was R'shiel té Ortyn, the Harshini demon child, who broke the lead wagon's axle. R'shiel who had alerted the bandits to the caravan's presence in the pass.

And R'shiel who had stopped time to prevent anybody dying, so she could force Death to confront her.

So far, the plan had worked well. She felt for the victims, but not enough to prevent her doing what needed to be done. R'shiel did not know how long she would live, but it was likely to be a thousand years or more.

Learning not to take on every human death she might be responsible for—either by accident or design—was something Brak had tried to warn her about.

She was learning the lesson the hard way.

There were more than a hundred souls here and they were all going to die—assuming she was successful—except for the one young woman— a Fardohnyan by the look of her—who must have been beyond the edge of her time bubble when she unleashed it. She would have to do something about the girl who'd seen more than anybody was supposed to and was staring at R'shiel with the stunned expression of someone witnessing more than her mind could cope with.

It might be kinder to extend the bubble to include her. Kinder to let her die with the others once she was done doing her deal with Death.

"You interfere with time at your peril, demon child."

R'shiel forgot about the young Fardohnyan woman as she turned to confront Death, who had appeared behind her. He wore a long white robe and the aspect of a tall, golden-skinned Harshini, but his eyes, instead of black-on-black pools of enchantment, were hollow orbs, and he didn't look happy. That, more than anything else, separated him from a true Harshini. They were always happy.

"It's not the first time a god has interfered with time to thwart you," R'shiel pointed out. The God of Thieves had stopped time to save her once. The deal Brak made following that day to keep her out of Death's clutches was the reason she was here now, trying to get him out of it.

"You are not a god."

"I am the demon child," she reminded him. "I suspect that's marginally worse."

Death glanced around at the bloody battle she had stopped in its tracks. There were injured and dying everywhere, frozen mid-stride, mid– sword thrust, even mid-rapine.

A lot of souls would meet Death this day. Assuming R'shiel allowed it.

"I know what you want."

"Then let us be done with this. Give him back to me."

Death shook his head. "Brakandaran made a bargain and he kept his side of it. You should stop trying to undo it and diminish his honor and his sacrifice by rendering it pointless."

"I'm sure Brak would rather have his life than his honor."

"If you think that, demon child, you do not know Brakandaran nearly as well as you think."

The argument was pointless. And she was getting annoyed. It would not help matters at all to get annoyed. "You took Brak body and soul, so you can return him to this life anytime you want." The agony of that moment a decade ago in the Citadel's Temple of the Gods still burned R'shiel with a pain that had barely dulled since then. Perhaps that was Kalianah's revenge—this unbearable loss of someone she loved. "Why would you do that if you believed Brak would want to stay dead?"

"Not all the seven hells are unpleasant places to be, demon child, and Brak's time in this life was . . . trying. I imagine he's enjoying the rest."

R'shiel shook her head in wonder. "Seriously? Are you telling me you won't release Brak because he's happy in hell?"

"I have no opinion on the matter, one way or another."

"Then let me ask him."

"No."

"But you just said you didn't care, one way or the other. Take me to him. Let me ask him myself. If Brak tells me he's happy where he is, I'll never bother you with this again."

"I said I had no opinion on the matter, demon child, which is quite a different thing from not caring. And why do you assume you can make deals with me?"

"Brak made deals with you all the time."

"Not as often as you think." He looked around at the carnage and then cocked his head curiously. "I wonder, demon child, if you want to join Brakandaran so badly, why you don't take the obvious course."

"What obvious course?" she asked. Surely, if there were an obvious course she would have discovered it before now.

"I could arrange for you to join Brakandaran in my realm, you know. That would solve your dilemma in one fell stroke."

"You'd kill me? Let me share the afterlife with Brak? I don't believe you."

"You think I can't take your life? Right here? Right now? Just by willing it to be so?"

"Of course you can," she said. "But you won't. I don't know why you let me live. Maybe you know something about the future I don't. Maybe it's because the gods went to so much trouble to bring me into this world that you're not prepared to risk their combined wrath by taking me out of it. But you haven't killed me yet, and I have a feeling you're not going to do it now."

"You risk a great deal on a feeling."

"It's my life to risk."

Death fell silent for a moment and then he shrugged. "Very well, I will give you what you want."

His sudden capitulation left her almost breathless. "You'll bring back Brak?"

"No. But I will tell you where to find him. If you can get to him. If you can locate him and get him to talk with you . . . if he expresses a genuine wish to return to this life, I will grant it."

If you can get to him. There was a sentence fraught with peril, if ever R'shiel had heard one. "What's the catch?"

"What do you mean?"

"I mean you don't let anybody out of hell for any reason, without making a deal of some kind. What is it? A life of equal value, like you made Brak promise when he traded his life for mine to save me?"

"It was Brakandaran who chose his own life over that of another, demon child. Do not blame that decision on me."

"Is that what you want?"

He hesitated before answering. "No. I think not. For you the decision would be too easy. Brak was far more principled than you, demon child. I suspect a decision such as that would not slow you down for a moment."

"What, then?"

"The life of a friend."

"*What?*"

"Assuming Brakandaran wishes to return to this life, you may have him back in return for the life of a friend."

"I don't have any friends."

"I think you do, demon child. In fact, to be sure you keep your end of the bargain, I will hold their lives in trust until you have made your decision."

"Hold in trust . . . What does that mean?"

Death refused to answer. "Release these people and let me do what I am here to do."

"You haven't told me where Brak is."

"He is in Sanctuary."

"That's impossible. Brak and I threw Sanctuary so far out of time, nobody will ever find it again."

"Then you have a problem, don't you, demon child? Release the time bubble surrounding this place now or I will change the terms of our deal to include the lives of *all* your friends, rather than just one of them."

R'shiel glanced at the frozen carnage around them and then looked over at the young woman standing just on the other side of the bubble, staring at them with wide, uncomprehending eyes. She looked around again, sickened by what she saw. Most of the caravan guards were dead—or at least they would be as soon as she released them—as were almost all of the wagon drivers and the merchants' families traveling with them. There were several women, and as far as she could tell most of them had already been raped and were about to be killed. One mother still clutched the limp body of a small child covered in blood where a bandit had crushed his skull with a boot rather than waste a sword thrust on the child.

The brutality of the attack shocked her. Some years ago, Brak had spent time in these mountains as a bandit. Surely he had never been party to such wanton violence.

A movement caught her eye and she realized the Fardohnyan girl was still watching her. She was only a step away from being raped and killed too, R'shiel guessed, if the spell were released while that bandit pursuing her was still within arms' reach.

"Is she on your manifest today?"

Death shook his head. "Life and death require a certain balance, demon child. There are a number of lives I must return with, to maintain that balance."

"So it's a numbers game, then, rather than a specific soul you seek?"

"That's one way of looking at it."

"Fine, then." R'shiel walked over to the edge for the bubble, snatched a sword out of another bandit's upraised hand and then turned the blade sideways, thrusting it with all her might between the ribs in the man's back and up through his heart. The bandit remained standing, sword protruding from his back. Not until she released the spell would he fall and die.

The Fardohnyan girl didn't flinch. That could mean she was too shocked to react or, possibly, that she was not worth saving.

She turned back to face Death. "Does that balance the books?" R'shiel wasn't sure why it was suddenly so important to save the girl. She didn't even know who she was. It just seemed it might compensate, somehow, for the rest of the lives here she couldn't—or wouldn't—save.

"She is of no concern to me now. Do what you will."

"Don't I always?"

But Death didn't answer. He was gone, leaving R'shiel alone amid the suspended battle.

She looked up. Outside the bubble, the sun was almost completely set, awaiting her whim to complete the task. Long shadows darkened the pass, while outside the bubble, another early summer blizzard was gathering in the west to unleash its fury on them as soon as she permitted it.

Still, it was done now. R'shiel turned to the dragon-meld. "Time we were gone from here, Dranymire."

"We have a passenger?" the dragon asked, turning his massive head to look at the Fardohnyan girl.

"Apparently we do."

"And where are we taking her?"

"Testra, I suppose," R'shiel said with a shrug. Beyond saving the young woman from Death, she really hadn't given her impulsive gesture much thought. "That's the closest city to the Sanctuary Mountains."

"You know how I feel about passengers, your highness."

She smiled as the dragon lowered his head to her. She reached up and scratched the bony ridge above his eyes, knowing how much the meld enjoyed it. "It's all right, Dranymire, I'll keep her unconscious until we get there."

But the dragon pulled back from her touch, not willing to let her coax the meld so blatantly. "And then what? You will abandon her, penniless and alone, in a strange city in a foreign country? She might have been better off if you let Death have her."

"I saved her from being raped and murdered."

"You saved her to assuage your own conscience, your highness. There is nothing noble in that."

"Why does everyone assume I'm even trying to be noble?" she muttered, mostly to herself. The gods had created her to kill one of their own, and she'd done exactly as they asked. And yet everyone she'd ever met, from the demons who melded to form her dragon, to Korandellan, the long dead king of the Harshini, believed she was filled with some inherent nobility of spirit.

She approached the Fardohnyan girl again, not sure how much the young woman had heard of the exchange, whether she had seen Death, just assumed R'shiel was talking to herself, or what she thought about what was going on.

R'shiel didn't have time to question her about it. She waved her arm and the girl collapsed, unconscious. Stepping through the barrier, she shivered a little at the sudden change in temperature. The wind whipped at her hair as she scooped the girl up, surprised at how light she was. Dranymire opened his wings and with one powerful beat, flew the short distance through the barrier to land beside her. He lowered his shoulder to aid her as she climbed aboard with the unconscious Fardohnyan girl, waiting until they were secure before he lifted off, much more gently than he would have done had it just been R'shiel on his back.

As the Widowmaker fell away behind them, R'shiel released the time spell, holding on to her lifeless passenger. The dragon meld banked to the left and headed around the storm clouds, north toward the city of Testra.

R'shiel tried not to think of the death and the scores of dying she'd left behind, just of the single life she had saved and the idea that finally, however impossible it might be to retrieve him, she knew where to look for Brak.

Part Two

15

IT WAS UNFORTUNATE when a man died under torture, Naveen Raveve mused as he stepped into the cool darkness of the underground caverns beneath Talabar Prison. But sometimes, it was even more unfortunate if he lived.

That might well prove the case here, he feared, although he knew nothing about the reason for this summons other than news that the prisoner had finally provided intelligence that was both important and extremely sensitive. So sensitive, the man responsible for torturing the information out of the former general, Meyrick Kabar, had refused to write it down.

A figure hurried forward out of the gloom as Naveen reached the bottom step of the caverns. It was Hagland, the prison warden. He wore a sleeveless shirt that left his hairy, meaty, and—most offensively—sweaty arms exposed. Naveen was quite sure he would pass out if he got downwind of the man.

The warden bowed to Naveen, even though he didn't need to. Nobody actually needed to bow to a slave. Wise men did, however. Smelly he might be, but Bril Hagland was a wise man.

"Lord Raveve."

"Master Hagland," he said, returning the bow, ever so slightly. He didn't bother to correct the man about his title. He rather enjoyed being referred to as *my lord*. "This had better be important."

"Mavos thinks so, my lord, if you'd like to come this way."

It was because Mavos thought so that he was here. He would not have come on the warden's word alone. Naveen raised the perfumed kerchief he was holding to his nose and followed the warden into the gloom. The rough walls down here were so different from Talabar's delightfully stuccoed pink walls outside. Here the dank, undressed stone on either side of the corridor wept with moisture and the whole place reeked of damp and mold.

Quite an unhealthy place to be, he decided, and then smiled at the irony of such a notion.

"The prisoner is in here, my lord."

Naveen followed Hagland into the unlocked cell, thinking security must be very slack if they didn't bother to lock the door. When he stepped into the cell, however, he understood why there was no need for a lock.

Meyrick Kabar was a broken shell.

Naveen remembered the general as a tall, proud man with unusual blue eyes, rare in a Fardohnyan and attributed to some long-forgotten Karien ancestor. This pitiful creature before him was barely recognizable. He was black and blue, the fresh bruises manifesting on top of yellowed skin of other bruises healing underneath. The man hung in chains secured to the ceiling, which was the only thing keeping him upright. His head lolled to the side and he wore the vacant look of a man pushed beyond the limit of sanity.

There was another man in the cell, standing beside Kabar. A slender, unassuming man, this was Mavos the Torturer. A slave like Naveen, he'd acquired the name years ago, when they were in training together. They had been suffering under a particularly brutal slave master at the time. Mavos, Naveen, Luka, Strayan, and a few others he still counted closer than brothers, even though most of them were dispersed across the continent now . . . they all owed their lives to Mavos, who had taken it upon himself to protect his brothers-in-suffering from any further pain. Mavos was an extremely imaginative man, as his victims—and that wretched slaver—could attest. Appointing Mavos to the position of official state torturer had been one of the first appointments Naveen made when he took over from Lecter Turon. It had felt very satisfying to repay—even in a small way—the debt he and his slave brothers all owed to this man.

Naveen nodded to Mavos as if they were nothing more than casual acquaintances and then turned his attention to Meyrick Kabar.

"Can he hear me?"

"Yes, my lord." Mavos smiled slightly as he spoke, a hint of irony in his tone. Only Naveen heard it and only Naveen could appreciate the reason for it.

"General? General Kabar? The warden tells me you have information for the king that might be of national importance."

With a visible effort, Meyrick raised his head and fixed his swollen eyes on Naveen. "I'm . . . sorry."

"What?"

He had barely any teeth left, making it hard for him to form words that made any sense at all. "Tell her . . . I said . . . I'm sorry . . ."

Naveen turned to Mavos. "Why is he sorry? Who is he talking about?"

"Tell Lord Raveve what you told me," Mavos prompted in a conversational tone.

Meyrick flinched at the sound of the torturer's voice. Naveen marveled at the man's ability to terrify a grown man with such a benign request.

"So . . . phany . . ."

Naveen had to lean in to hear him speak. "What?"

"Sophany."

"Sophany? *Princess* Sophany?" Naveen glanced at Hagland and then Mavos. "Why Princess Sophany? You brought me all the way down here because he wants to apologize to a woman he probably hasn't laid eyes on in twenty—Oh, dear . . ." Suddenly so many things became clear. Sophany's urgency to get her daughter out of the harem. Rakaia's unusual blue eyes. The timing was perfect, too.

Naveen knew Meyrick Kabar had been the Captain of the Harem Guard back before Rakaia was born. That was one of the reasons Lecter had taken him on as his apprentice. He had a memory for those sorts of details. And the ability to put two and two together and come up with a way to make it add up to anything his king wanted it to add up to.

Hagland nodded. "Now you understand why we called you here, my lord."

"Does anybody else know this information?"

The warden shook his head. "As always, my lord, it goes no further than this room until you order it so."

"What have you told Alaric?" He was the one who had ordered Meyrick Kabar arrested. He would want to know something.

"We've told the king's heir that Meyrick Kabar will die before he breaks."

Well, that's a lie, Naveen thought, glancing at the pitiful wretch hanging from the chains.

"General Kabar was a good man, Lord Raveve. It didn't seem right to destroy his reputation along with his body."

"I'm sure his reputation will be a great comfort to him as he rots down here with only me for company." Mavos was a surprisingly compassionate man, given his occupation—and the obvious delight he took in it.

Naveen turned to study the prisoner for a moment, puzzling over the dilemma of what to do with him. There was more at stake here than the confession of a man over a past infidelity, however delicate the affair may have been. Hagland was right when he claimed this news was of national importance. Hablet had just pledged a bastard to Frederak Branador for concessions to the Highcastle mountain pass, rather than the legitimate daughter he'd promised. There was a critical trade route to consider.

Not to mention Naveen's future retirement plans, which would be seriously threatened if Hablet decided to flay the Princess Sophany alive for cheating on him and then presenting him with another man's bastard, calling it his.

On the other hand, Naveen had no wish to torment the man longer than was necessary. That was just barbaric, and Alaric, perhaps, would benefit from a lesson in consequences when a good man and valuable general died as a direct result of one of his tantrums.

"End this," he ordered Mavos. "I'm sure all this torment must be putting an undue strain on Meyrick Kabar's previously unsuspected weak heart."

The torturer nodded in understanding. He had been at this game a long time. He did not need Naveen to be more specific. "It will be done before you get back to the palace, my lord."

Naveen turned to Meyrick Kabar and offered a sympathetic smile. "It will be over soon, General. I will see that people remember you well."

Kabar muttered something Naveen didn't quite catch. Mavos leaned in closer and asked the prisoner to repeat what he'd said and then turned to Naveen. "It's hard to understand him with his mouth busted up like that, my lord, but I believe he was saying something along the lines of 'eat shit.'"

Naveen sighed. "That's gratitude for you."

He turned for the door, handkerchief to his nose, adding, "Send his head to Alaric when it's done. I think our future king needs to see his handiwork up close and bloody, while we still have a few generals left."

Naveen headed back along the corridor, anxious to be out of this dreadful place, putting Meyrick Kabar's fate out of his mind.

He had bigger fish to fry this day, not the least of which was finding a way to break it to his king that the daughter he'd so recently sent to

Hythria to marry a cousin of the Hythrun High Prince was the bastard get of an affair with the Captain of the Guard and if word ever got out about it, their economically vital trade route through the Highcastle pass would be lost to them forever.

THE KING OF Fardohnya's eldest daughter had her own problems, and the imminent arrival of a younger sister she barely remembered was the least of them.

Her most immediate problem had arrived this morning in the shape of a smartly dressed, well-spoken young defender by the name of Caden Fletcher, the personal aide-de-camp of the Lord Defender of Medalon. As she strode the wide, tiled halls of the palace in search of her husband, her skin glistening with perspiration in the humid Greenharbour air, Adrina could feel her ire rising.

It wasn't that she didn't like their visitor. Or the man who sent him. Tarja Tenragan was an ally. More importantly, Damin considered him a friend.

And she knew, beyond doubt, that the Lord Defender of Medalon would not have sent his aide in person to deliver his message unless he considered it a matter of life or death. It followed, therefore, as sure as night followed day, that whatever Tarja Tenragan wanted of the High Prince of Hythria, Adrina probably wasn't going to like it.

"How bad is it?" she demanded as she slammed the door shut to her husband's study behind her, blowing a number of loose documents off the table with the small gust of wind she'd whipped up with her anger.

Damin was sitting at the long polished table that had served generations of Wolfblades as both desk, war council, and—on at least one occasion back when they were first married and still rather enchanted by the idea—a rather convenient place to make babies. The lurid, pornographic murals the last High Prince commissioned were long gone, replaced by much less distracting—not to mention tasteful—landscapes depicting scenes from each of the seven provinces that made up the nation of Hythria. Fortunately Damin was alone, no sign of his chamberlain, the envoy from Medalon, or, worse, his mother—the dread Princess Marla—anywhere in sight.

Her husband looked up from whatever he was signing. "Why do you automatically assume something is wrong, my love?"

"For one thing, Tarja wouldn't have sent his pet minion all the way to Hythria for something trivial," she said, leaning against the door. She liked to keep her distance from Damin when they argued. It was safer that way. "He could have asked the Harshini to send a message through the Seeing Stone."

"Tarja's a pagan," Damin reminded her with a shrug. "He doesn't believe in the Harshini or their magic."

"He's Lord Defender of a country ruled by a Harshini queen."

"A theological dilemma I'm sure he struggles with daily." Damin signed another document with a flourish and moved it to the pile on his right. It was quite a pile. He must have been at this all morning. "Don't read anything more into this than there is, my love. Tarja wants to invite me to the Citadel and sent Cade to deliver the invitation. That's all there is to it."

Adrina didn't believe that for a moment. Interesting, too, that Damin hadn't actually told her what Tarja's invitation was for, just that he'd sent one and chose his most trusted aide to deliver it in person. "Is this something to do with the missing lyre from the Temple of the Gods?"

"He might have mentioned it."

"Ha! I knew it!"

"Tarja thinks it's a Harshini problem. In fact, that's why he sent Cade here. He didn't want to bother Shananara while she tries to find it."

"I don't like it when Tarja tries to circumvent the Harshini."

"I'm sure he'll try to do better to please you in the future, my love."

"Don't patronize me, Damin."

"I wouldn't dare."

"Then don't try to placate me with platitudes. That's the third time in as many sentences you have called me 'my love.' Your disturbing lack of imagination when it comes to endearments notwithstanding, you only ever call me *my love* when you have to tell me something you know I'm not going to like."

"Am I really that transparent?"

"I can see right through you and admire the view on the other side, *my love.*"

He put down the quill and leaned back in his chair. Even the fact that he was *sitting* in that chair, dutifully signing piles of decrees and requisitions like a good little monarch, made her suspicious. Damin hated paperwork, and while he was conscientious enough not to ignore it completely, he had been known to go to extraordinary lengths to avoid it. This morning's sudden urge to be stuck inside on a glorious sunny Greenharbour morning reeked of a man getting his affairs in order.

He smiled at her, which just made things worse. Damin never smiled like that when he was doing something he considered a chore. "You must be looking forward to your sister's arrival."

"Don't try to change the subject."

"I wasn't. I just thought that with Rakaia here, you won't . . ." His voice trailed off warily, as if he were afraid to finish the sentence.

Now we're getting to the heart of it. "I won't *what*?"

"Miss me so much?" he said with a tentative smile.

"I knew it!" she said pushing off the door. "Tarja crooks his little finger and you're running off to Medalon, ignoring your responsibilities here in a time of crisis and leaving me alone with your mother."

"I could take my mother with me," he offered.

For a fleeting moment, Adrina wished he wasn't joking. The thought of a whole summer without Marla looking over her shoulder, waiting for her to make a mistake, reading dire motives into every little thing she did, was something about which she could only fantasize. But he didn't mean it. She knew that. Even if Damin took a blood oath to take Marla with him, she knew his mother would never countenance the rule of her beloved Hythria being left in the hands of her untrustworthy Fardohnyan daughter-in-law.

"Why don't you take *me* with you?"

"Because that would mean leaving Marla in charge. It's taken me a decade to convince my mother I can rule Hythria without her second-guessing every move I make. I wouldn't give her the keys to the kingdom for a week, let alone the couple of months I'll be away."

"So you *are* going away then?"

"I'm considering it."

"Why?"

"The treaty between Hythria, Medalon, and Karien is important."

"Is there going to be a problem with it?" she asked with a frown. "I thought we were all getting along swimmingly these days, and the renewal is just a formality."

"We are," he agreed. "And it is. But the Sisters of the Blade are out of power, not out of business. Tarja's afraid they're planning to use the negotiations to stir up trouble. He thinks a show of solidarity is in order. With this stolen lyre problem, things are . . . unsettled."

"Is that really the problem?"

"What do you mean?"

"Is Tarja really worried about the remnants of the Sisters of the Blade? Or is it the Harshini fear something might have happened to the God of Music?"

"It's just about the treaty."

"So the Lord Defender of Medalon is simply making the most of a chance to rub the Sisterhood's collective noses in the fact that when he crooks his little finger, the rulers of Medalon's northern and southern neighbors—both of whom are big enough to swallow Medalon whole and not notice the lump going down—dutifully come running."

"The latter, I suspect."

Adrina nodded thoughtfully. "I'd probably do the same if I were him."

"So you understand why I have to go."

Sadly, she did. It didn't make her any happier about him being away for so long, though. Not now. "How long will you be gone?"

"If I swing past Krakandar on the way to see how Starros is doing, it'll probably be winter by the time I get to the Citadel and back."

She folded her arms and glared at him. "I suppose swinging past Krakandar to see how Starros is doing will involve a great deal of hunting and drinking and carousing with loose women?"

Damin grinned. "That's my reward for getting Marla out of your hair for the summer."

Adrina stared at him in surprise as she walked around the table to his side. "So you meant what you said about taking Marla with you?"

He looked up at her and nodded. Her irritation faded quickly as she realized what that meant.

"I thought maybe Jaz and Marlie could come with us, too. They're old enough to visit Medalon without you, and it won't hurt to broaden their horizons with a bit of travel. Besides, it's always good politics to make the ordinary people fond of your heirs."

Although they'd been married for more than ten years, Adrina still forgot sometimes just how politically astute her husband was. He really had thought this through. It wasn't just that he was traveling to Medalon to help a friend retain power, or even that he would take the opportunity to catch up with another friend so precious to him he'd once done a deal with the gods to save him from certain death. Damin was serious about taking Marla with him, which—other than the obvious benefit of getting her out of Adrina's hair for a whole summer—meant he would have her advice during what might be some rather delicate treaty negotiations. There was simply no sharper political mind, or better negotiator, than Marla Wolfblade.

Even Adrina was willing to concede that.

Taking their two eldest children was a stroke of genius, too. Damin was right about it being good politics for them to be seen, but more importantly, Marla would jump at the chance to have unfettered access to her grandchildren, and probably not raise a whimper of protest about leaving Adrina alone in Greenharbour while they were gone because of it. For all that she despaired of her mother-in-law's perpetual mistrust, Adrina knew Marla would give her life for her grandchildren and they'd learn a great deal from her along the way.

"You'll miss the wedding."

"That can't be helped."

"People will wonder why."

"I think I'll be forgiven if it means they don't have to go to war."

"Marlie will be devastated. She's convinced she's going to be a wedding attendant."

"She'll get to see the Citadel. I'm sure she'll get over it."

"You'll have to formally name me regent in your absence."

"Of course." He was smart enough not to gloat. Ten years of some fairly epic fights had taught them both that simply conceding the point and moving on was the best way to deal with situations like this. It was more important to get the job done than to decide who was right and who was wrong.

"When are you leaving?"

"In about four days, if I can get everything organized."

She eyed him suspiciously for a moment. "Are you sure you're not fabricating this whole thing just to get out of spending time with my sister?"

He smiled and took her hand, drawing her closer. "Every cloud has a silver lining."

"Are you taking Rory with you?"

"I wasn't planning to."

"You should. A human magician you can trust would be useful. There might come a time when you need to emphasize your point during the negotiations, and the Harshini can be so prickly about smiting people where they stand."

He pulled her down onto his lap. "And this is why you're not coming with me. Medalon is an ally, darling. Tarja is a friend. There will be no smiting of anybody."

He kissed her, and she let him, because even though she knew he was shamelessly trying to manipulate her, being kissed by Damin was a very pleasant way to pass the time.

"I'm sorry," a sharp and anything but apologetic voice remarked from the door before their kiss could escalate into making another baby on the High Prince's desk. "Am I interrupting something important?"

Damin broke off the kiss, but he smiled at Adrina. For a fleeting moment, they remained close, foreheads touching, in a silent, shared moment of solidarity, and then they turned to face the door, although Adrina made no move to rise from her husband's lap. It was all part of the silent war they waged against Marla, this constant reminder that Damin loved his wife— the wife Marla had *not* chosen for him—and that she wasn't going anywhere.

"Good morning, Mother. It's good to see you up and about so early. How's the hip?"

"I got a message you wanted to see me, Damin." She made a point of not looking at Adrina.

Damin squeezed Adrina's hand and nodded almost imperceptibly. Adrina rose from Damin's lap and turned to face her mother-in-law, certain Damin would back her up. "Damin and I were wondering if you'd like to join him on his journey to the Citadel for the treaty renewal negotiations," she said. "I'm sending Jazrian and Marlie along for the experience. I thought they might benefit from your guidance."

Marla stared at her suspiciously as all the things Adrina had just been thinking must be churning through her mind. Damin said nothing and did nothing to hint this was anything but a joint decision. He knew what his mother was like.

"Who will rule Hythria in your absence?" Marla asked her son.

"Adrina, of course."

"Do you think that's wise?"

"Mother, if my wife were planning to open our borders to a Fardohnyan invasion, she might have done it long before now, don't you think?"

Marla didn't like it when Damin called her out so openly. The dowager princess nodded with ill grace. "Make sure you brief Kalan before you go. Without any formal training in governance, your . . . wife . . . will need the assistance of the High Arrion while you're away."

"I'm standing right here, Marla."

Marla looked at Adrina directly for the first time. "Oh, believe me, I know you are," she said, and then she turned on her heel and limped from the room, her silver-topped cane tapping sharply on the tiles as if spelling out her disapproval.

The door swung closed and Damin stood up, putting his arm around Adrina. "I'm sorry about that."

"You don't have to be. Did you see the look on her face when you told her I would be ruling Hythria in your absence? It was priceless."

Adrina had played this game for a decade. If anybody had been keeping score, she and Marla were probably about even.

She turned to Damin and added with a hopeful smile, "Although if you think Tarja might benefit from Marla's vast wisdom and political experience on an ongoing basis, I wouldn't mind at all if you left her in Medalon and came home without her."

17

CHARISEE WISHED SHE had time to grieve her sister, but she was supposed to be a princess of Fardohnya. She might lament the tragic loss of all those lives in the Widowmaker Pass, but it would have looked very strange if she gave in to her need to sob inconsolably. So she kept her tears at bay during the day, rode with her head held high, and tried to give the impression the loss of the Farmen Brothers' caravan to a bandit attack in the Widowmaker Pass meant nothing to her at all.

At night, however, when she was alone in the spacious silk tent Kiam Miar arranged to have erected for her each evening, after she'd eaten apart from the soldiers charged with her protection, she could retire. In the privacy of her tent, in the dull light of the coals glowing in the wrought-iron brazier, she could sob her heart out, both for the loss of her beloved Rakaia and for the stupidity of what she was attempting.

It amazed and relieved Charisee that since announcing she was her sister nobody had thought to question her identity. It made her realize how little people were judged by who they were, rather than what they seemed to be.

Every morning, as they headed ever downward toward the plains, the coast, and whatever fate awaited her in Greenharbour, Kiam Miar rode up beside her—Broos trotting faithfully at heel—to inquire about her welfare. As the days grew warmer and longer, he did the same thing every morning not long after they broke camp. He would ride beside her for a time, ask how she was, if there was anything with which he could assist her, and then tell her of their intended destination that day and when he planned to make camp that night. Their daily discussions were sometimes the only time she spoke to another human all day and she had come to look forward to them, and the time she spent with Kiam, rather more than she probably should.

She wondered what Rakaia would have thought of this handsome assassin who also happened to be the High Prince's stepbrother. *She'd probably tell him off for being too familiar.* And then Charisee remembered she would never be able to tell Rakaia anything, ever again. She would never be able to share her observations about Kiam—the way he smiled, the easy way he moved or the way he laughed or even the way he doted on that monster of a dog that followed him everywhere—and her eyes would fill with tears she couldn't explain to anybody.

Being a liar and a fraud, Charisee discovered, was a lonely occupation.

Her grief faded as the days passed, the excitement of her new life slowly overtaking—if not completely quelling—her guilt and grief at taking advantage of Rakaia's foolish generosity. But the loss of her sister and best friend would hit her unexpectedly at times, so she would ride in the van, her head held high, hoping nobody would notice she was crying.

They rode about thirty miles each day, depending on the availability of campsites and feed for their mounts. Charisee thought it odd they camped each night when they passed a number of perfectly serviceable inns along the way. When she asked the reason, Kiam explained they'd been expecting an entire Fardohnyan royal entourage, which few rural inns could cater to, so they'd brought sufficient provisions for making their own camps. Then he'd asked if she would prefer an inn, and she'd told him she would do whatever was easiest for him, which made him look at her very oddly.

It was only then Charisee realized her mistake.

She was a princess of Fardohnya. A spoiled and entitled young woman who expected mountains to be moved if they got in the way of her view. She was being far too accommodating.

So she called Kiam back and demanded they use inns from now on. Kiam nodded and smiled, although it didn't reach his eyes, and promised he would see she was accommodated in a manner befitting her status from now on.

He didn't speak to her for the rest of the day.

But this morning was different. After several days of him being distant and polite and sleeping in taverns of varying quality for the last three nights they had finally reached the plains. Kiam rode up beside her about an hour after they left the tavern in the small village of Somen, Broos faithfully padding alongside him, and let his horse—a magnificent golden sorcerer-bred mare—fall into step beside her much more sedate and ordinary mount.

"Did you sleep well, your highness?"

Charisee nodded. "Well enough."

"We'll be stopping in Warrinhaven this evening. Are you feeling better?"

She glanced at him sideways. It was a warm day and he was riding in shirtsleeves, his jacket thrown over the back of his saddle. He had the body of an assassin, lithe, muscular, and alert, even when he seemed relaxed. She'd caught herself watching him sometimes when he rode ahead of her, wondering how he managed to look so relaxed and tense at the same time. "Why do you assume I'm not well?"

Kiam was silent for a moment before he said anything, as if debating whether or not to answer her question. Finally, he took a deep breath and said, "I hear you crying yourself to sleep almost every night."

For a moment, Charisee didn't know what to say. She had thought her tears were her own secret. "I do not!"

"I've heard you."

"How could you hear me?"

Idiot . . . deny, deny, deny . . . you've just admitted you were crying . . . gods . . . what do I say now . . . Sorry, sir, but I'm just a bit upset because the real Rakaia is dead and I might have saved her if I'd said something about her running away?

"You sleep with one of the High Prince's own guard outside your door. It keeps you safe but the cost is your privacy, I fear." He looked at her with genuine concern. "Are you so terribly homesick, your highness?"

Homesick. That was her excuse. Kiam had handed it to her without realizing. She nodded, fixing her gaze straight ahead, certain he knew she was lying with every breath she took. "It's hard, being so far from home."

"But it's not as if you're gone forever. You'll be able to see Fardohnya from Highcastle after you're married. Perhaps your husband will take you home for a visit."

My husband. The old man with syphilis.

Gods, Rakaia, what have you done to me?

Charisee shook her head. "My father is an old man and my brother, Alaric, will take the throne when he dies in the not too distant future. Fardohnyan kings have a history of cleaning out the harem when they ascend to the throne, to ensure a clear succession. If I want to live, I can never go home." They were Rakaia's words—her oft-expressed fear—but they applied just as well to Charisee now.

"Cleaning out . . . ?" Kiam asked, and then it dawned on him what she meant. "Oh . . . Gods! That's barbaric."

"*You* think killing is barbaric?" She looked at him, not sure if he was teasing. "You're an assassin."

"That doesn't mean I don't think killing innocent women and children in cold blood is barbaric."

"But it's all right if you're being paid to do it?"

"Assassins don't kill innocent people."

She raised a brow at that. "Just those wealthy enough to attract enemies who can afford to hire someone like you?"

Kiam smiled. "Your highness, in my experience, anybody wealthy enough to attract enemies who can afford to hire someone like me is far, far from innocent by the time the Assassins' Guild comes knocking at his door."

"You *knock*? How terribly civilized of you."

Don't joke around with him, a little voice warned her. *The more you say, the more chance you'll say something stupid and give the game away. Don't talk to him. Don't kid around with him, and for pity's sake, don't* like *him . . .*

"You'd be stunned by how civilized I can be," he chuckled, in a rare good mood Charisee couldn't explain. "As my former stepmother is fond of telling me: *Just because you kill people for a living, Ky, doesn't mean you're allowed to have the table manners of a goat-herder just down off the mountain after a summer on his own.*"

"*Former* stepmother?"

"The Princess Marla. The one person in all of Hythria you do *not* want to fall afoul of."

Charisee had heard of Princess Marla. Everybody in the whole world had heard of Princess Marla. Her reputation was terrifying. "Is she really that scary?"

Kiam nodded, but Charisee got the feeling he wasn't nearly as afraid of her as he was making out. "I'd rather face a fleet of Trinity Isles pirate ships while armed with only a butter knife and a rusty spoon than cross Princess Marla."

"And what does she think of your profession?"

"She's fine with it," Kiam said, studying her as if he couldn't understand why she'd even ask such a question. "She was married to my father for a good number of years and he was an assassin, too, you know. In fact, they were good friends right up until he died."

"Then she doesn't have a problem with assassins killing people?" *Oh, for pity's sake, stop talking . . . you sound like a pompous, self-righteous old lady . . . You should be saying something sympathetic, you heartless fiend. He just told you his father died!*

"Not so's you'd notice . . . do you?"

"Well . . . isn't killing people . . . you know . . . *wrong?*" she asked, ignoring the stern voice of reason in her head completely.

Kiam stared at her in puzzlement. "Seriously? Who told you that?"

"I follow Kalianah, the Goddess of Love." *No . . . right now you're honoring the God of Monumental Fools.*

"Assassins honor Zegarnald, the God of War," he reminded her. "Old Zeggie doesn't have a problem with killing at all."

"Old Zeggie? Assassins actually refer to their god as *Old Zeggie?*"

Kiam smiled. "No . . . it's kind of a family thing with the Wolfblades. It comes from a friend of the family who's met Dacendaran and that's what Dace calls him."

"You have a friend who has actually spoken in person to the God of Thieves?"

"You sound surprised."

"I've never met anybody who's spoken to a god before."

"Well, I haven't spoken to one. Not directly. But Wrayan Lightfinger has. He's the head of the Greenharbour Thieves' Guild, hence the reason for his conversations with Dace. And there are any number of Harshini living at the Sorcerers' Collective in Greenharbour these days. They talk to the gods all the time, apparently."

Charisee shook her head in wonder. "The dread Princess Marla? Harshini? Gods? Thieves and assassins who are friends of the High Prince's family . . . what am I letting myself in for?"

Yes, Charisee . . . what are you letting yourself in for?

"Well, whatever it is," Kiam pointed out, his smile fading, "it's bound to be better than being butchered in a harem because your brother doesn't want any competition."

Or spending your life as a slave to the rest of your family because you were born on the wrong side of the blanket.

"There is that," she agreed with a thin smile.

"That's better."

"What?"

"You're smiling."

Charisee felt her face go red, thinking, *No, I'm not . . . I'm blushing . . .*

"You make me smile," she replied, before she realized how that sounded and hastily corrected herself. "I mean . . . you're *making* me smile. On purpose."

"Then my work here is done," Kiam said with a grin, and then kicked his horse forward into a canter to catch up with the two outriders leading their party before Charisee could respond and make an even bigger fool of herself.

18

Adrina's two older children, Jazrian and Marlie, were bouncing off the walls with excitement when she told them they'd be visiting Krakandar and Medalon with their father and their grandmother. The twins didn't quite grasp what "a few months" meant, so other than a momentary flash of envy that their older siblings were going on a journey, they soon got over their disappointment and ran outside to play.

Jaz was almost eleven now, his sister Marlie nine, going on sixteen. She was a precocious child, the inevitable result of being the daughter of Adrina of Fardohnya and Damin Wolfblade and having a grandmother like Marla.

Jazrian, on the other hand, was much more sensitive. If Marlie charged at a task like a bull at a gate, Jaz would stop and consider the gate's feelings before he charged anywhere. He wasn't weak. He could hold his own in any physical challenge his tutors put before him, but he would stop and think things through before acting, sometimes to the frustration of everyone around him, and particularly to his much more impulsive sister. Adrina couldn't imagine who he'd inherited such traits from—certainly nobody in her family. Adrina feared he took after Marla, which would make her mother-in-law even more intolerably smug if she realized Adrina saw anything of Damin's mother in her own son.

With the children planning their big adventure north, Adrina was heading back from the day nursery when she ran into Caden Fletcher in the wide, tiled corridor of the Greenharbour Palace.

He saluted her smartly as she approached. "Your highness."

"Good morning, Captain," she said, acknowledging his salute with a slight nod of her head. She liked Cade, but she didn't trust the reason he was here, or why he'd be in this part of the palace, which was restricted to members of the family, their trusted servants, and the guards who watched over them. "Are you looking for something?"

"Your husband sent me to find you, ma'am," he informed her.

Adrina raised a brow at that. "Really? We're using the Medalonian Defenders to run personal errands for us now?"

Cade smiled. "Actually, I think he was looking for a polite way to get rid of me for a while. But he does have a message, I believe. Something about word on your sister's arrival?"

"Why are you asking me? You're the one delivering the message." She didn't mean to sound so prickly, but she'd been on edge since Caden arrived. To have the Lord Defender of Medalon's personal aide arrive unexpectedly in order to invite the High Prince of Hythria north to a meeting made her uneasy for no reason she could readily explain.

Cade's smile vanished. He seemed quite taken aback. "I'm sorry, your highness . . ."

Adrina sighed. "No . . . I'm sorry, Captain. I don't mean to bite your head off. Do you know what the message said?"

"No, your highness, only that it came from a town somewhere north of here named Warrinhaven."

"I'll go see Damin, then. What are you up to for the rest of the day?"

"I've been ordered to visit the Sorcerers' Collective."

Knowing Cade was an atheist, his announcement made Adrina smile. "Will you be praying to the gods while you're there?"

"I doubt it, your highness."

"Still clinging to the notion they don't exist?"

"More wishing they didn't at this point," he said.

Adrina frowned. "So you think Shananara is right? That the gods are behind this stolen icon?"

Cade shrugged. "I really couldn't say, your highness," he said. "I only know the Lord Defender asked me to speak with the High Arrion about it while I'm here."

"Really? What light can Kalan shed on this that the queen of the Harshini cannot?"

"Tarja isn't looking for her guidance on the gods," Cade told her. "He wants the High Arrion's help."

"With what?"

"With finding R'shiel," Cade said, glancing over his shoulder to see if they could be overheard. The wide, tiled corridor was deserted. He seemed uncomfortable, but Adrina couldn't tell if that was because he feared they would be overheard or just that he didn't like anything to do with magic, the Harshini, or the Lord Defender's former lover—the only living being capable of destroying a god. He turned back to Adrina, adding in a low voice, "If there is a problem with the gods, your highness, Tarja doesn't think the Harshini will be much help at all."

"Which is why he wants to find the demon child."

Cade nodded.

"Nobody has laid eyes on R'shiel for a decade," Adrina reminded him. "She disappeared from the Citadel before Jaz was born. What makes you think you could find her now, particularly if she doesn't want to be found? Or that Kalan could help you locate her? I'm fairly certain if the High Prince's sister knew where the demon child was, she'd have mentioned it in passing. We dine together quite often, you know."

"I'm just the messenger, your highness," he told her with an apologetic shrug. "I'm to deliver Lord Tenragan's message, that's all. I'm sure the High Arrion will share that message with you, when next you dine, if she's so inclined."

Cheeky sod, Adrina thought, but she admired any young man who refused to be intimidated by her. "Will you be dining with us this evening, Captain?"

"I'd be delighted."

"You are dismissed until then," she decreed, and continued on her way without waiting for him to respond. After all, she was the High Princess of Hythria. Adrina always managed to have the last word.

DAMIN WASN'T IN his office when she went looking for him. She found her husband in the palace forecourt, looking over several magnificent sorcerer-bred horses being paraded for his approval. Adrina frowned when she saw them. The beasts were stunning, but if Damin was planning to head north on sorcerer-bred mounts, that meant he was in a hurry. Tarja had invited Damin to a treaty negotiation—so he claimed. In fact, it wasn't even that. It was a renegotiation of a perfectly functional treaty that nobody appeared anxious to meddle with.

Why the need to travel at speed with the aid of sorcerer-bred horses?

And worse, why would Damin risk Jazrian and Marlie, thinking they could handle such creatures?

A black-robed figure stood beside Damin, watching the horses, along with a white-robed Harshini woman. Adrina recognized them both. The Harshini was Yananara, their Harshini horse master. The black-robed sorcerer was Rorin Mariner, cousin to Damin's stepsister, Luciena, and the Lower Arrion of the Sorcerers' Collective.

"Really?" she asked as she strode up behind them. "You're going to travel on sorcerer-bred mounts?"

Damin looked up and glanced over his shoulder at her. "Adrina! So nice of you to join us. I was just telling Rory how it was your idea he come with us."

"Something about me being able to smite on command?" Rory said, grinning at her.

Adrina wasn't amused. "Why the horses?"

"They're pretty," Damin said.

"They're dangerous," Adrina replied. "And your traveling party includes two children and a woman who's already walking with a cane because she hasn't fully recovered from the last time she tried to prove she could manage one of these beasts, and is too stubborn to have it mended by the Harshini."

"I would never allow any harm to come to your children, your highness," Yananara said, her black-on-black eyes filled with despair at the very thought. "And I would never allow the horses to think of harming them, either."

"I know that, Yannie," Adrina said, smiling at the young woman. At least, Adrina always thought of her as young. She might be five hundred years old. There was just no way to tell with the Harshini. "I did not mean to imply you would be in any way to blame. It's my husband's complete lack of common sense or responsibility I'm concerned about."

Yannie smiled. "Oh . . . well . . . I understand now."

Even Damin bit back a smile at that. "Yannie, why don't you and Rory finish selecting the mounts?"

Yananara shook her head, stroking the proud muzzle of the golden stallion she was holding. "It is not up to me to select them, your highness. They must want to undertake the journey with us. We cannot force a sorcerer-bred mount to aid us."

"We'll ask them," Rory offered, with a wink at Damin, and then turned to the horse master. "The High Prince has princely things to take care of. You and I can take care of this."

That seemed to placate the Harshini. She began to lead the horses away, and the other dozen or so mounts turned to follow, obviously in response to some silent mental command Yananara had given them.

Rorin leaned across, gave Adrina a quick kiss on the cheek, whispering, "Don't worry, I'll keep the children safe and I'm an old hand at watching Damin's back," and then turned to follow the Harshini and her horses.

Damin watched them departing for a moment and then turned to Adrina. "What was Rory whispering to you about me?"

"Just that he agrees with me about your complete lack of common sense or responsibility. Are you really going to take Jaz and Marlie all that way on sorcerer-bred mounts?"

"Not on their own. They'll have an experienced Raider doubling with them and Yannie will be controlling the horses. They'll be safer than if they were on ordinary mounts. You're not worried about Marla?"

"Would your mother be worried about me?"

With a grin, Damin slipped his arm through hers as they headed back to the palace. "You know, my mother is right. You really are a terrible wife. I may have to put you aside for someone younger. Prettier. More respectful."

"I have a younger sister on the way," she offered. "Perhaps you'll find her more to your liking."

"Do you think so?"

"She's bound to be a better prospect, darling. You know my father . . . he never tries to rid himself of his *troublesome* daughters."

They'd reached the doors to the main entrance. The guards hurried forward to open the high double doors at the approach of their High Prince and Princess. Damin laughed, barely glancing at them. "Just what I need. Another conniving Fardohnyan princess for my mother to obsess over."

"Speaking of conniving Fardohnyan princesses, Cade said you'd received word about Rakaia's arrival."

He nodded as they stepped inside to the relative coolness of the palace lobby. The humidity was only marginally less in here, but out of the sun it was cooler, at least. "Ky sent a rather odd message, actually."

"Odd how?"

"It seems Rakaia sent her entourage back at the border and is heading here with an escort of less than a dozen men, no servants, no slaves, no handmaids, no *court'esa,* and no tantrums."

Adrina stopped and stared at Damin in surprise. "No. Surely not."

"That's what the messenger says. Ky sent him on ahead to warn us. Apparently our young Rakaia is quite an accommodating little soul."

"That can't be true."

"Why not?"

Adrina couldn't believe that after more than a decade living with her, Damin would need something like that explained. "Rakaia is Hablet's daughter. She wouldn't know the meaning of the word 'accommodating.' Besides, I remember her. She was a holy terror as a child."

Her admission seemed to amuse her husband greatly. "Can I quote you on that the next time you're accusing me of being inflexible, darling?"

She slapped his shoulder in annoyance. "I'm being serious."

"So am I," Damin laughed.

"Your highness?"

Damin was still laughing as he turned toward the guard who'd hailed him. Adrina glanced at the young man, thinking it odd he would address the High Prince so directly.

Time seemed to slow down as she turned. She saw the Raider's unshaven face. She saw him raise the knife, saw the look in his eye, the hatred, the sheer malice in his expression, and she heard a scream, although it took a moment to realize it was her own voice.

Damin saw the threat, too, perhaps even a split second before Adrina did. He'd been trained all his life to expect an assassin's blade, after all, but he was off-guard and not quite quick enough to avoid the unexpected attack.

Adrina watched in horror as the knife slashed down. Damin had his back to her, so she couldn't see where the blade connected, just heard him grunt in pain as it pierced him, and then there were Raiders everywhere and the assassin was beaten down. Adrina didn't know if Damin was dead, but it was certain his assassin soon would be.

"Don't kill him!" she cried out, as she dropped to her knees beside Damin. "We need to question him!"

Somebody, Adrina had no idea who, repeated her order, but she paid no further attention to the fate of the young man. She had Damin in her arms, saw the blood on his shirt . . .

He looked up at her, his eyes filled with pain. "Gods . . . that *really* hurt . . . ," he said, and then his eyes rolled back in his head and he went limp in her arms.

Adrina held him close, her vision blurred by tears as she swore a silent oath to every god she could name that she would invoke *mort'eda*—the ancient art of Fardohnyan revenge—to seek out those responsible for Damin's death and destroy every single one of them.

CADEN FLETCHER'S MISSION to Greenharbour was ostensibly to invite the High Prince to the treaty renewal negotiations.

It was only a part of what the Lord Defender had tasked him with in the southern capital. On the heels of a young apprentice sorcerer escorting him up a seemingly endless staircase, Cade was well on his way to fulfilling the second, and perhaps most important part of his mission.

So far, everything was going according to plan. Damin Wolfblade appeared to take the invitation to the treaty renewal negotiations at face value. The Princess Adrina was suspicious, but Cade couldn't tell if that was because she suspected he had an ulterior motive, or simply because she was Fardohnyan and suspected *everyone* of having ulterior motives.

The second task—and perhaps the most important one—Tarja had ordered him to undertake was to meet with the High Arrion and Wrayan Lightfinger, head of the Greenharbour Thieves' Guild, without raising any suspicion, to discuss the theft of the tiny golden lyre missing from the Temple of the Gods and not alert the High Prince before they learned if there really was a problem.

It had seemed a simple task until he realized the High Arrion was Damin Wolfblade's younger sister. Wrayan Lightfinger, in addition to being part-Harshini—which cast doubt in Cade's mind about where his loyalties lay—was so closely tied to the Hythrun royal family he was almost a de facto member of it.

His thighs burning from the four flights of steep stairs, Cade was admitted into the High Arrion's office by a pretty young apprentice. She was about sixteen, he guessed, with thick brown hair braided loosely down her back, as if she'd tied it back because it annoyed her, rather than any desire to enhance her appearance. She made no secret of the fact that she was not pleased to be escorting him anywhere. The pace she set was grueling. He tried to make conversation with her when they started the climb. By the fourth set of stairs, he didn't have the breath left to ask her anything.

The apprentice told him the High Arrion would be with him shortly and then left him alone in the office, closing the door softly behind her. Cade stepped into the office and glanced around. It was much less pretentious than he'd expected. There was the usual Hythrun geometric tiled flooring, a couple of straight-backed chairs, a cluster of cushions in the corner around a low table for informal meetings and a light-colored desk carved with doe-eyed demons facing the door. The desk was cluttered with formal scrolls and rather less formal stacks of papers, several large leather-bound books, and all the other paraphernalia of an overworked bureaucrat. The chair behind the desk was padded with sheepskin, but a serviceable seat, rather than the thronelike appliance Cade expected the head of the Sorcerers' Collective to own.

A gentle breeze stirred the beaded curtains hanging in front of the two open doors on either side of the desk leading to the balcony. Even through the curtains, Cade was impressed with the view. The Sorcerers' Collective compound occupied the highest point in the city and the High Arrion's office was on the top floor, which meant the entire white city of Greenharbour lay before her in all its glory. The harbor sparkled in the distance and this high above the noise and grime of massive wharves, one could appreciate the spectacle without having to smell it.

"It's a trap, this office," a voice said behind him. "It's very tempting to sit up here, look out that window, and believe the city is there for you to lord over at your whim."

Cade turned to find an attractive woman of indeterminate age standing in the doorway behind him, wearing a light green robe one might expect to find on a merchant's wife, her long fair hair pulled back into a loose braid. The only way Cade would have known this was the High Arrion was the large silver diamond-shaped pendant she wore and her resemblance to her older brother.

"Of course, the upside," she added, with a smile, "is that nobody who *really* doesn't have important business is prepared to tackle those stairs. It keeps the distractions at bay very effectively."

He bowed politely. Not just because she was the High Arrion. Kalan Hawksword was a princess in her own right. "Lady Kalan."

"You look surprised, Captain. Am I such a disappointment?"

"Ah . . . no . . . I was just . . ."

"Expecting the robes?"

He nodded a little sheepishly. "I suppose."

Kalan smiled. "Trust me, Captain, if you had to spend even a moment in those damned ceremonial sorcerer's robes in Greenharbour's heat, you'd understand why the Sorcerers' Collective has so much trouble finding new recruits." She walked to her desk and held out her arm to indicate one of the carved chairs opposite. "Please, have a seat. Much to the chagrin of the Collective's old guard, we don't stand on ceremony much around here unless we have to."

"Are you really having trouble finding new recruits for the Collective?" he asked as he took the offered seat. It really wasn't important, he supposed, but it seemed an odd problem and Cade had been trained to gather intelligence by Garet Warner. Odd problems, the old man maintained, were often the symptoms of a much greater calamity nobody was aware of yet.

Not unlike the problem that had brought him here today.

"Once the Sorcerers' Collective was the main center for humans and Harshini to share the study of magic," she said. "Then your wretched Sisters of the Blade drove them into hiding and it became more a university than anything to do with magic, which is certainly what it was when I joined. I mean . . . look at me. I'm the head of the Sorcerers' Collective and I couldn't work a spell if my life depended on it. Now that the Harshini are back, though, and are happy to share their magic again, we're no longer a simple university. Unfortunately, the number of people who can actually *wield* the magic the Harshini wish to share turns out to be rather low."

"Why is that, do you think?" Cade asked. The idea of a return to the past, when human magicians wielded enormous power—both political and magical—was one many in his country were unhappy with. It never occurred to him that there might be a problem finding anybody to wield that awesome power in the first place.

She shrugged and sat down to face him. "There are quite a few suggestions kicking around. The most popular theory at present is that humans simply can't wield magic at all."

"Then how do you explain the magicians the Collective used to produce?"

"Your wretched Sisters of the Blade tried to exterminate the Harshini mostly because they were too indiscriminate with their sexual favors."

Cade didn't respond to the accusation. Although he'd grown up under the Sisterhood's rule, he'd never been a supporter of their methods, or the way they ruled Medalon, so he was more than a little hazy about their origins. He'd joined the Defenders just before they were deposed by Tarja, the demon child, and the Harshini, with Damin Wolfblade's assistance, so he'd never had to spend hours learning the Sisterhood's history, or memorize the long list of brave Sisters who'd sacrificed themselves for the good of the cause—which was to rid themselves of a magical race who behaved with such unbridled lust. It was quite likely Kalan Hawksword knew more about Medalon's history during that era than he did.

"Since they've emerged from hiding," the High Arrion continued, "I gather the Harshini have learned their lesson. I don't know what it's like at the Citadel, but we've got hundreds of Harshini here in the city now and you hardly ever hear of them getting into even casual relationships with humans."

Cade nodded, thinking she was right. He'd not heard of any Harshini in the Citadel taking human lovers. "You mean the likelihood of future human sorcerers is under threat because the Harshini aren't making babies with humans any longer?"

"That is the popular theory."

"So the Sisterhood, even in defeat, may yet win the war?"

"Sadly," Kalan admitted. "But that's not the reason you're here, Captain. Nor why Lord Tenragan sent the request for this meeting via mundane channels, rather than using the Seeing Stone and risking the Harshini knowing about us meeting."

He nodded, grateful both Tarja and Garet Warner had warned him that even though they considered Damin the best Hythrun High Prince in living memory, the sharpest Wolfblade alive was probably his younger sister, Kalan—and that included Kalan's mother, the fearsome Princess Marla.

"You've heard about the theft from the Temple of the Gods?"

"The lyre representing Gimlorie?" She nodded. "Queen Shananara contacted us through the Seeing Stone not long after it happened to see if there had been any effect on the music."

"Was there?"

"If there were, nobody in Greenharbour noticed, although there are plenty of rumors swirling around the city about what the theft means, ranging from nothing to the end of life as we know it. Is there still no hint about who might have taken it?"

"None."

"How long did the loss of music last in the Citadel?"

"Only until the following morning. That's bothering Shananara, too, I suspect, although it's hard to tell what bothers a Harshini."

"And you're certain the Citadel Thieves' Guild didn't authorize the theft?"

Cade shrugged. "They say not, and we're inclined to believe them. They'll steal anything that's not nailed down, normally, but thieves take their god very seriously—even atheist thieves—and I gather Dacendaran is a rather hands-on sort of deity. Unless there is some conflict between the gods going on that we mere mortals know nothing about, there would be no reason for him to countenance such an act."

Kalan frowned. "I wouldn't dismiss a whole war between the gods idea out of hand. Who knows what they're fighting about among themselves at any given moment? But I've not heard anything about the gods being any more antagonistic toward each other than they usually are, either."

"And we're talking the God of Music here," Cade said. "I mean, what would stealing his icon be trying to prevent? People whistling while they work?"

The High Arrion seemed amused, but she gave Cade the impression she was listening to him out of politeness, rather than grave concern for what the theft of one tiny golden lyre might mean to the world of men. Perhaps if she'd been there when the music stopped, she'd have a better notion of the trouble this was liable to cause. "What does the Lord Defender really want from me, Captain?"

"Pardon?"

"You're trivializing this theft, Captain, but you have traveled a very long way to ask a question about it, I suspect."

"I came here to personally invite the High Prince to the treaty discussions."

"Was there any doubt he wasn't planning to attend?"

"I don't know."

"Did Tarja Tenragan really send you all the way to Greenharbour to issue an invitation that could have been handled by a courier? A raven? I'm sure the Harshini would gladly have conveyed the message via the Seeing Stone, had he bothered to ask."

"I'm not in the habit of questioning the Lord Defender's motives, my lady."

"Aren't you? Because I am." She leaned back in her seat and studied him for a moment. "Why don't we stop skirting the real reason you're in Hythria and tell me the truth? Be warned, if you *don't* tell me the truth, I'll have you turned into a toad. I'm the head of the Sorcerers' Collective. I have people who can do that, you know."

He smiled, thinking he really liked Kalan Hawksword. She was everything and more Tarja had warned him about. "The Lord Defender said you would be suspicious." *Along with a few other things it wouldn't be wise to repeat.* Despite her threat, Cade was still hedging, because he still wasn't sure how much of what he said to the High Arrion would end up dinner conversation at the palace, as Princess Adrina had suggested.

Kalan seemed to be losing patience. "Of course I'm suspicious. If the Defenders wanted information about the gods and the Thieves' Guild, you wouldn't have come to me. You would been sitting opposite Wrayan Lightfinger, questioning him."

"I was hoping you could arrange an introduction."

"I'll be happy to," she offered. "But so would the head of the Citadel Thieves' Guild. Wrayan is a part-Harshini thief, not a god, and it's a relatively small part, at that. So I ask again. What do you *really* want from the Sorcerers' Collective?"

"Information."

"About . . . ?" she prompted.

"Something called the Covenant."

Kalan frowned, but she looked puzzled, rather than alarmed. "In what context?"

"The Harshini. The gods."

"Why?"

"When we discovered the theft of the lyre, Queen Shananara was with us. She was frantic—at least as frantic as a Harshini can get. She said something about a Covenant being tied to the lyre."

"What else did she say?"

"That the Covenant gives gods the ability to walk among us. Then she said, *It is the Covenant that brought the Harshini into being.* When Lord Tenragan asked if that meant the stolen lyre was important, she said it was more important than he could possibly imagine."

"If that's the case, why don't you ask Shananara to elaborate?"

"We have . . . at least, the Lord Defender has. She refuses to discuss it."

Kalan studied him for a long moment before she replied.

"Captain, Medalon has a long and bloody history of going about their dealings with the Harshini the wrong way. Coming here, behind the back of the Harshini queen, and asking the Sorcerers' Collective to give you access to the Harshini archives to satisfy your idle curiosity, is hardly the way to improve that situation."

"*More than you could possibly imagine,*" he repeated. "Her exact words."

Kalan pondered the matter for a few more moments and then she sighed and leaned forward to pick up her quill. "I'll tell the chief archivist to see if he can find anything, but don't hold your breath. The libraries here are vast and they go back several thousand years, but Brakandaran cleaned them out with the God of Thieves just after the Harshini went into hiding a couple of hundred years ago, so a lot of the really meaty stuff is lost to us forever. In the meantime, I'll write you an introduction to Wrayan. I fear if you arrive in the Thieves' Quarter in a Defender's uniform without it, you won't get out of there in one piece."

"I believe the theory behind the Defenders' red jackets, my lady, is so our enemies can't see us bleed."

Kalan signed the introduction she was writing with a flourish and looked up with a grin. "Well, that also explains the brown trousers, then, I suppose."

She held out the introduction. Cade rose to his feet to take it from her, trying to think up a suitably witty and cutting rejoinder, when the young woman who had escorted Cade to Kalan's office burst in, her face flushed, as if she'd run up every one of those wretched four flights of stairs to get here.

"You have to come!" the girl announced.

"Excuse me, Julika, but I told you I was not to be disturbed." She turned to Cade and smiled apologetically. "My daughter is still adjusting to her new role as an apprentice sorcerer. I fear she's spent far too many years lording it over her cousins in Elasapine, which seems to have completely robbed her of any manners."

"It's perfectly all right, my lady," Cade assured her. "I wasn't—"

"Oh, for pity's sake, who cares what you think," Julika snapped. "Mother, you're needed at the palace. Now."

Kalan was obviously appalled by her daughter's rudeness. Cade was rather more interested in the fact that Kalan had a daughter he'd never heard of. She wasn't married, as far as he knew, and never had been. Julika didn't look like her mother at all, which meant she probably favored her father. Cade was very curious about who that might be, but was far too polite to ask.

"I will answer the High Prince's summons when I'm—"

"Uncle Damin didn't summon you, mother," Julika told her, impatiently. "Adrina did. And you'd better get there fast, because someone just tried to assassinate the High Prince."

"You sent Alaric a severed head," Hablet accused through a mouthful of broth, as Naveen arrived in response to his king's summons. "His mother was quite upset about it."

The king sat behind his desk with his foot elevated on a padded stool. Hablet was trying to ease his gout. The physics had suggested a bland diet consisting mostly of chicken broth, rye bread, and cider. Hablet was sticking to his physic's orders, but reluctantly. The Harshini ambassador, Belendara—who could have healed the king's pain in a moment with magic—was refusing to help. Her excuse was some nonsense about not interfering in the natural order of things.

The king's mood was not pleasant.

Naveen shrugged. "I thought he might benefit from a lesson in the dangers of acting on a whim, your highness."

"His mother doesn't agree."

"Are we paying attention to what your wives agree with now?"

Hablet shook his head. "Of course not. But I'd stay out of the harem for a while if I were you. Kabar's brains leaked all over the parquet flooring, I hear. You're not the most popular person in there at the moment."

"Your son is not the most popular person among your generals or your armed forces, your highness," Naveen reminded him. "Which is rather more problematic."

The king sighed and pushed away the broth with a grimace. "Damn physics. They're trying to kill me with culinary blandness."

Naveen was quite sure he wasn't required to respond to that.

"Did Kabar say anything incriminating before he died?"

As usual, Hablet ignored Naveen's not so veiled criticism of his son. The annoying thing was that Hablet knew Alaric was a spoiled brat, but seemed incapable of doing anything about it. At least openly. The fact that he seemed only mildly annoyed by the severed head was probably a good sign.

"If you're asking, was he plotting against you as your son maintains, then the answer is no. To the end, Meyrick Kabar remained a loyal servant of the crown."

The king's eyes narrowed. "If that's not the question I should be asking, what is?"

"Perhaps, your highness, you should be asking about the time he spent in Talabar as the Captain of the Harem Guard."

Hablet gave him a puzzled look. "That was years . . . decades ago."

"Two decades, to be exact," Naveen agreed. "He departed Talabar for a posting in Bordertown about six months before Princess Sophany gave birth to the Princess Rakaia, whom you so recently betrothed to Lord Frederak Branador, thus securing our clear access to the trade routes from the port at Tarkent through Highcastle Pass into Hythria, in perpetuity." Naveen thought it important to remind the king of that. Hablet was many things, but he was a dark-hearted merchant prince at his core. He'd happily put aside all thoughts of vengeance and retribution if there was a profit to be had.

Hablet was silent for a moment as he digested Naveen's news. "The blue eyes," he said finally. "Rakaia is a pretty little thing, but I always wondered about those damned blue eyes. Sophany told me it was something in my line. She even had me bring the blue-eyed whore's bastard . . . what was her name . . . ?"

"Charisee."

"Charisee . . . into the harem as a companion for Rakaia to remind me of it."

"A clever deception, as it turns out."

"Where is she?"

"Charisee?"

"No, of course not, you fool. Rakaia."

"Almost to Greenharbour by now, I would think."

The king shrugged, tearing a piece off the rye loaf and dipping it in the broth. "Have her killed as soon as she gets there. Execute Sophany while you're about it."

Naveen took a step closer to the desk, clasping his hands together. He took a deep measured breath as the king slurped up his soggy bread. "Your highness, is that *really* the most effective way of dealing with this . . . most delicate matter?"

"*Delicate* matter?" Hablet asked, wiping a drop of broth from his beard. "Gods alive, Naveen! The bitch passed off the get of a common-born soldier as my daughter. That's not a delicate matter. That's high treason."

"A most regrettable state of affairs, I agree, your highness, but in the small, unworthy hands of that common-born soldier's get lies the key to Fardohnya's future economic stability and prosperity."

The king frowned. Naveen could almost see the battle going on in his head as he warred between vengeance and profit. "What are you suggesting?" he asked after a time. "That I just ignore this?"

"Of course not, your highness. That would be unconscionable. But there is no reason to remove Rakaia until *after* the wedding, surely?"

Hablet nodded. "That's true enough. When are they scheduled to marry?"

"At the end of summer, I believe."

"I suppose we could wait until then."

"Might I also be so bold as to suggest we spend the coin to have this unfortunate matter taken care of by professionals?"

"Why would I involve the Assassins' Guild? They cost a fortune. Besides, they usually don't take commissions on members of a royal family."

"I believe the point here is that Rakaia is *not* a member of any royal family, your highness. More importantly, the guild can make her death look like an accident and not alert Frederak Branador—or his cousin, the High Prince—to the . . . awkward situation . . . in which we find ourselves."

Hablet thought on that for a moment and then nodded. "I suppose. Do you have a plan for Sophany as well?"

"My advice is to do nothing, your highness, to alert the princess to your knowledge of her affair until Rakaia has been dealt with and the trade routes through Highcastle are secured. You don't want her warning Rakaia, who, in turn, might alert the Hythrun."

"If I have the bitch summarily executed this afternoon," the king pointed out, "she won't have time to warn anyone of anything."

Naveen could feel his secret escape plan slipping through his fingers. He smiled at the king, hoping Hablet was in too much pain from his gout—or too angry over Sophany's betrayal—to notice his anxiousness. "Princess Sophany's unexpected execution, after so recently bestowing your favor on her daughter, would raise questions we do not wish to answer at this time."

With some reluctance the king nodded, conceding Naveen's point.

"What do you suggest, then? If I exile her, it will raise the same questions."

"Bide your time," Naveen advised. "Once Rakaia is taken care of, Sophany can be dealt with in a manner befitting her crimes."

"You have more patience than me, Naveen."

"I live to serve, your highness."

The king shifted uncomfortably in his seat. "Arrange with the guild to take care of Rakaia. But not until she's married and we have our own troops stationed at Highcastle. And send a message to the harem. Tell them I wish the Princess Sophany to attend me tonight."

Naveen doubted Hablet planned to bed the princess. "Is that wise? You haven't bedded Princess Sophany in a decade."

"Then she is long overdue for a visit, isn't she?"

"Sire, if she realizes you know . . ."

"Oh, Naveen, why do you treat me like I'm the fool? You said it yourself. Sophany is the honored mother of a daughter about to secure our future economic stability and prosperity. Why would I *not* bestow my attentions on her?"

Naveen bowed, accepting defeat. Perhaps there was some way to warn Sophany. He wasn't interested in saving the treacherous and unfaithful princess from a fate she richly deserved, but he had become quite attached to the thought of a safe haven if the king died and his position in the palace became less . . . tenable. "I shall arrange it, your highness. Will that be all?"

"For now."

Naveen turned to leave. He had his hand on the door latch when Hablet said, "I'm thinking of sending him to Medalon, you know. To the Defenders."

"Sire?"

"Alaric," the king explained. "I know he's spoiled rotten, Naveen. It's those damned women in the harem. They've let him run riot all his life."

As have you, your highness, Naveen was tempted to add.

"Anyway, with this treaty renewal coming up, I thought I'd take him with me to Medalon. The Defenders are the best-disciplined army in the world. They make my lads look like amateurs."

"I agree, sire, but . . ."

"They take their officer cadets in at twelve or thirteen, knock the stuffing out them completely, and turn them into real men. Perhaps a few years in the Defenders where nobody cares he's the Fardohnyan heir will knock some of the arrogance out of Alaric. It should buy him some respect in our army at the very least. I know we can't afford another incident like the one with General Kabar."

So Hablet *had* been listening all the times Naveen had tried to warn him of the dangers of a king's heir held in such contempt—and, after this unfortunate affair, actively despised—by a nation's standing army numbering close to a hundred thousand men. "But what if something happens to him? He's your only son."

"Then I will declare war on Medalon and wipe them off the map."

Naveen couldn't tell if the king was kidding or not.

Hablet laughed at his expression. "For pity's sake, Naveen, we're at peace. He won't be in harm's way. My son was a gift from Jelanna herself. The Harshini won't allow it."

"Have you approached Lord Tenragan about this?"

"Not yet. But I floated the idea with Belendara. She was so impressed by the suggestion, she said she might reconsider her refusal to allow magical healing of my . . . ailments, to expedite our journey."

Ah, that makes more sense. Hablet was doing this to get out of pain. Perhaps he was doing it to ensure he lived to see Alaric grown. As he'd heard nothing about this until now, Naveen wondered if it was the Harshini ambassador's idea, although the magical race was so incapable of violence it seemed odd she would suggest Alaric be sent to join anybody's army, let alone another nation's.

Maybe the Harshini just thought it politic for Hablet to stay on the throne until Alaric was grown, too.

"I shall tell the quartermaster to include his highness on the passenger manifest, your highness."

"He's a good boy, Naveen."

"Of course he is, your highness."

"You scared the living daylights out of him with that head."

"I'm sorry, your highness."

"No, you're not."

"You're right. I'm not."

The king grinned at him. "Wish I could have seen it. By all accounts he screamed like a little girl until someone took it away."

"Then perhaps the lesson was learned, your highness."

"I live in hope, Naveen," the king said with a sigh. "I live in hope."

21

RAKAIA WOKE UP in a strange room. She was lying on a comfortable—although hardly luxurious—mattress, sunlight streamed through the diamond-paned window, and there was a demon sitting at the end of her bed.

She had no idea how she came to be in the bed, where she was, or why there was a demon standing guard over her. Rakaia's last clear memory was of a dragon swooping down over the Widowmaker Pass.

She wasn't in the pass now, she guessed, or anywhere near it. The room was warm with no visible heat source other than the sunlight. The very air was warm, which meant there was no snow on the ground outside, nor the thin, chill air of the mountains.

Afraid to move, Rakaia studied the demon out of half-closed eyes. It perched on the bedframe like an odd-shaped bird, its large, liquid black eyes fixed on her with an unblinking stare. The demon's small, upward-pointed ears twitched back and forth. Its skin seemed gray and wrinkly from where she lay; like an old leather bag shoved in the bottom of a trunk for a few years, before being taken out and dusted off.

She moved her head a fraction. As soon as she did, the demon vanished, leaving Rakaia to wonder if she'd imagined the demon, puzzling over where she was and how she came to be here.

A quick inventory of her limbs reassured her she was whole and unharmed, although naked under the linen sheet and the thin woolen blanket. The realization she was naked panicked her for a moment as her last conscious memories surfaced. For an instant, the horrible specter of Aja being raped before her very eyes almost suffocated her with its vividness. It made her doubt her sanity. Was that a real memory and this place an imagined sanctuary she had retreated to inside her mind? Had her turn come? Was she really still in the Widowmaker Pass being brutally attacked by a bandit bent on taking more than the contraband he could carry off?

Or was this place real, and Aja's fate just a terrible, ghastly nightmare?

As if in answer to her question the door opened and a pretty, redheaded serving wench of about eighteen or nineteen walked in. She carried a tray with a pitcher and a bowl on it, kicking the door shut with her foot before she turned to look at Rakaia.

"You're not dreaming," the girl said.

Rakaia pushed herself up onto her elbows and looked around. The room was not very large, with plaster, whitewashed walls, a table with a water bowl and pitcher by the door. It wasn't a cell, so she probably wasn't a prisoner. Rather, the room had the impersonal feel of a place meant for travelers. This was an inn, she guessed, not somebody's home. "Where am I?"

"Testra."

"Testra!" she cried, sitting bolt upright. "How in the name of the gods did I get to Testra?"

The younger girl smiled. "On the back of a dragon, actually."

Rakaia opened her mouth to ask how, but another memory suddenly replaced the image of Aja and the bandit. A dragon. And a leather-clad, red-headed dragon rider.

"It's you!"

"That's a rather ridiculous statement, when you think about it."

"I mean . . . you. You rode the dragon. I remember now. We were in the pass. There were bandits. And then everything just seemed to stop, except you . . . and . . . and I . . . or how . . . or . . ."

"Shout it a bit louder," the girl said. "I don't think they heard you in Denika."

"Why am I in Testra?" she asked, in a somewhat less shrill tone.

"Because Testra happened to be in the general direction I was heading."

"Did anybody else . . . ?"

"Get out of the Widowmaker alive?" the girl finished for her. She shook her head and sat on the bed, offering Rakaia the tray. It turned out to be a pitcher of ale and a bowl of thick stew with a trencher of bread beside it. "Death had all of them on his dance card, I fear."

"Who are you?"

"My name is R'shiel té Ortyn."

Rakaia didn't know what to say. So she just bowed her head in awe and muttered, "Divine One."

"Stop it."

She looked up in surprise. "But you're the demon chi—"

"My name is R'shiel. I don't care who—or what—you think I am. Your payment for being rescued from rape and certain death in the Widow-maker is that you never mention that name again, fair enough?"

She looked about eighteen, but Rakaia knew the demon child had to be considerably older. And Rakaia was not about to defy someone so powerful. "Yes, your highness."

"My name is R'shiel. I don't need a title. I certainly don't need to be worshipped. What's your name?"

If I lie, will she be able to tell? Will she destroy me? Turn me into something with scales?

"Ra . . . Rakaia," she said, not prepared to risk it. No need to add family name, though.

Fortunately, the demon child didn't require any further information. "You should eat, Rakaia," she said, rising to her feet. "This inn belongs to a friend, so you're safe here. I'm going to head into town to find you something to wear. After that, I'll have to be on my way, I'm afraid."

"I was heading for Tarkent."

"I do apologize for disrupting your travel plans, your highness."

Rakaia experienced a moment of panic, thinking the demon child had guessed who she was, until she realized the R'shiel was mocking her. Smiling sheepishly to cover her fright, Rakaia shrugged. "I'm sorry. You saved my life. I must sound really ungrateful."

"You do, but you've been through quite a bit these last couple of days, so I'm prepared to cut you some slack, as they say on the riverboats. Will you be here when I get back?"

"I don't have any clothes."

"I'll take that as a yes," R'shiel said with a smile. "Dranymire?"

Rakaia started as the demon reappeared at the foot of the bed, splashing ale onto the tray and soaking the bread.

"Divine One."

"This is Rakaia," she said. "Will you keep her company until I return?"

"Do I have a choice?" the demon asked.

"Not really."

"Then it will be my pleasure, your highness. Why is she gaping like that?"

"She's not used to demons."

Rakaia heard, rather than saw, R'shiel leave. Her eyes were fixed on the leathery demon who returned her stare with his solemn, liquid black eyes, which made Rakaia certain he could see into her very soul.

Chapter

22

ADRINA WAS NOT a patient woman. She paced the tiled floor of the anteroom outside the royal bedroom in the apartment she shared with her husband until sunset, waiting for the Harshini healers to restore Damin to health. To while away the time, she amused herself with the many and various ways she planned to torture and kill the would-be assassin who had dared to attempt to take the life of the High Prince of Hythria.

"For pity's sake, Adrina, will you stop pacing?" Kalan asked. "You're worse than Julika."

"I can't. And I don't know how you can sit there so calmly."

"I'm amusing myself by imagining all the things I'd like to do to the man who did this."

"So am I," Adrina admitted, taking the seat opposite Kalan. "I have several methods in mind, all of them resulting in gruesome death." She fidgeted with her skirts as she spoke and realized the state of them. She should change before she spoke to the children. It would be difficult to reassure them Damin was fine if their mother was still covered in their father's blood.

"You can only kill him once, Adrina."

She jumped to her feet again to resume her pacing. "I haven't been able to settle on any one particular fate, so I thought I'd do all of them."

Kalan smiled sympathetically. "An interesting proposition. How do you plan to manage it?"

"I will make the Harshini bring him back to life over and over. Then I can kill him as many times as I please. Trust me, this assassin will learn the meaning of the ancient Fardohnyan art of *mort'eda*—the blood-oath of vengeance that has brought down entire dynasties. He will pay, Kalan, as will his parents, his children, anybody who has so much as glanced in his general direction . . ."

Kalan seemed amused, rather than threatened. "Gods, Adrina, no wonder my mother worries about you."

Before Adrina could answer, the main door to the apartment opened without a knock to request permission. She turned to give the miscreant a piece of her mind until she realized it was her mother-in-law, and she wasn't alone. Elin Bane, the Raven of the Assassins' Guild, was right behind her.

"Did you arrange this?"

"Don't be ridiculous, Adrina."

"I want to hear it from him."

The Raven closed the door and then turned to look Adrina squarely in the eye. "Not my guild, nor any branch of it I am aware of, ordered a hit on the High Prince of Hythria, or any member of his family." Then he turned to Kalan, who had risen to her feet and bowed politely to her. "High Arrion."

"Lord Raven."

Adrina believed him. In truth, she'd never seriously considered the possibility the Assassins' Guild was behind this. It was good to hear it stated aloud, though. For that alone, Adrina was grateful Marla had bought Elin Bane to the palace, despite the adverse gossip such an event might precipitate.

"How is he?" Marla asked Kalan. She displayed no visible emotion, unlike Adrina, who was quite sure the others could see her anger as a steaming, palpable thing. But then, this is what Marla was always like in a crisis. Calm and practical. To a fault.

"We don't know," Adrina said. "The Harshini are still with him."

"It's been hours."

"Does anybody know how long a magical healing like this takes?" Marla directed the question to Kalan. Her daughter was the head of the Sorcerers' Collective, after all. If anybody knew the answer, surely she would.

"It depends on the wound and how soon they got to work on it," the Raven told her before Kalan could say a word.

"Are you an expert in Harshini healing now?"

"The Lord Raven is here to help, Adrina," Marla said. "I know you're upset, but a bit of civility would not go astray."

The Raven wasn't offended. "Actually, your highness, I *am* something of an expert."

"When an assassin is commissioned to kill someone, they're instructed to make certain he's dead enough that the Harshini can't bring him back," Kalan explained.

Elin nodded. "If there is likely to be a Harshini in the vicinity, we have to kill the target in such a way that he is beyond healing."

Adrina was almost equally appalled and enthralled by this rare glimpse into the world of assassins. "Exactly what does that involve?"

"Bloody organs, mostly. They're the hardest to heal. The heart, the spleen, any of the major arteries . . ."

Princess Marla frowned. "Where was Damin stabbed?"

Kalan answered for her. "Barandaran says the left lung."

"Then he should be all right," the Raven said. "Once the Harshini are done with him."

"Assuming they *are* ever done with him," Adrina complained, glancing again at the locked bedroom door. She turned back to look at Elin Bane, her anger subsiding enough for her to think of other things. "Why are you here, Lord Raven, if your guild had nothing to do with this?"

"I thought he should interrogate the prisoner for us," Marla said. "The guild has . . . ways . . . of encouraging men to share what they know."

"I'll bet they do," Adrina agreed. "But why *ask* Damin's assassin anything? Why not just order Wrayan or one of the Harshini to take the information from his mind?"

"We did," Marla said. "I sent a message to the Thieves' Quarter the moment I learned of the attack. Wrayan's been with him these past few hours trying to do exactly that. He says there is nothing there except a song that keeps repeating, over and over, in his mind. He seems to think the song is a mask for something else."

"What song?"

"Some children's nursery rhyme, he says."

The news seemed to intrigue Kalan. "Didn't you have Wrayan do something similar to us when we were younger, to stop Alija reading our minds, Mother?"

Adrina stared at Kalan. "He did *what*?"

Marla shrugged, as if such a thing were quite an everyday occurrence. "What Wrayan did to us was more sophisticated than this."

Kalan turned to Adrina to explain. "Wrayan shielded all our minds against anyone reading anything deeper than the most shallow thoughts when we were children. The shields are still in place as far as I know."

"This is different," Marla told Kalan, almost, but not quite, excluding Adrina from the conversation. "Wrayan says it's like . . . noise . . . filling up the space to stop anything else but a single purpose taking hold."

"Is he a regular guard or an imposter who somehow managed to sneak into the palace?" Elin asked.

"He's a regular," Marla said. "Even worse, he's from Krakandar. He had a distinguished career in the Krakandar Raiders before he joined Damin's personal guard."

Adrina saw Kalan pale, and wondered how much that information would sting. Krakandar was the Wolfblade home and, more importantly, their seat of power. To hear Marla talk, the whole province would gladly lay their lives down for the Wolfblade family.

So much for that theory.

"Do we know where he's been?"

"What do you mean?" Kalan asked.

"I believe the High Princess is asking if this man has traveled anywhere recently, where he might have been infected with this . . . song," Elin said.

Nobody seemed to have the answer. "I'm hoping we'll know more after the Raven has spoken with him," Marla said.

Before she could say anything more, the door to the bedroom opened. Barandanan, the Harshini healer Kalan had brought from the Sorcerers' Collective, and his companion, Telenara, emerged from the room, shutting the door behind them. The Harshini were dressed in their traditional long white robes, but they were splattered with blood and both Harshini looked haggard, their black-on-black eyes dull, their tall, slender frames slumped with exhaustion.

Adrina headed for the bedroom door determined to assure herself Damin was alive. She was so certain he had died in her arms earlier, she wasn't going to be convinced her husband still lived until he told her so himself.

"A moment, your highness," Telenara said, still blocking the door.

"I wish to see my husband."

"And you shall, your highness," Barandaran said. "But we need to speak with you first."

"Does my son still live?"

"Yes, Princess Marla. He lives and we have healed him to the best of our ability."

"What's the problem, then?" Kalan asked, perhaps the only one in the room with the authority to take that tone with the Harshini.

"He's asleep," Telenara said.

"Then I promise not to wake him."

"Would that you could, your highness," Barandaran sighed.

"You can't wake him?" Kalan asked.

The Harshini shook his head. "Not at all."

"Let me try," Adrina demanded.

"There would be no point, your highness. He will not wake until Death is prepared to release him."

For a moment, everyone in the room went silent.

It was Kalan, the one among them who was most familiar with the ways of the Harshini, who asked the obvious question. "How do you know that?"

"We spoke to Death when we could not revive the prince, wondering if his time had truly come," Telenara explained. "Death assured us it had not, but he is holding the High Prince's life in trust."

"In trust for what?"

"He refused to say."

"Make him tell you!"

Telenara smiled at Adrina, which made her want to punch the lovely young healer, with her endless smiles, her golden skin, and her midnight-black eyes, in the face. "He did tell us one other thing that might be important."

"What other thing?"

"He mentioned the demon child."

"R'shiel?" Adrina turned to Kalan. "But nobody has seen her in years."

"Not since the last treaty negotiation," Marla reminded them. "Is Damin in any immediate danger?"

"Not at all, your highness. He rests peacefully and will come to no harm while in Death's care."

"Then I need to talk to the guard commander and ensure he's issued the order to seal the city. Until we've resolved this, I'll have to manage this crisis and find a way to keep this quiet. If the Warlords get wind of the fact that Damin is incapacitated in any way, they'll swoop down like vultures circling a corpse."

Listening to Marla issuing orders, Adrina had a sudden vision of her future. The future in which Marla ruled Hythria again and she became nothing more than an irritating—if somewhat decorative—presence at court, as she had been in her father's harem.

Damin trusted her. Damin appreciated her intellect. Damin had been prepared to make her regent while he was in Medalon.

And he would be furious if she let the reins of power fall back into his mother's hands because she was too busy grieving him to object.

"No."

Marla turned to Adrina in surprise. "I beg your pardon?"

"I said no."

"What possible reason can you have to—"

"Because you are merely the High Prince's mother, Marla. I am High Princess of Hythria, Damin's wife, and he has already signed the decree giving me the regency in his absence, in anticipation of his journey to Medalon for the treaty talks. You may advise me—in fact, I welcome your wisdom—but you will not be issuing orders to anyone in Damin's name, or mine, is that clear?"

Marla stared at Adrina in silence for a long moment. "I am sure Damin did not sign that decree expecting a crisis like this. He would want—"

"Adrina to act as regent," Kalan cut in, stunning Adrina with her support. "She's right, Mother. Damin appointed her regent, and I signed the decree off days ago. There's nothing you can do about it."

Marla was usually quite good at keeping her anger under control, but right now, she looked ready to burst something. "I will not stand by and watch one of Hablet's wretched daughters destroy everything I've worked for . . ."

"Then you needn't watch," Adrina said. "We still have to renegotiate this treaty with Medalon, Karien, and Fardohnya. Someone needs to represent Hythria at the Citadel, so it might as well be you. Damin had already decided he needed your counsel, so I see no reason why you shouldn't take his place."

"I am not leaving Greenharbour with my son in this condition."

"Actually, I think you should go, your highness," the Raven suggested.

Adrina was almost faint with shock at the idea of both Marla's daughter and the head of the Assassins' Guild siding with her.

"Nobody asked you, Master Raven."

"But I'm giving my opinion nonetheless. Adrina is right. That treaty is critical to the peace and prosperity of the whole continent. And I find it highly suspicious this has happened, with Death interfering so directly and suddenly talking of the demon child, when nobody has seen R'shiel té Ortyn since the last time this same treaty was on the table."

"You think they're connected?" Kalan asked.

"I'm not a great believer in coincidences."

"My son is dying, Elin."

"Actually, your highness, he's not dying at all," Telenara assured her. "As I said, Death his holding his life in trust. He will come to no harm."

"At least not until R'shiel fails," Adrina pointed out.

"What do you mean?" Marla snapped.

"Damin's life is being held in trust against *something*. Doesn't that mean if she fails, or loses the bet, or mucks up whatever the seven hells she's gone and promised Death she'll do, Damin may still die?"

Marla turned to Barandaran. The Harshini healer had listened silently to their argument and offered nothing. "How does one arrange a meeting with Death?"

"By dying, your highness."

"You know what I mean."

Both the Harshini shook their heads. "What you ask is not possible."

"I agree," Adrina said, filled with an unfamiliar sense of control—despite the very real possibility her entire life was, in fact, spiraling out of control and she had no way of stopping it. "We need to focus on what is possible, not what isn't. Marla, I need you in Medalon for the treaty, although I won't be letting the children accompany you. Until we know if this assassin was acting alone, we need to keep the children where they can be protected. Master Raven, would you see if you are able get anything further out of the assassin? If you can't, then we'll execute him. I don't plan to waste the food keeping him alive. Kalan, can you find the demon child?"

"I can try . . . but . . ."

"Find her, then. And bring her here. If we can't ask Death what's going on, she's the only other possibility."

"And what will you be doing," Marla asked, "while the rest of us are running errands on your behalf, my lady regent? Choosing flower arrangements for the wedding, perhaps? Approving the menus?"

Adrina let out a very unladylike curse she'd picked up years ago on the battlefields at Treason Keep, when she was fleeing her first husband, the crown prince of Karien. "Gods! I totally forgot about Rakaia."

"I'm sure your wretched father hasn't. Or the concessions he managed to extract from my fool cousin by dangling a bit of nubile young flesh in front of him."

Ignoring the jibe—which was pointless, because Frederak had not agreed to a damned thing Damin hadn't wanted him to—Adrina turned to her newest, unexpected ally for help. "My Lord Raven, can you use your guild contacts get a message to Ky on the road? Ask him to wait with Rakaia at Warrinhaven? I'd arranged for him to stop there anyway, until I'd sent word we're ready for her to arrive. He'll need to know why his stay is being extended."

"Of course."

"That's settled, then."

"What about closing the city?" Marla asked.

"To what purpose? It will panic the population and we don't even know if this attack was a conspiracy or just the act of a lone madman with a song stuck in his head."

"I still think—"

"We'll meet tomorrow," she announced, cutting Marla off. "In the council chamber straight after breakfast. We can discuss it then. In the meantime," she added, turning to the Harshini healers, "I am going to visit my husband and sit with him for a time, while I try to figure out how I am going to tell my children that Death is holding their father's life in trust, and I can't promise they will ever see him alive again."

Without waiting for anybody to respond to that, she turned toward the bedroom door. Telenara opened it for her and she stepped through with her head held high.

It wasn't until the door closed behind her and she saw Damin, laid out on the bed, so perfect and so lifeless, that she gave in to the despair. She leaned against the door for a moment and then sank down to the floor, sobbing as if Damin were already dead, because she knew, whatever happened from this moment on, her life, and the lives of her children, would never be the same.

Chapter

⊱⊰⊹⊱⊰⊹⊱⊰⊹⊱⊰⊹⊰

23

WARRINHAVEN WAS THE home of the baron of Charelle, Cam Rahan, his wife, Lady Saneyah, and their five sons under five. Adrina's orders were to rest her sister's entourage at Warrinhaven before finishing the journey to Greenharbour. She wasn't only being considerate of her sister's welfare, Kiam knew. The High Princess wanted advance warning of Rakaia's imminent arrival. Her instructions were to send a bird when he arrived at the Warrinhaven estate, and await further instructions before undertaking the remainder of the journey to the capital.

It was a bright spring day when they arrived, the sky a cobalt canopy dotted with fluffy white clouds, offering a spectacular backdrop to Warrinhaven's emerald, white-fenced pastures. Cam Rahan was a portly, middle-aged man, but more importantly, a good friend of the Wolfblade family. Although Kiam had never met him formally before today, the baron knew the family well enough that he wasn't required to explain who or what he was.

Lady Saneyah was a different matter. An Eaglespike from Dregian Province originally, she was too polite to refuse the High Prince's stepbrother a roof over his head—her husband would never have tolerated her turning away any member of the Wolfblade family, in any case—but she made only a token gesture of civility when they arrived and then excused herself almost immediately, claiming one of the children was ill and she was required to attend him.

Rakaia didn't seem to mind their hostess's absence. In fact, she almost seemed relieved by it.

Yet another puzzling reaction from this most puzzling of princesses.

For perhaps the thousandth time since meeting her in Winternest, Kiam tried to figure out exactly what it was about Rakaia that intrigued him to the point where he found himself thinking of little else. It wasn't her guileless blue eyes, or the way they lit up on the rare occasion he'd been able to make her smile. It wasn't her lovely face, her gentle way with Broos—who'd taken to trotting beside her all day and sleeping at the entrance to her tent at night—or even the way she treated each of his men like they were her chosen companions.

Before they'd even cleared the mountains she knew all of them by name and made a point of speaking to each one of them, every single day of their journey. Kiam didn't doubt any one of these hardened warriors would have laid his life down for Rakaia after only a few days on the road in her company. And these were men handpicked for their tough and uncompromising natures. Men he'd been sure would not fall under the spell of a manipulative little witch raised in the viper's nest that was the Talabar Royal Harem.

Rakaia was either completely untouched by the taint of her upbringing, Kiam decided, or the most brilliant actress ever to draw breath.

Either way, there was something about her that got under a man's skin in a very short time and even he, it seemed, was not immune to it.

Kiam wasn't looking forward to this break at Warrinhaven. He'd made a promise to Adrina and he feared he was in danger of breaking it if he didn't put some distance between himself and the enigma that was Rakaia of Fardohnya.

"Our seneschal, Kratys, will show you to the rooms we have set aside for you, your highness," Lord Rahan told the princess, once his wife had departed. "He'll see you have everything you need."

"Thank you, my lord."

The baron looked surprised to be thanked as he waved another slave forward. "Your men will be accommodated in the stables, if that's acceptable, Master Miar. Lortan will show them where they can unsaddle, and take care of their mounts."

"I'm sure they'll appreciate the relative luxury of a straw bed after three weeks on the road." Kiam motioned to the men to follow the Warrinhaven groom. With a nod, they led their own mounts, as well as their packhorses and the mounts Kiam and Rakaia had been riding, across the checkerboard paving toward the estate's vast stables. Rahan studied Kiam's golden sorcerer-bred mare as it was led away with open admiration.

"She was a gift from the High Prince," Kiam explained, before Lord Rahan could frame the question.

"No chance, then, I suppose, that you're interesting in selling her?"

"None at all, my Lord."

Rahan smiled, as if he'd expected Kiam's answer, and then turned to

Rakaia. "I trust you will find our humble home adequate, your highness. I would have made arrangements to provide more attendants for you, but we were expecting you to have your own."

They walked together up the broad, marble steps to Cam Rahan's palatial "humble home," overlooking a vast forecourt with a large fountain in the center of the delightful checkerboard paving. The household staff—freeborn and slave alike—awaited them like a guard of honor. Warrinhaven was a small barony, but a wealthy one. The racehorses they bred here were almost as prized—and certainly more affordable than—the sorcerer-bred mounts the royal family favored.

"I'm sure everything will be perfectly adequate," the princess replied graciously, although she declined to offer any explanation about why she had dispensed with her entourage back at the border. Kiam was hoping she'd say something to Lord Rahan, because he still didn't know why she'd done that. The closest thing to a reason he'd been able to get from her was she'd been afraid they'd be homesick, but that was patently a lie. Few people cared if a slave was homesick, least of all a Fardohnyan princess.

"Do you have a problem with Broos being in the house?"

Kiam's dog—traitor that he was—trotted along beside Rakaia as if he were her dog rather than his. When Rakaia stopped, Broos stopped too, sitting patiently beside her. Without thinking, she reached down and scratched him behind the ear. The dog was big enough that the princess didn't need to bend at all to rest her hand on his head, which was perhaps why the dog had figured out this was the best place to be sitting.

"Ah . . . ," the baron said, eyeing the large dog warily. "If that's what he's used to, then of course, your dog may stay with you."

"Actually, he's Kiam's dog, not mine. He's sort of . . . adopted me."

"If it's too much trouble, he can sleep in the stable," Kiam offered.

Although he didn't sound convinced, the baron shook his head and said, "No, if her highness wishes it, he's welcome inside. I'm sure he'll be fine."

"You are a most gracious host, my lord," Rakaia said, looking at him with those big blue eyes that could melt granite when she smiled. "And we are imposing on you at a very inconvenient time. I do hope your son is not seriously ill."

"Just one of those childhood fevers youngsters are prone to, your highness. He'll be better in a few days, I imagine."

"Probably just after we leave," Kiam muttered, not really meaning for the baron to overhear. Or perhaps he did mean it. Snobbery always brought out the worst in him.

Cam Rahan obviously did hear the remark. For a moment, he couldn't meet Kiam's eye. He, at least, had the good manners to be embarrassed by his wife's transparent excuse to avoid playing hostess to a common-born assassin—even one as well connected as Kiam Miar.

"Perhaps you would care to join me for some refreshments, once you're settled in?" Rahan said. "I have another houseguest from Greenharbour at the moment. Lord Erlon."

The name meant nothing to Kiam. "I'm not acquainted with Lord Erlon."

"Then we shall have to change that," the baron offered. "Lord Erlon is thinking of buying some racehorses. Perhaps you will join us this afternoon, inspecting the sale yards."

"I'd be honored," he lied, unable to think of a single thing more boring than two old rich men haggling about horseflesh neither of them was competent to control.

"Actually, you promised you would attend me this afternoon, Master Miar," Rakaia said. "To continue my lessons in Hythrun . . . court etiquette." They had no such arrangement. There were no lessons to continue. But she was staring straight at him, almost as if she were willing him not to object or reveal her lie.

"So I did, your highness," he agreed after a moment, trying to figure out what her game was. He turned to the baron. "Another time, perhaps, my lord."

"Of course. Kratys, show our guests to their rooms."

"Your highness, Master Miar," the seneschal said with a bow. "If you would follow me, please."

Kiam fell in beside Rakaia, with Broos trotting along contentedly between them. Rakaia waited until they were out of earshot of Lord Rahan before saying in a low voice—in Fardohnyan so the seneschal, even if he heard her, would not understand what she was saying, "Sorry about that, but you looked like you needed rescuing."

"Thank you," he replied in Fardohnyan in the same low, conspiratorial tone, marveling at the fact she had realized it. Either he'd been openly rude to Lord Rahan by revealing his true feelings, or this perplexing young woman could see right through him. "And you're right. I think I would rather have spent the afternoon sticking hot needles in my eyeballs. Damin loves his racehorses, but they bore me witless."

"Well, you're free to spend the afternoon with hot needles," she said with a suddenly coy smile as they entered the cool darkness of the passage leading to the west wing, where the guest suites were apparently located. "You don't really have to entertain me. I just said that to get you out of it."

It took his eyes a moment to adjust to the dimness, so he couldn't tell by looking at her if she was genuine or simply toying with him, like a cat tormenting a particularly juicy mouse.

"I'll offend our host if I do anything else," he told her, knowing even as he uttered the words that he was lying again. Rahan wouldn't care, and had probably only offered to have him accompany him and Lord Erlon as they haggled about horses out of politeness. "I'm afraid you're stuck with me for the afternoon, your highness—proof positive that no good deed goes unpunished."

"I don't think of it as a punishment," she said as they almost collided with Kratys, so wrapped up were they in their whispered conversation.

"This is your room, your highness," Kratys said with a disapproving look at the two of them. Kiam wondered what he must be thinking, as they'd followed him, heads close together, whispering in a foreign tongue. "I will have one of the women draw you a bath so you may freshen up before dinner. Master Miar, your room is this way, at the far end of the hall."

Rakaia turned her irresistible charms on the seneschal, and smiled at him. "Thank you, Kratys," she said in her faultless Hythrun. "You are too kind."

The old man seemed a little taken aback. "There is no need to thank me, your highness. It is my job to see my lord's guests are taken care of."

"Your status as a slave shouldn't deny you common courtesy," she told him. "I am grateful for your assistance, Kratys, and I don't mind thanking you for it."

The seneschal studied Rakaia for a moment, as if gauging her sincerity, and then he bowed. "Ask for anything you need, your highness, and I shall make it happen."

"Thank you, Kratys. Could we start with some water and something to eat for Broos?" She turned to Kiam and held out her hand. "Shall we meet in an hour, Master Miar? For my etiquette lesson?"

He took her hand and kissed her palm, holding on to it a fraction longer than was polite. The calluses were almost gone, her skin smooth, her hands more like those of a princess now than a serving wench's, as they had been the first time he kissed her hand. Then he let her go and bowed just as deeply as the now-thoroughly ensorcelled seneschal. "Your wish is my command, your highness."

For some inexplicable reason, his comment made her blush, and then she was gone, closing the bedroom door behind her, leaving Kiam with Lord Rahan's seneschal and some very confused feelings about Her Serene Highness, Rakaia of Fardohnya.

As he fell in behind Kratys, he glanced over his shoulder to ensure Broos was still with him, but the hall was empty. The traitor had followed Rakaia into her room.

Kiam shook his head in resignation. Even his dog, apparently, had fallen under her spell.

24

"HE KEEPS LOOKING at you."

"Who?

"The minstrel. He can't take his eyes off you." Rakaia chuckled softly, thinking how surreal it was to be sitting in this smoky tavern, joking around with the demon child. "I think he's in love."

The tavern was located across the street from the Testra inn where the demon child had brought Rakaia after rescuing her from the Widow-maker Pass. How she'd managed to land a dragon in the center of the town and get her unconscious passenger upstairs remained a mystery. R'shiel was not offering any explanation. Although she eschewed her title of the demon child, she didn't seem to mind the inevitable air of mystery that went with it. Outside it was pouring rain as a thunderstorm broke over the city. The tavern was warm, though, and filled with happy, mildly intoxicated patrons.

"I think *you've* had too much wine, my girl, and you're imagining things," R'shiel remarked as she tucked into the roast shank of lamb she'd ordered for both of them for dinner. The meal looked heavy and unappetizing to Rakaia, used to food prepared in a palace—food that had vegetables other than potatoes in it, and spices other than salt. Nothing so unrefined, overcooked, or so drowned in lumpy gravy was ever served in the Talabar Palace.

They'd come here for dinner on the recommendation of the inn-keeper. There was a traveling troupe of performers playing, and by all accounts they were quite entertaining.

They'd want to be, Rakaia decided, *to make up for the food.*

The juggler had been adequate—in that he didn't drop anything—and the dancing girls were really just thinly disguised whores working the crowd to find clients for after the show, but the young Karien minstrel had a voice as sweet as warm honey and he seemed to be singing directly to R'shiel.

"Anyway, even if I were in the mood for some horizontal

entertainment—which I'm not—he's far too young for me," the demon child said. "He's barely twenty, by the look of him."

Rakaia smiled. "So you *have* been looking at him." It surprised her how easy the demon child was to get along with. She was quite unpretentious, really, once you got past the fact there was no more powerful sorcerer alive. The demon child was—so the rumor had it—even more powerful than the Halfbreed. She'd killed a god.

And the Halfbreed, too, if the other rumors were true.

"He's rather hard to miss. And he can sing. I'll grant the lad that."

"You're not that much older than him, though."

"I'm older than I look."

"You look younger than me."

"How old are you, anyway?"

"Nearly twenty-two."

The demon child laughed. "You see, that's how I *know* I'm older than you. You're *nearly* twenty-two. You can't wait to be a year older. I, on the other hand, have already turned thirty. Notice how I'm not saying *nearly* thirty-two?"

Rakaia glanced around the crowded tavern to see if anyone was listening in before asking, "Will you always be so . . . young?"

"I get older every day, Rakaia. Just like you do."

"But you're . . . immortal, aren't you?"

That seemed to amuse her. "Sure . . . right up until somebody looking to make a name for himself succeeds in killing me."

"But I thought all the Harshini were immortal. They can heal themselves, can't they, so no wound is ever fatal?"

"They're long lived, Rakaia. Very, *very* longed lived. But they still die from fatal wounds like anybody else. And sometimes they just give up. A long life can be a curse as much as a blessing."

"But you're only just past thirty."

"I have it on good authority. Are you going to eat that?"

She looked down at the lamb shanks and frowned. She was hungry, but . . . Rakaia picked up her spoon and braced herself. Her days of fine food in the palace were behind her. She'd better get used to eating what the common folk ate or resign herself to starving to death.

R'shiel watched her eat with a curious expression. "You're not used to slumming it with the peasants, are you?"

"What do you mean?"

"I mean you claim you're a servant but you speak like you've been educated, you have the table manners of a noblewoman, and I'm going to take a punt here and suggest this is your first time in a tavern. Besides, you're grimacing like you've been served something from the sewers at a meal most commoners would consider a feast."

When Rakaia couldn't think up an excuse quickly enough, R'shiel unknowingly provided it for her. "So how did a nobleman's daughter wind up a slave in the Widowmaker Pass? What was it? Sold to cover your father's debts?"

Rakaia shrugged. That wasn't even far from the truth. "It would be fair to say it was my father's business dealings that caused my . . . change in circumstances."

"So now what?"

"Excuse me?"

"What are you going to do now? You're no longer a slave, Rakaia. I've freed you from that, so you've no need to return to Fardohnya. What will you do?"

Rakaia really hadn't thought about it yet. "I . . . I have no idea."

Her mother's plan had been for her to take refuge with her uncle in Lanipoor, but she was half a continent away from there now, thanks to the demon child. She had no money and no skills to earn a living to make the money required to buy passage back to Fardohnya. In fact, Rakaia had no skills other than those required to be a good nobleman's wife. She spoke several languages, played a lyre passably well, and had been *court'esa* trained to please her husband in bed, but that was a harsh way to make a living in the outside world, she thought, glancing at the two dancing girls working their way around the room.

"Well, you'd better think of something soon. The room at the inn is paid up until the end of the week, but after that, you're on your own, I'm afraid."

"Are you leaving?"

"As I said earlier, Testra happened to be in the general direction I was heading."

"When are you leaving?"

"Tonight."

"Where are you going?"

"That's really none of your business."

"I'm sorry," she said. "I know . . . it's just . . ."

"You're afraid?"

Rakaia nodded. "How did you know?"

The demon child smiled. "Because I've been where you are, Rakaia. It's scary. But also fun, if you decide to look upon it as an adventure rather than the end of the world. I mean . . . you're young, you're pretty, and you're not lying raped and murdered on the side of the road in the Widow-maker Pass. All these are things you should be celebrating."

"I have no money, no job, no family . . ."

"And now you're wallowing in self-pity." The demon child finished her meal and tossed a few coins on the table to pay for their meal. She rose to her feet as the tavern keep approached with two cups on a tray.

"A gift from Mica," he said, placing the tray on the table.

"Who?" R'shiel asked.

"The minstrel," the tavern keeper said. "He seems to think you ladies are the most beautiful creatures he's ever laid eyes on." He repeated the compliment with the disinterest of a man who had heard it all, many times before.

Rakaia glanced over to the corner of the room where Mica was perched on a high stool, singing a haunting ballad about a woman pining for her lost love. He was watching them intently as he sang—or rather he was watching R'shiel.

Does he know who she is?

"Then he's not been out much lately." R'shiel either didn't notice the young man's intense scrutiny, or she didn't care. "I have to go, but I'm sure my friend could do with a couple of stiff drinks."

Or maybe she did notice. Maybe that was the reason she was leaving Testra tonight, despite seeming to have no fixed timetable up until they'd stepped into this tavern for dinner earlier this evening.

R'shiel reached into her pocket and then tossed a small coin purse on the table. "I'll not need any coin where I'm going," she said. "That's all I can help you with, I'm afraid. It should see you through the next few days, until you figure out what you want to do."

"Thank you," Rakaia said, more grateful than she could find the words to express. "You've done more for me than anybody ever has in my life. And I don't even know you."

"Nobody ever really knows anybody, Rakaia. Trust me on that."

"Will I ever see you again?"

The demon child shrugged. "Who knows? It's a strange world we live in. Take care. And good luck."

With that, the demon child turned, headed for the door, and pulled up the hood of her cape before stepping out into the rain. Rakaia glanced at the minstrel, whose eyes never left the demon child for a moment.

Mica must have realized she was watching him. As soon as the door closed on R'shiel he turned his attention back to his audience and changed his song to a bright ditty about a farmer trying to count his chickens who kept escaping out of a hole in the wall of the chicken house and coming around to be counted for a second, third, and fourth time.

Rakaia smiled at the song as the rest of the patrons joined in, enjoying this brief moment of calm in the storm that was now her life. A clap of thunder broke over the town, reminding her that soon she would have to walk out of here, back to the inn where she had a warm bed and a roof over her head for only a few more days. She needed to figure out how she was going to survive, given her entire life now comprised the clothes on her back and the small coin purse the demon child had just left with her.

The jewels Rakaia had so carefully squirreled away to fund her trip through Fardohnya were tucked under the seat of the wagon she'd been traveling in, back in the Widowmaker Pass. The thieves who'd robbed the caravan had them by now.

She wondered what Charisee was doing at this moment.

Is she happy? Is she having fun being a princess?

Has Hablet discovered the truth by now about her paternity and ordered her killed?

A wave of guilt washed over Rakaia. However unknown or unknowable, she was alive and had a future. Charisee, on the other hand, would pay the price of Sophany's deceit in her half-sister's place, and never know the reason why.

She had no right to be wallowing in self-pity.

Rakaia picked up her spoon again, determined to finish her lamb shanks with their overcooked potatoes and lumpy, congealing gravy. Who knew how long it would be before she could afford a meal like this again?

She was a pauper now, but she was alive and that meant she could do something about it. She owed it to Charisee—and the demon child—to make the best of things.

"If you close your eyes and can't see the lumps, it tastes much better."

Rakaia started a little and looked up to find the minstrel, Mica, had finished his set and was standing beside her table. On closer inspection, he was a quite handsome young man with light brown hair and fair skin that looked as if he'd not spent a lot of time in the sun.

"Ah . . . yes . . . that's good advice."

Without asking, Mica sat down in the seat opposite, so recently vacated by the demon child. "What happened to your friend?"

"She had to leave."

"Will she be back?"

Rakaia shook her head. "I don't think so."

"My name is Mica," he said, studying her intently. "You're very pretty. Are you Fardohnyan?"

She nodded, a little bemused by his blunt manner. "Thank you . . . and yes."

"I knew another Fardohnyan lady once. She was very pretty, too." Mica smiled. "Had the treasonous black heart of a soul-eating viper, but she *was* pretty."

Rakaia had no idea how she was meant to respond to that. But apparently she wasn't required to. "Do you live here in Testra?" he asked, almost without taking a breath. "Or are you just passing through?"

"Just passing through."

"Where are you headed?"

"I . . . I don't know."

Mica's face lit up. "Excellent! You can come with us! We are heading to Bordertown next and then Krakandar. Have you been to Krakandar?"

"What?"

"Do you play an instrument? Sing? Dance?"

"I play the lyre," she told him, feeling more than a little overwhelmed. "But not that well."

"I can take care of that," he laughed, as if it was the best stroke of luck she had agreed to join them, even though she hadn't. He reached across the table, offering her his hand. "Welcome to Mica's Marvelous Minstrels!"

"Why?"

"Why not?"

"I mean . . . you don't know me . . ."

Still holding her by the hand, he leaned closer, until their heads were almost touching, and whispered, "Any friend of the demon child's is a friend of mine."

She pulled back in surprise. "You *know* R'shiel?"

He glanced around to ensure they weren't overheard, before adding in a low voice, "We're old friends."

"Why didn't you say something when she was here?"

"I doubt she'd remember me," he said with a shrug. "I was just a child the last time we met. I really didn't want to bother her. But truly, if the demon child found you worthy, then I do, too. Say you'll join us. We'll have so much fun on the road together."

Somewhat bemused—which seemed to be her normal state these past few days—Rakaia nodded. After all, what else did she have?

"I . . . I don't want to be a dancing girl," she said, noticing one of them leading a man by the hand toward the back alley out of the corner of her eye.

He smiled. "Nobody in Mica's Marvelous Minstrels does anything they don't want to do. I promise. What's your name?"

"Aja," she said on impulse. Rakaia was dead—a princess left behind at Winternest. She was Aja now. This was her new life. It deserved a new name.

And in truth, the real Aja had saved her life. She deserved to be honored.

"Welcome, Aja," Mica said. "I see great things ahead for us. Great things."

Before she could comment on that, or even object, Mica ordered another round of drinks and called the juggler and the other dancing girl over to join them, introducing her as Aja the Amazing, his new accompanist.

Nobody questioned her sudden inclusion in their troupe of players, or seemed anything other than welcoming. As the rain pelted down outside, they drank and sang and chatted long into the night, Rakaia's fears overwhelmed by their camaraderie. And she never thought to question that, either.

25

Charisee was required to attend dinner and couldn't think up a quick enough excuse to get out of it. She still hadn't mastered the I'm-a-princess-so-I-don't-need-a-reason attitude her sister was so easy with. Charisee was raised a servant, and one of the hardest adjustments to her new life was the expectation that others were meant to please her and not the other way around.

As it was a warm day followed by an equally pleasant evening, dinner was to be served outside on the paved checkerboard terrace overlooking the vast gardens at the back of the house. Charisee—used to the enclosed and manicured gardens of the harem, where even the bridle paths were always in sight of a wall—was quite overawed by their splendor. The gardens here—a riot of barely contained spring color—seemed to go on forever.

Lady Saneyah did not join them for dinner, and when Charisee arrived on the terrace, a step behind the silent slave sent by the seneschal to show her the way, the only guest in attendance was Lord Erlon. He proved to be much younger than Charisee was expecting—a smooth, well-dressed charmer with the jaded air of the excessively rich.

He introduced himself with a gallant bow, kissed her palm in the traditional Fardohnyan manner, and then offered to show her around the gardens while they waited for Lord Rahan and Kiam. Charisee wished now that Kiam really *had* been giving her etiquette lessons this afternoon, rather than just chatting to her like an old friend while they played with Broos. She was unsure if walking the vast Warrinhaven gardens with a single male to whom she was not related, unaccompanied by a chaperone, was something nobody in Hythrun society cared about or something that might ruin her forever.

Lord Erlon seemed to appreciate her dilemma. He smiled and beckoned the young woman who had escorted Charisee to dinner forward. "Wait here. The princess and I are going to take a turn around the gardens. If I try to ravage her serene highness, and you hear her screaming, you must immediately raise the alarm." He turned to Charisee. "Does that ease your mind?"

She nodded, feeling very foolish and provincial. He offered her his arm. Charisee slipped her arm into his and they headed off down the path. For no accountable reason, she felt safer, at that moment, than at any other time since she'd decided to pretend she was Rakaia.

"So, what do you think of Hythria thus far, your highness?"

"It's very beautiful."

"I meant the people, not the scenery."

"So far, they've been universally welcoming and kind."

Erlon laughed. "Never fear. That will change once you get to Greenharbour. Are you looking forward to your upcoming nuptials?"

"Of course."

"Liar."

Charisee snatched her arm from Lord Erlon's and turned to stare at him in shock. "*Excuse* me?"

"I said you're a liar." He said it without rancor. He almost seemed amused by the notion.

"I am not!"

He smiled even wider. "You delight me, Charisee, you really do."

"How can you say tha—*What* did you call me?"

"Charisee."

"I am Rakaia."

"No. You're Rakaia's base-born half-sister, Charisee," Lord Erlon replied with complete confidence. "And, ironically as it turns out, the true princess. Rakaia doesn't have a drop of Hablet in her. Much more captain of the guard than king of the realm is our dear, sweet Rakaia. Are you all right, my dear? You look quite pale."

Charisee feared she was about to throw up. Three glorious weeks her deception had lasted before her lies unraveled. How had Lord Erlon known? Was he one of the trade delegation to Fardohnya last year? Had he met Rakaia back in Talabar before they left?

"Here," he said, leading her to a small hedged alcove with a stone bench in the center of it, putting them out of view of the house. "Why don't you sit down before you fall down?"

"I . . . I . . . I'm Rakaia," she insisted. There was only one way out of this, she figured, and that was to brazen it out. Even if Lord Erlon knew the truth, how could he prove it?

"You are a delight, that's what you are," he said, smiling at her indulgently.

"My lord," she began, "I don't know what you think you—"

"Call me Jak," he cut in.

"What?"

"Call me Jak. That's my name, and as we are going to be such firm friends, and I know *your* real name, it's only fair you know mine, don't you think?"

Charisee couldn't keep up. He knew the truth. He must be planning to do something with it. But his manner was neither threatening nor sinister, despite what he had just revealed he knew about her.

"Jak," she repeated warily, with no choice but to play along until she figured out his game. Then she put the names together in her head and jumped to her feet. "Jak? Jak *Erlon?*" she gasped, with the sudden realization that she was either in the presence of a god or a madman. "*That's* your real name? *Jakerlon?* As in Jakerlon, the God of Liars?"

Still sitting on the stone bench, he bowed to her. "At your service, your highness."

"I don't believe you!"

"*Jakerlon,* you begged—with the most charming humility, I have to say," he said. "*Hear me, please. If I take on my sister's identity, I will be honoring the God of Liars for the rest of my life. Please watch over me, Jakerlon, God of Liars. Please keep me safe and I will not let you down.* I was moved. Truly moved by your sincerity. And the epic scope of your lie, I have to say. It's not every day I get one this good."

Even if this man was no god and had figured out the truth about her by ordinary means, there was no way he could know of her prayer to the God of Liars unless he was . . .

Stunned, she dropped to one knee and lowered her head. "Divine One."

"Come now," he said, urging her to rise. "We're friends. There is no need to stand on ceremony. Or kneel on it, either. Let's sit and talk a while."

Charisee had no choice but to comply. It wasn't as if she could outrun a god. She sat beside him, perched on the edge of the hard stone bench, bathed in a chill sweat born of fear and awe.

"So, let us talk about you being a princess."

"I . . . I didn't mean to . . ."

"Of course you did," he said, amused by her denials. "You chose this life, Charisee, and you are living a lie to maintain it. You will go through life deceiving kings and princes. I can't think of the last time anybody honored me so comprehensively."

"What do you want of me?"

"What do you think? I want you to keep honoring me," he said. "Not since Sophany of Lanipoor handed over a newborn babe to Hablet of Fardohnya and told him how much the babe looked like his beloved dead sister—whom he'd killed, incidentally—has anybody honored me with such a delicious swindle."

Charisee didn't know what to say. She was still trying to process the notion that she was sitting here talking to a god.

"Ah!" he said with a smile. "You didn't know that, did you?"

"Princess Sophany?"

"Mother," Jakerlon corrected. "You must always refer to Sophany as *mother*, not as Princess Sophany."

"I don't understand."

"If people hear you referring to her as—"

"No, I meant the baby. What baby?"

"Well, Rakaia, of course." He seemed a little confused by her puzzled expression and then he sighed as he realized she had no idea what he was talking about. "Fine. Let me explain. Rakaia is not Hablet's daughter. Never has been. Sophany had a fling with the captain of the guard and passed the resulting child off as a princess, a deceit that would never have been discovered, except by chance. I intend to speak to Jondalup about that, by the way, because I don't believe for a moment that it *was* chance . . ."

"You think the God of Chance had a hand in this?"

"I just said that, didn't I? Do try to keep up, sweetness. Anyway . . . where were we? Ah . . . Sophany. When she realized her lie was about to be exposed, she did what all my best disciples do—she lied some more. She lied to Naveen Raveve and offered him a safe haven should your father die an untimely death. She lied to you, telling you Rakaia was going to Hythria to marry this Branador character. And then she arranged for the best lie of all—which was to have you take over Rakaia's identity, enabling her daughter to escape unharmed. Hablet's not going to be happy when he finds out."

"But Rakaia didn't escape unharmed. She's dead."

"She's not dead," Jakerlon laughed. "The demon child arrived on the back of a dragon and heroically saved her in the nick of time." He leaned forward and patted her hand. "Don't worry about Rakaia. It's you who are honoring me, Charisee. It's you that I care about."

Charisee was quite numb. "Rakaia is . . . alive?"

He nodded, oblivious to the impact of his news. "I believe she's alive and well and having a high old time, gallivanting around central Medalon with a carnival troupe or something. To be honest, I don't really keep up with Rakaia these days. She *was* the lie, rather than the liar. Disappointingly, she was honoring Gimlorie last time I looked."

"What if she comes back?"

"She won't. Rakaia knows Hablet will have her killed as soon as he realizes he's been duped."

He said it so casually, for a moment Charisee didn't appreciate what he was telling her. "But . . . but doesn't that mean if I continue to pretend I'm Rakaia, he'll have *me* killed, as soon as he realizes he's been duped?"

Jakerlon smiled at her, like an immensely proud parent. "Don't you see how special that makes you? This lie you're living may cost you your very life. You are putting your life on the line for me. There can be no greater honoring of your god than something so dangerous."

"Is that what you want? For me to die honoring you?"

"Of course not! I don't want you harmed, Charisee. I'm here to help."

"Help how?"

"By making you see the truth."

"I thought you were the God of Liars?"

"All lies are just truths served more palatably."

"*What?*"

"Think about it. The lie you are living is that you are Rakaia, daughter of the king of Fardohnya. But the larger lie here is that Rakaia was ever any such thing. You, on the other hand, *are* a daughter of the king of Fardohnya, and yet to take your rightful place as a princess, you have to live a lie."

Charisee shook her head. "I'm confused."

"Do not despair, little one. I will be watching over you from now on. I just want you to do one thing for me."

Charisee nodded. How did one refuse a god? "What must I do, Divine One?"

"Enjoy yourself."

"Pardon?"

"Enjoy yourself, Charisee," the God of Liars ordered. "Shed this thorny cloak of guilt you're wearing with such noble self-sacrifice. It's suffocating me. You were placed in this lie because of Sophany's infidelity and the willingness of a sister you loved to selfishly put you in harm's way to save her own life. Embrace it. Make the most of it. Honor me every day by being glad you're living this lie."

"I'm not a liar."

"My sweet, you are the most wonderful type of liar there is, because the person you lie to most often is yourself."

"I don't—"

"Don't you?" he chuckled. "You lie to yourself about hating what you're doing, yet at every turn you've chosen the lie, in preference to confessing the truth in order to put an end to your supposed suffering. You could have said something at Winternest, but you wanted to have just one night with everything Rakaia had, didn't you? You tell yourself you're shattered Rakaia is dead, when in truth, just for a tiny, teeny moment, when you first heard the news about everyone in that caravan being killed, you felt a shiver of relief knowing she could never come back to expose you."

Her eyes misting with guilty tears, Charisee shook her head in denial, but they both knew that was a lie, too.

"Even now," Jakerlon continued relentlessly, "you're telling yourself you're doing the noble thing by pretending to be Rakaia."

"I'm not . . ."

"Of course you are! You're on your way to her wedding. You are going to allow yourself to be carried off by some lecherous old fool for the sake of a trade route negotiated to further enrich an obscenely wealthy king who would kill you in a heartbeat if he knew who you really were. And you're lying to yourself about the assassin, too, although that's more Kalianah's province than mine."

"The assass—*Kiam*? What do you mean?"

"Please, Charisee, I am the one creature in all of creation you can be honest with. You know exactly what I mean." He leaned back against the hedge, folding his arms above his head, looking very smug. "I have to say, trying to make his dog love you so he has to keep coming back to you to retrieve him is a fairly pathetic way of showing your interest in a man."

Charisee wiped her tears away with the heels of her hands, smiling faintly at the absurdity of it. There was no point, she'd begun to realize, in denying anything around the God of Liars. "Can everyone see through me like I'm made of glass, or just you?"

"Just me. And maybe the assassin. You should make the most of him, you know, while you have the chance. That would be the 'embracing it' philosophy I spoke of. If you're going to see this through, my pet, you'll want a pleasant picture in your mind to concentrate on when the lecher is having his way with you."

"He's the High Prince's stepbrother."

"I'm pretty sure that doesn't involve the removal of his manhood."

"But . . ."

"But *what*? You want him. He wants you—and he's lying to himself by pretending he's not tempted to break his promise to the High Princess. Neither of you can admit it openly, apparently, because gods forbid you were prepared to be honest about your feelings for each other. So . . . do what your heart is wishing for and then lie about it afterward. You'll be honoring both me and the Goddess of Love, if you do. How can that be considered wrong?"

She shook her head, not sure if she was denying his logic or his suggestion. "You twist everything around."

"It is the nature of truth and lies, my precious. And the best lies of all are the stone-cold truth."

Before she could respond to that, the slave who'd escorted her to dinner appeared from behind the hedge and curtseyed deeply. "Lord Rahan sent me to tell you that dinner is being served, your highness."

"Excellent," the God of Liars said. "I'm famished. And you heard nothing, just now, did you?"

"Not a word, my lord." The slave bowed and headed back toward the terrace.

"Did you do something to that girl?" she asked as Jakerlon rose to his feet and offered Charisee his hand.

"I just made sure she'll not report anything she may have overheard," the god assured her as she let him help her up.

Beyond trying to comprehend everything she'd learned in the last few minutes, Charisee wiped away the last of her tears, and then studied Jakerlon curiously for a moment. "You're a god. Do you even need to eat?"

"Not really."

"You said you were famished."

He laughed and slipped his arm through hers. "I think the thing I love about you most, Charisee, is that even now, knowing what you do about who and what I am, you're still surprised when you discover I'm lying."

Chapter

26

"I'VE BEEN THINKING, Naveen," the king of Fardohnya announced as he turned to wave at the loyal subjects lining the wharf in the rain to see him off.

"Perhaps if you were to lie down for a time, your highness," Naveen suggested, "the urge might pass?"

Hablet smiled at waved at the crowd. "Very droll."

"I aim to entertain, your highness."

He couldn't see Hablet's face any longer, but the king hadn't ordered him thrown overboard, so he'd probably gotten away with his quip this time. Coming up the slippery gangplank were Princess Sophany, stepping carefully to keep her balance, and Crown Prince Alaric, who was trying to make it bounce. The former looked worried—and not just because Alaric was trying to toss her off the gangplank. The latter was simply excited at the prospect of a sea voyage—however brief and close to shore— before they turned east and sailed up the mighty Glass River to the Citadel.

"I think it's time to start taking care of my legacy, Naveen."

Naveen leaned a little closer to the king. It was hard to hear over the noise of the sailors preparing to cast off and the cheering crowd on the dock—rented and paid for by the king, although he wasn't aware of the fact. "Sire?"

"This business with Sophany made me realize I need to start tying up loose threads."

Naveen had seen his predecessor, Lecter Turon, "tie up loose threads" for his king in the past. It usually involved someone dying. "Which particular *threads* did you want tied up, sire?"

"All of them."

"Excuse me?" He took a step closer, certain he'd misheard the king. "Did you say *all* of them?"

"Alaric! Come here, my boy!" Hablet called as his son stepped onto the deck. "Come wave to the people! The people like it when you wave to them."

"But it's raining."

"Then they'll think you even more wonderful for stopping to wave."

Pulling a face, the crown prince stepped up to the railing but was too short to see over it. Naveen motioned to a nearby sailor to quickly bring a box for the young prince to stand on, before he could throw a tantrum about it. At eleven, the lad was not particularly tall, but the gods had blessed him with a sweet face and large brown eyes framed with thick long lashes. He was almost too pretty to be a boy. Perhaps that was one of the drawbacks of the gods intervening in the creation of any human. Alaric was a gift from the gods; the direct result of a request from the demon child to the Goddess of Fertility to grant the king a son in return for his aid in expelling the Karien horde from the Citadel.

"Are they cheering for me, Papa?" Given the prince's generally cheerful demeanor, Naveen thought it safe to assume that Alaric had no inkling yet of his father's plans to leave him with the Defenders in Medalon.

"Of course they are, son," the king assured him. "One day you'll be their king."

"Why aren't there more of them?"

Perhaps the demon child could have been a little more specific when she made her request of Jelanna to grant Hablet a son, Naveen mused. *Listed a few desirable personality traits along with those pretty eyes.*

"We'd never have been able to get to the ship," Hablet told him, "if the crowd was any bigger."

Naveen could see by his frown that now Alaric had put the idea in his head, Hablet was wondering the same thing. Curse the child. Naveen could have hired more cheering peasants, but there was really only so much of the royal purse one could spend on stroking the ego of a king.

Hablet left the prince at the railing waving to the insufficient crowd and stepped back to speak to Naveen. "I'd like you to take care of these *loose threads* while I'm in Medalon."

"Sire, you need to be more specific."

Naveen could feel Princess Sophany's eyes boring into him from behind. She had been Hablet's constant companion since he'd revealed the truth about her daughter to the king, something that unsettled her immensely. Hablet had given her no reason for his sudden preference for her company, but she knew something was amiss. Every day she waited for the hammer to fall, and every day it didn't worried her more. Hablet was enjoying the game. He was playing with her, and the more tense and unsettled she became because of his apparently loving attention, the more Hablet thrived on it.

She'll be thanking me, he thought, *when she realizes what fate is in store for the rest of the harem.*

"There's no need to be excessive," Hablet said, lowering his voice so only Naveen could hear his instructions. "I just think we need to start . . . culling the herd."

"Did you have a particular preference for which of the . . . cows . . . you wish to cut from the herd?"

Hablet thought for a moment and then nodded. "The grandmothers."

"Sire?"

"Any of them whose daughters have been married off and given birth to sons. They'll be the ones with dynastic delusions."

Around them the sailors were preparing to cast off, Alaric was waving to the crowd, Sophany was staring at them suspiciously, while the numerous other slaves and courtiers accompanying the king to Medalon for the treaty negotiations hurried about their duties, tripping over each other in the confines of the deck. Naveen stood in the middle of the chaos, the soft rain running down his hair to pool uncomfortably under his collar, while his king instructed him to start the systematic extermination of his entire family.

The order didn't surprise Naveen—after all, Hablet had done the same to his father's harem when he took the throne—just the timing of it. He'd always assumed Hablet would be content to let Alaric do his own dirty work when he became king.

"Are you feeling unwell, sire?"

"No. Why?"

"No reason. Did you want the . . . heifers taken care of too?"

Hablet paused for a moment. Even he, apparently, wasn't able to order the murder of his own children without it giving him pause.

He did not pause for long, however. Hablet nodded. "It's time we started reducing the numbers. I'll let you decide which order. I love them all equally, you know. Not sure I could choose, to be honest."

Naveen let that comment slide, quite sure the irony was lost on Hablet completely. He bowed to his king, anxious to be gone from the ship so it could set sail and he could get out of this wretched rain. He was paying that crowd by the hour, too, and the longer he tarried, the more they were costing.

"It shall be done, sire."

He turned to leave. He had one foot on the gangplank when Hablet called to him, "Don't waste money on the funerals."

"I wouldn't dream of it, your highness." He bowed once more and then made his way down the slippery plank to the dock, grateful to be left in Talabar and not accompanying the king.

He turned and watched as the gangplank was drawn up into the ship and the captain began shouting the order to get the ship under way. He would not breathe easy until they were through the heads, Naveen knew, and not in any danger of returning for some time.

No matter how awful his orders, arranging the mass murder of Hablet's harem would be far less stressful than spending weeks in the confines of a ship with Alaric, he guessed.

Or being anywhere in the vicinity of the young prince's rage when he learned what his father had in store for him.

IN A PERFECT world, Adrina would have told nobody that her husband lay in a coma from which even the gods could not wake him.

This was far from a perfect world, however, so of course the news flew around the city at the speed only rumor can travel. Before long, Adrina was confronted with every opportunist and troublemaker in Greenharbour looking to take advantage of the situation. Added to the complication of Marla preparing to leave for the Citadel and the treaty negotiations, reports of Caden Fletcher meeting with the High Arrion of the Sorcerers' Collective far more than one would expect of a man who purported not to believe in magic, was the vocal disappointment of her children when they learned she had changed her mind about letting them accompany their grandmother to Medalon.

She was overwhelmed, and quietly terrified, a feeling not in any way helped by the fact that Marla had summoned her for a meeting before she left the city tomorrow. With a heavy feeling of impending doom, Adrina took a deep breath and accepted the hand of the guard to help her as she alighted from her carriage.

Marla's relatively modest, walled house was a few streets from the palace, staffed by loyal slaves who had been with her for years. The guards on the main door wore the livery of Krakandar, rather than Greenharbour Raiders, and in all the time Adrina had been married to Damin, Marla had never before invited her here. She usually stalked the halls of the palace, doing most of her interfering there.

To be invited to Marla's home was a rare honor indeed—if it was an honor. Adrina was not entirely convinced Marla hadn't lured her here to have her killed so there would be no danger of her evil Fardohnyan daughter-in-law being left in charge of her beloved Hythria while she was gone. It wasn't as if she couldn't arrange such an event without even raising a sweat. Marla had been married to the man who was once Raven of the Assassins' Guild, after all.

And with Damin in no position to stop her . . .

Adrina shook her head to rid herself of such a ridiculous train of thought. She knew she was being silly, and before she could give in to her paranoia, she stepped up to the front door and stopped before the two guards, who stood to attention as she approached.

"I am here to see Princess Marla."

The guard on the left bowed and opened the door for her. "She is expecting you, your highness."

"Wait here," Adrina told her own guards. She hated not being able to move about without an escort, but she wasn't going to tempt fate. Damin's attack had come out of the blue. There would not be another if Adrina had any say in the matter. She'd already had Kalan arrange for Harshini from the Sorcerers' Collective to scan and shield the minds of all the palace guard. There were no men in her service now, she was confident, with odd songs stuck in their heads.

Marla's ancient housekeeper, Cadella, led Adrina through the hall and a small but tastefully decorated reception room, out into a small walled garden where Marla was waiting, making the most of the slight breeze coming off the harbor. It was a hot and humid evening—there were really no other kind here in Greenharbour—and the princess had lived here long enough to know when to avail herself of what little relief was on offer.

As soon as she saw Adrina, the dowager princess turned to breathe in the aroma of a large flowering hibiscus, saying, "You should not have come."

Gods, nothing I will ever do will please this unforgiving old cow.

"You summoned me, your highness," Adrina pointed out in a voice as unemotional as she could manage. This time tomorrow, Marla would be well on her way to Medalon, she reminded herself. Adrina could maintain her poise for a few more hours.

"And you are the High Princess of Hythria, Adrina. You should have demanded I come to you."

"And if I had?"

Marla turned to look at Adrina with a thin smile. "I would not have come. But I would have respected the effort."

"What have I ever done to make you distrust me so, Marla?"

The princess returned to studying the hibiscus. "You'd like a list?"

"Gods, you *have* a list?"

Marla continued to study the plant, but she spoke as if she'd rehearsed this speech for decades. "Your father spent a good portion of Damin's early life trying to have him killed, Adrina. You were raised at the knee of a man who murdered his own family when he took the throne, and is undoubtedly encouraging your brother to do the same when his time comes. You betrayed your first husband, cheerfully committing adultery—with my son, I grant you—and but for the intervention of the demon child would have brought the entire continent to war."

"My marriage to Damin stopped a war, and that marriage was also at the behest of the demon child. My father was ready to invade Hythria when we married. And he would have done, until I married Damin and he was forced to withdraw. You know that."

Marla nodded. "I do. And, when I'm feeling generous, I'll even concede the wisdom of it. But that's not why I don't trust you, Adrina."

"Then why, for pity's sake?"

"Because Damin listens to you."

Adrina opened her mouth to respond, but couldn't think of anything intelligent to say to that.

Marla turned to face her again. Her mother-in-law seemed amused by Adrina's loss of words.

"I have spent every waking moment since I was fifteen years old protecting my family, Adrina. First for my brother, Lernen, who was barely worthy of the name Wolfblade, and then my children. I haven't done a damned thing for the past forty years that wasn't directly related to that goal. It cost me the man I loved, the dearest friend I have ever known, and every soft place in my soul. I made this country what it is, Adrina, so Damin could inherit something worth having." She took a step forward and leaned on her cane with both hands. "And then the Halfbreed and the demon child come along and the next thing I know, Damin has abandoned his province to go haring off to the Medalon-Karien border to fight on the side of the Defenders, and when he finally comes home, it is with the daughter of my sworn enemy as his bride."

"Have I ever counseled Damin to ignore your advice?"

"Perhaps not," Marla conceded. "I don't know what you two talk about in bed at night. But even if you haven't, it doesn't mean I don't expect you to. Every single day."

Adrina was getting very tired of this. "You must be exhausted, Marla, expending all this energy on waiting for me to destroy everything you've ever worked for."

"I am."

"Then I wish you a safe journey, your highness," she said, with a curtsey that managed to be more sarcastic than courteous. "Don't forget to write."

Adrina turned on her heel and headed for the door, wishing that rather than come here, she'd sent back a message telling Marla what she could do with her summons.

"That's more like it."

"Excuse me?" Adrina stopped and turned to look at Marla.

The princess limped back into the reception room after her, the silver cane tapping on the tiles. "You never push back, Adrina."

"You and I fight all the time."

"No, we don't. We dance. We snipe. We hedge. We're polite for the sake of the children, when I know what you would really like to do is tear my head off with your bare hands, and scream at me to stop being such an interfering old bitch."

"And if I had done?" she asked, appalled that Marla might have seen through her so easily. "What would it have achieved?"

"I would know you have the spine for what lies ahead."

"What?"

"Damin is incapacitated, Adrina, but he appointed you regent because he trusts your judgment. Strange as it may seem, it is that which gives me hope. I did not raise a fool, and if you were as shallow and dim as I once feared, he would not have spared you the time of day. My son trusts you and I trust *his* judgment. I just never see what he sees in you and now I have to leave and hand you the keys to the kingdom. I am terrified, because if you can't stand up to me, how are you going to deal with the Warlords?"

Adrina was shocked to hear Marla say anything complimentary about her, even if it was in such a backhanded fashion. This might well be the first time since she'd arrived in Greenharbour that Marla had conceded anything positive about her daughter-in-law at all.

"When you ran Hythria in your brother's name, Marla, keeping up the pretense that Lernen was in charge, did you tear the heads off your enemies with your bare hands and scream at them?"

"Of course not."

"Then why do you fault me for having the same modicum of self-control?"

"Because I don't know if it's self-control, Adrina, or simply a lack of fortitude."

Adrina took a deep breath. "Which is your problem, Marla, not mine. I am far more capable than you imagine, and I can stand up to anybody I have to. Ironically, the only two people I seem to be incapable of standing up to are you and your son."

Marla scoffed at that notion. "Damin is putty in your hands, Adrina."

"Only when he wants to be, Marla. A child died once because I couldn't reason with Damin. You'd not be so certain your son was my willing puppet if you'd been there the day *that* happened."

For a moment, Adrina found herself back in northern Hythria, on the road with Damin and his army going to save the Citadel from the Kariens. She'd thought the memory long buried, but Marla's question brought it all flooding back.

"What child? What are you talking about?"

"Do you recall the young Karien lad in my service when I first arrived in Greenharbour?" she asked, wishing she'd said nothing. The memory was so painful she'd done her best to bury it in the deep dark recesses of her mind, where it was unlikely to ever see the light of day.

Marla shrugged. "Vaguely."

"Damin never told you about what happened to Mikel?"

"I really don't know what you are talking about, Adrina."

"It happened on the way to Medalon to relieve the Karien occupation of the Citadel," she said. "Brak and R'shiel had just found us. They arrived on the backs of dragons, if you can believe it. We were having dinner. I remember Damin telling everyone about lifting the siege on Greenharbour. Mikel served R'shiel a drink, but he stayed behind her, just watching. Perhaps that was what tipped off Brak that the child had just served R'shiel wine laced with jarabane."

"The attempt failed, obviously."

She nodded. "Brak was the one who realized what was happening. He threw himself across the tent to stop R'shiel drinking the poison and then caught Mikel before he could run away."

"What reason would a child have to kill the demon child?"

Adrina shrugged, not wishing to relive that awful night, sorry now that she had even mentioned it. "Apparently R'shiel traded his soul to the God of Music so he could learn the Song of Gimlorie and turn back the Kariens who were pursuing me—and Damin—back to Hythria after the Medalonians were ordered to surrender on the border. Until then, Mikel was a disciple of the God of Thieves. According to Dacendaran, her interference made the child vulnerable and the Overlord, Xaphista, was able to get inside his head."

"So the child Damin killed was the tool of the Overlord? My question would be, Adrina, not why you were not able to stop him, but why you would try to stay his hand in the first place?"

"He was a child, Marla, and the fault for his vulnerability to manipulation was R'shiel's, not his."

Her eyes filled with tears as she struggled to go on. Marla sat down, her hands resting on her cane, before asking, "I take it you were unable to dissuade him?"

Adrina shook her head. "Neither could the Halfbreed or the demon child. I've never felt so helpless. Nobody tried to stop him, Marla, even with magic. "

"Let me guess: Damin offered them a choice," Marla said. "Go to the rescue of those in the Citadel waiting for his help or interfere with his justice. The good of the many invariably outweighs the interests of one small child. I'm sure Damin learned that at my knee."

She nodded, quite certain Marla was right about that much. "I remember that night so vividly. We all stood there—even the Harshini who had come to aid the Hythrun in their quest to relieve the Citadel. 'You can't order this,' I recall R'shiel shouting as he led Mikel away. 'You can't ask a man to execute a child!' Do you know what Damin said then?"

"Something along the lines of 'I don't ask anything of my men I wouldn't do myself'?" Marla allowed herself the slightest of smiles. "I know my son, Adrina."

"I tried to stop him, Marla. I grabbed him, but he shook me off and told me I didn't have to watch. Then R'shiel yelled something else about him being reasonable, and he turned on her. I'll never forget the look on his face or how cold his voice was. 'Define *reasonable*, demon child,' he said. 'Is it reasonable I let this child live so he can turn on you again? It is reasonable that I let an assassin reside in the heart of my family? Suppose Adrina had taken that cup? Suppose Brak hadn't noticed something was wrong? What the hell do you expect me to do?'"

"I can't say I am surprised at his reaction, Adrina. Thanks to your father and a few others I've taken care of over the years, Damin has lived with the threat of assassins all his life."

Adrina nodded. "That's what Damin said. He was adamant his own children would not be raised the same way. 'I want the whole damned world to know what I'm capable of if they dare to threaten me or mine.' That's what he said."

"And then he killed the child?"

Adrina shook her head. "Brak did it in the end. The Halfbreed summoned Death to take him body and soul. It was kinder that way."

"And you think because you weren't able to bat your eyelashes at my son and undo a lifetime of conditioning against the threat of assassins, he is somehow immune to your manipulation? If only you'd told me of this incident sooner, Adrina. I might have been much less harsh in my assessment of your insidious power over him."

"I tried to stop him, Marla."

"But you were unable to," the princess replied. "That you tried to save someone you considered innocent speaks well of your character. That you were unable to change Damin's mind on such an important matter speaks even more about his. Perhaps Hythria is not lost after all." Marla leaned forward and rang a small silver bell on the table beside her chair. "Have a seat, Adrina. Join me for supper."

"Really?" she asked, rather ungraciously. "You're inviting me for supper?"

"I'm looking after my interests," Marla told her, settling back into her chair. "If you are to rule Hythria in my absence with Damin incapacitated, there are things you must know. Things I would never commit to paper. People you need to be wary of. Other people who will help you if you need it. Quietly. People on whom I rely that even Damin is not aware of."

A little bemused by Marla's change of heart, Adrina took a seat as Cadella opened the door and entered the room wheeling a small silver cart with a selection of fruit and pasties laid out, as if she'd been waiting for her mistress's signal.

Marla saw Adrina's doubtful look and smiled. "In this house, if I ring the bell three times, Cadella knows to bring the gold cart. That is the one with the poisoned supper on it."

For a moment, Adrina feared Marla was serious, until she caught the smirk on the old slave's face as she parked the cart beside Marla.

"Silver cart good, gold cart poison," Adrina noted. "I'll remember that."

Marla smiled again, a much more genuine smile than Adrina was used to seeing from her mother-in-law, and then she turned to Cadella. "Have some refreshments sent out to the High Princess's coachman and guards. Let them know we'll be a while yet, so they might as well relax."

"Of course, your highness."

Cadella shuffled off, leaving Adrina alone with Marla, a little stunned by the fact that for the first time she could recall, Marla had referred to Adrina as "the High Princess" without lacing the title with enough scorn and sarcasm to smother a small child.

"IF YOU COULD wish for anything, Aja," the minstrel asked, "what would it be?"

Still not used to her assumed name, it took a moment before Rakaia realized Mica was talking to her. She turned from looking out over the moonlit stillness of the mighty Glass River to study the minstrel in the darkness. Out here on the barge the world was silent, but for the soft grunting of the ferryman as he pulled on the rope that spanned the broad expanse of water between Testra and Vanahiem on the southern side. Rakaia still wasn't sure how Mica had convinced him to cross the river at night, or why he'd offered to do it free of charge.

All she knew was that Mica had a knack for getting people to do things for him that she would not have believed possible had she not seen it for herself.

"I don't really know," she said, unable to think of any single particular item she wanted for, right at this moment.

"Then you must be the happiest person alive," Mica told her.

"How do you figure that?"

"Because you want for nothing."

"I have nothing."

"And that is why you're so happy. When you have nothing, you have nothing to fret over losing, either."

Rakaia wasn't sure she agreed with Mica's latest, somewhat simplistic philosophy—and he had plenty of them, she'd discovered these past few days.

"I'll have *my* wish now," Irma announced, coming up behind them. She was one of the dancing girls.

The other one, Olena, was her daughter, something Rakaia was shocked to discover. She couldn't imagine being a traveling whore with a child you'd then recruit into the business, but neither woman seemed unduly bothered by their career choice. Perhaps it was because they were Medalonian, where a whore was just another profession like any other, taxed and regulated the same way a baker or fishmonger might be.

Rakaia had thought the women were permanent members of the troupe, but apparently they had joined Mica at the Citadel only a few weeks ago, for the promise that he would grant them a wish whenever they wanted it. Rakaia had no idea why the women would agree to such a ludicrous arrangement, but in the week she'd been a part of Mica's Marvelous Minstrels, she learned that people came and went in Mica's life, never staying longer than a few weeks, always leaving—so Mica claimed—happier than when they arrived.

As if to prove his point, Norn, the juggler, was already on his way back to the Citadel with plans to put together his own juggling troupe. Mica had promised it would happen, and that his new venture would be wildly successful, although how he knew that, or why Norn believed him, Rakaia could not fathom.

They'd all had a drink to celebrate Norn's departure, Mica had sung a special song he composed for the occasion, and they had all parted the best of friends several hours ago. It was then that Mica had announced, unaccountably, they would be leaving for Vanahiem tonight, and he was sure, if he offered to sing for them, the ferrymen would agree to launch their barge, despite the late hour.

"What is your wish, Irma?" Rakaia asked.

Irma jerked her head in the direction of the burly ferryman pulling on the rope. He was a large young man with a body toned and tanned by long hours hauling the barge across the wide expanse of the Glass River across the current. "Him."

Mica smiled. "You want a *ferryman*?"

"Not any ferryman," she said, lowering her voice. "That one."

Rakaia looked across at the man, who was chatting to Olena as he worked. The younger woman was leaning against the railing, her hands grasping the polished rail behind her, which thrust her bosom forward, almost as if by accident. The ferryman on the rope couldn't take his eyes off her.

Good thing the barge is attached to that rope taking us to the other side, Rakaia thought. *If he's meant to be watching where he's going, we'll be in Bordertown before he notices.*

"Isn't he a bit young for you, Irma?" Mica asked. He seemed just as bemused by the request as Rakaia was.

"I don't want him for me. I want him for Olena."

"Why would you waste your wish on something for your daughter?"

"Because that's what mothers do," Rakaia said, with a sudden flash of insight. She'd never really considered, until now, what risks Sophany might have taken to get her daughter safely out of the harem before the king learned the truth about Rakaia's paternity. What deal had she done with Naveen Raveve that would make him put her daughter's name forward to marry a Hythrun border lord over all the other harem mothers jostling for the same privilege? She pulled her shawl around her shoulders, not at all certain it was simply the cold breeze that gave her chills.

Oh, Mama, what did you do?

"The Fardohnyan is right," Irma said. "Olena wants a husband, and she likes that one."

"But you don't know anything about him," Mica pointed out.

"He has a job," Irma said. "And a good heart."

"You don't know that. He might beat her senseless every night as soon as they're married and throw you out into the street."

"That's Olena's part of the wish. You have to make sure he'll be good to her."

Appalled by the naïve superstition of the Medalonian woman, Rakaia opened her mouth to scoff at the very suggestion, but Mica seemed to take the request quite seriously. "Do you mind if we wait until we've docked on the other side?"

"Just do your thing, little man," she said, "and we'll be even."

Irma turned and walked back to where Olena was leaning against the railing and began chatting to the ferryman again, who seemed in no need of any wish-granting to be utterly enchanted by the young whore.

That wasn't what intrigued Rakaia, though. She was far more interested in what Irma had said to Mica. "What did she mean about being even?"

"Irma did me a favor at the Citadel."

"And she really believes you're going to repay her for this favor by granting her a wish?"

"I *will* grant her wish. And Olena's." He studied the ferryman in the moonlight for a moment as the man leaned forward and pulled the rope, hand over hand, to inch them ever closer to the lights of the dock on the other side, and then he shrugged. "I'd aim a little higher, if it were my choice, but to each his own."

"How?" Rakaia asked. "You can't grant wishes. You're not Harshini."

Mica smiled, looking quite smug. "I will sing to him in such a persuasive fashion, he will have no choice but to propose to Olena on the spot and offer his new mother-in-law a home with them for as long as she wants it."

Rakaia laughed aloud at that. "I don't believe you."

"You'll see," Mica said, supremely confident he was right. "Would you like to accompany me?"

"What?"

"You said you played the lyre passably well."

"I lied," she said. "In truth, I'm not very good at all. I used to threaten to have my instructor whipped if he didn't give my mother glowing reports of my progress."

"Ah, another crack in the veil."

"What veil?"

"The veil behind which you hide, Aja. The veil behind which lies the reason someone like you, who acts like she is a noblewoman born and bred, finds herself penniless and on the road with someone like me for company. The reason someone like you, who counts the demon child among her acquaintances, has nowhere to go and no one to watch over her."

"How would you even know what a noblewoman acts like?" Rakaia asked, hoping to divert Mica's questions with questions of her own. She hadn't told Mica anything about who she was—or had been—because she really wasn't sure she could trust him. She liked him well enough. She liked being around him. But, sweet as he was, pretty as he was, she suspected he was simply a clever con-man, swindling his way through the world on the promise of wishes he couldn't deliver. She wasn't about to entrust someone like that with her life story.

"I've known a few princesses quite well in my time."

"Really?"

"One, then," he admitted. "But she was more than enough princess for anybody to deal with."

"Who was she?"

"You tell me your secret, I'll tell you mine," he said, his eyes reflecting the moonlight as they fixed on her with an uncomfortable level of scrutiny.

"Maybe," she said, looking away. "One day."

"Then I shall await that day with great anticipation," he said, lowering his lyre case from his shoulder. "Here, why don't you show me something you can play?"

"Now?" she asked as he opened the case and pulled out his instrument. It was a battered old thing. The sound-chest was made out of turtle shell. The two raised arms appeared to be made from some kind of animal horn that curved both outward and forward, connected near the top by a carved wooden yoke. An additional crossbar, fixed to the sound-chest, made the bridge, which transmitted the vibrations of the strings and gave the instrument its tone. The strings were yellowed and made of various types of gut. They were stretched between the yoke and bridge, to a tailpiece below the bridge where the bone tuning pegs were located. It was nothing like the gilded instrument she had learned to play in the palace, and yet she'd never known any instrument to make such deliciously sweet music.

But it seemed too old and fragile to loan to an amateur like her. She was almost afraid to touch it, for fear of damaging the instrument beyond repair.

"Aren't you worried about the moisture getting to it on the river?"

Mica shook his head. "This old thing is more robust than you think," he said, thrusting it at her. "Here. Play me a tune."

With some reluctance, Rakaia took the lyre, cradling it in her left arm against her chest so she could pluck the strings with her right hand. Mica's bone plectrum was tied to the corner of the instrument with a red ribbon. She took it up and cautiously ran it across the strings to see how it sounded.

Mica applauded her loudly. "Brilliant! A true talent has been discovered here tonight! Bards will sing of this moment! Parents will tell their—"

"If you're going to make fun of me, I'll toss your wretched lyre into the river."

"I'm sorry," Mica said, his apology somewhat negated by the grin on his face. "Play something."

"Play what?"

"I don't know. What did your instructor at the palace teach you?"

"I never said I grew up in a palace."

"My mistake, Aja. Please, play something your personal lyre instructor taught you while you were scrabbling to stay alive in the slums of Talabar."

She couldn't help but smile at him. But she was suddenly self-conscious about her skill—or lack if it—in front of the minstrel.

"Do you promise not to laugh?"

"No."

She decided to ignore that. He was baiting her now, however gently, and she didn't want to disappoint him. He was right about that much. Even though she now counted the demon child among her acquaintances, without Mica and his band of minstrels—what was left of them, at least—she would be on her own. Rakaia was still too unfamiliar with the world outside the sheltered security of the Talabar harem walls to contemplate making her way back to Fardohnya across hundreds of miles and two foreign countries on her own, in the hope that her uncle was still prepared to offer her safe haven.

She closed her eyes and tried to recall the Fardohnyan folk song her instructor had been trying—with little success—to teach her before she left Talabar. She had only plucked at a few notes before Mica placed his hand over hers, silencing the strings.

"Try using a second note with the note of the melody," he suggested. "Add a little strum between phrases, every now and then."

"You say that like I know how."

"I will teach you," he offered softly, his head close to hers, his eyes staring into her eyes as if he could see through her lies and into her very soul. And then he straightened up and glanced toward the shore. "We'll be there soon. Do you know how to play *The Moneylender's Daughter*?"

Rakaia nodded. It was a simple tune most novices—even in Fardohnya—learned in their first lesson.

"Then that will have to do." Turning his back on her, Mica addressed the ferryman. "A song for your heroic efforts, my lad," he announced theatrically.

The ferryman didn't answer him. He was too busy trying to impress Olena.

Amused, Mica turned to Rakaia and nodded. She began to pluck out the notes of the simple melody as Mica's honey-sweet voice rang out over the water, singing of love, of hearth and home and family, in a way that brought tears to Rakaia's eyes. The words he sang were not the words of the bawdy song she knew, but something Mica must have composed himself. They left her longing for someone to love so badly there was a physical ache in her belly at the thought of it.

As his voice faded away, Rakaia brushed the tears from her eyes in time to see the ferryman let the rope go and drop to one knee in front of Olena, who nodded happily in response to a question Rakaia was too far away to hear, and then the young whore threw her arms around the ferryman and began kissing him furiously.

Irma watched the young couple for a moment and then turned and nodded to Mica; a simple thank-you for a promise delivered.

"No," Rakaia said, shaking her head.

"I told you so."

"You staged this. You're playing a prank on me."

"If you say so," Mica said, taking the lyre from her. He carefully placed it back into its case and then slung it over his shoulder again before making his way across the barge to congratulate the lucky couple . . . and perhaps remind the ferryman that his hands belonged on the rope and not on Olena as they neared the Vanahiem dock.

Rakaia watched them, almost as if she were caught in a rising fog, not sure where she was or what had just happened, only certain that if what she had just witnessed wasn't a prank staged by the minstrels to amuse themselves at her expense, there was something far deeper, and darker, about Mica the Minstrel. If she had any brains at all, Rakaia suspected, she'd get far, far away from him while she still could.

But then Mica turned and smiled at her and beckoned her forward to join him and Irma congratulating Olena and the ferryman on their betrothal and all thought of leaving Mica or running away from him faded from her mind.

Chapter

29

THE SANCTUARY MOUNTAINS were named for the hidden Harshini fortress they had protected for several thousand years. Located on the border of Karien and Medalon, they were home to a number of scattered settlements of woodcutters and fur trappers on the Medalonian side, and a few hardy souls who preferred to live far from the trappings of civilization.

The closest settlement to Sanctuary used to be a village named Haven, where R'shiel té Ortyn—daughter of the Harshini king, Lorandranek, and the Medalonian peasant girl, J'nel—was born. The village no longer existed. As the demon-melded dragon she rode swooped down over the remains of the village, R'shiel could see nothing but snow-covered shapes that might once have been houses, with the occasional charred skeleton of a stone chimney poking through.

The destruction of the village pained her. It had been destroyed to hide the secret of her birth from those seeking to find the demon child. She had no memory of the place. She was only days old when Joyhinia Tenragan offered to take her off the villagers' hands after her mother died giving birth to her.

Fly on, Dranymire, she told the demon controlling the dragon meld. *There is nothing for us down there.*

As you wish, the demon replied, banking left and upward toward the mountain's peak. R'shiel watched the small village clearing disappear behind them. It wouldn't be long, she knew, before the forest reclaimed the site completely and there would be no trace left of her birthplace.

Maybe that was a good thing. She didn't want people finding it and turning it into a shrine to something they thought she was—a burden of being the demon child she loathed. R'shiel had come to accept who she was these past ten years or so, but she had never been happy about it. It wasn't her fault the gods had decided the only way to deal with Xaphista was to create a being capable of destroying the demon who had managed to elevate himself to the status of a god. And having achieved her divine purpose before she turned twenty-one, she was quite certain the gods had not given much thought to what she was meant to do for the rest of her unnaturally long Harshini lifetime.

So she'd kept her head down and stayed as inconspicuous as she could while she sought out Death. She had completed the quest the gods created her for, and now she had one of her own. R'shiel had traveled the world, had seen wonders most people had only heard about in stories, as she tried to force Death to face her. It was ironic that it was here, only a few miles from where she was born, that she would finally find what she was looking for.

They flew on toward the peak, past the sheer precipice where she had once sat, debating whether or not to throw herself off and end it all, when Brak had found her and talked her into living. R'shiel smiled as she remembered Brak's answer that day when she'd asked him if not thinking about the future was how he coped with being a halfbreed Harshini.

"That and large quantities of mead," he'd told her.

R'shiel had tried the large quantities of mead method. It hadn't helped. She tried forgetting who she was. She'd even debated announcing what she was to everyone she met and making a living out performing miracles, except the very idea seemed rather seedy and unwholesome. What she really wanted was a chance to be as normal as being a now-surplus-to-requirements-being-capable-of-killing-a-god would allow her to be.

And the only way that would happen, she knew, was if she could bring Brak back.

It won't be long now, she thought as Dranymire and the demon-meld headed toward the peak where Sanctuary once stood, before she would step into Death's realm. Then she could find Brak and convince him to come back.

R'shiel didn't kid herself that Brak would automatically agree, even if he still remembered her name after almost a decade in the afterlife. He might be perfectly happy where he was and see no reason to return to this imperfect world. R'shiel was prepared for that. She loved Brak enough to want him to be happy, even if it meant sacrificing her own happiness to achieve it.

But she needed to hear it from him. The deal Brak made with Death to trade his life for hers was made long before he could admit that he loved her, long before they became lovers. He would never have made such a deal, she was certain, had he loved her then the way he loved her by the time he died helping her destroy Xaphista.

With a powerful beat of his wings, the dragon landed on the snow-covered peak, sending a flurry of snow in all directions. R'shiel jumped from the dragon's back and stepped forward to examine the pristine peak. The air was icy and thin, but she hardly noticed the temperature, glancing only briefly over the spectacular view her position afforded her. She was so high, the sky so clear here, she could make out the thin ribbon of the Glass River glinting in the far distance.

Of Sanctuary, the grand palace that had once perched on this peak, no trace remained.

That was something of a relief. She and Brak had flung Sanctuary so far out of time and space it would have been unsettling to discover there existed another being in this world able to bring it back.

"How will you find it?"

R'shiel glanced over her shoulder. The dragon was gone and in its place were the scores of demons who had melded to form it, some of them winking out of existence as soon as they were free, the others—probably the younger demons—gamboling in the snow. The demon who'd spoken was Dranymire. He was perched on an outcropping of rock behind her, loftily ignoring the antics of his less dignified brethren as they reveled in being released from the meld. His large eyes studied her curiously, his leathery face creased with concern. He and his demon brethren had been loyal to a fault, but he clearly did not agree with what she planned to do next.

"Don't look at me like that."

"I am not looking at you like anything," the demon said. "I am merely curious as to how you intend to do this."

"I have a plan."

"And I'm waiting to hear it."

"You think I can't bring Sanctuary back on my own, don't you?"

"I think it is foolish of you to try."

"Why?"

"The dead should remain dead."

"Not when they die before their time."

"Are you so certain it was not Brak's time?"

She nodded. "Absolutely. He traded his life for mine. If he hadn't, he would still be alive."

"And now you have traded the life of one of your friends for his."

"Not really," she said, her assurance sounding hollow, even to her own ears. "Brak has to agree to return first. By then I will have figured a way around that whole 'friend's life in return' complication."

The demon blinked at her, unconvinced. "You are fooling yourself, demon child. And one of your friends will die because of it."

"No, they won't," she insisted. "Everything will be fine. Are you coming with me?"

He shook his head. "I cannot follow where you are going. If we enter any one of the lower hells, there is no coming back for my kind and no deal you can broker with Death to change that."

On impulse, she stepped across the snow to the outcropping and hugged him. The demon wiggled uncomfortably in her embrace, almost yelping with disgust when she planted a large kiss on his forehead. "I love you, Dranymire."

"You are embarrassing us both, your highness."

"Will you wait for me?"

"Not at all," he said, shaking her off. "I will return to the Citadel and Queen Shananara, where my brethren and I shall relish the opportunity to serve a té Ortyn who knows how to behave like Harshini royalty."

"You'll miss me, though, won't you?"

"Not in the slightest."

R'shiel didn't believe the little demon for a moment. She leaned forward and kissed him again and then turned around to face the mountain peak where Sanctuary had once stood—and where she intended to make it stand again.

"It took the combined power of you *and* Brak to send it out of time," Dranymire reminded her.

R'shiel had forgotten that. What she had done, however, was think of little else since Death had told her how to find Brak. There was a solution here. She might not be able to reach Sanctuary alone, but a god could. Or a goddess.

She just needed to call on the right one.

"Kalianah!"

"You're summoning the Goddess of Love to aide you?" Dranymire sounded horrified.

She glanced over her shoulder at him and grinned. "Never underestimate the power of true love."

"I never do."

R'shiel spun around to find the goddess standing behind her in her favorite manifestation—that of a little girl. She had thick blond hair and wore a thin white shift, oblivious to the cold winds swirling around the peak of the mountain.

R'shiel bowed to the goddess. "Divine One."

"Why have you summoned me?"

"I need your help."

"I offered you help once and you spurned it."

R'shiel took a deep breath. "I did not spurn your aid, Divine One. I didn't know that asking the demons to possess Tarja while he healed would break the geas you put on him to love me."

"Nobody ever broke a geas I placed on them before."

"And probably never will again, Divine One," she assured the goddess. "It was a unique set of circumstances that will likely never be repeated. But Tarja's happy now, isn't he? With Mandah?"

"Mandah is dead," the goddess informed her flatly.

"Oh . . ." R'shiel hadn't heard about Tarja's wife dying. She felt bad for Tarja, but had always been jealous of Mandah, even though the poor woman was probably the most selfless person R'shiel had ever met. Perhaps that was why she'd always been suspicious of her. Nobody was that perfect. "I didn't know . . ."

"Well, I suppose she's not really dead . . . any more than Damin Wolfblade is . . . but—"

"Hang on . . . what are you talking about, Kali?"

The little girl rolled her eyes. "What do you *think* I'm talking about, demon child? You, of course, and this ludicrous deal you have done with Death to get Brak back."

"Is Damin dead?" Her stomach churned at the thought Death might have taken Damin Wolfblade's life on her account.

"Death is holding their lives in trust until you decide if you truly want to bring Brak back."

"Then what has Mandah got to do with it? The deal was for the life of one of my friends. Damin is, but Mandah's never been my friend."

"Mandah is Tarja's wife, though," Kalianah reminded her, "and the mother of his children. If you trade her life for Brak's, how do you suppose Tarja—your friend—will react to that?"

Tarja has children. R'shiel had been away so long, she didn't know that.

"Well . . . I suppose he'd blame me," she admitted, thinking if Death had thought Mandah one of her friends, then the choice of whose life to trade for Brak's would be a simple one indeed. There was no comparison, in R'shiel's mind, between the worth of Brak and that too-sweet-to-be-true opportunist who had worked her way into Tarja's bed almost as soon as the geas that made him love R'shiel was shattered. The fact that R'shiel loved someone else, and had rejected Tarja's love as artificially imposed, did not, for some reason, mitigate her jealously of Mandah.

"Tarja would do more than that," the goddess warned. "He'd not just blame you. He'd blame the Harshini and all their gods, and so would every citizen in Medalon still looking back kindly on the good old days when the Harshini were a forgotten memory and the Sisterhood ruled their lives. You helped destroy the Sisters of the Blade, R'shiel, but you left Medalon to fend for itself."

"There has been peace for a decade now," R'shiel reminded the goddess.

"And that's about all you can take credit for," Kalianah said. "You took away Medalon's government and gave them a military dictatorship supporting a Harshini monarchy they'd been trained all their lives to despise and eradicate."

Kalianah might well be speaking the truth, but R'shiel had never known the Goddess of Love to pay even the slightest attention to politics. She was all about who loved whom. Not why. "Who have you been talking to?"

"What do you mean?"

"I mean you haven't even asked me yet if I love you. Rather, you've delivered a political lecture Zegarnald would be proud of."

The goddess looked down, kicking a small divot in the snow with her bare foot. "I may have spoken to Zeggie about it . . ." Then she looked up, scowling. "Love is love, R'shiel. If the people of Medalon don't love their government, that affects me too, you know."

"Does *anybody* love their government?"

"All governments are loved by enough people to keep them in power," the goddess announced. "Now, what did you want? I have other places to be."

"I want you to help me bring Sanctuary back."

"Why? It's perfectly fine where it is. It's not bothering anyone, is it?"

"It's the gateway to the Seven Hells. Actually, the more I think about it, Sanctuary might actually *be* one of the Seven Hells—just the one closest to this world. That's why humans can survive there for limited periods and how the demons can live there. It's how the Harshini could make it disappear at will when they were in hiding. And why they had to bring it back every spring, or they really would end up dead."

"Did Death tell you that?"

"He hinted at it."

Kalianah shook her head. "He is a fool."

"Will you help me?"

"Why should I?"

"Because there can be no greater act of honoring the Goddess of Love than to enter the Seven Hells to bring back someone I love."

"Or no greater act of selfishness."

"I will not force Brak out if he's happy," she promised. "If he wants to stay, I will return to this world without him and never mention it again. You have my word."

That seemed to satisfy the goddess, as R'shiel suspected it would. Once this became about honoring the Goddess of Love, any political awareness the God of War might have managed to instill in his little sister was forgotten.

"Very well," the goddess said. "But don't blame me if this folly brings you nothing but pain in the very hollows of your heart, demon child."

"I've had nothing but pain in the very hollows of my heart since Brak died helping me sort out your mess," R'shiel said, thinking it was probably unwise to antagonize the goddess just as she was agreeing to help.

But Kalianah didn't seem to notice her tone. "Do you love me?" the goddess asked.

"Of course I do."

"So be it," she said and abruptly vanished into thin air, only a tiny white feather settling to the snow to indicate that she had ever been there.

R'shiel bent down to pick up the feather. As she straightened up, she became aware the sun was suddenly in shadow. Turning to look at the peak behind her, she discovered the reason why.

She might need a god's help to bring Sanctuary back out of time, but the gods obviously did not need hers. The tall, elegant white towers of a palace now blocked the sun, reaching up toward the heavens from the top of the mountain as if they had been there for a thousand years.

The sight took R'shiel's breath away.

Its gates open and unguarded . . . Sanctuary had returned.

Part Three

Chapter

30

DACENDARAN, THE GOD of Thieves, had no formal place of worship. To honor him simply required one to steal something. He really didn't mind what his followers stole, nor was he a particularly jealous god. He knew his worshipers often prayed to other, less venal gods, as if that somehow made them better people. But every time one of those worthy souls cheated a merchant of a few coppers, kept something they'd found that didn't belong to them, or even stole the heart of an unsuspecting lover, Dace had what he wanted.

He didn't care if nobody prayed to him. In fact, he preferred it that way. Prayers were a lot of work and always required some measure of effort on the part of the deity in question to answer them. There was the additional problem of whose prayers to answer and whose to ignore, until it all became just too much effort.

Better to take the quiet, stealthy honoring of ordinary, everyday dishonesty, and let the other gods deal with all that tedious prayer answering.

If Dacendaran had a temple, however, and if that temple had a high priest, it would have been Wrayan Lightfinger.

Wrayan was a rare creature. Like Rorin Mariner, he was part-Harshini, which meant he had enough of the magical race's blood in him to be able to wield true magic. He had, in fact, spent his formative years apprenticed to a previous High Arrion of the Sorcerers' Collective, until he ran afoul of an ambitious young woman named Alija Eaglespike. Thanks to her unsuccessful attempts to cauterize his brain, the Halfbreed—at the request of the God of Thieves—had rescued him and taken him to spend the next two years living in the magical hidden settlement of Sanctuary among the Harshini.

The God of Thieves' intervention was the result of a foolish prayer. Wrayan was living proof of the perils of having one's prayers answered.

Years before his confrontation with Alija, he'd met a young, naïve princess named Marla Wolfblade and accidently frozen time around her. With no idea of what he'd done or how he'd done it, it took the intervention of a god to undo the spell. It wasn't so strange that he'd asked Dacendaran for help. Wrayan's father had been a Krakandar pickpocket of some considerable renown. He'd grown up actively worshiping Dacendaran, so when Wrayan had accidentally struck down the only sister of the High Prince on the night of her betrothal to the king of Fardohnya, Dace was the first god Wrayan had thought to call on.

The consequences of that night had eventually brought him here, to his current position as head of the Greenharbour Thieves' Guild, a position, given the longevity of his Harshini ancestors, he was liable to hold for a long time yet.

Not that he was unhappy with his lot in life. He lived well, enjoyed the respect of his peers, and counted the High Arrion and the High Prince's mother among his closest friends.

But there were times when he wished he'd never been plucked from obscurity in the Krakandar markets, where he'd been making a tidy living scamming rich merchants with his magical tricks, by the old High Arrion, Kagan Palenovar, who brought him here to Greenharbour to join the Sorcerers' Collective. He would not have met Princess Marla, not traded his soul to a god nor have had to deal with the man he was waiting for now.

It wasn't that Wrayan Lightfinger had any specific prejudice against Medalonians in general or Captain Fletcher in particular. But by agreeing to meet with Cade, he was dabbling in affairs his gut told him he was better off staying out of.

The High Arrion had asked him to meet with Cade as a personal favor to her. For reasons few people in this world understood, Wrayan found it difficult to deny Marla Wolfblade's daughter anything.

When the door opened, Wrayan was a little surprised—and more than a little annoyed—to see the Medalonian captain wearing his uniform, as he knew Kalan had advised him not to walk the streets of the Thieves' Quarter wearing anything so obvious.

"I'm here to meet with Wrayan the Wraith," the captain said as he stepped into the office. It was sumptuous room, every item in it, from the heavy wooden desk to the delicate dragon-scale letter opener, stolen—at one time or another—from someone wealthy and careless in Greenharbour.

"I am Wrayan Lightfinger. I don't go by the other title much, these days."

Caden Fletcher studied him for a long moment, clearly skeptical of the claim. "Wrayan Lightfinger must be sixty years old if he's a day. You might be his grandson, but—"

"I'm part Harshini," he reminded the younger man. "Given you live and work side by side with the Harshini in the Citadel, I'm surprised you need to be reminded of what that means."

The captain, to his credit, didn't seem in the slightest bit intimidated. "I'm sorry, I thought immortality was something reserved for halfbreeds."

"I'm not immortal, Captain," he said, indicating the young man should take a seat opposite the desk. "Just long lived."

"How do you know?"

"That I'm long lived? I would have thought the answer was self-evident."

The Medalonian smiled. "I mean how do you know you're not immortal? Didn't you already die once?"

"I almost died," he said. "Which is quite a different thing. But you didn't risk your very life walking the Thieves' Quarter in a bright red Defenders uniform to ask me if I'm immortal."

Fletcher took the offered seat as Wrayan resumed his chair, nodding. "Did Lady Kalan tell you anything?"

"Just that you were asking about something called the Covenant?"

"Have you heard of it?"

"Not until Kalan brought it up."

"Are you sure?"

"What reason would I have to lie?"

The captain shrugged. "I'm not sure. The only thing I know for certain is that when we asked the Harshini queen if this Covenant was important, she said it was more important than we could possibly imagine. Fair to assume, then, that someone who lived with the Harshini in Sanctuary for a couple of years might know something about *why* it's so important."

"What does the Collective librarian say?" Wrayan asked, genuinely puzzled by Caden Fletcher's questions. He never a heard a word uttered about any covenant when he was in Sanctuary. Of course, he was a guest there, and hardly privy to all the Harshini's secrets, but still, it was reasonable to assume he might have heard of something so important, even in passing.

"The same as you. Never heard of it. He claims the Harshini cleaned out their library of anything that might be used against them before they went into hiding in Sanctuary and that what useful stuff was left, Brakan-daran removed after you had your . . . accident."

"What happened to me was no accident," Wrayan, with a faint grimace at the memory of that painful—and nearly fatal—encounter with Alija Eaglespike almost forty years ago. "But he has the right of it. Brak made sure there was nothing left that might endanger the Harshini."

"Did the Halfbreed never mention the Covenant?"

Wrayan shook his head. "Not at all. Did Shananara say anything else?"

"Nothing useful. She did seem upset, though."

"How could you even tell?"

"Exactly," Cade said. "The fact that the Harshini queen was visibly upset might give you some idea of how much the loss of Gimlorie's token—and this Covenant it seems to be connected to—means to her people."

"What was it that was stolen, exactly?"

"A tiny golden lyre. A trinket, really, and certainly easy enough to smuggle out of the Citadel."

"I can speak to my people," Wrayan offered with a shrug. "In case someone tries to fence it. But if it was solid gold, it may have been melted down already."

"The Lord Defender suggested that possibility to the queen," Cade told him. "She was adamant no human had the power to harm it, nor do anything to it at all."

"Other than steal it," Wrayan reminded him.

Fletcher nodded. "Other than that."

Wrayan rose to his feet, not sure what else he could do for the Medalonian. "Well, I'll get my people onto it and see if we can find it for you. If this golden lyre has made it to Greenharbour and someone is hoping to profit from it, sooner or later it will come to my attention."

The captain stood and offered Wrayan his hand. "Thank you. Lord Tenragan said you would help."

"Did he? I'm not sure why. He hardly knows me."

"I believe the High Prince vouched for you, too."

That made sense. Wrayan had known Damin Wolfblade all his life. "You can assure the Lord Defender the Hythrun Thieves' Guild will do what they can to retrieve the Harshini's stolen property and return it to its rightful owners."

He rose to his feet and offered the Medalon captain his hand. Fletcher accepted the handshake, but he wasn't done yet. "The Lord Defender had another question for you, Master Lightfinger."

"I'll answer if I can."

"About the demon child."

"You're asking if I know where she is."

Fletcher nodded. "Lord Tenragan seemed to think you had ways of communicating with . . . other immortal creatures who might know how to find her."

"You mean he wants me to ask the demons?"

"Lord Tenragan wasn't specific."

Wrayan smiled at that. "Ah, how difficult it must be for an atheist living in a world populated by gods and immortal beings."

The captain smiled back, as if he were quite aware of the absurdity of his situation. "Nonetheless, can you ask them?"

"I can and I have, Captain, on more than one occasion. I'm sure you appreciate that when given a choice over whom they wish to please—the indescribably powerful only child of their beloved King Lorandranek or a mostly human Hythrun thief who just happens to have enough Harshini blood in him to wield a little magic—they're going to pick R'shiel every time."

"Do you have any clue as to where she might be?"

"No. But if I had to make a guess, I'd say she's out there somewhere, looking for Brak."

"The Halfbreed? But he's been dead for a decade or more."

"R'shiel is likely to consider that merely a minor inconvenience."

"So where do I find her?"

He shrugged. "If I knew I'd be going after her myself, to find out why Damin is still unconscious." He really had no answers for this young man. "I have no idea what she's up to or where she's doing it. But if she's determined enough, she could well be fighting her way through the Seven Hells to find him, even as we speak. I wouldn't pin my hopes on solving this mystery about the stolen lyre on R'shiel appearing in the nick of time to save the day, because even if she did come back, there are other people here who need her more than you do."

ONCE THE MEDALONIAN captain had left, Wrayan sat down, leaned back in his chair, placed his booted feet on the desk, and closed his eyes.

He didn't waste any time wondering where R'shiel might be. She would return in her own good time. He was more interested in trying to recall if he had ever heard anything about a covenant when he was in Sanctuary.

It seemed odd that he hadn't heard something about it, if it was so important. At the very least, the Harshini never lacked for an excuse to celebrate. They had a festival to honor every god in the pantheon. There was no Festival of the Covenant. Not in the two years Wrayan had spent with them. Nobody had breathed a word about a covenant. Not even the Halfbreed.

"You're not going to keep that promise, are you?"

Wrayan opened his eyes to find a young lad standing on the other side of his desk. Fair, tousle-haired, and almost glowing with power, he was dressed in a motley selection of cast-off clothes, although he seemed a little taller, a little better dressed, than Wrayan remembered.

"Divine One. To what do I owe this singular honor?"

The God of Thieves glared at him. "Are you being sarcastic? I'm never sure what sarcastic sounds like, but that might be it."

Wrayan lowered his feet from the desk and sat up straighter in his chair. He should know better than to mock his god. "Of course not, Divine One. I am genuinely honored you have come to visit me. I can't remember the last time you honored me with your presence. Certainly not when I asked for your help a few days ago when I needed help interrogating the man who tried to assassinate the High Prince."

"I've been busy."

Dace didn't even comment on the attack, which was suspicious. At the very least, Damin Wolfblade was a favorite of Zegarnald, the God of War, a god Dacendaran spent an inordinate amount of time trying to best. To hear the protégé of his nemesis was lying at Death's door should have evoked some reaction in the God of Thieves, even if it was only to gloat.

"You haven't been stealing Harshini artifacts from the Citadel, perchance?" Wrayan suggested, wondering if that was why the God of Thieves was not interested in what had happened to Damin Wolfblade. A theft of something truly valuable to the Harshini would empower him more than any other act of honoring.

Little wonder he didn't want Wrayan to help the Medalonians retrieve it.

"I didn't steal the lyre," Dacendaran said. "Nor did any of my followers."

"Doesn't the mere act of stealing something make the thief one of yours?"

"Not in this case."

"So you know who stole it, then?"

"Of course."

"And it's important?"

"More than you could possibly imagine."

Wrayan studied the god for a moment and realized he wasn't imagining things. Dace was all but pulsing with the power this theft had bestowed upon him. "Why don't you want me to find it?"

"Because you will weaken me if you return it."

Wrayan watched his god closely, not sure how Dacendaran's newfound power had changed him. Whatever it had done to him, it probably didn't auger well for the mere mortal sitting on the other side of the desk, appearing disrespectful. "The Harshini want it back, Divine One."

"The Harshini want world peace, too. That's never stopped Zegarnald stirring up a war every time the opportunity arises for a bit of mischief."

"What do you want me to do about it, then?"

"Nothing," Dacendaran said. "Don't look for the lyre. Don't ask about it. It's stolen and it's better for everyone if it stays that way. Besides, the lyre protects itself. You won't find it by looking for it."

"That makes no sense."

"Nevertheless, it's the truth. Was that all you wanted?"

Wrayan nodded—there was really nothing much else he could ask. "Oh . . . what about the Covenant?"

"The Covenant is between the Harshini and the gods. It has nothing to do with mortals. You need to leave that alone, too."

"Do you know where the demon child is?" Perhaps, if Dacendaran weren't willing to help recover the lyre, he'd help them locate R'shiel. It was her deal with Death, apparently, that had placed Damin in the magical coma currently holding the High Prince in thrall.

But Dacendaran simply shrugged. "Not really."

"What do you mean, *not really*? Can't you sense her? Can't you feel her presence from across a continent?"

"Usually."

Gods, Wrayan thought. *This is like pulling teeth.* "Why *usually*? Can't you feel her now?"

"No."

Chilled by the thought R'shiel might have already lost her wager with Death and that Damin was doomed, he asked, "Is she dead?"

Dacendaran shook his head. "I doubt it. We'd all feel that. It's like she's just . . . faded away."

Before Wrayan could ask what that meant, someone knocked on the door. Dace vanished before he had a chance to tell whoever was outside the door to go away.

His visitor didn't wait for permission in any case. The door opened and Willos, the large doorman who stood guard at the entrance to the Thieves' Guild headquarters, opened the door a crack and stuck his head through the gap.

"*What?*"

"That Medalonian lad that was just here."

"What about him?"

"Some thugs have set upon him at the end of the street."

"Is he all right?"

"He seems to be giving a good account of himself."

Wrayan shook his head and cursed softly under his breath. "Why don't you go and help him out?"

"That's what I came to ask, boss. Is it all right for me to—"

"Of course it is, you fool. Go! Help him. Preferably before someone kills him!"

"Serves him right for wearing that ridiculous uniform around the Thieves' Quarter," Willos muttered as he closed the door.

Damn fool Defenders, Wrayan thought. They supposed that wretched uniform of theirs made them impervious to harm. Here in Greenharbour it was liable to have quite the opposite effect.

Still, Caden Fletcher wasn't his problem right now.

He glanced around the office, but Dacendaran had not reappeared, and didn't answer when he called to him.

Wrayan leaned back in his chair again, puzzling over the problem he now faced—not the problem of explaining how the envoy of a foreign government came to be beaten up in the streets of the Thieves' Quarter, but how he was going to find out about this mysterious Covenant and locate the Harshini's stolen lyre without the God of Thieves discovering what he was up to.

And what in all the Seven Hells had the God of Thieves meant when he said the demon child had just faded away?

Chapter

31

THE DAY AFTER Charisee's encounter with Lord Erlon, she woke to find he'd left Warrinhaven, and hardly anybody remembered him being there. By the following day, it seemed nobody could recall him, and by the day after, it was as if he had never been to Warrinhaven at all. Charisee was the only one who remembered the visit of the God of Liars.

Now she was left with the dilemma of what to do about his advice.

The God of Liars told her to make the most of her deception. Only he would say something like that.

The God of Liars and Rakaia, she reminded herself, as she headed off toward the horse paddocks, Broos padding faithfully along beside her. Kiam was in a meeting with a guild courier who'd arrived in the early hours of the morning with a message for him. Lady Saneyah and Lord Rahan were busy with family matters, which left only Broos to keep her company. Not that she minded. The dog was the safest companion she knew.

He could be trusted, at the very least, not to repeat anything Charisee told him.

The grass was damp and lush with the onset of spring, and spongy underfoot as she headed away from the house down to the paddocks where the foals were kept with their mothers. Charisee had never seen a real, live foal. She'd grown up in a walled harem, learned to ride on a bridle path on her sister's horse that was brought into the harem stables, broken and ready to be ridden. The horse breeding, the foals, and even the stallions were kept far away from the harem in the king's stables—a place no resident of the harem ever had the opportunity to visit.

But here in Warrinhaven, surrounded by Lord Rahan's extensive horse stud, it was spring and there were foals everywhere one looked. Until this morning, Charisee had only seen them from a distance. With nobody interested in entertaining her or even checking on her whereabouts, she decided to take the opportunity for a closer look.

Although Broos seemed obedient enough, she wasn't sure enough of his reaction to being close to a foal—a creature not much larger than he was—so she tied one of her scarves around his neck and held him on a loose lead as they walked. Although he'd objected a little when she first tied it on, he seemed accepting of it now, and plodded along quite happily beside her as they headed down between the whitewashed paling fences separating the various paddocks.

At the very least, Charisee wanted to get away from the house. She needed to clear her head. Jakerlon's words about embracing her circumstances still rang in her ears, and had kept her awake at night ever since he'd spoken to her.

Honor me every day by being glad you're living this lie, he said.

What she was doing didn't seem nearly so bad when she thought about it like that. And Jakerlon was right. There was no point in pretending to be Rakaia if she was going to agonize over it every single day, worrying herself into an early grave over the right of it. The deed was done and she could either embrace the opportunity and learn to enjoy it, or confess now and put an end to the charade once and for all.

It seemed a simple choice until she recalled Jakerlon's prediction about what awaited her when she reached Greenharbour.

If you're going to see this through, my pet, you'll want a pleasant picture in your mind to concentrate on when the lecher is having his way with you.

In truth, she realized now, she hadn't thought that far ahead, perhaps because she was unconsciously expecting to be exposed at any minute. Somehow, the idea she could keep up the charade long enough to actually make it to Rakaia's wedding hadn't really occurred to her. When she'd walked into dinner with Kiam and Valorian Lionsclaw in Winternest, pretending she was Rakaia, she certainly hadn't thought past wondering what it was really like to be her sister.

"Is my life really going to be so awful if I marry Lord Branador?" she asked Broos.

The dog looked up at her, tongue hanging out as he walked beside her, but offered no opinion on the subject.

"Am I really going to let some disgusting old man use my body for his pleasure, just so other people will treat me like I'm special?"

When she said it out loud like that, Charisee realized she'd almost be better off as a slave. At least slaves knew their jobs. She wasn't a *court'esa,* so she'd never been expected to provide sexual favors for her mistress, the king, or anybody else in his employ. The harem where she'd spent her entire life was staffed almost exclusively with eunuchs or *loronged court'esa*—male slaves who had survived drinking the vile poison *loronge*, which guaranteed they were sterile.

She hadn't been trained, like Rakaia was, in the arts of pleasing a man, which also included lessons—so her sister had assured her—in how to divert unwanted attention. Charisee knew only what Rakaia had chosen to share with her after her sessions with her own *court'esa*.

Until Jakerlon had pointed it out to her, it had not occurred to Charisee that she lacked the single most significant skill for which the king of Fardohnya's daughters were renowned.

Still fretting about how she was going to get away with pretending she knew anything about pleasing a man on her wedding night, Charisee passed a work gang of slaves, who looked at her oddly as she absently waved to them.

Fool, she told herself, when she realized why they did not return her greeting. Not only did she lack the training to please a lover, but she should know better than to wave to a slave gang fixing the fences.

A princess would have looked straight past them as if she hadn't seen them at all.

That was another problem she was having: it was proving much harder to act like an arrogant member of the ruling class than she'd imagined.

Charisee soon forgot about being arrogant, untrained, or anything like it, however, as she spied several mares grazing beside their new foals in the paddock on her left.

"Broos! Look!"

She ran to the fence, the dog having no choice but to follow, as she dragged him along by his makeshift lead. Two mares grazed beside their foals close by the railing, the closest a piebald filly with a dark patch over one eye. She climbed up onto the bottom rail of the fence to watch, Broos tugging at the lead.

"Oh, Broos! They're so gorgeous!"

The hound didn't share her enthusiasm. He was tugging on the lead, trying to get her to drop it. Charisee tightened her grip and scolded him to be still. The last thing she needed was Broos deciding the foals were prey, jumping over the fence, and deciding to make a meal out of one of them.

She turned back to the foals, her heart almost bursting at the sight of them. They were so sweet. So innocent. She envied the simplicity of their lives, with nothing to do but nurse from their protective mothers and gambol in a sun-kissed meadow . . .

Her moment of tranquility shattered abruptly as Broos started barking.

At the sound, the startled mares and the foals dashed toward the fence on the other side of the enclosure, as far from the noise as they could get.

She jumped down from the fence to better control the dog, and discovered the reason he was so excited. Kiam was heading toward them on foot, striding as if he had a purpose, rather than going for an idle walk, as Charisee had been doing.

As he neared her, she saw the look on his face and knew something was terribly amiss. "Kiam? What's wrong?"

He didn't answer immediately. First, he bent down to pat Broos and take the makeshift lead from her before he spoke. When he looked up, his expression was grim. "I'm sorry, your highness, but we have to stay here in Warrinhaven for a while longer."

They know, she thought, feeling the blood rush from her face as she saw how serious Kiam was. *Somehow they know. That's what the courier came to tell him. Did they find Rakaia? Is she in Greenharbour already, exposing me as a liar?*

"Has . . . has something happened?"

Is this what you call "looking out for me," Jakerlon?

"Someone tried to kill the High Prince."

Charisee had to consciously stop herself from letting out a sigh of relief.

"Wh—who?" she managed to stammer, hoping she seemed shocked at such dreadful news and not relieved that, yet again, she hadn't been exposed as a fraud.

"The messenger didn't say."

"Is Prince Damin all right?"

"He's in a coma. They're not sure when he'll wake."

"Then you must leave now," she said, certain that was what Kiam had come to tell her. "At a time like this your family will need you."

Kiam shook his head. "That would have been my first choice, but Adrina—and the guild—wants me to stay here with you. She's afraid this might be the first wave in an attack against the whole Wolfblade family."

Charisee tried not to appear too pleased about that news either. *Gods! I am the most horrible, horrible person!*

"Then surely you are more of a target than me?"

A thin smile flickered over his face. "It's nice of you to think that, your highness, but really, I think Adrina is worried more about you than me."

Charisee nodded in understanding. Although she hadn't seen Adrina since she was a small child, it was easy enough to figure out her older half-sister's reasoning. This was unlikely to be about a threat to Rakaia the princess so much as the High Princess not wanting to deal with a houseguest in the middle of such a crisis. "Of course. The last thing Adrina needs right now is an irritating younger sister underfoot. Are we to stay here?"

"I've spoken with Lord Rahan," Kiam told her. "His wife isn't too happy about the filthy assassin remaining under her roof, but Cam's an old friend of the Wolfblades. I hope you don't mind the delay."

"I'm the last person anybody should be worrying about at a time like this," she said, mentally kicking herself for sounding like such an idiot before the words were even all the way out of her mouth. That was Charisee the slave, not Rakaia the princess, speaking.

Kiam studied her face for a moment, almost as if he didn't believe her. "How did someone like you manage to come from a viper pit like the Talabar Royal Harem?"

Charisee shrugged because she didn't know how else to answer that question. "Just lucky, I guess."

Kiam considered her in silence for a moment, his expression impossible to read.

Is he looking at me like that because he likes me, or because he can tell I'm a fraud?

"There was one other thing. Lady Saneyah wants to know if there is anything you need, now that you're staying longer? She's happy to give you your own handmaiden while you're here, but she wanted to know if she needs to provide you with . . . anything else?"

"Like what?" She couldn't imagine what he was asking her. And he *was* asking her something, she realized. Something she didn't understand.

"Ah . . . I think her ladyship wants to know if she needs to arrange your own *court'esa* for you. She doesn't keep her own anymore, so I gather it's going to be something of an inconvenience to find a suitable one out here in the country on short notice, but she did offer."

Say yes, the sane voice in Charisee's head yelled silently, feeling an even bigger fool for not understanding what Kiam had been hinting at.

Here's your chance. Tell Lady Saneyah you insist she provide a loronged court'esa for your entertainment and then make him teach you everything you need to know—every skill Rakaia spent the last four years perfecting—before you get to Greenharbour.

Get him to show you how to make Lord Branador not want you.

"Aren't you *court'esa* trained?"

As soon as she uttered the words, Charisee felt her face go red. She wanted to die. Even if she hadn't just blurted the question out like a stupid slave girl, Kiam was a member of the High Prince's family. He was probably so insulted that she'd implied his position was equivalent to a slave's he would never speak to her again.

"I'm sorry . . . ," she said, shaking her head, as if that could somehow undo the damage. "I didn't mean to imply . . . I mean . . . it's not that I thought . . . I know you're a free man. Your stepbrother is the High Prince. You're a guild assassin. I really didn't mean to insult—"

"I'm not insulted."

She risked looking up at him, terrified of what she might see, but he was smiling faintly, looking at her as if he could see right through every one of her many, many lies.

And then he reached out and brushed the loose hair from the side of her face. "Actually, I'm kind of flattered."

His touch was electric, but Charisee didn't believe him for a moment. He was toying with her. Letting her dig herself in deeper and deeper until she was so far down this hole of embarrassment and offense that she'd need a rope to climb out of it. "But . . . I just suggested you were a whore."

He shrugged. "In my line of work I've been called far worse, your highness."

"I really didn't mean . . ."

"That you want to sleep with me?" he said, lowering his hand. He smiled. It was a small, intimate smile, the sort of smile one reserved for a lover, not a princess one was supposed to be guarding as a duty. "Pity, your highness. I thought that was exactly what you meant."

Rakaia would have slapped him, Charisee knew. She'd have some witty rejoinder that would cut this well-connected assassin down to size and walk away with her dignity intact.

All Charisee could do was try not to look like a fool and wonder what it would be like if Kiam kissed her. Wonder if the God of Liars was right. Wonder how she was going to survive the next few months when she couldn't even handle a simple question about how she'd like to entertain herself during this unexpected delay in their journey.

I should just confess now, and get it over with.

But she didn't. Almost as if Jakerlon had taken possession of her, she smiled up at the assassin just the way Rakaia would have done and stepped a little closer to him. "Well, you did say my wish was your command."

His gaze was fixed on her with an intensity that made her want to melt. "I did say that, didn't I?"

"And I wouldn't want to put Lady Saneyah to any trouble."

There was a moment, Charisee knew, where he was telling himself to step away. She could see it in his eyes—that fleeting moment of caution—but it only lasted a moment and then his mouth was moving slowly toward hers.

Charisee closed her eyes and raised her face to him. *I'm honoring Jakerlon*, she told herself. *He said I should embrace my lies . . .*

She could feel the warmth of his breath on her cheek, the anticipation almost making her heart stop—

Only to have it skip a beat completely when Broos barked loudly at them, impatient with being made to sit on a lead, with so many interesting things to chase so close at hand.

Charisee squealed with fright as she jumped back and then burst out laughing in her awkwardness.

Kiam grinned at her and tugged on the lead to silence the dog. Their moment was lost, however, and would probably never return. He glanced around. They were alone but for the distant slave crew mending the fences. As he turned back to her, she thought he seemed more than a little disappointed, but that might be just her own regret reflected in his eyes.

"Perhaps I should head back to the house," he suggested, his voice unaccountably raw.

"That might be wise," she agreed. Whatever Kiam was feeling, her frustration was a palpable thing.

But then he added in a toneless voice that filled her with hope. "Shall I tell Lady Saneyah you have no need for any . . . additional . . . companionship?"

She searched his face, looking for the answer. "If you think I can find . . . other ways to kill the time, then I suppose . . ."

Kiam took her hand then, and lifted it to his mouth, placing a lingering kiss on her palm. "Your wish is my command, your highness."

Charisee couldn't think of anything intelligent to say because all her concentration was required to keep her weak knees from folding underneath her.

He never gave her the opportunity to spoil the moment, in any case. Without waiting for her to reply, the assassin turned and strode off toward the distant house, Broos still on the lead beside him, leaving Charisee clinging to the fence for support, wondering how it was possible to be so terrified and so excited about what her future might hold, all at the same time.

32

MICA WOKE SCREAMING almost every night from his nightmares.

Rakaia discovered this disturbing fact the first night of their journey after leaving Vanahiem. Until then, Rakaia had always been in the company of the other members of the minstrel's troupe and she was never close enough to him at night to hear him crying out. But once they boarded the barge for Bordertown, and Rakaia found herself in the next cabin, it was impossible to ignore his tortured slumber.

By day, Mica was charming, amusing, and endlessly entertaining. He couldn't seem to help himself. Without being asked, as the barge sailed south with the current on the broad silver river that cut Medalon almost in two, he entertained the crew and the other passengers—a sour Blue Sister from the Citadel named Delana and an elderly couple from Brodenvale on the way to visit their daughter in Bordertown—with songs and jokes and clumsy magic tricks that didn't work almost as often as they did, although he bungled his attempts at magic tricks so good-naturedly, Rakaia wondered if it was all part of the act. Nobody seemed to mind. Mica was the sort of person you just naturally fell in love with, and Rakaia was no more immune to his charms than anybody else on the boat.

But at night, through the thin walls of the barge's cabins below decks, his songs became cries of torment.

Two nights of Mica's pain were all she could take. On the third night, as soon as Rakaia heard him cry out, she slipped from her narrow bunk and felt her way through the darkness to the door.

"Are you going to him?" a weary voice asked from the other bunk. She was sharing her cabin with the Sister of the Blade, a dour, middle-aged woman who seemed to mightily resent how far her order had fallen this past decade, and who'd made little attempt to socialize with her cabin-inmate.

"I didn't meant to disturb you," Rakaia whispered apologetically, as another agonized cry rent the quiet night.

"It's that racket he's making that's disturbing me," Delana grumbled. "Probably disturbing everyone in a five-mile radius."

"I'll quiet him down," she promised, with no real idea how she might do anything of the sort.

"Stay with him," Delana advised. "The boy sounds like he needs a hug. At the very least," she added, as she turned to face the wall, "you'll be close enough to smother him with a pillow if he doesn't shut up."

Rakaia figured Delana wasn't expecting a response. She unlatched the door, closing it softly behind her, and made her way along the companionway to the master's cabin in the stern, which Mica had somehow managed to sing the captain into surrendering.

She opened it and poked her head through the doorway, not sure if Mica would welcome her visit or send her away.

"Mica?"

The only answer was a mumbled cry from the bunk. His words seemed to be gibberish and she wasn't even sure if Mica was answering her or still lost in his nightmare.

She slipped into the cabin and closed the door behind her. In the moonlight coming from the window in the stern, she could just make out Mica's sleeping form on the bunk. The cabin was about twice the size of the one she was sharing with Delana. So was the bunk.

"No! Don't leave me here alone!" Mica cried out suddenly, sitting bolt upright.

Rakaia hurried to his side. "Mica? Wake up! You're dreaming."

He turned to stare at her, but his eyes were blank and she realized he was probably still asleep.

"Mica?" With some trepidation, she placed her hands on his shoulders and shook him gently, not sure of the etiquette for waking someone caught in a nightmare. Should you wake them at all? Was it better just to let the dream run its course?

But then he blinked and the blankness faded from his eyes and he seemed to become aware of his surroundings.

"Mica?" she asked gently. "Are you all right?"

"Um . . . I suppose . . ."

"Do you know where you are?"

He nodded, glancing around. "On a boat."

"That's right. We're heading for Bordertown."

He was silent for a moment and then he cocked his head slightly. "Why aren't we moving?"

"We're docked for the night. Remember what the captain said? Nobody in their right mind sails the Glass River in the dark."

"I remember," he said. "Is something wrong? Why are you here?"

"You were having a nightmare."

He didn't seem surprised. Perhaps Olena or Norn had heard him cry out before and said something to him when they were in his company.

"Did I wake you?"

She smiled in the darkness. "I think you woke everyone between here and the Trinity Isles."

"What was I yelling about?"

"The only words I understood were 'don't leave me here alone,'" she told him, taking a seat on the edge of the bunk. The master's cabin had quite a large window. Even with no light, the moonlight outside was sufficient, once her eyes adjusted to the darkness, for her to see the tears on his cheeks and the pain her words evoked in his eyes.

"I'm sorry I woke you."

"Do you remember what you were dreaming about?"

He shook his head, wiping his eyes. "No."

Liar, she thought, but didn't press the matter. She understood he might not want to talk about it.

"You should try to go back to sleep." She rose to her feet, wondering if it was a good idea to leave him alone.

Mica grabbed her hand before she could move away from the bunk. "Will you stay with me?"

Rakaia hesitated, not sure if that was advisable. She'd known Mica for barely a month. She wasn't sure how he'd interpret her agreeing to spend the night with him, however innocently. "Are you sure?"

"The nightmares only happen when I'm alone."

She debated the wisdom of agreeing for a moment and then thought of the others on the boat. If he kept up yelling out like this every night, the captain might simply refuse to take them any farther and then she'd never get back to Fardohnya. "Move over, then," she instructed with a sigh.

Mica threw back the covers and pushed himself back against the wall to give her room. She climbed in beside him, the two of them barely fitting side by side on the captain's bunk. He threw the blanket over her once she was lying beside him and then somehow managed to work his head under her arm until she was holding him like a mother holding a frightened child with his head resting on her breast.

She stiffened a little with the intimacy of their embrace, but she could feel Mica relaxing beside her so she held him in silence for a while, while he clung to her like a small child, as if her very presence could drive his demons away.

"Will you sing to me?" she asked, to relieve the uncomfortable silence as much as a desire to hear him sing.

"No."

"Why not?"

He lifted his head and looked up at her, his eyes glistening in the moonlight. "Because you like me."

"Everybody likes you, Mica."

"Everybody likes my *singing*," he corrected, in a small voice that almost broke her heart. "You're the first person I've met since I came back who likes me because I'm me." He settled his head on her breast again and said nothing more.

Rakaia didn't know what to say to that, but in the end, she didn't need to say anything. Before long Mica's breathing slowed and deepened and she knew he was asleep.

Rakaia stayed like that for the rest of the night, keeping his nightmares at bay simply by her presence, until she fell asleep too, comforted by the unusual experience of being needed for herself and not her value as one of the king of Fardohnya's daughters.

Her last thought before she fell asleep was yet another unanswered question about Mica. He'd told her, before he fell asleep, *You're the first person I've met since I came back who likes me because I'm me.*

The question Rakaia wondered about was, *Back from where?*

Chapter

>─┤◆├─◇─┤◈├─┤◈├─◇─┤◆├─<

33

THE RAVEN OF the Talabar Assassins' Guild was a small, nondescript man with a balding pate and the unassuming air of a servant. Arguably among the most powerful men in Fardohnya, one would never know to look at him. One's eyes might slide straight past him and not notice him at all, Naveen thought as he was led into the Raven's presence.

He was also not the same Raven who'd been in charge the last time Naveen had anything to do with the guild. Perhaps the rumors of trouble in the ranks, or rather the leadership of the guild, had some truth to them.

They were meeting on the Raven's turf, something Naveen abhorred the necessity for. He was well aware that much of his power came from the fact that any edicts he delivered on behalf of the king seemed so much more authoritative when they were delivered from a palace. But he could not invite the Raven of the Assassins' Guild to the palace, and even if he had, the Raven would have refused the invitation.

The Assassins' Guild prided itself on its political neutrality.

Naveen had come in disguise to this warehouse in the weaving district of Talabar, where the sour smell of felting wool hung in the air and the constant clickety-clack of weavers' looms in almost every street played like a never-ending symphony in the background. He was led through a maze of stacked wool bales by a silent young woman, his eyes slowly adjusting to the darkness as he was taken further into the building, until they finally reached a clearing in the bales where the Raven sat at a small wooden table with a three-legged stool waiting on the other side.

"I thought the Raven was a woman," Naveen said, after studying the balding little man for a time.

"I thought the great Naveen Raveve was a man," the Raven responded. "That wig looks ridiculous, you know."

Naveen snatched the dark wig from his head, glad of an excuse to be rid of the wretched, itchy thing. "I am well known in the city," he explained, stuffing the wig into the pocket of his homespun and equally itchy trousers. "I thought it prudent not to announce we are doing business together."

"It remains to be seen if we *are* doing business together," the Raven said, indicating Naveen should sit on the stool. Then he looked up at the young woman who had escorted his guest. "Wait outside. I'll call you when it's time to take him back."

The girl bowed without saying anything and retreated into the darkness, leaving Naveen alone with the assassin in the small pool of yellow light cast by the single lantern on the table beside the Raven.

Naveen took the offered seat and studied his adversary for a moment. The man looked so harmless, it was hard to believe he had the balls to squash a fly, let alone take a man's life.

They sat in silence for a long moment, each one waiting for the other to speak. It was a game, Naveen knew, and the loser was the one who broke first. He was good at the game—very good at it—but he was also acutely aware of not being gone from the palace for a second longer that he had to. His absence would be noted and things that were noted in the palace invariably meant questions he would rather were not asked in the first place.

"I have a job for the guild," he announced, deciding to act as if he didn't even know the game existed. "One that will require a modicum of delicacy."

"We don't do royalty," the Raven stated flatly. "You know that."

"The . . . target . . . in this case is not royal. In fact, that is rather the issue. The target has been posing as someone of royal blood, accepting all the wealth, rights, and privileges that go with such an elevated station under false pretenses. My king . . . *our* king . . . wishes to have this situation . . . remedied."

"Why doesn't Hablet just denounce the imposter and have him executed for treason?" the Raven asked. "After all, he is, you know, the *king.*"

Naveen shrugged. "The imposter has managed to ingratiate themselves into the royal family in such a way that publicly denouncing them would have unfortunate political ramifications the king would rather avoid."

The Raven smiled, revealing a row of surprisingly well-fitted wooden teeth. "Gods . . . he wants one of his daughters killed."

Actually, he wants all of them killed, Naveen was tempted to reply, but that wasn't a job he could outsource to the Assassins' Guild. He would have to take care of the bulk of the harem deaths himself. Rakaia, however, was in Hythria and effectively out of his reach. For that he needed the Assassins' Guild.

"The imposter in question is . . . well, yes . . . posing as one of his daughters."

"Which one?"

"Rakaia."

"The one Hablet just married off to the Hythrun border lord? No wonder he doesn't want to denounce her publicly."

"I'm glad you appreciate the political delicacy of the situation."

"Political delicacy is expensive," the Raven said.

"I expected as much," he said, resisting the urge to mop the sweat from his brow in this stifling, closed-in place. "The king would like the imposter's death to appear accidental. An obvious assassination will raise questions better left unasked."

"That will cost more."

"I know."

"Do we have a deadline—no pun intended?"

"It must happen after her wedding but before she can give birth to an heir. Too soon after the ceremony might be suspicious, but certainly before the end of next winter."

The Raven frowned. "Then it will have to happen in Hythria. That means involving Elin Bane and the Hythrun guild."

"I suspected as much."

"They're even more expensive than we are."

"Of course they are," Naveen said, making no attempt to disguise the sarcasm in his voice. "Will you take the job?"

"Yes."

"How much?"

"Ten thousand gold rivets."

Naveen could feel the blood draining from his face. "I could buy one of the Trinity Isles for that."

"I don't doubt it," the Raven agreed. "But you're not asking for anything nearly so simple. You want us to kill a young bride everyone believes is the daughter of the Fardohnyan king in a foreign country, make it look like an accident, and I'm guessing in a way that does nothing to jeopardize any concessions Hablet gained for access to Highcastle Pass as part of her dowry agreement. When you look it at like that, Lord Raveve, ten thousand is a bargain."

"Is the price negotiable?"

"No," the Raven stated flatly. "It may even go up, depending on what the Hythrun guild wants for their services."

Naveen rose to his feet, certain the Raven would use that excuse to inflate the cost of this assassination even more. "I'll have the deposit sent to you in the usual fashion."

The Raven looked up at him, shaking his head. "No. This will require payment in full up front."

"That's not how you usually do business."

"It is in this case."

Naveen debated arguing the point. After all, no self-respecting Talabar merchant accepted any price without some sort of haggling. But something about the set of the Raven's shoulders warned him the man wasn't lying when he said the price was not negotiable.

"If the job is not done exactly as required, the king will expect a full refund," he warned, aware of what a hollow threat that was to someone like the Raven of the Assassins' Guild.

The Raven smiled. He knew it was a hollow threat, too.

"You tell his highness we're taking care of it," he said. "Our work is always guaranteed."

"It had better be," Naveen warned. He turned on his heel, intending to make a dramatic exit, until he realized he had no way of finding his way out of this stinking maze of wool bales in the darkness. He took a deep breath and turned back to the Raven, wishing he could snuff the little worm out for the smug smile he was wearing. "Please call my escort. I have more important things to be doing."

"I'm sure you do," the Raven replied with a knowing smile, and then yelled for the girl so loudly, it made him jump. *"Lilleh!"*

The girl appeared out of the darkness a moment later and looked to the Raven for her instructions. She still hadn't uttered a word.

"Show our illustrious visitor out, would you, pet? He has important things to be doing."

The girl nodded and pointed to a gap in the bales, obviously expecting Naveen to follow.

"Master Raven," he said with a short bow as he pulled the wig from his pocket and positioned it back on his head. Then he turned to follow the young woman into the darkness, silently cursing the exorbitant cost of this contract, but relieved at least one important task his king had charged him with was taken care of.

Now he just had to figure out how he was going to dispose of the rest of Hablet's unwanted wives and daughters.

Naveen sighed, keenly feeling the burdens he carried on behalf of his king.

"It's hard, sometimes, being King Hablet's most trusted aide, you know," he told his silent escort. "Some days, I swear, it seems like my work will never be done."

The girl glanced over her shoulder at him with an odd expression, but she made no comment, offered no sympathy for his plight. She just turned back to leading him out of the warehouse, vanishing into the night as soon as they stepped outside.

Chapter

34

CHARISEE USED THE excuse of returning Broos to his rightful owner to visit Kiam's room. The hall was dark, lit only by the moonlight checkering the patterned hall runner with light from the large window at the end of the hall. The rest of the house was asleep and far out of earshot from the guest wing. She led the dog along the hall, glancing over her shoulder to ensure there was nobody else about, although she had her story prepared if anybody challenged her right to be wandering Warrinhaven Palace in the middle of the night, dressed in nothing more than her nightgown.

The halls were deserted. She wasn't challenged. Her carefully prepared excuses were unnecessary. As she reached Kiam's door, rehearsing the conversation she planned to have in her head with him, Jakerlon's words kept interrupting her thoughts.

"You are the most wonderful type of liar there is," he'd told her, *"because the person you lie to most often is yourself."*

She knew she was lying to herself. She knew Broos didn't need to be escorted back to Kiam's room. But somehow, it seemed less dishonest to pretend she had a reason to visit him other than a selfish concern for her very survival.

That was the other lie she was telling herself—that she was only here at Kiam's door in the middle of the night because of the danger she would be in on her—or rather Rakaia's—wedding night.

Her hand shaking with a mixture of fear and anticipation, Charisee glanced up and down the hall once more and then forced herself to knock on Kiam's door. A few moments later it opened to reveal the assassin wearing only his trousers, barefoot and obviously fresh from bathing. He had the broad shoulders and narrow hips of a fighter, Charisee noted, as she consciously forced her gaze upward to look him in the eye.

"I brought Broos back for you."

"Is he giving you trouble, your highness?" His eyes were gray—like a stormy winter sky. She'd never been so acutely aware of that before. He was looking at her as if he knew exactly what she was doing here, but was going to make her go through the charade of pretending he didn't have a clue.

"Not really . . . Can I come in for a moment?"

He stood back to let her enter. "Are you sure?"

She nodded and stepped across the threshold, waiting until he closed the door behind her before she said anything more. Broos bounded over to the bed and claimed it by stretching out across it sideways, leaving no room for any human occupants.

Charisee smiled at his antics, and then turned to Kiam. He was studying her curiously, waiting for her to explain the reason for this late-night visit.

"I need your help," she said, walking a little further into the room, as if putting some distance between her and the assassin would make this easier. She had to tell Kiam at least a version of the truth if she hoped to merely survive her wedding night. That was another thing Jakerlon had taught her, words now branded in her brain: *the best lies of all are the stone-cold truth.*

"I think we've already established that your wish is my command, your highness," he said with a wry smile.

"What I said earlier today . . . about not wanting a *court'esa* . . ."

Kiam remained standing by the door, his hands behind him on the latch. Charisee tried not to look at him, finding his bare chest more of a distraction than she would like.

"I remember."

So did Charisee. She could feel her face growing warm at the memory.

"I said I didn't want one because . . ." *Take a deep breath, Charisee. You can do this.* "Because I've never been with one. A *court'esa*, I mean."

Kiam seemed puzzled by her confession. "What do you mean?"

"I mean I'm not *court'esa* trained. I don't know the first thing about sex or men or how to make a husband happy."

"You're still a virgin?" Kiam sounded genuinely shocked at the idea. "How is that possible?"

She shrugged, not able to meet his eye. "I just never . . . I mean there were plenty of *court'esa* in the harem, but my father has so many other daughters I didn't expect I'd ever be married. I expected to spend my entire life there . . ."

The best lies of all are the stone-cold truth.

"I guess I wanted to wait until I found someone . . . special. Someone I . . ."

"Loved?" he asked. There was a smile in his voice, but Charisee was too afraid to meet his eye to find out if he was amused, or mocking her naïveté.

"I must seem like such a romantic fool."

She looked up in time to see him nodding. "I think it's a very sweet ambition, actually. Certifiably insane, perhaps, but kind of sweet."

"Then you'll help me?"

"To do what, exactly?"

"Show me everything a *court'esa* would teach me."

To his credit, Kiam didn't even flinch at the suggestion. "Lady Saneyah has already offered you a *court'esa* to do exactly that, your highness, although I fear you've left your run a bit late. If you want to know everything a *court'esa* can teach you about the human body, you should have started taking lessons in this sort of thing years ago."

She shook her head, certain it was the worst thing she should do. "Any *court'esa* employed by Lady Saneyah will report back to her. I'd rather my . . . inexperience . . . remained a secret."

"And you think you can trust *me* to show you the ropes? You do remember what I do for a living, don't you, your highness?"

She nodded. "In spite of your profession, Kiam, I believe you are a man of honor."

"You don't know anything of the kind about me."

"You have been nothing but honorable the whole time I have been in your care."

He seemed amused by her reasoning. "My stepbrother is the High Prince of Hythria. He would flay me alive if I merely contemplated the thought of doing anything else. You shouldn't mistake pragmatism for honor, your highness."

She squared her shoulders gamely and finally looked up at him, trying to figure out if this was the smartest thing she'd done since becoming Rakaia, or the stupidest. "Nevertheless, I believe I am a sufficiently good judge of character to risk asking you to aid me." Another lie. Charisee was an appallingly bad judge of character. She hadn't seen Rakaia's escape coming, or suspected Princess Sophany of being an adulteress, or even the urbane Lord Erlon of being the God of Liars.

If her future relied on her ability to see the true character of others, she was in dire straits indeed.

Kiam took a step closer to her. Charisee held her ground. She didn't know what he would do. He might help her—gods, how she wanted that more than anything. But he might just as easily take advantage of her and then betray her to Adrina. It was her royal half-sister who had commissioned this man to guard her, after all, and when he spoke of Adrina he did so with fond familiarity, suggesting their relationship was far from simply that of distant relatives who only meet a few times a year at formal family gatherings.

He reached out, gently moving a stray strand of hair from her face as he had done down by the foals. Her skin burned where he touched her, raising goosebumps along her bare arms.

"Exactly what do you want me to teach you, your highness?"

"Every . . . everything, I suppose."

"That might take a while."

"Do you have anything better to do?"

Kiam smiled at her, and took her hands in his. "You're trembling."

"It's cold in here."

"No it's not. What are you frightened of?"

The best lies of all are the stone-cold truth.

Charisee took a deep breath. "I'm frightened of what will happen when Lord Branador finds out I don't know the first thing about how to entertain him in the bedroom," she said, the words tumbling out of her before she could stop them. "I'm frightened my first time is going to be horrible and painful at the hands of a lecher old enough to be my great-grandfather. I'm frightened because I don't know how to make him not want me. I'm frightened that when I'm lying in his bed, night after night, doing my duty for king and country, I won't have any pleasant memories to get me through it." She was crying by the time she got it all off her chest. Every world of it was true. She was a slave. *Court'esa* were only available for the high-born, not their servants. All she knew about sex came from what Rakaia had told her about her lessons. Charisee was a fool, and an innocent one at that, but when she tried to turn away, Kiam gathered her into his arms and held her while she sobbed.

He didn't say anything, just let her cry, until she pushed him away and sniffed inelegantly. "I'm sorry. I should never have come here and asked this of you. I should go."

In response, Kiam bent his head to hers and kissed her.

Charisee's knees almost buckled. It was as if the room were suddenly devoid of air. She closed her eyes and slipped her arms around his neck, reveling in the glory of it. For a moment he held her in his arms, his broad bare chest pressed against her, his warm firm lips covering hers, kissing her the way no trained *court'esa* would ever dare kiss his mistress . . .

And then he broke away. With a great deal of reluctance, he pushed her away from him and held her at arms' length.

"I'm sorry," he said, his voice ragged.

Why is he apologizing? Did I do it wrong? "I'll get better with practice."

That made him smile. "I'm sure you will."

"Do we need to start with something else?"

He shook his head. "We're not starting with anything, your highness. I can't play this game with you."

"But . . . you said you'd help me."

"Not with this, your highness. I'm sure you're bored here and need some sort of distraction, but I made a promise to your sister to see you safely to Greenharbour. She was quite specific about where my duties began and ended."

For a moment Charisee was so surprised to learn Adrina might have warned Kiam off Rakaia, she almost forgot herself. "Why would Adrina do that? She doesn't know anything about Rakaia."

"She knows what it is to grow up in the Talabar harem," he said, dropping his hands to his side. "And I have to say, you're very good."

"Good? Good at what?"

He walked to door and held it open for her. "This whole innocent ingénue routine you have going here. It's flawless. Real tears and all. If I didn't know who you are, your highness, and where you come from, I'd believe every word of it."

Gods, Charisee thought with despair. *He thinks I'm playing some sort of stupid game.*

This Hythrun apparently couldn't imagine any daughter of Hablet's would be allowed out of the harem without the full benefit of expert *court'esa* training.

And he was right. Hablet would never have permitted it.

Charisee burned with the humiliation of her error in thinking Kiam would believe her. Or help her.

Or that she had so badly wanted him to.

She also realized, with a sinking feeling in the pit of her belly, that even truth wouldn't help her now. Even if she confessed every sordid little detail about the deception she and Rakaia had pulled in switching identities, Kiam would think she was playing yet another game.

With nothing left but the need to escape with what little shred of dignity she had left, Charisee wiped away her tears and smiled at him. "Worth a try, though, don't you think?"

He smiled at her, so certain he was right. Charisee could feel her heart shattering into little shards so small and sharp they were actually painful.

"Worth a try," he said, opening the door for her. "Goodnight, your highness."

With her head held high, she walked to the door, waiting for him to stop her, waiting for him to pull her into his arms and tell her he was only teasing, and that of course he would make love to her.

But he didn't move. Didn't say another word as she stepped past him.

Not until she was out in the hall did he softly call, "Rakaia."

He'd never called her by name before, and for a moment she didn't react, momentarily forgetting it was now her name.

"What?" she asked, looking over her shoulder at him, when she realized he was addressing her.

"If you weren't you, and I weren't me . . ."

She nodded. "I understand."

"Goodnight, your highness."

"Goodnight, Master Miar."

With all the strength she could muster, Charisee walked back toward her own room at the other end of the hall, feeling Kiam's eyes on her the whole way.

It wasn't until she was alone in her room, the door firmly locked, that she was free to throw herself on to her bed and punch the pillow angrily, over and over, cursing herself for being such a fool.

And cursing the God of Liars for putting ideas in her head, which angered her even more as she discovered how solidly her lie had become her truth.

There was no way out of this now, short of death.

238 · Jennifer Fallon

Or Rakaia returning to denounce her.

The bitter irony of her situation was made even worse by the realization that because Kiam was a commoner and an assassin, he would never be permitted to become the consort of a princess. Had he known who she really was, there would be no social impediment to taking a lover who was a slave and a bastard of the Fardohnyan king.

I hate you, Rakaia.

RAKAIA SLEPT WITH Mica every night as they sailed southwest toward Bordertown, after the first night she'd tried to relieve his nightmares. They did nothing else. Mica made no attempt to molest her or otherwise take advantage of her proximity. He simply cuddled into her on the captain's narrow bunk, laid his head on her breast, and slept peacefully for the first time—she suspected—in years.

The effect on him was remarkable. With no nightmares disturbing his sleep, Mica bounded through each day, full of energy and purpose. He delighted in their journey. He even clambered up the mast once and sang at the top of his voice from the apex. At every opportunity, he entertained the other passengers with funny songs he seemed to make up on the spot. He serenaded the crew with dirty ditties that had them laughing as they worked. Each evening when they anchored near the riverbank for the night, if the weather was fine, they gathered on the deck. Mica would pull out his battered old lyre after their evening meal and sing haunting songs of loneliness and a far distant home that brought a tear to everyone's eye. Rakaia even caught Delana, the humorless Sister of the Blade, wiping her eyes on more than one occasion as Mica's last, melancholy note faded into the night.

Rakaia couldn't remember a time in her life when she'd been so happy.

The politics of the Talabar Royal Harem were far behind her. She no longer listened for noises in the night, wondering if it meant someone was coming for her or her mother. She hadn't spared Charisee a thought in days. It was liberating, not being a princess. There was no rank on the boat other than passenger or crew, all lorded over like a benign dictator by the captain of the *Maera's Daughter*, a brusque, white-haired Fardohnyan named Drendik.

The crew knew she was Fardohnyan, but seemed to have no curiosity about where exactly in Fardohnya she came from. She supposed they were used to carrying all sorts of passengers up and down the river. It really wasn't their job to inquire into their passengers' lives or business. They assumed she was Mica's wife—or at the very least, his lover—and when Mica did nothing to disabuse them of their assumptions, Rakaia decided to play along. As disguises went, there probably wasn't a much better one for a runaway princess than to be thought of as the wife of a penniless traveling troubadour.

They reached Bordertown some ten days after they sailed from Vana-hiem. By then Rakaia was firmly entrenched as Aja, the Fardohnyan wife of the young Karien minstrel, who had entertained them so willingly on their journey. They left the boat, waving to the crew as they stepped down the gangplank, shouldered their few belongings, and headed into the town to find an inn prepared to trade a meal and a bed for the night, in return for the entertainment Mica could offer.

The Bordertown docks were huge and busy and quite frightening for a girl raised in the sheltered world of a royal harem. She slipped her hand into Mica's as they pushed and shoved their way along the wharves for fear of losing him in the crush. There must have been a score of boats tied up, in various stages of loading or unloading, both river craft and sea-going vessels. The air reeked of fish and was filled with so much yelling, haggling, and cursing that Rakaia had to shout at Mica to be heard when she asked if he knew where they were going.

Nominally located in Medalon, the town—although it was large enough to be called a small city these days—sat close to the northern border of Hythria, the western border of Medalon and the southern border of Karien. The population was an almost equal mix of the three national-ities, along with a large contingent of Fardohnyans who sailed their goods to Bordertown, where they were either loaded into river barges for their journey into Medalon, freighted south into Krakandar by caravan, or loaded onto seagoing vessels destined for Yarnarrow in the north.

Rakaia and Mica were almost to the end of the docks when a line of smart red-coated Defenders halted them, marching in perfect unison toward the docks under the command of a mounted officer, and quite a few other mounted dignitaries, including one man wearing a long green robe and a large medallion on a heavy silver chain that marked him as the town's mayor. They stopped to watch the troops march by, impressed by their discipline and precision. Fardohnyan troops weren't quite so sharp or so well dressed, Rakaia thought, although she couldn't say for certain. She'd only ever stood on the walls of the harem and watched them pa-rade from a distance.

"Where do you suppose they're headed?" she asked Mica as they waited for the road to clear.

Mica grinned. "The docks."

She punched his arm. "You know what I mean."

Still grinning, Mica shrugged. "Maybe they've gone to arrest someone. Maybe, since the mayor is coming along, somebody special is arriving." He turned and looked back the way they'd come. The crowd was falling away from them, moving back toward the river, following in the wake of the smartly turned out soldiers. Unable to see over the heads of the crowd, Mica climbed up onto the half-loaded bed of a nearby wagon to find out what all the excitement was about.

After a moment, he bent down and offered Rakaia his hand. "Here. Come see."

She let him pull her up to the wagon bed, which afforded them a clear view over the crowd to the river beyond. The Defenders had spread out to clear one of the wharves and lined the dock to ensure a clear path to the road. Out on the river, a ship was approaching. It was a huge seagoing sailing ship, being towed toward the wharf by two oared tugs, each manned by a dozen or more brawny, dark-skinned men who looked to come from the Trinity Isles or even somewhere further south, like Denika.

She studied the ship for a moment, feeling the blood drain from her face.

She knew that ship. On one of the rare occasions she had been allowed out of the harem, she had sailed the Talabar harbor on it.

"We have to go," she told Mica, jumping to the ground.

"What's the hurry?" he asked, looking down at her with a puzzled expression. "Don't you want to find out whose ship that is?"

"I know whose ship that is," she told him. "And I'm leaving. Now. You can come with me or not."

Without waiting to see if he was following, she shouldered her pack and headed away from the wharves, feeling ill to the pit of her stomach.

A moment later, Mica caught up with her. "What's the matter?"

"Nothing."

"Whose ship is it?"

"It doesn't matter."

"You said you knew," he said, not willing to drop the subject. He skipped ahead and planted himself in front of her. "It's Fardohnyan, isn't it?"

"You could tell that from the flags," she said, pushing past him.

"Is it someone you know?" he called after her.

"Of course not."

He skipped ahead again, and stopped her with a wide grin on his face. "I think you do. I think you know whose ship that is and you want to avoid him."

"That's very clever of you, Mica. Get out of my way."

His grin faded. "Has he hurt you in some way, Aja? I can take care of him for you if he has."

"He hasn't hurt me, Mica. It's not what you think. I'm just tired, and hot, and you said we'd find somewhere to sleep that's not rocking as soon as we got to Bordertown. I've had enough of the Glass River and I don't care who else is sailing on it. Can we just go? Now? While all the crowds are down at the docks?"

He studied her curiously for a moment and then nodded. "On one condition."

"What?" she asked in exasperation, aware that every moment they lingered, the ship was getting closer to the dock.

"Tell me who is on that boat."

Rakaia debated arguing the point, and then she shrugged in defeat. He wasn't going to let this go until she answered him. "The ship is called *Wind Dancer*. It's the royal Fardohnyan flagship," she told him with a sigh.

"What's a flagship?"

"It's the king's own ship, Mica," she explained.

"Then king of Fardohnya is on that ship?"

"More than likely."

Mica stared at her for a time and then took her hand. "Come on, then, we need to get some supplies."

She almost stumbled, he jerked her forward so unexpectedly. "Supplies? What supplies?"

"We need to change your hair color," he told her as he hurried her along the road toward the large central marketplace. "Maybe even cut it shorter."

"What . . . why would I do that?"

He stopped and looked at her. "Because you don't want to be found by the king of Fardohnya."

Rakaia didn't know what to say. She didn't know whether to be alarmed or relieved that Mica had so easily figured out her secret. At the very least, even if she hadn't just given most of it away, he suspected enough of the truth to want to help her hide.

Impulsively, she leaned forward and kissed him. "I just love you sometimes."

He beamed at her. "One day, you'll love me all the time."

His grin was infectious. It made everything seem like a grand adventure. She laughed as he pulled her forward again, no longer afraid, but rather exhilarated by the thought that Hablet was approaching Bordertown with no idea the daughter he thought was on her way to Greenharbour was in the same town, traveling with an itinerant troubadour, and having the time of her life.

36

ADRINA TOOK TO hearing petitioners in the main hall of the Green-harbour Palace. Usually reserved for receptions and balls of the grandest kind, the hall was lit by sixteen massive chandeliers made—ironically, Adrina always thought—from Fardohnyan crystal. The chandeliers were not lit during the day, relying on the tall geometrically patterned stained-glass windows lining the walls to illuminate the hall, which could comfortably accommodate almost a thousand people.

Holding court here, making supplicants to the High Prince walk all the way down the empty hall to the twin thrones at the far end, gave Adrina time to gauge their mood, their demeanor, and their level of respect for their foreign-born High Princess.

It was important people realize she held the regency and acted with Damin's full authority, even with him incapacitated. The long walk gave petitioners time to contemplate the importance of the person to whom they were about to speak. Adrina could tell by the confidence of their stride and the set of their shoulders if they were here to ask a boon of the High Princess or demand it.

Adrina sat on Damin's throne—rather than the smaller one on the right that she normally occupied during formal court sessions—watching the next supplicant approach, hoping he was thinking exactly that.

"Lord Foxtalon," Darvad announced.

She glanced up at Damin's step brother-in-law, rolling her eyes. "Oh, goody."

Darvad smiled. She liked the earl of Dylan Pass. He was married to Damin's older stepsister, Rielle, and had come to court at Damin's request when the previous Lord Chamberlain retired some six years ago. Adrina had wanted her base-born half-brother, Gaffen, the current lord of Green-harbour Province, to take the job, but Damin had denied her request. They'd had a blazing row over it at the time, but she had come to see the wisdom of her husband's choice. Although he was now officially a Hythrun citizen, sat on the Convocation of Warlords, had adopted the Hythrun

House name of Sharkspear, spoke Hythrun, lived like a Hythrun, had a Hythrun wife and four gorgeous Hythrun children, and had never done anything to suggest he held any lingering loyalty to his Fardohnyan roots, Gaffen was still an object of mistrust. Damin had already taken a Fardohnyan wife, he reminded her. He wasn't going to get away with his closest advisor being Fardohnyan too without causing all sorts of trouble he could easily avoid by picking a Hythrun.

Fortunately, Darvad was a practical and pragmatic man, and a good diplomat with little desire to be a politician. He was Damin's cousin on the Bearbow side in addition to being his step-brother-in-law. That made him family and in Hythria, it also made him trustworthy.

The contrast between her own family, where treachery was a game she'd learned to play before she could walk, and the Wolfblades, who were so loyal to each other—and to Damin—that she sometimes found it unsettling, never ceased to amaze her.

"Please tell me he wants an audience to announce he's migrating with his entire wretched family to live in a tent on the steppes of southern Denika."

"Chance would be a fine thing," Darvad replied in a low voice. "He claims to be here to offer his help."

"Chance would be a fine thing," Adrina repeated with a sour smile, and then turned and smiled down from the podium at the lord of Pentamor Province as he stopped at the foot of the dais.

"Lord Foxtalon," she said. "To what do we owe this honor? I thought we wouldn't see you again in Greenharbour until the end of summer for the convocation."

"Under normal circumstances, you would not, your highness," he said, bowing out of politeness, rather than respect, Adrina was quite sure. "But these are hardly normal circumstances."

"Is there something afoot of which I am unaware?" she asked, feigning ignorance.

"I speak of the absence of the High Prince, your highness."

"My husband is not absent, Lord Foxtalon. He's upstairs."

"In a coma on the brink of death, if one listens to the rumors, my lady."

"Perhaps, if one didn't listen to rumors, one would have nothing about which one needs to be concerned," she suggested.

Foxtalon was not amused. "You are treating this like it's a joke, my lady."

"Not at all," she said, rising to her feet. Darvad made to follow her, but she signaled him to stay put. Foxtalon was a weak man, if one in a position of some influence. He lived only because he'd had the wit to change sides at the last minute in the brief conflict following the death of the last High Prince over a decade ago. But he was an easy man to flatter. Sometimes, it was easier to let men like him think they were more important than they really deserved to be.

Adrina walked down the steps until she was standing before him, and then she held out her arm. "Let's walk while we talk," she suggested.

Looking a little bemused, Foxtalon fell into step beside Adrina as they did a turn of the great hall. Once they were out of earshot of Darvad, who remained standing loyally behind the throne, she slipped her arm through Foxtalon's and whispered, "How widespread is this rumor, do you think?"

"It's everywhere, your highness."

She sighed with relief. "Thank the gods."

Foxtalon faltered for a moment. "Excuse me?"

"We were worried nobody would believe such a preposterous tale."

"I . . . I don't understand."

"Can I tell you something in confidence, Lord Foxtalon, and ask you to keep the secret on your honor as a Warlord of Hythria?"

"Of course."

"Damin is . . . on a mission for the demon child," she confided, choosing her words carefully. If Foxtalon marched straight from here to the Sorcerers' Collective to verify her story with the Harshini, who couldn't lie, even if they wanted to, she had to make sure he was asking the right questions.

"What mission?" He sounded skeptical at best.

"I don't know," she answered in all honesty. "I just know the demon child needs him to do something for her, and he has answered her call."

"Nobody has seen or heard of R'shiel té Ortyn for a decade," Foxtalon reminded her.

"You and I haven't seen her," she agreed. "But Damin is honored by the gods. He's met more than one of them in person. His dealings with the demon child do not usually involve me."

"So you're saying Damin Wolfblade is off gallivanting about with the demon child? What about the man who lies unconscious upstairs, your highness?"

"Jeck," she said with a sigh.

"Pardon?"

"His name is Jeck. Sweet man. Wouldn't harm a fly. Dumb as a bag of hair. Gaffen found him in Yarnarrow when he was in Karien last year. Couldn't believe his eyes. The man could be Damin's twin."

Foxtalon didn't appear to be buying a word of her outrageous tale. "You're telling me the unconscious man currently ensconced in the High Prince's bed being tended by the Harshini, and visited every day by his children, is an imposter?"

"I'm sure you understand now why I asked for your oath."

"But that's . . . that's . . ."

"I agree," Adrina sighed. "It is far from an ideal solution to our predicament, but R'shiel was adamant we not reveal Damin's involvement in her . . . well, whatever it is she's up to. And it wasn't like we could just teach poor Jeck a few names and pertinent facts. The man doesn't speak a word of Hythrun. A coma seemed like the best solution. I mean . . . if Damin's not back by the end of summer, how do I explain to my little sister that her brother-in-law, the High Prince, is not prepared to give her away at her wedding because he can't speak the required words at the ceremony?"

Foxtalon took a moment to process that. He was starting to come around, she could see. Dropping Rakaia's name helped. He wouldn't believe she was doing anything to protect Hythria, but he'd happily believe anything she said when it implied she might be doing something for a member of her own Fardohnyan family.

"So the wedding is still going ahead?"

"Of course, why wouldn't it?"

"Your sister is not here, your highness. My sp— . . . informants tell me she has come no closer to Greenharbour than Warrinhaven."

"My sister requested a break in her journey, my lord, to prepare herself for her arrival. She is young and not used to long-distance travel. Why would my husband not allow her to have it?"

They had reached the end of the hall. Adrina had, ever so subtly, led him to the door as they talked.

"Well, yes, I suppose . . ."

She smiled at him, turning her full, wide-eyed charm on the hapless warlord. "I knew you'd understand, Lord Foxtalon. Damin will not forget your discretion when he returns."

Foxtalon glanced at the door and realized he was being dismissed.

Before he could start objecting, Adrina leaned forward and kissed his cheek. "You are a true Hythrun, my lord. I now see what Damin means when he speaks of your honor and your intelligence. Please remember me to your lovely wife and your charming daughters when you return to Pentamor."

"Um . . . yes . . . of course, your highness."

Adrina tapped on the door. A moment later the ponderously large double doors swung inward, opened by the guards on the other side.

Not quick-witted enough to find a polite reason to stay, Foxtalon bowed, much more respectfully this time, and left the hall.

"Close it," she ordered the guards. "I'll send word when I'm ready to receive the next petitioner."

The guards did as she bid. Adrina turned and strode back toward the throne.

Darvad stepped down to meet her. "What did you tell him?"

"That Damin is off gallivanting about in parts unknown with the demon child on some divine mission I know nothing about and the man upstairs is a Karien imposter named Jeck."

"Why Karien?"

"Because he doesn't speak Hythrun. That's why he's pretending to be in a coma."

"Clever. Inspired, even."

"I swore him to secrecy on his honor as a Warlord."

"Which means we've got an hour, maybe less, before it's all over the city."

She smiled. "Will it take that long?"

"Probably not," he chuckled. "Marla would be proud of you."

"Let's not get carried away now," she said, picking up her skirts so she could climb the dais and resume Damin's throne. "Who's next?"

"A delegation from the Weavers' Guild. I believe they want Damin to declare a public holiday."

"For what?"

"To celebrate their contribution to our city."

"They can't do that without shutting the aforementioned city down while they get drunk on a heady mix of cheap beer and their own importance?"

Darvad shrugged. "Apparently not."

"Send them in," she said, smoothing her skirts as she resumed her seat.

Darvad was almost at the bottom of the steps before added, "Oh, and before I forget. We need to get the wedding plans under way. People are wondering why Rakaia is not here yet. Can you send Kiam a message and tell him it's time to bring her home?"

"To Greenharbour you mean?"

"Yes," she said, a little surprised. "Of course."

"Sorry . . . but you said *home*."

"This is my home, Darvad."

He smiled. "My apologies for thinking anything else, my lady."

He turned and marched the length of the long hall, his footsteps echoing off the walls. Adrina closed her eyes for a moment, hoping Rakaia was not going to be the trouble she feared . . .

. . . And wondering how Foxtalon had known the children were visiting their father every day. He had a spy in the palace, obviously. Perhaps more than one.

So too, it would be safe to assume, did every other Warlord in Hythria.

The thought of a palace riddled with spies didn't bother her as much as it would bother Darvad when she told him. Adrina had grown up in the Talabar Royal Harem. She was used to dealing with spies, the key to which, she had learned at a very young age, was being aware the spies were all around you in the first place.

37

THERE WAS NO avoiding the fact that the King of Fardohnya was in town. Bordertown was full of Fardohnyan sailors, and although the king deigned to grant the mayor an audience on board, he did not leave his ship. Rakaia and Mica walked through the markets listening to the gossip swirl around them as the good people of Bordertown speculated on why the king had not yet left his ship while it was being resupplied. Rakaia could have told them the reason had she not been too afraid to speak and be identified as Fardohnyan, too.

It was simple, really. Her father was a king and he wasn't going to tolerate being formally welcomed to a foreign country by any lesser personage.

A mayor simply didn't make the grade.

Hand in hand with Mica, Rakaia followed the minstrel with her face shaded by the hood of her cloak as he led her through the crowded markets, following the directions he claimed one of the *court'esa* at the inn had given him. They'd been at the inn for two days now, long enough to earn some coin and for Mica to befriend some of the working *court'esa,* which he seemed to do wherever they went. Women were drawn to Mica. There was an innocence about him that for some reason whores, in particular, found almost irresistible.

They were lucky to have found any rooms at all. With a foreign king docked at the wharves, there was almost nothing to be had. Mica sang for their room, entrancing the innkeep and everyone in the taproom. He sang a song about being lost in a desert and dying of thirst. Rakaia thought it an odd choice until she realized everybody in the taproom had ordered another drink by the time he finished the song. The innkeep noticed it too. He assured the minstrel and his young wife they could stay as long as they liked, if his songs continued to have the same effect on business.

Mica had only asked for one room and their meals in payment, and to be allowed to pass around a basket for donations after his performance. Rakaia didn't make an issue of their sleeping arrangements. Even if it didn't reinforce the notion she was his wife, she figured he was still afraid of the nightmares and wanted to keep her close.

"This is it," he said, pointing to a low, grubby, foul-smelling tent tucked in between a furrier selling rabbit skins and another selling rounds of hard cheese that didn't seem to smell much better than the herb-woman's tent.

"Are you sure?"

"This where Elliene said she gets her hair dye."

Rakaia frowned. She wasn't sure she like the idea of permanently changing her hair color. Particularly not on the advice of a whore whose hair was the color and texture of used stable straw. "You know Elliene's not a real *court'esa*, don't you?"

"What do you mean?"

"I mean she's just a whore. They call them *court'esa* in Medalon, because they don't understand the difference between a whore and a proper *court'esa*."

"*Court'esa* do naughty things to people for money. So do whores. What's so different about that?"

"Naughty things?" She had a bad feeling Mica wasn't trying to be funny.

"You know what I mean."

"Gods!" she said. "You're actually blushing!"

He looked away, embarrassed. "I am not."

Rakaia stared at him for a moment, as it dawned on her Mica had probably never been with a woman in his life. Her smile died as she realized how embarrassed he must be to admit such a thing. He was at least the same age as she was, if not a year or two older. Where had he grown up for such a thing to happen—or not happen, in his case?

As was the custom in most civilized societies, she had been trained since the age of sixteen by specialist, highly trained *court'esa*—slaves who taught her languages, etiquette, and all manner of useful skills both in and out of the bedchamber. She found it almost inconceivable that a young man like Mica had somehow sailed through life without making love to anybody, woman or man. "I'm sorry, Mica. I didn't realize."

"It doesn't matter."

She let the subject drop. He pushed back the tent flap and bent down to enter the tent. Rakaia followed, squinting in the darkness once Mica let the tent flap drop back into place. She pushed back the hood of her cape and glanced around. The interior reeked with such an overwhelming mixture of aromas that her eyes began to water. As she wiped her eyes, she spied an old woman sitting in the corner, cross-legged on the ground. Rakaia wasn't sure if the woman didn't get up to greet them because she was comfortable, or just wasn't physically capable of it.

"Knocked her up, have you?" the old woman asked Mica, eyeing them both with a jaded expression.

"No! Of course not," Mica exclaimed, when he realized she was asking if they had come for an abortifacient. "My wife wants to change the color of her hair, that's all."

"Your wife?" The herb-woman cackled in amusement. "Damn, boy, you married a long way up, didn't you? Shade?"

"Excuse me?"

"What shade . . . what color do you want? Red? Black? Dark brown? Blond?"

"Blond," Mica said, before Rakaia got the chance to offer her opinion.

The woman nodded and poked around in the baskets surrounding her on the ground. After a moment she tossed a small, cloth-wrapped pouch at Mica. He caught it and studied the pouch for a moment before looking up. "What is it?

"Ashes of burnt vine, the chaff of barley nodes, licorice wood, and sowbread."

Mica handed Rakaia the pouch. Somewhat dubious, she looked down at the old woman for instructions, not sure what a bit of ash and some old bread was supposed to do. "What do I do with it?"

"Wash your hair with it," the old woman said. "Boil the chaff and the sowbread in water. Then mix in the other ingredients. Let it cool down and sit for a few hours. Once it's cool, you can drain off the liquid and wash your hair with it . . . the liquid that is, not the sowbread mash. You should go quite a few shades lighter than you are now. Don't leave it on too long, though. With your complexion you'll look ridiculous if you go too light."

"How much do we owe you?" Mica asked.

"Ten rivets," the woman said.

Rakaia had never had to deal with money until she met Mica, so she had no real notion if ten rivets was a good or a bad price for hair dye. Mica didn't seem bothered, however. For once he didn't try to settle his debt with a song, just counted out the coins Rakaia had collected during his performances at the inn and handed them over without argument.

The woman snatched them from his outstretched hand. "You need to learn to haggle, lad," she advised. "I'd have let you have it for half that much, if you'd bothered to try."

"Give half of it back then," Rakaia suggested.

The old woman chuckled at the very notion. "I don't think so, deary. Tell you what, though, I'll throw something else in for you." She scrabbled around through the baskets for a moment and then tossed another packet to Rakaia.

She caught it and lifted the small packet to her nose. Rakaia sniffed the minty aroma, recognizing it immediately for what it was.

"What is it?"

"Your lady knows," the old woman said with a smug grin. "Proper *court'esa* trained, she is."

Rakaia wondered how the old woman could tell, just from watching her sniff a pack of herbs.

"What is it?" Mica asked Rakaia.

"Pennyroyal," she said. "Mixed with wild carrot."

"See. She knows."

"What it's for?"

To stop me getting pregnant, Rakaia almost said, but she decided against it. If she said anything like that, Mica might ask *how* she was going to get pregnant and then this whole charade about being his wife would fall apart. "It's to help me. With my monthly cycle."

Despite the dimness of the tent, she could see Mica blushing. She turned to the herb-woman. "Thank you for this. And the dye."

"No need to thank me. You've paid dearly for the privilege."

"Come on, Mica. Let's go."

Looking a little bemused, Mica let Rakaia push him through the tent flap before he could ask any foolish questions. Once outside, blinking in the bright sunshine, Rakaia pulled up the hood of her cloak to shade her face, in case she ran into to someone who might recognize her—more than a possibility with Hablet's ship docked at the Bordertown wharves.

They had only gone a few steps when her worst fears were realized. Their way was blocked by a couple of large Fardohnyan sailors and an officer from the king's personal guard.

"Are you the minstrel?" the officer asked in Fardohnyan.

Mica looked at them blankly.

"Are you the minstrel?" the officer repeated, this time in Medalonian.

Mica nodded warily. "Who wants to know?"

Beside him, Rakaia's guts were turning to water with fear. She kept her head down, shadowed by the hood of her cape, praying the officer had never seen her before and would not recognize her now. She didn't know him, and given how many daughters the king of Fardohnya owned, it was unlikely he knew what even a quarter of them looked like, but the risk was still there.

"The king of Fardohnya wants you to perform for him and his family tonight," the officer said. "The resupply is taking longer than anticipated, and the young prince is bored. Word about town is that you're quite good for a tavern brawler. You'll get paid. Bring your dancing girl with you."

"She's not a dancing girl," Mica said. "She's my wife."

"Bring her anyway," the officer said. "Be at the ship at sundown." The man stepped a little closer. "Don't make me come and find you, lad."

"Will it just be the king's family?" Mica asked. "No Harshini advisors who also want to hear my songs?"

The officer shook his head. "His highness doesn't like traveling on water with the Harshini on board. Says they stir up the gods and make the trip too rough. Why?"

"I was hoping for a truly musically educated audience."

The man scowled at Mica. "Whatever . . . just be there."

"We'll be there," Mica promised.

The officer seemed satisfied Mica would do as he'd ordered, so he and his escort turned to head back through the markets to whatever other king's business they were on. Mica waited until they were out of earshot before he turned to Rakaia. "Are you all right?"

She shook her head, feeling almost faint. She was clinging to the rough wooden support of the furrier's stall to maintain her balance. "Why . . . why did you agree to perform for Hablet?"

"Because he wasn't asking."

"I can't go on that ship, Mica."

"Yes, you can."

"No, you don't understand . . ."

He took her by the hand, and stepped closer to her, his eyes boring into hers. The market around them faded to a dull noise in the background as she was caught in his hypnotic gaze. "It's you who don't understand, Aja. There are no Harshini on board, so I can keep you safe. You just need to tell me the truth."

"I have told you the truth."

"Then you need to tell me the king's truth."

Although she was trying, she couldn't seem to break the hold he had on her gaze. "I don't know what you mean."

"I can sing away the danger to you, Aja, but I need to know exactly what that danger is. If you lie to me, if you leave out one tiny but important detail, it won't work."

"You don't know what you're asking, Mica."

"Is it worse than boarding that ship this evening and having the truth you don't want me to know come out anyway?"

She shook her head. "Can you really protect me, Mica?'

"Nobody in the mortal realm can protect you better," he promised.

"Hey! If you ain't buying, you ain't lingerin'," the furrier snapped at them. "Move on. You're blockin' the payin' clientele."

His words seemed to break the spell. Mica stepped back and took Rakaia by the hand. They walked back to the tavern in silence, Rakaia not sure what frightened her most—the prospect of confronting Hablet or telling Mica who she really was, and why putting herself in front of the Fardohnyan king might well end her life.

38

THE HARDEST THING Charisee ever did in her life was come down to breakfast the following morning after throwing herself at Kiam and being so comprehensively rejected.

She debated asking to have her breakfast served in her room, but that was just being cowardly.

She had to face him sometime.

Today was as good a time as any.

Once she'd finished sobbing like a heartbroken child, Charisee had lain awake until the small hours of the night, reassessing her situation. She felt as if up until now she had just been playing a silly game with Rakaia, which would end at any moment with Princess Sophany marching into the playroom to tell them off, insisting they put an end to this nonsense, and apologize to their father, the king, for confusing him with their little charade.

But Sophany was nowhere in sight. Rakaia was long gone.

This wasn't a game. Even the God of Liars had tried to tell her that.

At some point in the night, when she had cried all the tears of humiliation and grief she had in her, Charisee wiped her eyes, sat up, forced herself to take a deep breath, and decided to take stock of her situation.

Only then did it occur to her how foolish she was. She was trying to be Rakaia, and that lie was something she simply couldn't sustain.

Jakerlon had tried to explain that, too.

The best lies of all are the stone-cold truth.

She could be a princess. She was Hablet's daughter. But she had to be Charisee, not Rakaia. If that meant people thought her odd, then so be it. If they thought her unnaturally considerate of her slaves and servants, then that would just be her way. People would ascribe her odd behavior to many things, she was beginning to understand, but that she might be a slave and the real princess had run away to join a traveling minstrel show was unlikely to be one of them.

Charisee wondered what Rakaia was doing. She hoped her sister was happy and well, but her consideration of her sister's plight was fading with the increasing complexity of her own. Rakaia had put her on this path and she had no choice now but to follow it wherever it might lead.

Kiam's rejection—once she pushed past the humiliation and embarrassment she felt whenever she recalled the look on his face as he'd kicked her out of his room—gave her another idea. He had shown her the way to deal with her husband on her wedding night.

The best lies of all are the stone-cold truth.

She would not try to fake experience. She would do exactly what Kiam accused her of doing. She would tell Frederak Branador she liked to play games and the game was that she was an innocent and it was up to him to teach her what to do.

With a renewed sense of purpose, Charisee headed down to the dining room, almost looking forward to facing Kiam. He knew nothing of her inner turmoil and need never know. In fact, it was important she didn't give him any hint of how much his rejection had hurt her.

Kiam Miar could live the rest of his life thinking Rakaia the princess liked to play games. There was no reason for him to ever know that Charisee the slave was hopelessly in love with him.

Charisee the slave did not exist in Kiam's world and never would. She was as dead as Rakaia was supposed to be. And so were any silly flights of fancy she might be entertaining about the handsome assassin sent to escort Rakaia the princess to her wedding.

Broos bounded over to greet her when she arrived in the dining room. Lady Saneyah was already there, and so was her husband. Despite Broos's presence, there was no sign of Kiam.

Charisee was both relieved and disappointed.

"Good morning, your highness."

"Good morning, my lord, my lady. Is Master Miar not about?" she asked as she bent down to pat Broos.

"He was," Cam Rahan said, "but a courier arrived for him from the capital just now. I'm sure he won't be long."

"How does one even guess how long assassin business takes?" Saneyah asked, making no attempt to hide her feelings about being forced to entertain one. "Do you think they're planning to murder someone in this house?"

"Please excuse my wife, your highness. Several members of her family have been eliminated—"

"He means murdered. Don't beat about the bush, Cam. Name it for what it is."

". . . murdered . . . by the guild."

"I understand. But I was just wondering if you'd like me to return Broos to Master Miar's room," she offered. "He can be a bit much when there's a breakfast table full of food on offer."

"Glad I'm not the only one who thinks that monster should be in the stables," Saneyah muttered, but Lord Rahan shook his head.

"I'm sure he'll be back soon, your highness. Please, won't you join us?"

Charisee took the proffered chair and waited patiently as the slaves in attendance hurried to seat her, feed her, and ply her with freshly squeezed fruit juices. Broos padded happily along beside her and flopped at her feet to wait for her to pass him a tidbit. She selected the spiced pigeon eggs and the soft, still warm bread, with a silver goblet of apple juice. She had barely taken a bite before Kiam came back into the dining room. Broos abandoned her immediately for his master.

"Good morning, your highness. I trust you slept well?"

"Like a baby," she assured him, forcing an air of nonchalance she really wasn't feeling. "You?"

"Very well, and I have news I'm sure you've been waiting for."

"News?"

"I have orders to resume our journey, your highness."

"Has Damin recovered from his wounds?" Cam asked.

"The courier didn't say, my lord. Just that the High Princess Adrina awaits her sister's arrival, and that we are to make our way to Greenharbour as quickly as possible."

Before Charisee had a chance to react to the news, Lady Saneyah tossed her napkin on the table and rose to her feet. "I will have the cooks prepare food for your journey," she announced. "We should be able to get you away before lunch."

Charisee noticed Cam Rahan biting back a sigh at his wife's unseemly haste to be rid of her houseguests.

Kiam bowed graciously. "Your generosity is most appreciated, my lady."

The lady of the house didn't bother to reply, already on her way to ensure her household staff did whatever it took to rid herself of the assassin she had been forced to host these past few weeks.

Kiam turned to Charisee, addressing her as formally as he had done the first time they met. "Your highness, is an early departure acceptable to you? We should be able to make it to Remon Falls by sundown. There is an inn there you might find adequate. We should be in Greenharbour in a few days after that."

"I am in your hands, Master Miar," she said without looking up at him.

There was a moment of silence, one of which only she and Kiam were aware, and then she saw him bow out of the corner of her eye. "Your wish is my command, your highness."

Charisee's heart skipped a beat and then he was gone, Broos by his side, leaving Charisee to her breakfast and the sickening realization that a few days from now, after he handed her safely over to the High Princess for her wedding to Frederak Branador, she might never see Kiam again.

39

RAKAIA LEANED BACK in the rickety chair of the inn's bathhouse and closed her eyes. Mica stood behind her, a basin and several buckets of water at his feet, massaging the dye into her scalp. It was foul smelling and disgusting, and Rakaia doubted it would work, but she had seen Mica perform miracles before. If he thought changing her hair color would help protect her tonight on Hablet's ship, even for a few moments while Mica worked his unique brand of magic, she was willing to give it a try.

"My real name is Rakaia," she said, as Mica's strong fingers lathered the foul concoction into her hair.

"That's a pretty name."

"Is it? I never really thought about it."

"And the rest?"

"What do you mean?"

"You promised the truth, Aja whose real name is Rakaia. What else goes along with that pretty name? A title?"

"Sort of."

"As I suspected. What are you? A duchess? A baroness?"

"A princess."

"Even better," he said, not sounding the least bit surprised. "So King Hablet of Fardohnya is your father? That makes Adrina of Fardohnya your sister."

"Yes . . . no . . ."

"Which one is it?"

"My true father, apparently, was a captain of the guard."

"Aha . . . the plot thickens! Does King Hablet know about your true father?"

"Maybe . . . probably, by now."

"And that's why you ran away?"

She nodded, but his fingers didn't stop working the lather into her scalp. "My mother found out her lover had run afoul of my little brother,

Alaric. She was certain he would break under torture and reveal my secret in lieu of anything else he had to confess."

"And did he?"

"I don't know," she admitted. "Mama was so worried about what Hablet might do when he found out, she arranged for me to marry a Hythrun border lord and leave Talabar before it was too late."

"So, now it really gets interesting. There's a Hythrun border lord out there somewhere, on the warpath because he's lost his wife."

Rakaia shook her head. "I changed identities with my base-born half-sister. We look alike enough to pass casual inspection and she has blue eyes, too. I ran away and left her at Winternest pretending to be me."

"Can you be sure she hasn't betrayed you?"

"Why would she? I gave her the chance to be a princess instead of a slave."

"Does she know why?"

"No."

"Well, as the taverns aren't full of gossip about a slave being arrested in Hythria for posing as a princess, and nobody seems to be looking for you, I'd say we can take comfort in the idea that your ruse has been successful. What do you think her reaction will be when she learns the truth?"

"What do mean?"

"Well, I assume you ran away because when Hablet learns the truth about you, he'll kill you. So now your base-born sister . . . what's her name?"

"Charisee."

"So now Charisee is no doubt going to suffer the fate destined for you—assuming she hasn't already."

Rakaia had been trying very hard to convince herself that would never happen. It seemed unlikely when she heard it stated in such a matter-of-fact way.

"She won't die," Rakaia insisted, to convince herself as much as Mica. "All she has to do is tell Adrina the truth. The High Princess will protect her. She has to."

At the mention on Adrina's name, Mica hands fell still. "You mean the High Princess Adrina?"

"Of course," Rakaia said. "Who else would I mean?"

"Do you know her well?"

"Hardly at all, actually. I remember her being in the harem, but I was barely ten when she left Talabar to marry Prince Cratyn in Karien."

Mica was still for a moment longer and then he stepped back. "That should do it. Close your eyes." She heard him pick up the bucket behind her. "This might be a bit chilly."

Chilly was an understatement. The water was icy. Rakaia yelped as he upended a freezing bucket of water over her head, drenching her almost completely.

Behind her, Mica laughed. "And again!"

He dumped another bucket over her before she had a chance to catch her breath. He seemed to think it was hilarious.

Water dripping from her hair and face, her shirt translucent from the water, she jumped off the stool, sending it clattering across the chipped tiles of the bathhouse. Rakaia was sodden and chilled to the core. Mica was holding his sides, he was laughing so hard. Furious, she grabbed the rope handle of the other bucket, swept it up and tossed the entire contents at Mica.

It caught him full in the face. His shock was so genuine, she burst out laughing.

Laughing almost as hard as Mica, they both spied the last remaining bucket of water at the same time. Rakaia pushed her long, dripping hair out of her eyes and lunged for it as Mica did the same. They collided heavily on the slippery tiles and fell, one of top of the other.

Somehow, Rakaia managed to land on top. Miraculously, the last full bucket remained standing. Sitting astride Mica she pushed herself up, reached out to drag the full bucket over and then lifted it high, poised to dumped on it his head.

"No! Wait!" Mica cried, tears of laughter mingling with the water on his cheeks.

Rakaia hesitated, bucket held high. "Do you yield?"

"I yield!"

She glared at him for a moment, to gauge his sincerity, but Mica wasn't looking at her face, or even the threatening bucket. His eyes were transfixed by the sight of her breasts and her cold hard nipples poking through the sodden fabric of her all-but-translucent shirt.

Rakaia lowered the bucket, her smile changing from one of mirth to one of genuine curiosity.

"Mica, have you ever been with a woman?" She'd held him against her breast to calm his nightmares every night for the better part of two weeks and he had never laid a hand on her. Either he didn't like women at all, or didn't know what to do. She'd lain close enough to him at night to know he wasn't a eunuch and everything seemed to be functioning quite normally when he was asleep, even if he didn't realize it.

Mica's face turned bright red at the question. "Of course."

"What was her name?"

"I . . . I don't remember."

"Was she a whore?"

"I don't remember."

"How old were you?"

"I don't remember."

"Everyone remembers their first time, Mica."

He looked away, unable to meet her eye, and tried to sit up. "We should be getting ready for the performance tonight."

"Would like to touch them?" she asked gently, pushing him back down.

"What?"

"My breasts. You can't take your eyes off them. Do you want to touch them? Or do you prefer boys? I don't mind if you do, I'm just curious, that's all."

Mica tore his gaze from her chest and looked at her face, as if trying to tell if she was teasing him or making a genuine offer. "Why would you let me do that?"

She shrugged. "Because I like you. Because I see the way you look at me when you think I don't notice. Because without you I would be lost in a foreign country with no money and no way of ever finding my way home. And be—"

He looked away, as if her words pained him. "You don't have to let me molest your body just to be sure I won't abandon you, Rakaia."

She smiled, unaccountably pleased he had called her by her real name. "You didn't let me finish, Mica. The last reason, and the most *important* one, is because I want you to."

"You're a princess."

"Ex-princess," she corrected.

"But you're *court'esa* trained."

Rakaia smiled, reached down, picked up his hand and brought it to her breast. "Then aren't you the lucky one."

Mica was hesitant at first, almost as if he thought she was trying to trap him, but when he tentatively squeezed her breast and she let out a small moan of pleasure, he grew more bold. With his lips slightly parted, his breathing shallow, he brought his other hand up to caress her breasts through her wet shirt, wide-eyed with wonder.

Rakaia smiled and leaned forward, offering him her breast. Mica took her nipple in his mouth through the drenched shirt and sucked the moisture from it. The combination of the rough cold fabric and Mica's hot mouth against her nipple almost drove her insane. Rakaia cried out, wondering why, with all her training, no *court'esa* in the employ of her father had made her feel so ravenous for the touch of another human being. Before she went mad with the torment, she pulled her breast from Mica's gasp and sat up so she could remove her sodden shirt.

She tossed her shirt aside. She could feel him growing hard beneath her. Mica stared up at her in wonder, and then moaned as she rotated her hips against him. He took her breast in his hands again as she lifted her skirts so she could reach the laces of the front of his trousers. Mica didn't try to help. Perhaps he didn't notice what she was doing, so entranced was he by the feel of her breasts. With a deftness wrought of years of *court'esa* training, Rakaia managed to undo the laces of his trousers with one hand. She leaned forward so he could take her nipple into his mouth again, then rose up slightly and guided Mica into her. The young minstrel cried out with shock, pleasure, and surprise as Rakaia began to move up and down.

And then he did something completely unexpected. He began to sing.

The rhythm of his song perfectly matched the rhythm of their bodies, but the song he sang reached in to caress Rakaia's soul. She didn't hear the words, didn't even know what language in which he sang, but the song amplified her pleasure to incomprehensible heights. Soon she was so lost in it, she forgot the world around them . . . the messy wet floor with its foul-smelling dye, the fact that it was the middle of the afternoon and someone might walk in on them at any moment—it all seemed irrelevant as the song transported Rakaia from somewhere in the mundane world to some place she had never even glimpsed in her dreams.

And then it faded as Mica's song turned to cries of a much more primal kind as he arched his back and then collapsed, spent and stunned by the sheer insanity of their coupling. Her body still throbbing from the power of their shared experience, she collapsed on top of him, utterly drained, utterly exhausted, unable to do anything as Mica held her while he cried silent tears for the void left behind by the loss of whatever the magical thing they had just shared was.

Chapter

40

SANCTUARY WAS A lonely place with the Harshini gone. R'shiel preferred to remember the magnificent fortress city when it was full of life, full of music and full of smiling Harshini in their long white robes who didn't know how to be anything else but happy, even when they were trapped here and dying, because the outside world was too dangerous for them.

R'shiel tried not to think of the purges that had all but eradicated the Harshini. She preferred to remember the times when she was happy here, after Joyhinia had tried to kill her and Brak made the gods bring her to Sanctuary to be healed. She didn't have any memories for a while after that. For a few idyllic months, she was as ignorant and blissfully contented as a newborn babe in this place.

It remained the happiest time of her life.

Then Brak arrived and her memories came back . . . and nothing was ever quite so wonderful again.

With the memories had come the pain and the realization that she wasn't just R'shiel Tenragan, rebellious but unimportant daughter of the First Sister of Medalon—she was R'shiel té Ortyn. Harshini royalty. Heir to the Harshini crown. A halfbreed capable of wielding an unthinkable magical power. A tool of the gods.

A demon child.

The gatekeeper was no longer watching over the gate. With Sanctuary sent out of time, there was no need to supervise the comings and goings of any beings, real or corporeal. The scrying bowl used to watch the surrounding forest was still, showing nothing more than silent trees and the occasional drip of water as the last remaining pockets of snow succumbed to the onset of summer.

R'shiel wandered the empty halls, her heart aching as she recalled the last time she'd wandered them with Brak. It was just as still and silent then. They'd made love here, that time, just before they threw Sanctuary out of reach. That moment was one R'shiel had never forgotten.

The only other moment in her life she could truly call happiness.

The moment she discovered the true magic of being even half-Harshini and sharing that bond with another of her kind.

Pushing the memories away to concentrate on more immediate concerns, she walked ever downward through Sanctuary's perpetual twilight into the valley around which Sanctuary was constructed. R'shiel sometimes caught a movement out of the corner of her eye as she walked. Occasionally she imagined a sound, like a leaf being swept past on the wind, but there was nothing to see. Once she felt something akin to butterfly wings brush her cheek, but when she swatted the irritation away, there was nothing there.

As she walked through the wide, glowing halls taking the winding stairs to the lower levels, she ran her hands over the smooth white walls, hoping to feel the essence of Sanctuary; to connect with the living presence that imbued this place and others like it built by the Harshini. If Sanctuary was still here—if she could wake him from his slumber—she had a much better chance of finding the entrance to the underworld.

Surely, if Sanctuary wasn't one of the Seven Hells, then it was the entrance to them. Both Kalianah and Death had told her as much.

Perhaps the gatekeeper was watching over more than the Harshini, she mused, *when they were hiding from the Sisterhood's purges.*

Perhaps he marshaled other souls through this place and into the underworld, as well as stopping mortal beings with evil intent.

Perhaps that was the other reason Sanctuary had to reappear each year— to allow new souls through the gate.

No wonder people thought the Sanctuary Mountains were haunted.

R'shiel stopped, tempted to retrace her steps and head back to the entrance, to see if there was any clue to what she was looking for back there. She never remembered seeing any souls pass through Sanctuary on their way to the next life when she lived here. Did they enter the halls and delightfully decorated chambers, and pause to have a look around on their way through? Did they hover about the amphitheater and listen to the unearthly Harshini songs as the magical race acknowledged the gods who brought them into being?

She was about to turn back when she heard a sound below her. It wasn't a figment of her imagination this time, but a definite sound of banging. R'shiel ran to the balcony and looked down into the valley. The terraced levels with their glowing balustrades and wildflowers climbing over them did strange things to sound here. At the far end of the valley, the water-fall still tinkled musically down the rocks, spraying rainbow-colored light over the lush clearing surrounding the deep pool at its base.

R'shiel waited, wondering if the sound would come again. A few moments later her patience was rewarded—the unmistakable sound of banging on something wooden, followed by a distinctly female cry of frustration.

And then she caught a movement in the trees near the amphitheater. R'shiel pushed off the balustrade and broke into a run, taking the remaining ten flights of stairs to the floor of the valley in record time. She burst through into the garden and ran along the graveled path toward the amphitheater, hoping to catch whoever it was down there before they could vanish into the ether, something more than likely in this place stuck between here and now.

"Is anybody there?" she called, wondering if she was chasing a ghost and, if she was, how she expected them to hear her. Sanctuary had been locked away for a decade, accessible only to Death and the Primal Gods. There could be no living being here other than one sent here by the gods.

"Hello!"

"R'shiel?"

She stopped and turned, stunned to find a fair-haired woman with pale green eyes standing behind her. The woman was dressed in a green, Medalonian-style robe—high-necked and gathered just below the bust, and she carried what seemed to be a broken-off branch. She was surrounded by an aura of crimson light and although she was solid enough, there was something incorporeal about her. The woman was older than R'shiel remembered, but then, she hadn't seen her for a decade and she'd borne several children in that time by all accounts.

"*Mandah?*"

"I might have known it would be you. I suppose it's your fault I'm trapped in this wretched place."

The bitterness in her tone was not just over being trapped here, R'shiel guessed. They had both loved the same man for a long time, and thanks to the interference of the Goddess of Love, Tarja had loved R'shiel back for much of that time rather than Mandah—the woman he ultimately settled down with; the woman who bore his children.

"Have you to come to rescue me, demon child?" she asked. "Come to take me back to Tarja and earn his undying gratitude for saving the mother of his children?"

"How did you get here, Mandah?"

"As if you didn't know."

"Truly, I have no idea."

"I went to bed feeling poorly." She glanced around at the empty fortress and then fixed her gaze on R'shiel. Her eyes glistened with unshed tears. "The next thing I knew I was here and I couldn't find a way out of this place."

"How long have you been here?"

"I don't know. Time seems to stand still here. I might have been here a few days or my children might be all grown by now."

R'shiel recalled what Kalianah had told her about Mandah's life being held in trust by Death, to ensure she would not renege on their deal. She felt a momentary spasm of guilt, but it was easily overcome by the thought this really was the right place to enter the Seven Hells, if Death had trapped Mandah here while he waited for R'shiel to find Brak.

It also meant Mandah wasn't the only one here. Death held Mandah's life in trust for the moral dilemma R'shiel faced if she chose to trade Brak's life for this woman's. The other life he held—at least according to Kalianah—was someone R'shiel counted as a true friend.

"Are you alone here?"

"I don't know. This place is huge. I hear things sometimes, but . . ."

"Where? Where do you hear things?"

"I don't know . . . by the waterfall . . . the library . . . not that I've been in there much. I'm afraid if I enter that rabbit warren of a place, I'll never find my way out."

The library. Mandah was right about it being a rabbit warren, but the Damin she remembered was a man of action, not learning. Would he be there, or somewhere else? Not that there was much to entertain a man like Damin in this place of no weapons and no hint of violence.

But even if I can find him, how much help could he be?

And then another thought occurred to her and she looked at the branch Mandah was still holding. "What were you banging on, by the way?"

Mandah pointed behind her. "There's a door in that cliff over there. It's recently started opening for a moment or two with a blaze of blinding light, and then it closes before I can get to it. I've tried leaving by the entrance at the top of this place, but I keep running into some sort of invisible wall. I was hoping it might be a way out of here."

"Show me."

Mandah shrugged and led R'shiel the short distance to the cliff wall. Sure enough there was a simple, arched wooden door set into the cliff. R'shiel must have passed it a hundred times on her way to the amphitheater when she lived here.

Not once had she seen it open. But then, when she lived here, Sanctuary was hidden out of time. Kalianah had brought it back for her. Did that mean all the souls waiting to enter the Seven Hells were finally able to do so now that it was back?

It also made her wonder if Brak had known about the door when he helped her throw Sanctuary out of time. The notion raised a disturbing thought. Had Brak helped her, knowing then he was going to die in the quest to destroy the god, Xaphista, and locked Sanctuary away to expressly prevent R'shiel coming to find him after it was done?

She pushed the thought away. Brak loved her. He would never do such a thing. He was probably as ignorant of Sanctuary's true purpose as she was.

"How often does it open?"

"Who can tell? There's no way to keep time in this place."

R'shiel studied the door for a moment longer, and then decided it could wait until she found Damin. After all, if it opened regularly, she could afford to miss a time or two.

"Can you open it?" Mandah asked.

R'shiel shook her head. "I doubt it. But I'm pretty sure I can go through it. Have you seen Damin around since you arrived?"

"Damin *Wolfblade*? Founders, R'shiel, do your schemes and machinations involve the High Prince of Hythria as well?"

"Not on purpose." She didn't mean to sound quite so defensive. Mandah just always seemed to have that effect on her.

"It never is on purpose with you."

"I need to find him."

"Why?"

"Because that door is the gateway to the Seven Hells, Mandah, and if I'm going in there, I'd like someone I trust at my back."

"You don't trust me?"

"Do you trust me?"

Mandah tossed the branch aside and shrugged. "I trust you to do what you set out to do, R'shiel. Whether that is good for the rest of mankind remains to be seen."

"Then help me find Damin," R'shiel said, "so we can find out."

"How did you meet the demon child?"

Mica asked the question as they walked, hand in hand, toward the docks and their appointment to entertain the king of Fardohnya. Mica held Rakaia's hand fast, as if he were afraid to let it go. The Glass River on their left was painted red by the setting sun, and the temperature had dropped enough for her to be glad of the cloak Mica had bought her in Vanahiem.

Mica bounded along beside her like an excited child. He hadn't stopped grinning since they left the bathhouse.

His question irritated Rakaia a little. After what they had just shared— and Mica's reaction to it—she expected to be the only woman in his thoughts. "I thought you wanted to know everything about me."

"I know about you now," he said, his strong musician's fingers holding her hand tight. "You used to be a princess and now you're not. That doesn't explain how you came to be in the demon child's company."

She placed her head on his shoulder as they walked, the leather strap of his lyre case so old and supple it felt like velvet against her cheek. "Who cares about the demon child? You do understand that Hablet will kill me tonight as soon as he realizes who I am, don't you?"

Mica brought her hand up and kissed it, and then he hurried her over to the window of a milliner's shop, displaying an array of finely crafted felt and feather hats. He made her face the window for a moment, so she could see her reflection.

A stranger stared back at her. Rakaia's once waist-length, light brown hair was cut off just below her shoulders and golden honey in color. Now it was dry and much shorter than before, the natural wave in her hair was allowed some freedom, and her face was scrubbed clean of the heavy eye makeup she usually wore.

"Couldn't we just run away, Mica?" she asked, refusing to acknowledge how different she looked. "Why even stay here in Bordertown? We could head south for Krakandar and be miles from here by the time they realize we're not coming if you sing someone into giving us a couple of horses. You said Krakandar is where we're going. Why delay that just to entertain a bored child?"

"The king won't have a clue who you are."

Reluctantly, Rakaia conceded he might be right. She barely recognized herself. "You *are* going to sing away his suspicions, aren't you?" Although she had seen him make people do some remarkable things with his songs, the idea that her own father—or at least the man she'd grown up believing was her father—would not know her when she was standing right in front of him was still a hard pill to swallow.

"I hardly need to, but of course. I told you. He won't have the foggiest idea who you are."

"What about Alaric?"

"Who is Alaric?"

"My brother. Well . . . the king's son, at any rate. He knows me. And he's a brat. He'll say something even if he only suspects something is awry."

That's how her real father had been arrested and tortured. Thanks to Alaric.

"Then I will make him forget you, too."

She smiled. "Can you make him less of a brat while you're at it?"

"I suppose."

"Suppose someone else on the ship recognizes me?"

"I promise you. They won't."

"How can you be sure of that?"

"Because even if you stood in front of them without a disguise, my lovely, they believe Princess Rakaia is a thousand miles from here, getting ready for her wedding to Lord Lecherous the Leering. They are not expecting you. So they won't see you." He stood behind her, holding her by the shoulders, forcing her to look at her reflection. "Look at yourself, Rakaia. You are nothing like you used to be."

"Then you'd better not call me Rakaia when we get there. That might be pushing our luck."

He spun her around, kissed her on the lips, and then took her hand again. "Come then, wife Aja. We have a king to entertain."

AS THE WEATHER was clear, and there really wasn't room below deck, Mica's impromptu concert was held on *Wave Dancer*'s foredeck. Mica and

Rakaia were shown to a small circle of three chairs, for the king and his family, already set up and waiting. The sailor who told them where to stand informed them the king was currently having his dinner with his family and would be out when he was ready. Around them, other sailors lit the deck with lamps against the closing darkness.

Rakaia's heart was pounding. Mica calmly removed his lyre from its case and began to tune it, strumming a few notes, his eyes closed, as he checked the instrument's pitch and tone. Rakaia stood behind him, her palms sweating as she tried to find a space in the shadows between the lanterns where nobody would notice her.

They waited nearly an hour before the king deigned to appear. He led the way with Alaric close behind, looking around at everything as if he owned it. The woman behind Hablet and Alaric, however, made Rakaia's heart skip a beat.

Although a sheer, pale blue veil covered half her face, Rakaia would have recognized her anywhere.

The woman with Hablet was Princess Sophany.

Mica rose to his feet as the king approached. This was the danger period, Rakaia knew. Mica could sing stars down from the heavens, but he hadn't sung a note yet. There was plenty of time for Hablet to recognize her. Or Alaric. Or her mother.

The minstrel bowed extravagantly to the king as he took his seat. "Oh, mighty king," he cried, "greatest of all monarchs living and dead! Thank you for allowing a poor minstrel such as I the chance to bask in your presence and perchance, to entertain you for a moment or two."

"He's full of shit," Alaric announced as he took his seat at his father's right hand.

"Aye, lad," Hablet agreed. "That's part of what they do."

"Can we kill him if he doesn't please us?"

Little monster, Rakaia thought as she watched him from the shadows, an unexpected surge of hatred for this child she no longer had to pretend was her adored only legitimate brother. *You haven't changed a bit since I left, have you?*

Turning from Alaric, she focused on her mother, reading the fear in Sophany's rigid posture. Why had Hablet brought her with him on this trip? As far as Rakaia knew, he had not called for her mother in years. Hablet tended to lose interest quite quickly in wives who only gave him daughters.

"Ah, noble prince," Mica exclaimed. "If I fail to entertain you, there will be no need to take my life. I will throw myself on your sword for the disappointment I have caused you."

Hablet chuckled. "You're right, son. He is full of shit." Then he turned to look at Mica and noticed Rakaia standing in the shadows behind him. "Perhaps the dancing girl will make things more interesting. Step forward, girl. Give us a look at you!"

Rakaia couldn't move. She was frozen to the spot in fear. Mica took her hand, however, and coaxed her forward. "This is no dancing girl, your magnificence. This is my wife, Aja."

Mica led her forward a few steps. Rakaia curtseyed as low as she could manage, keeping her eyes downcast, but she was trembling so hard she stumbled and landed on her knees, which Alaric thought was hilarious.

"She looks like Rakaia," he said, laughing. "If she was a peasant with no breeding or wit. Don't you agree, Mama Sophany?"

The princess was staring at Rakaia with wide, horrified eyes as Mica helped her up. There was no need for her to say anything. She knew.

Hablet studied Rakaia for a moment and then shook his head. "You think so, Alaric? I suppose there is some resemblance, but it's tenuous at best. Does she sing?"

"Alas, the gods have played a cruel jest on me, your worthiness. While the Great Gimlorie gifted me the voice of an angel, he chose not to give my precious Aja a voice at all."

"She's a half-wit, is she?" Alaric asked.

"Mute, O mighty prince, that is all."

Hablet seemed to be growing bored with the discussion. "Let us hear this voice, then" he said, settling back into his seat. "I will tell you when you're done if it belongs to an angel or not."

"As you command, O precious one," Mica said with a bow. He took Rakaia's hand and led her back to the railing. She didn't say a word, couldn't even think of anything intelligent to say. Once she was safely behind him, he picked up his lyre and began to sing.

Rakaia wasn't sure what song he sang first, although she was sure she'd heard it before, and at sometime in the night she heard the familiar strains of the song Mica always sang as she was passing out the collection hat.

He sang until his voice cracked and Alaric was nodding off in his chair. When he was done, apparently entertained, Hablet ordered his captain to pay them and send them on their way.

He left them then, Alaric close on his heels—yawning and surprisingly silent—to pack up and leave.

Princess Sophany waited until her husband and stepson were below decks before she stepped forward to address them.

"You have a rare gift, minstrel," she said, although Sophany's eyes never left Rakaia.

"Thank you, my lady."

"Is it a happy life you lead, this life of a traveling minstrel?"

Mica glanced at Rakaia and smiled. "It has its compensations, my lady."

"Then I wish you both well in the future," she said. And then she reached up and took the emerald earrings from her ears and handed them to Mica. "Consider this a bonus. For the . . . comfort you have bought me this evening."

Before either of them could reply, Sophany hurried below, leaving them staring after her.

Mica opened his hand and studied the earrings, mouth agape. They were worth more than he earned in a year. "Why . . ."

Rakaia was supposed to be mute, so she couldn't answer him. She tugged on his arm and indicated they should leave the ship. Bewildered by the princess's unexpected largesse, he nonetheless nodded and took her hand.

As soon as they were down the gangplank and wrapped in the darkness away from the ship, Rakaia broke into a run. She didn't stop until they were three streets away.

When she finally halted, she leaned against the wall of the tannery to catch her breath. Mica was only a step behind her, grinning. "Why so anxious to be gone? I told you nobody would recognize you. Although we came close when your brother first saw you. Quick thinking, by the way, being so clumsy."

"I wasn't being clumsy," she said. "I fell. And he's not my brother. He's a spoiled little monster."

"Well, whatever the reason. It worked. Why do you think the princess gave us such prize?"

"Because she recognized me."

"She didn't say anything."

"Of course she didn't say anything. She's my mother."

Mica didn't seem to have an answer for that.

"Can we go now?"

"Go where?"

"Krakandar," Rakaia said. "Tonight. Thanks to my mother we have enough there now to buy a whole herd of horses and the stable to go with them. I want to be gone from this place."

Mica nodded and took her into his arms. Rakaia laid her head on his shoulder, surprised at the comfort she felt, knowing he was with her. "We'll leave tonight then," he promised. He took her face in his hands and kissed her then before adding with a grin. "I did what you asked, by the way."

She pushed him away. "No you didn't. You said you would sing away any chance anybody on that ship would recognize me. Sophany knew exactly who I was, even after you were done."

Mica shrugged and shouldered the lyre case a little higher. "That's because I didn't know she was your mother. You can't sing away a parental bond like that easily, and I didn't know I had to. But that's not what I was talking about."

"What, then?" she asked as she fell into step beside him, unable to think of any other boon she had asked of Mica, other than Hablet not recognize her and have her put to death.

Mica took her hand and smiled at her. "I tried to make Alaric less of a brat," he said.

42

KIAM STOPPED ON the hill overlooking Greenharbour to give Charisee her first view of the city. She gasped with surprise when she saw it. The vast, white-walled city with its sparkling harbor beyond spread out over coastline almost as far as the eye could see, dominated by the domed cupola of the Temple of the Gods and the Sorcerers' Collective compound in the center.

She rode up beside Kiam and reined in her horse, staring in wonder for a time, the enormity of what she was attempting assaulting her all over again, just when she thought she'd gotten used to the idea.

"Behold the city of Greenharbour," Kiam said. He was smiling at her reaction, which was a marked improvement on his attitude since they'd left Warrinhaven. Ever since her foolish visit to his rooms he'd treated her differently, as if she'd disappointed him somehow.

"It's . . . very big."

"Not that much bigger than Talabar."

"Have you been to Talabar?"

"Once or twice."

She eyed him curiously. "On business?"

He smiled. "Ah, now that would be giving away guild secrets. Did you want to stop and freshen up before we arrive, your highness?"

"Would you mind?" she asked, a little surprised he had even thought of such a thing. She had the gown Rakaia intended to wear on her arrival tucked into her luggage and if she was going to enter Greenharbour and confront her sister Adrina, she had better look the part. That meant dressing like a princess, wearing the small amount of jewelry Rakaia had left her, and applying the traditional Fardohnyan eye makeup that only a rare Fardohnyan woman would dare venture into public without.

"Your wish is my command, your highness," he said.

He's mocking me, she thought. But she wasn't going to let him know how much it hurt her.

"Then if you would be so kind as to have your men set up a screen, fetch me some water to wash, and fetch my red bag, I would very much like to prepare to meet my sister."

"And your future husband?"

"Naturally. Him, too."

"Your wish is my command, your highness," he repeated, wheeling his horse around, leaving Charisee to stare at the vast city of Greenharbour and wonder how she was going to survive it.

KIAM SENT ONE of his men on ahead to warn the city they were arriving so as they approached the huge open gates of the city the silver-liveried guards stood to attention as another troop of soldiers, with an officer and a civilian in the lead, rode out to greet them.

The troop stopped and parted, lining the way into the city with a guard of honor, while the civilian rode forward. As he neared them, Charisee's palms began to sweat. Although he was dressed like a Hythrun lord, he was Fardohnyan.

The man reined in his magnificent, golden sorcerer-bred horse and bowed to Charisee. "Welcome to Greenharbour, your highness."

"Thank you, Lord . . . ?"

The man smiled. "I'm sorry, where are my manners? I am Gaffen Sharkspear, Warlord of Greenharbour and half-brother to the High Princess Adrina. I believe that makes me your half-brother too, Princess Rakaia."

Of course. This was Gaffen. Hablet's bastard son who'd followed Adrina to Hythria, lifting the siege on the city that almost cost Damin Wolfblade his throne. The man had been rewarded with a province and a seat on the Convocation of Warlords.

While he wasn't exactly a forbidden topic in the harem, Charisee had only ever heard him spoken about in whispers, and certainly nobody in their right mind reminded Hablet of what his eldest living bastard was up to these days.

"I'm so sorry, Lord Sharkspear. I didn't recognize you."

"That's perfectly understandable," he said. "I wouldn't have recognized you either had I not been told you were arriving. You must have been, what . . . only nine or ten . . . when I saw you last?"

"I really don't remember, my lord."

"Well, you've certainly grown since then. What happened to your little friend?"

"Little friend?"

"As I recall, you used to be joined at the hip to another one of father's bastards. Pretty little thing she was. Had blue eyes, like you. What was her name? Sharilee . . . Marilee . . ."

"Charisee," she told him. "Her name was Charisee."

"That's right." He glanced over the rest of Kiam's small troop with its distinct lack of entourage or any of the trappings of a traveling Fardohnyan princess. "Did you not bring her for company?"

Her mouth dry, Charisee gripped her reins until her fingers cramped and shook her head. "She was never going to be happy here. It seemed cruel to force her to come."

"That's remarkably considerate of you," Gaffen said, nodding with approval. "And please, there is no need to keep calling me 'my lord.' We're family, after all."

Fortunately, Charisee wasn't required to respond, because Gaffen turned to Kiam then, leaning across his horse to grip Kiam's arm in a firm handshake, which was a relief, because she had no saliva left in her mouth at all and doubted she'd be able to get out another word for a while.

"Welcome home, Ky," Gaffen said, obviously a friend of the assassin's. "Good journey?"

"Good enough," Kiam replied, glancing at Charisee. "How are things here?"

Gaffen's smile wavered for a moment. "Interesting," he said, after a very telling pause. "I'm sure Adrina will fill you in. Shall we proceed?" He looked back at Charisee and resumed his friendly, welcoming smile. "Your highness?"

"Ready when you are . . . Gaffen."

He wheeled his horse around and made a signal to the rest of the guard of honor. Some of them remained by the road waiting for them to pass, while others took up formation in front.

Charisee rode in the center of the guard of honor, flanked by Gaffen on her right and Kiam on her left with Broos trotting faithfully beside him, the rest of the troops falling in behind as they entered the momentary cool darkness of the entrance before emerging on the other side into the chaos that was Greenharbour City.

* * *

IT TOOK ALMOST an hour to reach the palace, an hour in which Charisee's senses were assaulted from every side by the sheer size and vibrancy of the city. Many people stopped to watch the unusual sight of a Fardohnyan princess riding by; just as many paid her no attention at all. The roads were cluttered, the streets full of people who all looked to have something to do and somewhere to be. Every building in the city was white, crafted from stone quarried farther down the coast—so Gaffen informed her—even the new buildings in the poorer quarter of the city. A lot of the city had been rebuilt since the siege, he explained, giving him a chance to rethink the layout of the streets in the destroyed districts and allowing some long-term thought regarding the city's plan. Although the city was the capital of Hythria and the seat of its power, as Warlord of Greenharbour it was Gaffen and not the High Prince who was responsible for its upkeep and services. As he spoke, her half-brother seemed inordinately proud of what he'd achieved since coming here.

She soon forgot about Gaffen's civic pride, however, as they approached the gates of the palace, a massive, white three-story building with large paved forecourt. As they rode through the gates Charisee could already see the welcoming party gathering on the steps.

"Is this all for me?" she asked, a little surprised at how many people had gathered to greet her,

"Of course," Gaffen said. "It's not every day we have a real Fardohnyan princess come to visit."

Charisee decided not to say anything else, for fear of looking a complete fool. Rakaia would have been asking why there weren't fireworks.

But I am not Rakaia and I am not going to be.

As the troops in front peeled off to either side to allow them closer to the palace steps, a woman stepped forward and walked down to greet them, stopping halfway.

Charisee reined in her horse, allowed Gaffen to help her dismount, and walked up the steps, her knees shaking, to greet her half-sister, the High Princess of Hythria.

Adrina was everything Charisee feared and admired. She was a stunning woman in her prime, with emerald eyes and thick dark hair, filled with poise and a confidence Charisee could only dream of. The

High Princess commanded simply by standing there, waiting for her little sister to arrive.

Charisee stopped on the step below Adrina and dropped into a deep, respectful curtsey. The noise of the city fell away. "Your highness."

"Welcome to Hythria, Rakaia. Let me look at you, little sister."

Charisee stood up and raised her head to meet Adrina's critical gaze. "You grew into quite a beauty, didn't you?"

How do I answer a question like that, for the gods' sake?

By telling the truth, she could almost hear Jakerlon whispering in her ear. *The best lies of all are the stone-cold truth.*

"I am my mother's daughter, your highness. What small amount of beauty I possess, I owe entirely to her."

Adrina smiled, as if the answer pleased her. "I remember you as a holy terror in the harem. You and your shadow, Charisee."

Interesting that while Gaffen couldn't remember Rakaia's companion's name, Adrina could.

"I've grown up a lot since those days, your highness."

"Good thing, too. She's not with you?"

"Charisee deserved more than a life as a drudge in a draughty mountain keep, your highness," she said.

Adrina held out her arm, smiling. Weak-kneed with relief that she had passed this first, critical hurdle, Charisee placed her trembling hand in her sister's steady one. "I fear a draughty mountain keep will be your fate for a while," she said, a trace of sympathy in her tone for Rakaia's future as the lady of Highcastle. "Was Kiam an adequate escort?"

"More than adequate, your highness."

Adrina turned and together they climbed the remaining stairs until they reached the landing. At the top, Charisee looked over her shoulder at Kiam, who stood at the base of the stairs, holding the horses with one hand, his other on Broos's collar, staring up at her.

She felt she ought to say something to him. Thank him at the very least.

Running down the steps, throwing herself into his arms and smothering him with kisses, she supposed, was completely out of the question.

"Be careful, Rakaia."

She turned to Adrina, afraid her astute half-sister had guessed the direction of her thoughts.

"Your highness?"

"It all seems shiny and new here, I know, and it's wonderful being freed from the harem, but try not to be too enchanted by it. Greenharbour is a dangerous place, as you will learn soon."

With that dire warning ringing in her ears, Charisee followed Adrina into the palace to begin her life proper as Her Serene Highness, the Princess Rakaia.

Princess of Fardohnya. Lady of Highcastle Keep. Liar.

Part Four

Chapter

43

THE CLOSER THEY got to Krakandar, the more animated Mica became, as if there was something great waiting there for him. When Rakaia asked why he was so excited by the prospect of visiting the city, he shrugged and grinned and said he was expecting some good news when they got to Hythria, but would not elaborate.

"Have you been to Krakandar before?" she asked as they rode side by side on the horses Mica had bought in Bordertown with one of the emerald earrings her mother had given them.

"Once."

"What's it like?"

"You'll see."

"You seem really excited about going back."

Mica leaned over and kissed her. "You'll see."

She smiled at him. Rakaia had never been worshipped before. Not the way Mica worshipped her. It was possible his infatuation was entirely centered on sex. She knew that. They'd made love every single night since their first encounter in the bathhouse. Mica was voracious. He wanted to learn everything Rakaia could teach him.

Rakaia was happy to oblige, almost as enchanted by Mica as he was with her. She'd been taught well by her *court'esa*, but one thing she was only just beginning to understand was the difference between having sex and making love.

That latter, she was discovering, was much more fun.

By the time Krakandar finally came into view and they'd joined the line of people waiting to enter through the city gates, Rakaia was starving. For some reason the road leading toward the city was jammed with travelers, and there was some holdup at the gate.

The northernmost city in Hythria was a grand sight from a distance, built in a series of concentric rings that all peaked with the palace perched on the hill in the center of the sprawling metropolis. While not as large as Talabar or Greenharbour, it was an important center of commerce in the north and pretty much all the trade that happened between Medalon and Hythria came through here.

Rakaia sighed when she realized it would be hours before they reached the gates. The red-bricked walls of the city were still a mile or more ahead of them, and because the surrounding countryside had been cleared of vegetation to prevent a sneak attack, it was hot, there was no shade, and more than once they passed both men and women squatting down to relieve themselves on the side of the road as they inched their way forward.

"Is it always this busy?" she asked Mica.

"Something important must have happened," Mica replied as if he knew something she didn't.

Before she could answer him, she spied an enterprising food vendor walking toward them, weaving his way through the line of wagons and pedestrians, all patiently waiting to enter. "Sweatmeats! Meatballs! Spicy jerky!"

Mica glanced at Rakaia. "Are you hungry?"

Her tummy rumbled in answer. Mica laughed and hailed the man over. He wheeled his small cart to them, revealing a selection of dried meats and pastry-covered balls filled with dried fruit.

"Is something happening in the city?" Rakaia asked the vendor, as Mica dismounted to closer inspect the man's wares.

"The Princess Marla arrived yesterday," the man explained. "She's on her way to Medalon, they say, for the treaty negotiations."

Mica selected a few pieces and handed them up to Rakaia, saying, "I suppose the whole city is still in mourning."

The man shook his head, puzzled. "Mournin'? Mournin' for who? Princess Marla is alive and well."

"I meant for the High Prince."

The food vendor looked at Mica like he was mad. "The High Prince ain't dead," he said. Then he leaned forward and added in a low, conspiratorial tone. "Word is he's off on a special mission with the demon child, but you didn't hear that from me."

Mica stared at the man. He looked stunned. "What do you mean, he's not dead? Are you certain? Maybe the news hasn't reach Krakandar yet?"

The food vendor shook his head. "We'd know an hour after it happened, lad, if something befell our Damin. There's Harshini here now, same as there are in every city since those evil bitches in Medalon were tossed out on their arses and it was safe for them to come back. They talk through them stones to each other all the time. 'Sides, can you imagine Princess Marla galavantin' off to Medalon if the High Prince of Hythria had just passed on?" The man laughed, "Ye gods, lad, you need to stop listenin' to silly rumors. That'll be four rivets, thanks."

Mica seemed too shocked to speak. "What . . . ?"

"Pay the man, Mica," Rakaia urged, worried about how pale he suddenly looked.

"Oh . . ." Mica fished some coins from his purse and tossed them on the food vendor's cart.

"Thanks, lad." He pocketed the coins with a grin and then turned to keep working his way up the line. "Sweatmeats! Meatballs! Spicy jerky! Sweatmeats! Meatballs! Spicy jerky!"

"Mica, what's wrong?"

He didn't answer. He just swung up into his saddle and gathered up the reins, staring into space as if she weren't even there.

She reached out to place her hand on his arm. "Mica . . ."

He reacted to her touch as if he'd been burned, turning his horse's head so savagely Rakaia winced for the poor beast's mouth. Without another word, Mica kicked his horse with a soundless cry and galloped off in the opposite direction, away from Krakandar.

It took Rakaia nearly an hour to catch up with Mica, another half hour to find him, and by then the sun was moving toward the horizon and she realized they would not be entering Krakandar City today. The gates would be closed for the night before they got back.

She spied his horse first, grazing on the side of the road near an outcropping of rock. Rakaia dismounted and led her horse over to Mica's, picking up the reins and draping them over the saddle so the poor thing couldn't step on them. He was lathered and had obviously been run until he almost foundered, but there was no sign of Mica.

She petted him for a moment to calm him down, whispering sweet nothings to him as she led the horses to a nearby sapling, where she tied them both. Rakaia smiled fleetingly at the thought of how proud Charisee would be of her, for being so considerate of the horses for once, before she turned and called out for Mica.

There was no answer, although she was certain he must be nearby.

"Mica!"

Other than the echo of her own voice from the rocks, there was no reply.

"Mica! Please! Don't leave me out here on my own! It'll be dark soon!"

She waited for a moment and then she heard a faint call.

"Over here."

"Over *where*?"

A hand appeared above the rocks a hundred paces or so to her left, waving briefly before it disappeared.

With a sigh of exasperation, Rakaia picked up her skirts and headed over the rough ground to where he was hiding, still unable to imagine what might have made him gallop off like that. She could conceive a person being that upset on learning a loved one had died, but he seemed ridiculously upset to learn the High Prince of Hythria was alive and well.

"Mica! Please . . ." she called, after crossing a small creek narrow enough for her to step over.

"Over here," he called again.

Now that she was closer, she could hear him better and only a few minutes after crossing the creek she rounded an outcropping and found him sitting in a small shallow cave formed by a hollow in the rocks.

He looked up as she blocked the sun with her approach. She was shocked to discover his face streaked with tears. In his hands he held a fine gold chain with a tiny golden lyre hanging from it. She'd seen it before. He usually wore the chain around his neck.

"Are you all right?"

"Not really." He wiped his tears away with the heel of his hands, as if he was embarrassed for her to see him like this.

She squatted down so she could look him in the eye. "Why did you run off like that?"

"Because it's all gone, Rakaia. Everything I had planned. It should have happened by now."

She moved around until she was beside him and then sat down with her back to the rocks and put her arm around him. "What did you have planned, Mica?"

"This," he said, holding up the lyre necklace. "Zegarnald said it would fix everything."

She smiled at that. "So the God of War is the one at fault here?"

"He said he'd help me. Help me get even . . . or even things up . . . I'm not even sure now." He put his head on her shoulder. "But nothing has gone the way he said it would. The only good thing that's happened to me lately is you, and he didn't mention you at all."

"The God of War didn't mention me? How rude."

He turned his head to look at her, his expression pained. "You don't believe me."

"I'm sure you talk to the gods all the time, Mica. I certainly do. I just don't expect them to talk back to me."

"They talk back to me," Mica insisted. "At least they used to talk to me. Kali would come visit me sometimes. I know Jakerlon and Dace and Zegarnald and . . . Gimlorie . . . I even knew Xaphista once."

"Well, I'm not surprised you know Gimlorie," she said. "You sing like the God of Music chose you himself."

Mica shook his head. "He never chose me . . . it was the demon child who made him teach me his song."

Having heard Mica sing and seen what he could do with his songs, that was one claim she wasn't prepared to dismiss out of hand. "Is that how you know the demon child?"

He nodded. "I knew them all, once," he said. "Princess Adrina, the High Prince, Brakandaran the Halfbreed, the demon child . . . I was only a small boy, but I knew them . . ."

Somehow, Rakaia realized, no matter how bizarre his story, Mica was telling the truth. "So what happened? How did you end up here?"

"It all started," Mica said, wiping away a fresh bout of tears, "when Damin Wolfblade ordered me put to death and Brakandaran the Half-breed killed me."

ONCE CHARISEE WAS accepted by Princess Adrina as her sister, it removed the last chance anybody might question her identity. Rakaia was one of a dozen legitimate sisters and a score of bastards raised in the harem. They hardly knew each other. Adrina already had her first *court'esa* by the time Rakaia was born and she'd left Talabar more than a decade ago.

There wasn't a single question Adrina might ask her sister that Charisee couldn't answer. It gave her a sense of renewed confidence.

To Charisee's immense relief, Adrina didn't throw a banquet to welcome her to Greenharbour the day she arrived, although she assured her one would be held in due course. Adrina didn't sound particularly enthusiastic about the idea, which suited Charisee just fine. She wasn't so full of confidence yet that she was ready to be the main attraction at a royal gala.

They ate an informal dinner in the nursery so Rakaia could meet her nieces and nephews. Although it would have been nice to think Adrina was considering Rakaia's feelings, she quickly deduced the informality of the occasion was for the children's sake, not hers.

Adrina had arranged a dinner table set up in the large playroom. There Charisee met Jazrian, the eldest, a bright, tousle-haired eleven-year-old who seemed to study everything around him quite intently before making a decision about anything. Marlie, his nine-year-old sister, was much more outspoken. Charisee got the feeling it was Marlie who ruled the nursery, not her quieter older brother.

The two youngest, Tristan and Kimarie, were twins. They were four, as different as two siblings could be, and rather intrigued by the notion of having yet another aunt. The Wolfblades were a large extended family, and it seemed they knew all their aunts and uncles by name. It took Adrina quite some time to convince them Rakaia was another aunt they had only just met.

Being the youngest, they had eaten earlier, and were carried off to bed by their nurses once the introductions were over, leaving the two older children to share their dinner with their mother and their new aunt.

Marlie, in particular, was very excited at the prospect of being an attendant at the wedding.

"Have you decided what color we'll be wearing," Marlie asked as they took their seats on the cushions around the low dinner table.

"Wearing for what?" Charisee asked, a little confused.

"The wedding, of course."

"Marlie seems to think you're going to want her as your head attendant at the wedding," Adrina explained as she began to help herself to the food, which was the signal that everyone else could eat. "I have been trying to explain to her that a bride's head attendant is usually much older, and her cousin, Julika, is the most likely candidate. The decision is yours, of course. I haven't yet convinced Marlie she shouldn't presume any such thing."

"I'd be delighted to have Marlie as an attendant." Charisee forced herself to smile as the looming reality of her wedding to a man old enough to be her grandfather became horribly real. "Who is Julika?"

"Aunt Kalan's daughter," Marlie informed her before her mother could answer. "She's apprenticed to the Sorcerers' Collective. Jaz says it's because her mother is the High Arrion. I think it's because her papa was a Harshini prince and she's a real sorcerer."

"Don't be stupid, Marlie," Jaz scolded. He turned to Charisee, shaking his head. "Don't pay any attention to her, Aunt Rakaia. She's making it up. Nobody knows who Julika's papa is."

"Oh," Charisee said, not sure how to react to the news that the High Arrion of the Sorcerers' Collective had given birth to a bastard.

Adrina smiled. "Welcome to the Wolfblade family," she said. "As I'm sure you'll learn soon enough, the Wolfblade women—Kalan in particular—are fond of defying convention. There's a lesson in that, actually. Don't assume anything about the people you meet here. They are not always what they seem."

Charisee smiled at the irony of Adrina's advice. "Well, I'm going to be terribly boring, I'm afraid, doing exactly what convention requires of me and marrying Lord Branador."

"Maybe you'll get lucky," Jaz said, "and Uncle Frederak will die of old age before the wedding."

"Jazrian, that's a terrible thing to say!"

"I didn't say it," Jaz told his mother calmly. "Nana Marla said it. She said Grandpapa Hablet breeds daughters like cattle, and he trades them like cattle too so he can—"

"That will be quite enough about what Nana Marla says," Adrina scolded. She turned to Charisee. "I'm sorry. As you'll soon learn when you meet her, my mother-in-law is inflicted with an unreasonable prejudice against all things Fardohnyan in general and very specifically against all things relating to our family."

"That must make life here difficult for you."

Her response seemed to surprise Adrina. "It has its challenges. Fortunately, you'll be living in Highcastle after the wedding. You shouldn't have to weather *Nana* Marla's animosity more than two or three times a year."

"We can come and visit you at Highcastle, too," Marlie offered. "Can we, Mama?"

"I'm sure a visit can be arranged. If you haven't driven Rakaia mad by the wedding, pestering her about how you think it should be done." She turned to Rakaia and added with a smile. "Marlie is one of nature's little organizers. She's never happier than when she is ordering people about. We're considering a career in the military for her. She'd make an excellent general."

"But you and Papa said I couldn't train with the Raiders like Jaz does, Mama."

"That doesn't mean you wouldn't make a wonderful general, darling."

"Is Princess Rakaia's wedding still going ahead, Mama?" Jazrian asked, his expression too grave for one so young. "With Papa still so ill?"

"Of course it is."

"If it would be easier on you to delay it, your highness . . . ," Charisee began, still not comfortable calling this intimidating woman by her given name.

"Easier, yes," Adrina agreed. "But politically foolish. And we live by politics in this place."

"How is the High Prince?" she asked cautiously, wishing as soon as she said it that she'd not asked the question in front of the children. "Is he recovered from his wounds?"

"He's better than expected, worse than I'd like," Adrina replied cryptically. "After dinner we'll visit him so you can pay your respects."

* * *

THEY LEFT THE nursery an hour or so later. By then Marlie had explained all her plans for Rakaia's wedding, what she should do with her time in Greenharbour, and how she should manage her household when she got to Highcastle. Jaz said little, just rolled his eyes a lot as Marlie chattered away. Adrina didn't seem to say much either, prepared to let Marlie do the talking while she watched her sister out of the corner of her eye.

This was a test, of sorts, Charisee realized.

She wished she could tell if she'd passed it or not.

As promised, Adrina took Charisee to meet her husband after dinner. They walked in silence along the wide mosaic tiled hall toward the royal suite on the second floor. Charisee didn't mind the silence, quite certain any attempt she made to fill it with small talk would only end in disaster.

It was Adrina who broke the silence, surprising Charisee with a compliment. "You were very patient with Marlie tonight."

"She's a sweet child."

Adrina seemed amused by that. "You say that because you've only just met her. Still, it's not often a grownup gives her many and varied opinions so much weight. You've made a friend for life there, I suspect."

"Then I'm pleased to know I have made my first new friend in Greenharbour."

Adrina didn't answer. They had reached the large double doors at the end of the hall carved with a massive wolf's head. This, Charisee guessed, was the royal suite where the High Prince was recovering from his wounds.

"How much did Kiam tell you about my husband's injuries?" Adrina asked as she waved to the guards on duty to open the door.

"Not much at all," Charisee said as they stepped into the anteroom. It was a large room, but furnished in a way that made it feel quite cozy and lived in. Charisee suspected Adrina and her family spent a lot of time in here. On the far side of the room was another set of large double doors with yet another wolf's head carving. "I gather they were quite serious."

Adrina nodded, indicating Charisee should sit. With some trepidation, she did as Adrina asked.

Apparently they were not here to meet the High Prince, after all.

Once she was seated, Adrina looked down at her and crossed her arms. "Who are you, Rakaia?"

"Excuse me?"

"Are you Hablet's daughter? Or your mother's?"

Charisee felt her blood run cold. *What sort of question is that? Does she know? Does she suspect something? Did I say something over dinner that gave me away?*

"I . . . I'm both, of course."

"Did our father ask you to spy on me?"

Charisee didn't know the answer to that question, but she could guess. "Yes."

Adrina didn't seem surprised. "And are you planning to?"

"I'm not sure I can answer that question to your satisfaction, your highness."

"You're evading the question."

The best lies of all are the stone-cold truth.

"If I say yes, then you will never trust me, your highness. If I say no, you will assume I'm lying and you'll trust me even less."

Adrina was silent for a moment, and then she smiled. "That's a pretty good reading of the situation. Are you usually so clever?"

"I don't think I'm clever at all."

"I think you do yourself an injustice, Rakaia."

"My lady, I have not come here to cause you trouble. I'm to marry the lord of Highcastle because your husband and our father did a deal that gives the same value to possession of a single woman's body as it does a number of trade concessions." Charisee clamped her mouth shut, horrified she'd voiced such an opinion aloud.

Adrina, however, burst out laughing. "Dear gods, you and Marla are going to be firm friends! You sound just like her."

"I'm . . . I'm sorry, my lady, I should never . . ."

"You're right, Rakaia. You shouldn't have said that. Not unless you want to be thought of as some sort of anarchist. You're perfectly entitled to think it, though, and if my mother-in-law and I agree on anything, it's that things need to change. But changing something so . . . ingrained, takes time. You won't win any friends undermining the efforts of those of us actually working to change things by being dismissed as a troublemaker."

Charisee forgot she was trying to be Rakaia. The slave answered. The outraged slave who had watched her friends—both slave and high-born—taken from the harem time and again to seal trade deals or enrich their father. "Then you condoned the deal that married one of your own sisters to a man sixty years her senior in return for a few trade concessions?"

Adrina nodded. She was unapologetic. "Do you know why?"

Charisee could think of quite a few reasons, but none of them was complimentary, and she was dangerously close to making an enemy of the High Princess. She wisely shook her head and said nothing.

"Then I will tell you. It's because one of the trade concessions we traded you for, little sister, was the right for unaccompanied Fardohnyan women to travel to Hythria without a customs official confirming that a male relative has permitted her to travel before they let her across the border."

Charisee didn't know what to say. She'd imagined the trade concession concerned timber, or wool.

Adrina was no longer smiling. "Do you think you're the only woman who ever sat in that wretched harem, cursing the accident of birth that made her a tradable commodity?"

"I'm so sorry, your highness," she said, trying to figure out how she was going to repair this fragile new relationship that appeared so close to fracturing before it had even begun. "I don't want you to think that I think—"

She was interrupted by a knock at the door, which was probably a good thing, because she appeared to be digging herself deeper and deeper with every word she uttered.

"Actually, Rakaia, I will soon know exactly what you think. Enter!"

Before she could ask what Adrina meant by that, the door opened and a tall, brown-haired young man walked in. He was dressed simply, but his clothes were well made, his boots tooled from the finest leather, and he seemed quite at home in this inner sanctum of the royal family. For a moment, Charisee wondered if this was Damin Wolfblade, but then she realized he was far too young. Damin was a man in his forties. This man didn't seem much older than her.

Adrina turned and smiled at her guest, holding her hand out to him. "Wrayan. Thank you for coming."

Wrayan took her hand, kissed the High Princess's palm, and then turned to study Charisee. "And this must be Rakaia?"

"Rakaia, Princess of Fardohnya, I'd like to introduce you to Wrayan Lightfinger, head of the Greenharbour Thieves' Guild."

Charisee was starting to wonder if she was going mad. "The Thieves' Guild?"

"Your highness." Wrayan Lightfinger took her hand, kissing her palm with the same respect he'd shown Adrina, and then he turned to the High Princess. "You didn't tell her I was coming?"

"Of course not; that would spoil the surprise. Have a seat."

Wrayan did as Adrina bid, facing Charisee.

"Wrayan is an old family friend," Adrina explained, although she remained standing behind Wrayan. "Do not be fooled by his youthful appearance. Wrayan is part-Harshini and quite a bit older than my children's grandmother."

"I . . . would never have guessed," Charisee said, not certain what she was supposed to say to that.

"I asked Wrayan here tonight, Rakaia, because in addition to ensuring none of his fellow guild members rob the palace blind, he provides another service for the Wolfblade family."

Am I supposed to ask what service? Why is he looking at me like that?

"I'm going to look inside your mind, your highness," Wrayan said, as if saying the words gently somehow mitigated the invasion. "I'm going to confirm for the High Princess that you are no threat to her family, and then I'm going to shield your mind so nobody else can influence you, or try to use you to threaten or harm them."

Charisee felt the blood drain from her face. "You can *do* that?"

"I don't have many magical gifts, your highness, but that is one of them."

She looked up at Adrina who was staring down at her with an implacable and entirely unsympathetic expression. There was no help to be had from that quarter. Far from it. This was clearly Adrina's idea.

"Will it hurt?" she asked, her mind racing. The moment she let Wrayan into her mind, she would be exposed.

Why didn't you warn me this might happen, Jakerlon?

Where are you now . . . when I need you the most?

"Only if you try to push back," Wrayan assured her.

"And if you do, we will assume it's because you have something to hide, Rakaia, so I suggest you submit without complaint. It only takes a few minutes and then I won't have to wonder if I can trust you; I will know."

Charisee nodded. She had to appear compliant, but inside she was a seething ball of panic. "What do I need to do?"

"Get comfortable," Wrayan said. "Then just close your eyes and try to relax."

"May I use the garderobe first?" she asked. "I drank far too much cordial at dinner, I'm afraid."

"Of course." Wrayan glanced up at Adrina. "Is that all right with you?"

"I'll have the guards show you to the nearest facility," Adrina offered.

Charisee smiled and climbed to her feet. Adrina opened the door, asked one of the guards to show her the way to the nearest bathroom, and then closed the door behind her, leaving Charisee in the hall.

She followed the guard down the corridor to the garderobe, thanked him when he opened the door for her, and then collapsed against it and sank to the floor as soon as she was alone.

Charisee was shaking so badly she couldn't think straight. She could barely breathe. A quick glance around the room and she realized there was no escape here. The window above the garderobe was too small to climb through, and besides, they were on the second floor. There was no escape that way.

Calm down! Think!

Perhaps she could just walk out of here, pretend nothing was amiss and head downstairs as if that was where she was meant to be going. She was a princess, after all. Who would think to question her?

How far will I get before Adrina starts to wonder where I am?

Charisee wanted to cry. It wasn't going to end like this, surely? It was too unfair to have come all this way, only to be exposed now.

Jakerlon, you answered my prayer once. I need you to do it again.

If you want me to keep honoring you, then cause an earthquake, or make the sky fall in the next few minutes because a part-Harshini thief is about the steal the truth from my mind, and there's nothing I can do to stop him.

"Your highness?" a muffled male voice asked through the door. "Are you alright?"

Charisee wiped her eyes and took a deep breath. "I'll be out in a minute!"

She rose to her feet, walked to the washbowl, and splashed some cool water on her face. Charisee looked at herself in the mirror. A stranger stared back at her.

"You can do this," she told the princess in the reflection. "Whatever he finds in your mind he will believe. So think the right thoughts and you might just get away with this."

After all, the best lies of all are the stone-cold truth.

Charisee smoothed down her skirt, opened the door, and smiled at the guard. "Could you take me back now, please?"

"Of course, your highness."

She followed him back to the door of the royal suite. He knocked on it twice and then opened it without waiting for permission. Charisee squared her shoulders, forced a smile onto her face, and stepped inside.

Adrina and Wrayan Lightfinger were waiting for her.

"Shall I lie down?" she asked. "Or would you prefer I sit?"

"Whatever makes you the most comfortable, your highness."

"I suppose lying down would be best." She walked back to the cushions and sank down gracefully, rearranged a few of the pillows, and then stretched out. Before she closed her eyes, she turned to Wrayan. "I hope you don't get lost in here, Master Lightfinger. According to my sisters, I am rather scatterbrained."

Wrayan smiled reassuringly. "I'm sure I can manage, your highness. Would you close your eyes, please? And try to relax."

Charisee did as he asked. She took a deep breath and then opened up her mind, forcing every early memory of Rakaia she could manage to the surface, until the only thing filling her head were memories of two little girls playing pranks on everyone in the harem by each pretending to be the other.

Until the requested earthquake or skyfall happened, it was the only thing she could think of to do to protect herself.

"Don't you mean when Brakandaran the Halfbreed *tried* to kill you?" Rakaia asked.

Mica shook his head. "No . . . he had me killed."

"And yet . . . here you are . . ."

He looked at her, his face filled with pain. "I knew you wouldn't believe me."

"I want to believe you, Mica, but what you're saying doesn't make sense."

He took a deep breath. "It's a very long story."

"Well, we're not going to make it to Krakandar tonight, so we might as well do something to pass the time," she said.

"I can think of something," he said with a small smile.

"*Other* than that, you fiend. I think there's some cheese and the last of that loaf we bought in Walsark left in the saddlebags. There's a stream a little way back so we can water the horses. Why don't you get a fire going, I'll take care of dinner, and then you can tell me all about how you died?"

"But you think I'm mad."

"That doesn't mean you're not entertaining."

He smiled faintly. "You know, the only other real friend I ever really had was a god."

"You see, you can't go making statements like that and not offering some sort of explanation. So . . . dinner and a tale of gods, adventure, and coming back from the dead?"

He nodded. She took her arm from around him and climbed to her feet. "You get the fire started. I'll be back in a few minutes with the horses."

Rakaia headed back toward where she had tied the horses, shaking her head at her own folly. "I should mount up right this minute and ride away from here," she told the horses when she reached them in a low voice. "He's mad as a cut snake and the only reason I've come this far with him is because . . ."

Because he's saved me from Hablet, and without him I would be lost. Because he adores me and I . . .

Rakaia gathered up the reins, not prepared to finish that thought, even silently. "Come on, girls," she told the mares. "Let's get you something to drink."

THE BREAD WAS stale, the cheese dry, and the water from the creek of dubious quality, but Rakaia hardly noticed, as Mica, with a great deal of reluctance, began to explain his bizarre claim that Brakandaran the Half-breed had killed him.

"I grew up in Kirkland," he began once he'd finished his cheese. Rakaia sat opposite him, the small fire they'd made between them more for comfort than for warmth. As darkness fell, the fire became their only illumination. It threw shadows up onto Mica's face that made him seem far more sinister than the Mica Rakaia knew in the cold light of day. "It's a province of Karien, ruled over by Lord Laetho."

"Was it a happy childhood?"

He shrugged. "Happy enough. My father was a steward on Lord Laetho's estate. That's what I was going to be when I grew up, too. A steward on Lord Laetho's estate."

"I had much higher aspirations," Rakaia joked. "I was going to be a princess. Look how that turned out."

Mica smiled. "So neither of us ended up where we expected."

"Well, I know how I got here. What's your excuse?"

"War," Mica said. "We went to war."

Rakaia didn't have an answer for that, but she didn't need one. Mica continued his tale without any further prompting.

"My brother Jaymes and I went to war with Lord Laetho. We were just supposed to be there to wait on Lord Laetho and his knights. You know . . . fetch and carry, polish armor, that sort of thing. Nothing else. But Prince Cratyn was anxious to get the war done before winter so Lord Laetho told me and Jaymes to see if we could sneak over the border into the Defenders' camp and report on what was going on."

"How old were you?"

"Ten. Jaymes was fourteen."

Rakaia shook her head at the stupidity of men at war. "Is that when the High Prince ordered you put to death?"

"Damin Wolfblade wasn't the High Prince then. His uncle Lernen was still on the throne. He was just a Hythrun warlord off to fight someone else's war for a bit of a lark, I think. At least, he never seemed to take it as seriously as the Medalonians did."

"You were captured, though?"

"Of course we were. Jaymes and I . . . we were stewards, not spies. We weren't across the border more than a few hours before Damin Wolfblade's Krakandar Raiders found us."

He stopped long enough to throw another few sticks on the fire. Rakaia was almost afraid to ask what happened next, well able to image the fate of two young spies in the war camp of an enemy. Mica surprised her, however, by smiling at the memory.

"They separated us, of course. Jaymes stayed in the Raiders' camp and I was sent to the keep to wait on Sister Mahina. I think that was the first time I was truly warm and not hungry since we reached the border. It really wasn't that bad. Mahina was gruff, but she was kind and I had the run of the place, truth be told."

"Didn't you try to escape?"

"Tarja Tenragan threatened to cut Jaymes's fingers off if I tried. I don't know if he really meant it, but I believed he'd do it, so no . . . I did exactly what I was told, when I was told. Jaymes had it even better than me. The Raiders adopted him like a pet and he ended up joining them. He's probably still with them, for all I know. And then, one day out of the blue, they sent me home."

"Because you were eating so much?"

He smiled. "Not exactly. The Medalonians decided to try and sue for peace, so I was sent back with the offer."

"A prisoner of war and diplomat, all by the age of ten. You *are* an accomplished young man, aren't you?"

"I was just as much a prisoner when I got back to my side of the border as I was in the Medalonian war camp," he told her, his smile fading. "You joke about the food, but they didn't see the funny side of it. Being well fed almost got me killed. They thought I looked too well fed to have been a prisoner. I probably would have wound up dead if Princess Adrina hadn't intervened."

"Adrina? My sister Adrina, you mean?" Strictly speaking, Adrina wasn't her sister, now that she knew the truth of her paternity, but Mica knew what she meant.

He nodded. "She was still married to Prince Cratyn then. Gods . . . I remember thinking she was the most beautiful, pious, noble woman Xaphista had ever created."

"You followed Xaphista?"

"Everyone in Karien followed Xaphista until the demon child destroyed him."

"I know . . . it's just . . . I can't imagine piling all the woes of the world at the feet of a single god."

"None of the gods are much use to humanity when it gets down to it," he said. "But I didn't know then what I know now. Adrina rescued me from the war council and I became her servant, and I would have walked over hot coals and broken glass in bare feet to do her bidding."

Mica's tale fascinated Rakaia. Like every one of Adrina's sisters, she knew somehow Hablet's eldest daughter had managed to wed the crown prince of Karien and the High Prince of Hythria's heir, all within a matter of months. The details of how it came about remained vague. One of her regrets about swapping places with Charisee was that she would never have the opportunity to ask Adrina what happened.

"Mind you, I thought Cratyn was a proud and noble prince too, and he turned out to be a real weasel. Anyway, after the first serious battle, Adrina's captain was killed—"

"Tristan," Rakaia cut in, still able to recall the sadness she'd felt on learning of his death. She was no older than Mica was when they sent him off to war when the news reached Talabar about her bastard half-brother's death. "He was father's eldest bastard. I remember him. Everyone said if Papa . . . Hablet . . . didn't sire a legitimate son, he'd make Tristan his heir one day."

"His death changed Adrina," Mica said. "She was . . . I want to say angry, but that seems too insignificant a word. She was beyond anger. That very night she left the Karien war camp with me and her servant, Tamylan. We crossed into Medalon under cover of darkness, rode straight across the battlefield while they were still burning the dead . . . and ran smack bang into Damin Wolfblade and Tarja Tenragan."

"And that's when he ordered you killed?"

"No. He took Adrina and Tamylan prisoner and sent me back to wait on Sister Mahina. But it wasn't long after that I met Dace and Kali."

"Who are they?"

"Dacendaran and Kalianah."

She'd believed every word he'd told her so far, but he was wandering into the realms of fantasy. "Really? You met the God of Thieves and the Goddess of Love?"

"Dace took it upon himself to save me from Xaphista. Kalianah hangs around with him a lot. I'm not sure why. Maybe because they both prefer to appear to mortals as children . . . I don't know. I just know that Dace very quickly became the best friend I'd ever had and spent all his time trying to get me to steal something."

Rakaia wasn't sure what to believe. It seemed easier to just play along and pretend it was real. "Did you?"

"Eventually. I stole a bird's nest, if you can believe it. He convinced me the eggs wouldn't survive unless we took the nest away from where the mother bird had built it."

"And that's it . . . now you're a follower of Dacendaran?"

"It doesn't take much."

"But what about Adrina? How did she go from prisoner of war to High Princess of Hythria?"

"I'm not even sure of that myself," Mica admitted. "When we first arrived in Medalon, Adrina didn't have a good word to say about Damin Wolfblade, and he looked at her like she was infected with the plague. A couple of months later and they can't keep their hands off one another. I snuck up on them once, in the stables, you know. They were kissing each other like there was nobody else in the world, in between telling one another how much each one didn't like the other."

Rakaia hadn't heard this version of the story. Not for a moment did she imagine Adrina and Damin had married all those years ago because they were in love. That just didn't happen to people in their position. "We were told the demon child made them get married because it meant my father couldn't invade Hythria through Krakandar Province via Medalon. Once his daughter was married to the warlord of Krakandar, he was forced to withdraw."

Mica shrugged. "I don't know the politics behind it. I just know that when R'shiel suggested it, nobody objected too loudly."

"But Adrina was still married to Cratyn."

"Not for long. The demon child killed him."

"Oh. I didn't know that."

He nodded. "After that, things got a bit muddled. I think Medalon had surrendered to Karien by then and there was an army marching down on top of us, and we had the army Cratyn brought with him being held prisoner. Damin wanted to put them to the sword, I think, but R'shiel said it would be a bad idea. She came up with the idea of magically coercing them to return home, to avoid any further bloodshed. I think she had the power to make it happen herself, but the coercions she can work don't hold for long. The Song of Gimlorie, however . . ."

"Gods . . . I thought that story about the Song of Gimlorie was a fairy tale . . ." Even as she said the words, she realized how foolish they were, how often she had seen Mica do exactly that—coerce people into doing exactly what he wanted when he sang to them.

His wild tale didn't seem anywhere near so wild all of a sudden.

Mica shook his head. "It's real. And the effects can last for years . . . sometimes a lifetime. But you have to learn the songs from Gimlorie himself. The main problem with his coercion, though, is that most people can resist it if they know it's happening to them. R'shiel knew she could never get close enough to any of the Karien soldiers to sing the song without one of them putting a blade through her, but they wouldn't be suspicious of a child."

"So she had Gimlorie teach it to you . . ."

He nodded. "She knew the danger. She had Jaymes there to keep me anchored so I didn't get lost in the song, and I did what she wanted. I sent the army back, and no more lives were lost that day."

Any other story like this might end there, with a relatively happy ending, but Rakaia knew that all of this had been preamble to the real story of how Mica came to be here.

"Then what happened?"

"I came to Hythria with Damin Wolfblade, and Adrina, and the demon child."

"I still don't understand why Damin sentenced you to death."

"Well, that was because while the demon child was busy saving Médalon from the Kariens, she kind of forgot about what learning the Song of Gimlorie might do to me. She also forgot, I think, that Xaphista was still around and quite desperate to get rid of the demon child before the demon child got rid of him."

"Xaphista got to you."

"I didn't know it—and I probably wouldn't have understood what it meant if you'd told me at the time—but I was wide open to any god bending me to his will after that. I don't know if R'shiel didn't know, or didn't care. All I know is that Xaphista found me one night on the way to Green-harbour and after that, all I wanted to do was kill the demon child."

Finally, Rakaia understood. "And that's why Damin Wolfblade sentenced you to death."

Mica had tried to kill the demon child.

46

"SHE'S HIDING SOMETHING," Wrayan told Adrina once he was done probing Rakaia's mind.

The young woman in question remained stretched out on the cushions of her private sitting room. She was asleep now, peaceful, serene, and innocent. Wrayan had done that for her too, partly to prevent her developing a headache and partly to give them the opportunity to speak in private.

Adrina walked to the sideboard and poured them each a goblet of wine. Hearing news like that, she felt in need of a drink. "You couldn't tell what she was hiding?"

He shrugged as he accepted the goblet from the princess. "This is your sister, your highness, not the man who tried to assassinate Damin. I was trying to be careful."

"But if she's hiding something . . ."

He took a sip of wine and asked, "Who is Charisee?"

"Rakaia's shadow," Adrina told him, lowering herself to the cushions beside him. "One of father's countless bastards who grew up in the harem with us. I think her mother was a *court'esa*. She was assigned to serve Rakaia when she was about six, the theory being that as they grew up together, Charisee would learn to serve and Rakaia would learn to lead. It's a common enough practice in the harem." She smiled, looking down on her unconscious sister. "As I recall, things didn't go according to plan, with those two. They became fast friends and wreaked all manner of havoc for a while. I was surprised when Rakaia turned up without her, to be honest. I thought those two couldn't be separated without magical intervention."

"Did you ask why she didn't bring Charisee to Hythria with her?"

Adrina nodded, and took another sip of wine. "She told me she thought Charisee deserved better than a life as a drudge at Highcastle. Truth is, Frederak wouldn't have allowed her to keep her own slave anyway, so it was probably the best decision in the circumstances. Is she hiding something to do with Charisee?"

Wrayan shrugged. "Her thoughts are full of Charisee. But not now, oddly enough . . . when they were younger. And something about Rakaia being Charisee and Charisee being Rakaia. She was right about the scatterbrained thing. I couldn't really make head nor tail of it."

Adrina smiled as a long forgotten memory burbled to the surface—a rare happier time in the harem when someone other than her was causing trouble. "Actually, that's one thing that does make sense. Rakaia and her little friend used to swap identities all the time when they were younger. Thought it was hilarious, they did. I don't know that they ever fooled Princess Sophany, but father's other wives often fell for the prank, and if I'm not mistaken, they even conned Hablet more than once."

"Perhaps she's just missing her sister, which is why she dredging up all those memories of happier times." Wrayan didn't seem unduly alarmed by what he'd seen in Rakaia's thoughts.

"But she's still hiding something?"

"Most definitely."

"Is it going to be a problem?"

"I doubt it," Wrayan said, although he didn't sound entirely convinced. He took a sip of wine and added, "She certainly bears you or your family no ill will. Quite the opposite. She's in awe of you."

"What's not to love?" Adrina asked with a thin smile. "But what is she hiding?"

Wrayan hesitated. Adrina could tell there was something more he wasn't telling her. "Out with it, Wrayan."

He leaned forward and placed the wine on the table, even though he'd only taken a few sips. "Well, there was something else . . . I just don't want to accuse anyone of something when it may just be the wild fantasies of a lonely young woman."

"Accuse away, Wrayan. I'll decide if it's something to be concerned about."

Wrayan hesitated a moment longer before he took a deep breath and appeared to brace himself for her reaction before saying, "It could have something to do with Kiam."

Adrina frowned. She knew Kiam and trusted him, far more than she knew this girl. "Did he hurt her?"

"Not intentionally."

Adrina sighed. "Oh, dear . . ." She looked down at Rakaia's lovely, peaceful, sleeping face, shaking her head. "You silly, silly girl. Is she in love with him?"

"Hard to say. She was trying to bury those thoughts as hard as she could."

"That explains what she's hiding then, I suppose," Adrina said, wondering how big a problem this was going to be. "And also why she offered to delay the wedding the moment she got here. Out of consideration for me, of course."

"Of course," Wrayan agreed with a smile. "What are you going to do?"

"Speak to Ky first," she said, downing the rest of the wine in a gulp, "before I jump to any conclusions. He may know nothing about this."

"Oh, he knows," Wrayan told her with absolute certainty. "She has a memory of kissing him that's burned into her thoughts, and it's not in a bad way."

Adrina cursed in a very un-princess-like fashion. "I warned him. I told him to be careful . . ."

"Kiam would never betray your trust, your highness. This might just be as innocent as Rakaia fancying herself in love with Ky, and he's done nothing to encourage it."

Adrina couldn't help feeling responsible for this. She had put the two of them together, after all. "I should have sent someone other than a handsome young assassin to escort her to Greenharbour. Someone old, unattractive . . . who chews with his mouth open."

"You mean like the man you've arranged for her to marry?"

She glared at him, not amused at all. "Don't even joke about it, Wrayan."

"Sorry, but I don't know what else to tell you. She's not on a mission to destroy you, and if Hablet has instructed her to do anything nefarious, I can find no trace of it in her thoughts. If anything she's glad to be out of the harem and intends to make the most of her new life here. She's obviously missing her sister, and she has a crush on Damin's stepbrother. That's not so awful in the general scheme of things."

"You think it wouldn't be awful if Frederak Branador thinks his new bride has been amusing herself with a common assassin on her way to marry him?"

"And yet he's perfectly fine with the idea that she's entertained herself with any number of *court'esa* until now?"

"I don't make the double standards in this world, Wrayan, I just suffer under them like everyone else. Did you shield her mind?"

He nodded and climbed to his feet. "Nobody but a god could get to her now."

She sighed as she also rose and walked him to the door. "If that happens, we've a lot more to worry about than Rakaia's infatuation with Kiam Miar. At least now, though, I can let her in on the big family secret."

Wrayan glanced at the wolf's head–carved doors leading to the bedroom where Damin still lay unconscious and unmoving. "No change, I take it?"

"None at all. I don't suppose you've had any luck finding R'shiel?"

"Not even Dacendaran seems to know where she is. Or if he does, he isn't telling. I heard a rumor, though, in the city the other day. Apparently, that man in there is a Karien imposter named Jeck and Damin is really off helping the demon child with some secret mission on which the fate of the whole world depends."

Adrina laughed at that. "Really? The whole world depends on it?"

"You've heard the rumor?"

"I started it."

"Well, it's got legs now."

"If you've heard it already, and it's been embellished so much, then it has more than legs, Wrayan. It has wings."

He nodded in agreement. "Then I shan't deny it, if anyone asks. How are you bearing up?"

"I have good days and bad days. This felt like a good one . . . until now."

He glanced back at Rakaia and then smiled. "I really don't think you have anything to worry about, your highness."

"I hope you're right, Wrayan. How long will she sleep?"

"The rest of the night, if you can move her without waking her," he said.

Impulsively, Adrina leaned across and kissed Wrayan's cheek. "Thank you. I know you're only here because Marla told you to keep an eye on me, but I do appreciate your help."

Wrayan took her hand and kissed her palm. "I would help you anyway, your highness, even if Princess Marla forbade it."

Adrina didn't believe that for a second, but she smiled as if she did. "You will let me know if you hear any news about the demon child?"

"The moment I hear something," he promised.

Adrina opened the door for him, said goodbye to Wrayan, and then ordered one of the guards to fetch some help to move Rakaia to her room.

After that she closed the door and walked back to the cushions. She looked down and studied her sleeping younger sister for a moment, wondering if she should mention what Wrayan had told her or keep it to herself.

In truth, she didn't begrudge Rakaia her infatuation, just wished it was focused on someone less problematic.

She needed to speak to Ky, Adrina decided, and get his side of the story first, because the sooner Rakaia was married, away from temptation and out of her hair, the sooner she became one less problem the High Princess of Hythria had to deal with.

Chapter

47

MICA THREW THE last of the wood they'd gathered onto the dying flames. Rakaia had no idea what time it was. She suspected it was edging close to dawn. But while she understood a lot more about Mica's history, there was still more to be told.

And nothing yet explained why he'd fled on the Krakandar Road earlier, so distraught and disappointed.

"What did you do?"

"Poison," he said. "Xaphista visited me again in Greenharbour. He gave me the idea. It took me a long time to find the right opportunity. I had to wait until I was serving the demon child and that wasn't easy. R'shiel and Brak left Greenharbour not long after we arrived. She only stayed long enough to bully the other warlords into line and help Damin secure his throne, then she flew off on the back of a dragon with Brak to convince Hablet of Fardohnya he had to change sides." He closed his eyes for a moment. "Gods, I can still remember how determined I was. How proud I was that nobody guessed my intentions."

"What went wrong?"

He shrugged. "I really don't know, to be honest. Everything was going according to plan. R'shiel and Brak finally caught up with us on the road back to Medalon. Damin was taking a force to relieve the Karien siege of the Citadel by then. I remember everybody sitting around the tent, laughing and joking . . . I remember putting the jarabane I'd kept hidden in my pocket for weeks into the wine I was about to serve to R'shiel . . . then next thing I know, Brak is yelling, the wine is spilled, Damin has his sword at my throat, and Adrina is begging for my life."

Mica stopped, his eyes misting with tears. This part, it seemed, was almost more than he could bear.

"Mica . . . it's alright. If you don't want talk about it . . ."

He wiped his eyes impatiently, shaking his head. "It's not that. I want to tell you . . . I do. I've never told anyone before. Never had anyone to tell, truth be told . . . it's just . . . can I sing it for you?"

"Sing it . . . you mean tell me in verse?"

"No, I mean show you. I can sing it so much better than explain it."

Rakaia's heart skipped a beat. "You mean you want to use the Song of Gimlorie on me."

"Not to coerce you, Rakaia. I would never do that to you, I swear. Besides, it's like I told you . . . if the listener knows they're being influenced, they can block it out."

"If I can block you out, then what's the point?"

"Because this isn't coercion," he assured her. "I can just make you see what I saw, what I felt . . . then you'll understand." Her hesitation seemed to wound him. "I love you, Rakaia. I would never do to anything to hurt you."

"Now you're trying to manipulate me."

"I could have just started singing and not warned you at all, if I wanted to do that," he pointed out. "I think you're afraid."

"Of course I'm afraid."

"Of what?"

"What do you think? You can wield the power of a god, Mica. And now you want to use it on me."

"Take this, then," he said, leaning across the fire to hand her the little golden lyre on its fine gold chain.

The gesture amused her. She accepted the necklace and held it up to examine it in the dying firelight. "You think you can bribe me with this cheap trinket?"

"It's not a cheap trinket," he said. "It's the God of Music's Covenant token." Mica spoke as though his words should impress her.

"Is that supposed to sway me?"

"I stole it from the Temple of the Gods in the Citadel."

"So it's a stolen trinket. You're not exactly making your case here, Mica."

"When the gods brought the Harshini into being, they made a pact with each other," he explained. "They realized their wars were getting out of hand, so they agreed to let the Harshini act as . . . I don't know . . . like a bridge. They allowed the Harshini to use their magic, to petition them on behalf of humans . . . That's why they can't lie, why they can't get angry or even really sad. The gods didn't want them to be anything other than evenhanded." Then he added with a smile, "It's why there are demons, by the way. They're little and harmless and by nature are all the naughty bits the gods wanted to remove from the Harshini."

"I know all this, Mica. It might be a revelation to someone raised to believe in the Overlord, but in Fardohnya, we're taught all this at our mother's breast."

"I'll bet you don't learn about the Covenant."

"What is it? A treaty?"

"It's more than a treaty," he said. "It's a magical bond that holds the Covenant of the Gods together. All the gods had to surrender something of their essence to forge it. If it's ever broken, the deal would be off and the Harshini would cease to exist."

"What about the gods?" Rakaia asked, still not sure she believed a word of this.

"The Primal Gods would still be there, but they wouldn't be able to interact with humans the way they do now. And I suspect a lot of the Incidental Gods would cease to exist, because most of them started out as demons, and if the Harshini were gone, they'd be gone, too."

She held up the necklace and examined it more closely. It still looked like a cheap trinket to her. "And you think this bauble is the essence of the God of Music."

"I know it is. That's why he can't find me. It protects the wearer from his influence. It will protect you when I sing for you. It's how I was able to escape."

"Escape from *where?*" she asked in exasperation.

"Let me sing for you, Rakaia, and you'll understand."

Rakaia stared at him in the dim light of the fire, wishing she knew if Mica was as genuine as he seemed or a master manipulator. The trinket in her hand might be no more than a placebo, and she was walking into his trap like a blind fool.

But then, she'd been on the road with Mica for weeks now. Surely, if he wanted to mess with her mind, he could have done it any time before now. She'd held him as he slept to calm his nightmares. She'd listened to him sing a thousand times. She made love to him over and over and she was certain to the core of her being that she had chosen to do so of her own free will, not because he'd made her do it.

But most of all, she was filled with doubt. And it was that which reassured her. She'd seen the ferryman propose to Olena. There hadn't been a doubt in his mind once Mica had sung to him. If Mica were forcing her to do anything against her will, the first thing he would rid her of, she reasoned, would be doubt.

She nodded slowly, gathered up the necklace and chain, and closed her fist over the tiny golden lyre. "Alright, then," she said. "Sing to me, Mica. Show me what happened."

She expected him to reach for his lyre, but it seemed he needed no accompaniment to work his magic. He closed his eyes and began to sing, a haunting, lilting song in a language Rakaia didn't understand.

She waited, not sure what she expected to see, beginning to doubt Mica had any magic at all, but then she realized she was no longer sitting in the lee of a rock outcropping. The temperature grew colder and she glanced around.

She was in a tent, held fast in the grip of a strange man. She was paralyzed with fear. A trickle of blood oozed from her neck where the man held the point of his sword to his throat, ready and determined to run him through.

I am Mica, she realized. *I am seeing this through his eyes.*

"Damin, Brak and I need to take care of this," a woman's calm and reasonable voice said behind them.

The man holding her—Mica—was Damin Wolfblade. "This child is a member of my household. He tried to kill a guest under my roof. Even if you weren't the demon child, R'shiel, the penalty for such a crime is death."

"If you kill him, Damin, we won't be able to question him."

"What's to question? The child is Karien. He obviously follows the Overlord. What more do you need to know?"

"We need to know why he turned from Dacendaran," a voice said. The speaker moved in front of Damin and Mica and Rakaia realized she was facing the legendary Brakandaran the Halfbreed. He proved to be something of a disappointment. Given the stories she'd heard about him, she'd expected him to be ten feet tall. But he was really just a little taller than a normal man with dark hair and a pleasing face, seemed to be aged somewhere between twenty and forty, and was otherwise quite unremarkable. "The God of Thieves took a personal interest in this boy, and somehow he's been subverted. I don't want to interfere with your idea of justice, Damin, but if you harm that boy before we have a chance to talk with him, you'll regret it."

Damin glared at Brak. "Are you threatening me?"

"Yes, Damin," the Halfbreed replied. "That's exactly what I'm doing."

For a long, tense moment, Rakaia waited as Damin Wolfblade stared at Brak, then he lowered the sword and thrust Mikel at him. "You have an hour, Brak. Ask him what you want, do what you want. But in one hour that child dies for what he's done. R'shiel, I hope you will forgive this grievous insult." He sheathed his sword as Brak caught Mikel, who was shaking so badly he could barely stand. "Oh, and by the way, don't think to leave this camp with him," the High Prince added with an icy glare at Brak. "If you do, I will simply turn around and go home. I'll call off my Warlords, and the Medalonians can face the Kariens on their own and to hell with them."

Damin Wolfblade strode out of the tent without another word. In the distance, Rakaia could still make out the strains of Mikel's strange song, but she was quickly becoming lost in his memories.

Brak pushed Rakaia down onto the cushions and looked over at Adrina. Mikel followed her gaze and saw that Adrina was heavily pregnant.

"Can you talk him out of this?" the Halfbreed asked her.

Adrina shrugged helplessly. "I don't know. I've never seen him so angry."

"You've got an hour, Adrina," R'shiel pointed out.

The demon child had not changed at all since Rakaia had last seen her in Testra.

Adrina nodded. "I'll do what I can, but he may not listen to me. I was the one who brought Mikel here."

"Then you'd better do something about keeping him alive, hadn't you?" the demon child said unsympathetically.

The dream faded for a moment, and Rakaia found herself back in front of the fire. Mica still sang, but his cheeks were wet with silent tears. The moment was fleeting and she was back in Mica's body, seeing the world through his eyes as the God of Thieves appeared.

R'shiel must have summoned him. She sat huddled on the cushions, her knees drawn up under her chin, tears streaming silently down Mikel's face. In the warm glow of the candlelight he was an island of misery and dejection.

"What do you want, demon child?" Dacendaran asked as he materialized behind R'shiel.

"What's the matter with you?" she demanded as she spun around to face him.

"I'm busy," Dace muttered, scuffing the rug with a boot that did not match the other he wore.

"I want to know what happened to Mikel."

"You stole him from me."

"I *stole* him from you? Don't be ridiculous! I'm not a god! How could I steal him?"

"You gave him to Gimlorie."

"Oh," R'shiel said, suddenly looking guilty. "That."

Brak glanced at R'shiel for a moment and then looked down at Mikel. "Why did you give him to the God of Music?"

"I needed to make sure the Kariens would leave, so I asked Gimlorie to help."

"What exactly did you do, R'shiel?" Brak asked.

"I asked him to teach Mikel a song that would instill an irresistible longing for home in the Kariens. I knew it might be a little bit . . . dangerous . . . so I asked Gimlorie to make his brother Jaymes his guardian. That way, if he got lost in the song, Jaymes would be there to pull him back."

Brak muttered a curse. "R'shiel, have you any idea what you've done? A guardian is only effective if he's in touch with his ward. Once Jaymes left his side Mikel was vulnerable to this sort of manipulation."

"Hey, how come suddenly this is all my fault? *He* tried to kill *me*!" Neither Brak nor Dace answered her. "I needed to turn them back," she added. "It seemed like a really good idea at the time."

"Gimlorie's songs are dangerous, R'shiel. They can twist men's souls around. You should never have taught one to this boy."

"I didn't teach it to him. Gimlorie did. He didn't seem to mind when I asked him."

"Of course he wouldn't mind. Every soul who hears it hungers for him more. But it's what it has done to Mikel you should be concerned about."

"Are you saying Gimlorie is the one who turned Mikel into an assassin?"

"No," Dacendaran said. "Gimlorie wouldn't do that. But what you *did* do was leave Mikel vulnerable to Xaphista."

"Humans need faith to believe in the gods, R'shiel," Brak added in a lecturing tone. "What you did was take away Mikel's freedom to believe or not believe. You destroyed his free will and made him a creature of the gods. Any god."

R'shiel turned to Mikel and stared down at him impatiently. "Is that what happened, Mikel? Did you go back to worshipping the Overlord?"

Rakaia could feel Mikel shake his head silently, too distraught to speak.

"Then why? Who told you to do this thing?"

"The old man," she replied in a voice so low even Dacendaran had to strain to hear him.

"What old man?" Brak asked.

"The one in Hythria. At the palace. He told me to give the demon child a gift. He said it would help her see the truth."

"What old man is he talking about?" R'shiel asked Brak.

"It was probably Xaphista himself," Dace shrugged.

"Can he do that?" The God of Thieves gave the demon child a withering look. "Oh, well, I suppose if you can do it, so can he."

She turned and studied the miserable figure hunched on the cushions for a moment, then turned to Brak. "Why Mikel?"

"Because he's young, he's impressionable, he's feeling guilty for turning away from his god in the first place, and," he added with a frown, "you left him wide open to manipulation when you opened his mind to Gimlorie's song."

"Well, how was I supposed to know it would do that? The Harshini sang it all the time in Sanctuary. It didn't seem to bother them."

"The Harshini are already a part of the gods, R'shiel. But even they will only share it among themselves. No Harshini would ever share the song with a human."

"So what do we do with him?"

"I don't know, but we've got about half an hour to make up our minds," he reminded her grimly.

"Dace? Can't the gods do something?"

The god shook his head. "You can't un-teach him, R'shiel, and he's done the Overlord's bidding. None of the gods has any interest in saving this child."

"But he was your friend, Dace!" The god stared at her. His smile faded and for a moment Rakaia saw the true essence of his being. Mikel whimpered with fear.

Even the demon child took a step back from Dacendaran in fear.

"Do what you want with the child," Dacendaran said in a voice that chilled Mikel to the bone. "His fate is of no concern to the Primal Gods."

Dace vanished, leaving them alone in the tent. R'shiel appeared to be having trouble breathing. Mikel had still not moved.

The vision flickered again, and Rakaia became aware of Mica's voice wavering. This was taking a great deal out of him, to show her this. She wanted to tell him to stop, to turn away from the terror of a small boy fully aware that he was about to die for a crime he was not responsible for, even if it was one he had tried to commit.

And then she was back in Mica's body, seeing the world through his eyes, feeling every terrified moment of his past.

They were no longer in the tent. The hour must be up, she realized.

Damin Wolfblade had come to kill her.

"I'll do it," Brak said, stepping forward into the torchlight.

The demon child rounded on him in horror. "Brak!"

"I'm sorry, R'shiel, but Damin has a point. If he doesn't deal with this, he'll never put an end to it. The child needs to die. He has to make an example of him."

Damin looked stunned to find such an unexpected ally. "I cannot ask a Harshini to do this. I won't even ask it of my own men."

"I'm a halfbreed, Damin, and it won't be the worst thing I've done." He turned to the Harshini watching in at the edge of the clearing. "Take the others away from here, Glenanaran. Just pray to the gods that watch over this child that Death comes quickly for him."

The Harshini stared at him for a moment. Then Glenanaran nodded solemnly. "We will pray for the child."

The Harshini turned and vanished into the darkness. Brak made sure they were gone and then walked across the clearing and took Mikel by the hand.

Damin stood beside the demon child. He seemed surprised and more than a little suspicious of Brak's willingness to kill. "How do I know this isn't a trick?"

"This is no trick, Damin." He grabbed Mikel by the arm and pulled him clear of the guards, then drew the dagger from his belt. He turned it for a moment in his hand as if testing the weight, then he glared at Damin. "Are you planning to watch?"

"Yes."

"You're a sick son of a bitch, aren't you?"

"No, just a distrustful one. I don't believe you'll do it."

Brak looked down at Mikel. Rakaia couldn't move. Mica had moved beyond fear and stepped over into paralytic terror.

"Are you ready to meet Death, Mikel?" he asked gently.

In the distance, Rakaia heard Adrina choking back a sob. Even the torches were hissing loudly in the unnatural silence.

But almost as soon as the words left his mouth, the air was filled with unnatural, crystalline music. Mikel's knees gave way as the figure of Death appeared in the clearing. He wore a long hooded cloak, blacker than the night surrounding him. His face was a pale skull, his hollow eyes radiated light, and he actually carried a scythe in his left hand.

"This is the child you wish me to take?" the specter asked in a musical voice that boomed through the clearing.

"Yes, my lord."

"You presume a great deal, Brakandaran."

"This is necessary, my lord."

Death glanced around the clearing until his eyes alighted on R'shiel.

"Demon child," he said, with a slight bow in her direction.

"Divine One."

The creature swiveled his fearsome head toward Mikel then and held out a skeletal arm to the child. "Come."

Rakaia couldn't resist the compulsion to follow him. In a trance, she felt Mikel walk toward Death, unable to resist his song. And she felt Mikel's fear fall away as he realized this wasn't Death at all, but Gimlorie, the God of Music.

The Harshini must have intervened. Perhaps that's what they did when Brak asked them to pray for him.

Mica smiled up at the specter as he realized this wasn't Death. It was theater.

Gimlorie was taking him somewhere safe. Somewhere he'd never be hurt again. He took the god's hand willingly as Gimlorie—posing as Death—cast a withering gaze over the stunned humans and disappeared, taking Mikel with him.

CHARISEE WOKE THE next morning to discover there did not seem to
have been an earthquake recently and by the strength of the sun streaming in her window, the sky was exactly where it was meant to be.

And yet she was lying in a comfortable bed in an exquisitely furnished
room rather than a dirty straw mattress in a dungeon.

She tried to recall what had happened last night, but after Wrayan
Lightfinger told her to relax and close her eyes, everything was a blank.

Charisee was still trying to figure out what had happened when the
door opened and a slave entered the room wheeling a cart laden with
delicious hot food that she could smell from the other side of the room.
She pushed herself up on her elbows, thinking either the Hythrun were
astonishingly kind to their prisoners, or she had actually managed to get
away with her deception yet again.

"I'm sorry, your highness, I didn't mean to wake you."

"That's alright . . . is all that for me?"

"Yes, your highness."

"What time is it?"

"Mid-morning, your highness."

"Already?"

"Princess Adrina instructed me to let you sleep."

"That was . . . kind of her. Do you know if my luggage has found its
way here yet?"

The girl moved closer. She was a slave, with dark hair and a plump,
cheerful face. She seemed no older than Charisee. "I put everything away
yesterday while you were at dinner, my lady. Is there something specific
you wanted to wear today?"

"I'm not sure. What's your name?"

"Brinnie, your highness. Lord Branador sent me to look after you while
you're here in Greenharbour."

"He's your master?"

She nodded, a little uncomfortable with the question.

Gods, this would have been my replacement. If Rakaia had stayed, we would have come to Greenharbour together and as soon as I got here, I would have been reassigned at best, sold off in the slave markets at worst, because Frederak Branador had already arranged for his future bride to have a handmaiden of his own choosing.

She forced a look of idle curiosity, hoping none of her thoughts were reflected on her face. "What's he like?"

Brinnie shrugged. "I hardly know him, your highness. He seems nice enough."

As if you'd tell me any different, Charisee thought. "Can you find the gray silk skirt and the blue bodice to match it? My blue slippers, too."

Brinnie dropped into a low curtsey. "Of course, your highness. But didn't you want me to serve breakfast first?"

She smiled. "I'm sure I can manage on my own."

The girl looked uncertain, but she curtseyed again and then hurried out of the room to fetch Charisee's clothes.

Stretching luxuriously, Charisee smiled, a little amazed she was here and not in chains. Or down in the slave markets waiting for the next auction. She threw the covers back and climbed out of bed. On impulse she dropped to her knees beside the bed and closed her eyes. "Thank you, Lord Jakerlon, for watching over me."

"Much as I'd like to take the credit, sweet Charisee, you managed this latest feat of wonder without any help from me."

Charisee started with shock and turned to discover the God of Liars lifting the lids on the food cart to see what was on the menu.

"Is that blue-finned arlen?" he asked, leaning closer to take in the delicious aroma. "My, my, you *are* an honored guest, aren't you?"

"How . . . how did you get in here?"

"Did you miss the part about me being a god?"

"But . . ."

"Deep breaths, Chari," he advised. "Just take deep breaths. After your amazing performance last night, you're going to have to get used to me popping in to visit you more often. I don't think I've ever been honored like that before."

"But you saved me . . ."

"Hardly. You saved yourself, sweet thing. Quite a remarkable feat considering it was Wrayan Lightfinger doing the probing. I mean . . . he's no Harshini, but the lad knows how to get the job done."

"But I have no magic. How could I stop him from seeing the truth?"

"Because the best lies of all, my precious . . ."

"Are the stone-cold truth," she finished for him. "I still don't understand how I survived someone looking into my mind and not learning . . . everything about me."

"Wrayan Lightfinger is by no means omnipotent, sugarplum. Ask him about Luciena Mariner sometime."

"I don't understand."

He shrugged and sniffed the contents of the teapot. "You gave them enough of the truth to satisfy them, and they filled in the rest for themselves, I suspect. Children do it all the time."

"Princess Adrina and Wrayan Lightfinger aren't children."

"Of course not. They're as susceptible to jumping to conclusions as any child, however, which brings us to why I'm here."

"To frighten the wits out of me?"

He smiled. "You're not frightened of me, honeycomb. Look at you . . . trying to be witty."

Charisee climbed to her feet and faced the god who now owned her soul. "Why are you here, Divine One?"

"To save you from yourself."

"But you said I saved myself already."

"And you did, buttercup. In the most spectacular fashion. But they know you're hiding something, and your big sister even thinks she has a fair idea what it is. So in about thirty seconds, when she walks through that door to ask you what you're hiding from her, you'd better have something to confess."

"But I haven't done anything!" As soon as she said it, Charisee realized how ridiculous her protestation of innocence sounded. "Well . . . except . . . you know . . ."

Jakerlon smiled and replaced the cover on the teapot. "Perhaps the assassin could be of some help."

The door to the bedroom opened before Charisee had a chance to say another word, and sure enough, as Jakerlon predicted, Adrina walked in.

"You're up, I see."

She curtseyed to the princess; rather inelegantly given she was wearing a nightdress, although how she came to be wearing a nightdress remained a mystery along with how she came to be in this room.

Jakerlon was gone, vanishing the moment the door cracked open.

"Good morning, your highness."

"You can call me Adrina, Rakaia. Particularly when we're in private. Have you eaten yet?"

"Not yet . . . Adrina . . ."

The princess closed the door and walked over to the window, throwing the curtains back wide, saying, "Please, don't let me stop you. It will go cold if you don't eat it soon."

"Thank you."

Charisee hurried across to the cart and lifted the first lid to reveal a stack of freshly baked buns glazed with dried fruit. She selected one and took a bite, hoping Adrina would not expect her to talk with her mouth full.

"I heard you talking to someone as I arrived," Adrina remarked, turning to lean against the windowsill. She seemed so confident, so sure of herself, and so beautiful. Charisee didn't think she could ever be like that, not with a dozen lives to pretend she was a real princess.

"I was talking to my god," Charisee said.

The best lies of all are the stone-cold truth.

"And to which god do you pray, Rakaia?"

"Whatever god will listen, truth be told, your highness."

Adrina laughed. "That's an excellent philosophy. I should adopt it myself. Did you sleep well?"

She nodded, concentrating on the bun.

Adrina's smile faded. "Are you afraid of me, Rakaia?"

"No," she said, shaking her head. When Adrina did nothing but continue to look at her with a skeptical expression, she added, "A little . . . maybe."

That made her sister smile again. "See, isn't it better when you tell the truth?"

Charisee nodded and took another bite of the bun, not sure where this was going.

"Then perhaps we can agree to always tell each other the truth. I won't lie to you about what your future holds here in Hythria, and you won't lie to me. About anything."

"You had a sorcerer look into my mind to be sure I was being truthful, my lady . . . I mean, Adrina." *Gods, if you keep sounding like a frightened rabbit, she'll know something is amiss.* Charisee swallowed hard, put down the half-eaten bun, and faced Adrina, squaring her shoulders with determination. "Actually, no. I do mean, *my lady.* Or your highness, or whatever title you're owed. You're not treating me like a member of your family. You're treating me like you suspect I'm an enemy spy. When have I lied to you?" she asked. *The best lies of all, after all . . .* "I let you probe my thoughts, I haven't done anything to make you mistrust me . . ."

"Ah, now that's where you're wrong, Rakaia," Adrina said, not in the least bit offended, apparently, by Charisee's defiant manner. "Wrayan was able to establish you haven't been sent here to murder us all in our beds, true enough. But you are hiding something, and if you ever want to be a part of your new Hythrun family, I want to know what it is."

I knew this wasn't going to last.

Her defiance began to falter almost as quickly as it flared into life. "I . . . I don't know what you mean . . ."

"I'm quite sure you do, Rakaia."

"I . . ." *I am doomed.*

"Yes?"

Give it up, Charisee. Tell her the truth and maybe she'll have you executed painlessly.

Adrina was growing impatient. "If you don't tell me, I will make Kiam tell me. And I'll be more inclined to believe his version of events."

Perhaps the assassin could be of some help. That's what Jakerlon said. *Gods, this is not about me being an imposter at all! Wrayan saw I was hiding something about Kiam Miar.*

"Kiam acted with nothing but honor as my escort, your highness."

"I don't doubt it," Adrina agreed. "So what are you hiding about him?"

The best lies of all are the stone-cold truth.

"When I said he acted with nothing but honor, I wasn't lying. He did more than that. He was wonderful. He was kind, considerate . . . and . . . I think I'm in love with him."

"Does he reciprocate you feelings?"

"No." *And that* is *the stone-cold truth.*

"Have you slept with him?"

"I tried. He sent me packing."

Adrina laughed, but it wasn't an unkind laugh. If anything, she sounded quite sympathetic. "You poor thing. I really should have sent someone less . . . engaging to collect you, I suppose. I just never thought a sister of mine would look at a common-born assassin as anything but so far beneath her, he wasn't worth considering."

"He may be common-born, my lady, but Kiam is a nobleman at heart."

"Oh, my, you do have it bad, don't you?"

"What are you going to do?"

"About Kiam? Nothing, provided you promise to put any thought of him out of your head, and stay focused on your future husband. Can you do that?"

She nodded, unable to believe that was all Adrina expected of her. Where was the tyrant of the harem, feared by all who knew her? Charisee had grown up hearing horror stories about what a first-class bitch Adrina could be. It was the reason Rakaia had admired her so much.

Maybe Adrina swapped places with someone reasonable along the way, too. Charisee couldn't help smiling at the thought. "I can try . . . Adrina."

Adrina walked across the room to where Charisee was standing. She took Charisee's hands in hers and smiled encouragingly. "I know this is hard, Rakaia. I've been where you are now, believe me. But sometimes you just need to have a little faith things will work out for the best."

"Like they did for you?"

The High Princess shrugged. "I could argue my life at the moment is far more complicated than I'd like, but it's certainly a better life than the life I expected when Hablet put me on that boat for Karien, all those years ago, to marry Prince Cretin the Cringing."

Charisee's eyes widened. "You *called* him that?"

There was a mischievous gleam in Adrina's eye, as she nodded. "They used to think it was my accent."

"That's . . . terrible. And wonderful."

Adrina squeezed her hands. "Are you going to be alright, Rakaia?"

Charisee nodded. "I'll do my duty, Adrina. And I won't seek out Kiam, or do anything else foolish. At least not on purpose."

"That's all anyone can ask of you," Adrina said, embracing her. And then she stood back and eyed Charisee critically for a moment. "And speaking of your duty, make sure you dress . . . appropriately, this morning."

"Appropriate for what?"

"To meet your new husband's family."

Charisee's heart skipped a beat. "Lord Branador is here?"

Adrina shook her head. "No. He won't be here for another couple of weeks. His son, Braun, is here, however, and Lord Branador's grandson, Olivah. We'll be joining them for lunch."

49

"So, ARE YOU finished babysitting and ready to go back to your day job?" Elin Bane asked as Kiam let himself into the Raven's office the evening of his return to Greenharbour. He'd been sure the Raven would be in. He never seemed to leave the building.

"I have no choice but to respond to the command of my High Prince," Kiam reminded him as accepted Elin's handshake. "You know that."

"Firstly, it wasn't the High Prince but his wife who ordered you off on this little jaunt to collect her sister," the Raven said as he resumed his seat, indicating Kiam should take a seat opposite. Broos bounded over to Elin and tried to lick his face. The Raven pushed him away impatiently. "Secondly, your oath to the guild outweighs any and all family ties, even *your* family—I'm sure you remember that bit when you swore it. And thirdly, what is that wretched dog doing in my office?"

"He likes you," Kiam said, calling Broos to heel with a wave of his hand. "And if you're so worried about my oath, why did you let me go?" Broos padded back to Kiam's side and dropped to the floor.

"Because I like the idea of the High Princess owing the guild a favor. How was it?"

"As you'd expect. What's been happening here?"

"You know about the High Prince?"

Kiam nodded. "Only inasmuch as I was asked to wait in Warrinhaven because Damin was attacked and Adrina didn't want her sister getting underfoot while she dealt with the aftermath."

Elin raised his brow. "Warrinhaven, eh?"

"Yes."

"Isn't Cam Rahan married to . . . ?"

"Saneyah Eaglespike," he finished for him. "Yes. He is."

"That must have been awkward. Did you say anything?"

"Say what? 'Good morning, Lady Saneyah, I'm the assassin who garroted your brother'? Didn't seem like a very friendly conversation starter."

Elin chuckled. "I suppose not. Did she suspect it was you?"

"She acted like I was infected with Malik's Curse, but I don't think it was personal. I think she just despises all assassins on principal. I'm not sure she would have acted any differently if she'd known, to be honest."

"Funny how people forget what the dead were really like," he said, leaning back in his seat. "By all accounts, her brother made her life a living hell and she hated him with a vengeance when he was alive. We certainly weren't contracted to take him out because of his charm and long list of charitable works. Did you speak to Adrina when you delivered her sister?"

Kiam shook his head. "I thought she'd rather spend some time with Rakaia first. I was planning to visit her tomorrow."

"You mean you came to visit me first? I'm touched, Ky. Next you'll be wanting to give me a hug."

"What happened to Damin's assassin?" Kiam asked, ignoring the comment. Elin was a hard man, but Kiam had known him all his life and he had been handpicked by Galon Miar to succeed him as Raven. Unfortunately, Elin fancied himself quite the comedian. As there were few people in the world prepared to put the head of the Assassins' Guild straight on that point, one had to put up with Elin trying to be funny and resist the urge to groan.

"He's dead."

"So nobody had a chance to interrogate him, then?"

"Oh, never fear on that score. He was interrogated to within an inch of his life. Quite literally. And what Wrayan Lightfinger couldn't take from his mind, we persuaded him to reveal by more . . . traditional means."

"You tortured him."

"We persuaded him it was in his best interest to tell us everything he knew. There were hot pokers involved, I'll admit. And screaming."

"And what did he know?"

"Sweet fuck all," Elin said with a sigh. "According to Wrayan he had a song stuck in his head. It wasn't even anything particularly sinister. Just some children's nursery rhyme, and that's all he could remember since returning from leave in Krakandar a couple of months before the attack."

"If something happened to him in Krakandar, why wait so long?"

"Because that's how long it took before he was in the same room as the High Prince."

Kiam frowned. "What do the Harshini say? I mean, surely one of them looked into his mind?"

"They got no more out of him than Wrayan did."

"But there was magic involved."

"That's the consensus," Elin agreed. "Trouble is, nobody knows how, or why."

"And is Damin recovered? I didn't see him at the palace this morning when I delivered Rakaia, and Adrina's message was just to come home. She didn't go into specifics."

"Damin is still in a coma."

Kiam was on his feet before he realized, heading for the door.

"Sit down, Kiam!" Elin ordered.

He stopped with his hand on the door latch, and turned to look at Elin, torn between his loyalty to the Wolfblades and his loyalty to the guild. "He's my brother, Elin."

"Stepbrother," the Raven reminded him. "And a former stepbrother at that. Besides, unless you know the whereabouts of the demon child, lad, there is nothing you can do for him."

With some reluctance, Kiam returned to his seat. "What are you talking about?"

"The Harshini cured him, Ky. Waggled their magical little fingers and fixed him up good as new."

"Then why is he still in a coma?"

"Because apparently the demon child has done some sort of deal with Death, and he's holding Damin's life in trust until this deal—whatever it is—is done."

Kiam slumped back his chair. "Are you serious?"

"I know . . . it sounds crazy, but I was there. Trust me, it's the truth."

"Then we have to find the demon child and tell her to call off the deal."

"*We* don't need to do anything, Kiam," Elin corrected. "*We* are the Assassins' Guild. Adrina has Harshini advisors in the palace, she all but owns the Sorcerers' Collective, thanks to Kalan Hawksword being the High Arrion, and I'm quite sure Wrayan Lightfinger talks to the God of Thieves in person on a regular basis. Adrina doesn't need the guild's help and she's had all the help from you she's getting for quite some time."

Kiam shook his head when he realized what that meant. "No . . . you haven't got another job for me already, have you? I just got back."

"And if you'd just got back from guild business, I'd be paying for you to lie on a beach in the Trinity Isles surrounded by naked dancing girls for a month," he said. "But you didn't. You've had your break, and I need you back at work."

"Can't Arex do it?"

"The White Fox is in Pentamor, reducing the population of cheating husbands by one." The Raven shook his head, frowning. "I swear, better than half the commissions we get these days are from disgruntled middle-aged wives looking to rid themselves of useless husbands. There's a cautionary tale in that somewhere, let me tell you."

"Elin . . ."

"There's no point bitching about it, lad. This job requires your special talents."

"Oh . . . now I have special talents?"

"Well . . . family connections, then. It needs to look like an accident."

There was no getting out of this, he realized, and if he tried, Elin would just get angry, and one did not anger the Raven of the Assassins' Guild lightly. Perhaps it would be an easy job. Accidents weren't all that hard to arrange. He sighed. "Who is it?"

"Chap by the name of Gidion Narn. He's a spice merchant."

"Another disgruntled wife?"

"Business partner," Elin said, "and that's all I'm going to tell you about who commissioned the job. Suffice to say the client was adamant his death appears accidental. Apparently they have a clause written into their partnership agreement that prevents the other partners profiting from a suspicious death of any one of them. If anyone suspects foul play, we won't get paid."

"Trusting little souls, aren't they? What have my family connections got to do with it?"

"Are you kidding? Rodja Tirstone controls more of the spice trade in Hythria than anybody else. He's another one of your uncountable former stepsiblings, isn't he? Go pay him a visit. I'm sure he wants to hear all about your trip to Winternest to collect Adrina's sister."

"Seriously? You want me to kill someone while I'm a guest at Rodja's and Selena's home?"

"Don't care where or how you do it, lad, just get the job done by the end of the month."

Kiam pushed himself to his feet, conceding defeat. "What do you have on him?"

Elin pushed a folded piece of paper across the desk to him. "It's all there. Where he lives. Where he drinks. Where he keeps his mistress. Shouldn't be too difficult. He's a man of predictable habits."

"So are you, Elin. Come, Broos."

The Raven smiled as Kiam let himself out. He seemed to think Kiam meant it as a compliment.

His smug expression annoyed Kiam. There was one way to remove it, though. He turned to Elin before he closed the door. "I'm curious about something, Elin."

"What?"

"You said you're quite sure Wrayan Lightfinger talks to the God of Thieves on a regular basis."

"So?"

"Just wondering why Zegarnald doesn't talk to you in person. I mean . . . you're the head of the guild that honors him the most in peacetime. You'd think he'd be a bit more, I don't know . . . interested in you. I wonder what makes Lightfinger so special?"

He didn't wait for an answer, content that Elin would be up half the night, trying to come up with a suitable rejoinder.

"So, your real name is Mikel."

Mica shook his head, refusing to look at Rakaia as they rode, side by side, on their way back to Krakandar. The sun was just creeping over the horizon, painting the low-hanging clouds a dazzling shade of crimson, and it was already hot. Hopefully the line to enter the city wouldn't be quite so long this early in the morning.

"Mikel died," he said. "Mikel was a victim and a fool. Gimlorie knew me as Mikel. I am Mica now. Just like you are Aja and not Rakaia."

Rakaia could have argued her reasons for assuming a false name were quite different from Mica's, but she was still feeling a little fragile from everything she'd seen and heard this past night. The images of Mica's supposed death, and the aching loneliness he'd lived with in the years until he escaped Gimlorie had washed over her like a tidal wave, drowning her in his misery, fear, solitude, and perhaps a touch of madness.

For the first time in her life, Rakaia felt the urge to fiercely protect another being from pain. She'd loved Charisee like no other, but what she felt for her sister was dwarfed by whatever it was she was feeling for Mica. She couldn't even name it. It was somewhere between love for him and anger for what had been done to him.

Who would do that to a child?

Who would abandon a small boy to such an existence?

"Mica it is, then," she agreed. "You still haven't told me why you ran off like that yesterday."

"Because Damin Wolfblade is still alive."

Rakaia waited, certain there was more to that statement.

Mica took his time, but eventually he filled the silence with an explanation of sorts. "I swore if I ever escaped, I would kill all the people who sentenced me to life as Gimlorie's prisoner."

She reached out to grab his arm, not certain she'd heard right. "Did you hire an assassin to kill Damin Wolfblade?"

He shook his head and her hand off his arm at the same time. "Of course not. Why would I hire an assassin? They're far too expensive and the Wolfblades own the Assassins' Guild anyway."

"What did you do?"

"I sung to one of his guards and told *him* to kill Damin for me."

"So you created your own assassin?"

"I suppose."

Rakaia was appalled. "But . . . that's . . ."

"What?" Mica asked, looking at her with a wounded expression. "Wrong? Unfair? Cruel? Hmmm . . . where have I heard those words before?"

"You probably sentenced that man to death, Mica."

"Then I have honored Zegarnald."

They didn't speak for a while after that. Mica seemed to be sulking, and Rakaia was still getting her head around just how serious Mica was in his desire for vengeance. But it was eating him up. She'd seen the raw open wound that was Mica's soul when he sang to her last night and showed her what had happened to him. That wound would never heal while he burned with such a self-destructive need for revenge.

"Who else is on your list," she asked after a time. There was no point in trying to tell him he was wrong, but it would be useful to know if she'd placed her trust in the blood-drenched hands of a homicidal madman.

"The demon child," he said, with the conviction of a man rehearsing an oft-repeated list. "Princess Adrina. The Halfbreed . . ."

"You've missed out there, I'm afraid. Brakandaran is already dead."

Mica sighed with disappointment. "Are you sure?"

She nodded. "It happened at the Citadel when the demon child killed Xaphista. I think helping R'shiel killed him because of the power she was channeling. I really don't know the details. I was only a child when we got the news in Talabar, so I didn't pay much attention to the—Gods! That's why you came up to me in that tavern in Testra, isn't it? You thought I'd be able to help you find the demon child so you could kill her. Or were you planning to sing me into an assassin?"

He didn't try to deny it. "That plan didn't work out as I imagined either." He looked at her for the first time since they'd left their impromptu campsite and grinned, the first she'd seen of the old Mica all morning.

Impulsively, Rakaia leaned across and kissed him. "You are a terrible, terrible person."

He put his hand behind her head and pulled her closer, kissing her soundly before he broke off the kiss, saying, "Then I'm in good company, my love. You left your sister to be raped by an old man, and probably killed for being a bastard in your place."

Stung by his brutal words, she punched his arm. "That's an awful thing to say."

"True, though."

This time it was Rakaia's turn to sulk. She tried so hard to convince herself Charisee was happy, that she was looking forward to the wedding and the fabulous life of privilege and wealth stretching out before her. But there was barely a night she hadn't lain awake, thanking the gods for bringing her Mica instead of the man her mother had arranged for her to marry.

They rode in silence the rest of the way. The road into the city was cluttering up quickly when they arrived, mostly with farmers bringing their goods to market. With only themselves and a few saddlebags to declare, they were waved through with a cursory glance by the guards, who were more interested in what might be lurking in those wagons.

They dismounted not long after, finding it easier to lead their horses than try to negotiate the crowded streets. Rakaia wasn't sure where they were going. Although Mica appeared to have a destination in mind, she was too angry with him to ask where it might be.

Around mid-morning they finally arrived at a tavern with a swinging sign over the front door announcing it was the Pickpockets' Retreat. Rakaia frowned when she saw the name. They were in the Thieves' Quarter.

"Is this where we're staying?"

"It doesn't have fleas, princess."

"I didn't mean that. I just thought you'd want to stay in the . . . Musicians' Quarter?"

"Krakandar City doesn't have one," he told her. "And even if it did, I would still stay here."

"Why?"

"Because if there was a Musicians' Quarter, that's where all the musicians would be. We need somewhere I can perform. There's less competition here. More thieves, you see. Less musicians."

Rakaia rolled her eyes. There was no arguing with him. "It better not have fleas," she warned as they crossed the street to where a young lad waited outside, already calculating what he could charge to look after their horses and prevent them from being stolen. This was the Thieves' Quarter, after all.

"Mind ya mounts for ya, me lord, me lady?" the lad asked, doing his very best to appear honest and trustworthy. He was a tousle-haired lad of about nine. He reminded Rakaia of Alaric. Only with charm. And manners.

"How much?" Mica asked.

"Ten rivets," the lad announced with not a shred of shame.

"I could almost buy another horse for that," Mica pointed out.

"Aye," the child agreed. "And for anythin' less than ten rivets, ya may have to. I get offers all the time, ya know, when I'm mindin' things. Ten rivets will make 'em easier to resist."

Mica frowned but handed over the coin. The lad tucked it into his belt and then took the reins of both their mounts.

"That was straight out extortion," Rakaia complained under her breath as they walked into the cool darkness of the tavern.

"This is the Thieves' Quarter," he reminded her. "His mother is probably very proud of him. I'm sorry."

"For what?"

"For what I said about your sister. I know you didn't mean her any harm."

"It kills me that you might be right," she said, slipping her hand into his. "Are you going to be alright?"

He shrugged. "I suppose."

"It won't change anything if you kill everyone who ever hurt you, Mica."

"No," he agreed. "But it will stop them hurting anyone else." He let go of her hand and approached the man behind the counter to negotiate their lodgings and meals in return for entertainment.

There is no arguing with him on that point, she thought. *At least not at the moment.*

But Rakaia knew she wouldn't stop trying until she had convinced Mica that the person he would hurt most by pursuing vengeance against a family as powerful as the Wolfblades, or someone as formidable as the demon child, was himself.

And her. Already the thought of a life without Mica in it was becoming unthinkable.

But how could she convince someone as hurt and hurting as Mica to walk away from the chance to even the score with those who had caused his unbearable pain in the first place?

51

Olivah Branador was a slender, fair-haired, handsome young man a couple of years older than Charisee. He smiled when they were introduced, kissed her palm, and greeted her with an altogether too charming smile. She couldn't say why, but he set her teeth on edge.

His father was much easier to assess. She simply disliked him on sight. He was a brute of a man, barrel-chested and red-nosed from a life of excess by the look of him. He lacked any guile at all, along with not owning any discernable manners.

"Gods, what a prize you turned out to be," he announced after Adrina introduced her. "You're going to be wasted on my father."

"Please, my lord," Adrina scolded as they took their seats at the table. "My sister has just arrived. Don't frighten her off on her first day in Greenharbour."

Charisee grabbed her wine and took a good mouthful, quite certain the only way she was going to get through this next hour or so was with plenty more of it.

"I'm right, though," Braun insisted as he drank down his own wine in a single gulp. He wiped his mouth with the back of his hand, glaring at Adrina. "Given the concessions your husband insisted we cede to your father, your highness, I'd expect the girl to have a pussy lined with solid gold."

Charisee almost choked on her wine, but Adrina was either used to this man's crudeness or had a nerve of tempered steel.

"I would imagine if one required something like that, one could have one made and use it at their leisure. In private. Without the need for my sister to be attached to it."

Even Braun had decency to look a little shamefaced. Charisee was certain her face must be as red as the wine.

Olivah grinned at her obvious discomfort. He seemed to be having a grand old time. He leaned across to Charisee, smiling. "Shall I call you Grandmother?"

Charisee had no idea how to respond to that. She looked to Adrina for help.

"Does she not speak Hythrun?" Olivah asked his father when Charisee didn't answer. "Surely someone thought to put a clause into this wretched agreement that insisted my new granny spoke basic Hythrun?"

"I'm sure, Olivah, that as soon as you say something civil, my sister will be glad to respond."

"It's alright, Adrina," Charisee said in Fardohnyan, anger and humiliation lending her courage. She turned to Olivah and replied in flawless Hythrun. "You may not call me Granny. You may call me *your highness*."

Out of the corner of her eye, Charisee caught Adrina's smile of approval.

Braun did more than approve. He bellowed out loud at her comment, leaving Olivah looking rather foolish.

"Ha! She has you there, son," he laughed. "Maybe this girl won't be so awful after all."

"Even if I'm not lined with gold?"

Neither Braun Branador nor his son had an answer for that.

Adrina skillfully drew the conversation away from Charisee's physical attributes after that, keeping the conversation on more mundane topics like the state of the roads to Highcastle and the timber exports Highcastle was now able to send to Fardohnya.

As she listened and said nothing, Charisee learned a great deal. Highcastle was losing revenue from border taxes in this deal, but it was a timber-rich province that had always struggled to sell its product to its neighbor just on the other side of the pass. This was in no small way, she discovered as she listened to Adrina and Braun argue about it, to do with another deal Hablet had done years ago, when he traded Adrina in marriage to the Karien crown prince in return for access to vast quantities of Karien timber. Although the treaty was long dead—along with the crown prince of Karien—the timber deal had remained in place.

Charisee began to get a hint of the politics involved in wedding another daughter of Hablet's to secure this deal, which would make Highcastle richer than it had ever been, and strengthen the High Prince's coffers, too, no doubt. The Kariens had put a price on their timber, and that price was one of Hablet's daughters. Now that the price was set, there was no chance any other deal was going to be taken seriously unless it came with the same payment.

Adrina knew all of this, Charisee was quite sure. She may even be feeling a little guilty about it. Perhaps that's why those other conditions about free travel for Fardohnyan women were added into the agreement. If Adrina had to stand by while one of her sisters suffered the same fate as she had done, all those years ago, perhaps the knowledge that others might benefit somehow eased the sting a little.

Or Adrina was simply a ruthless politician who didn't give a damn about what any of her sisters might suffer at her hands.

Charisee didn't really know her well enough to tell.

BRAUN AND OLIVAH took their leave a couple of hours later. Charisee's silence during Adrina's discussion with Braun and his son had probably given them the impression she was a brainless trophy bride looking for a shelf on which to sit. She smiled and said the right things as they left, planning to escape to her room and ponder the least painful way she could kill herself rather than spend a lifetime sharing a home with those two.

She wasn't allowed to escape, however. As soon as the men left, Adrina turned to Charisee and indicated she should resume her seat. "You did well."

"Braun Branador is a brute," Charisee said before she could stop herself. "If that is the son, I'm afraid to even guess what the father is like."

"Frederak Branador is the least of your problems, Rakaia," Adrina told her, refilling Charisee's wine with her own hand. "He's an old man. Really old. He raised my children's grandmother, for pity's sake, and he's really quite sweet when he remembers what day it is. If he does anything more than share your bed for the sake of appearances, I will be astonished. But you needed to meet Braun and his son before you get to Highcastle. They are your real problem, because it's Braun who effectively rules there. Not his father."

"Then why wasn't the deal done with Braun?"

"Two reasons," Adrina said. "The first is that Braun is already married to Olivah's mother, so he wasn't available for a marriage, and the second is that I fought tooth and nail to prevent you from ever becoming Olivah's wife."

Charisee frowned. That made no sense. Admittedly, her first impression of Olivah was a sleazy charmer far too aware of his own good looks, but surely that was preferable than being married to a man old enough to be her great-grandfather?

"Why would you do that?"

"Are you questioning me, Rakaia?"

"No. I just want to understand."

Adrina leaned back and took a sip of her wine. "Frederak will be lucky if he lives another three years. That means in three years you will be free to marry whomever you like. You will be Frederak Branador's widow, at that point, not the king of Fardohnya's daughter. He has an heir and his heir also has an heir, so even if you conceived a child, it wouldn't stand to inherit much in the way of titles or wealth. If you married Olivah, on the other hand, you would be stuck with him for life. I know his type, Rakaia. I was married to a man like him once. There is no chance I will be a party to that happening to one of my sisters."

Adrina made a lot of sense. And it might only be three years. Perhaps less. It hardly seemed like any time at all.

Charisee nodded in understanding. "I won't let you down, Adrina."

"And I'll do my best to make your time pass as comfortably as possible," she promised. "I know Frederak sent Brinnie to serve you, but she's a kitchen wench elevated by Braun as some sort of prank, I'm sure. I'll find you someone more suitable. Someone you can trust. I could send for Charisee if you want."

Deep breaths, Charisee, deep breaths . . .

"Thank you, but I think my sister is happier where she is. Besides, another Fardohnyan would not make matters any easier for me in High-castle, I suspect. I'm happy for you to choose someone appropriate."

Adrina nodded, accepting the wisdom of her suggestion. "We shall have to get you your own *court'esa*, too. Someone who can double as a bodyguard wouldn't go astray, either."

"Do you have your own *court'esa*, Adrina?"

The question made her sister smile. "No. When you meet Damin, you'll understand why."

"Is he jealous?"

Adrina laughed. "Not in the slightest. He's just . . . well, you'll see when you meet him."

"I hope it's soon. I'd like to meet the High Prince before the wedding, if it's possible. He will be giving me away, after all."

The smile faded from Adrina's face. "That's something we need to talk about, actually, Rakaia."

"Is there a problem?"

"Why don't we visit Damin now," Adrina said, putting down her wine and rising to her feet. "And you can see for yourself."

52

CADEN FLETCHER LOOKED out over the city of Krakandar, high above the red rooftops here in the palace, counting the days until they crossed the border into Medalon. It was only since they'd arrived in Krakandar that it had occurred to him how much he wanted to get home to the Citadel.

All this traveling on sorcerer-bred horses, able to travel farther and longer than any normal beast when linked with the minds of their Harshini handlers, was a hard thing for a man skeptical of all things magical to accept.

It wasn't that Cade didn't like the Harshini. They were really quite delightful, once you got to know them, and he'd yet to meet a Harshini woman he wouldn't have traded his soul to spend an hour in bed with. Since they'd returned from Sanctuary there were hundreds of them in the Citadel. So many nobody even glanced at them oddly any more. But Cade had grown up being taught the Harshini and their pet demons were evil, and even though the logical part of him knew that was far from the truth, old childhood prejudices were harder to put aside than he imagined they'd be.

"Why the long face?"

Cade turned from the window to find the warlord of Krakandar and Rorin Mariner, the Lower Arrion of the Sorcerers' Collective, entering the sitting room. For some reason, they'd both changed since dinner. Rorin had long since shed his official robes, but Starros Krakenshield was dressed in old clothes, the kind a workman might wear if he was heading out for a night on the town. He looked anything but the dapper, well-dressed lord who had greeted them on their arrival yesterday.

"I'm sorry, my lord, was I looking miserable?"

Starros smiled. "You might be. Or it might be your natural expression. Hard to tell with you Medalonians. Would you like a tour of the seedier parts of the city?"

"Excuse me?"

"Starros has certain commitments to the God of Thieves," Marla announced, walking into the room behind Starros and Rorin. She still carried the cane she was using when he first met her, but not because she needed support. The necessity of spending long days in the saddle had changed her mind about Harshini healing on her fractured hip. Now she carried the silver-topped cane, Cade suspected, just because she liked it. "I'm sure they conflict with his duties as the warlord of this province, but as it was my son who put him in this predicament, I have no choice but to turn a blind eye to whatever it is he's up to."

Marla walked to the sideboard and helped herself to the refreshments laid out for the Warlord's guests. Cade knew he was missing something here, but wasn't sure how to go about asking for an explanation.

"You'll want to get rid of that uniform," Marla suggested as she poured herself a cup of wine. "Remember what happened the last time you wandered the Thieves' Quarter of a Hythrun city flaunting the fact that you're an officer of the Medalonian Defenders?"

Cade remembered all too well the beating he'd received until the doorman from the Thieves' Guild had arrived to even up the odds a little. He didn't realize Princess Marla knew about it, though.

Still, a chance for a night off duty was a rare opportunity and he'd be a fool to turn down the invitation. They still had a long way to go, even with magical horses to expedite the journey. "I'm sure, in Lord Starros's company, I'm safe from being set upon by a bunch of cowardly thieves."

Marla laughed out loud at that, but offered no explanation for her mirth.

"Excellent," Starros said. He was grinning, as if he knew what Marla was laughing about, but didn't offer to explain the joke. "I'll have some ordinary mounts saddled and meet you downstairs."

"Cowardly thieves or not, no point tempting fate with a sorcerer-bred mount," Rorin explained before Cade could ask what was wrong with the horses they'd arrived here with. And then he glanced at Starros with a grin. "There's a *lot* of thieves out there."

Starros smiled, but didn't seemed offended by the Lower Arrion's thinly veiled accusation. He turned to Marla, adding, "Don't wait up."

Marla sighed. "I remember when you were the sensible one, Starros, and Damin was the lunatic. What happened to those days?"

Starros walked over to Marla and kissed her on the cheek. Whatever the relationship between these two, it was obviously a long-standing and very fond one. "We grew up, Marla. And Damin became a High Prince."

"That explains Damin," Marla agreed, as Cade headed out into the hall with Rorin. "What's your excuse?"

Cade didn't hear the rest of the exchange, but it did make him wonder. Perhaps, while they were touring "the seedier parts of town," Starros or Rorin might explain why the fearsome Princess Marla treated the Warlord of Krakandar like one of her own children.

"HAS MARLA BEEN giving you merry hell?" Starros asked once they were well away from the palace.

"Actually, she's been far better than I was expecting. Princess Adrina painted her highness as something of a shrew."

"I think Adrina's take on her mother-in-law's character is a little skewed," Rorin chuckled.

Starros nodded in agreement. "Marla's a tough old bird, Captain. Don't let her fool you into thinking anything else."

"You know her very well?"

"All the Wolfblade children grew up here in Krakandar," he said, which explained quite a bit. "Me among them. Marla wasn't exactly the mother I never had, but she was probably the favorite aunt I never had. Are you looking forward to getting home?"

Subject nicely changed, Cade thought. "Very much."

"Well, I hope Lord Tenragan isn't too disappointed to find himself on the other side of the negotiating table with the dread Princess Marla rather than his good friend, the High Prince."

"I'm looking forward to seeing what Hablet's going to do when he finds out who is negotiating for Hythria," Rorin said.

Cade was about to ask what the Lower Arrion meant by that, when he and Starros reigned in their horses and began to dismount. He looked around and realized they were outside a tavern. The sign announced it was the Pickpockets' Retreat. The windows glowed yellow from the candlelight inside and the sweet voice of a minstrel spilled into the street leading a chorus in a cheerful song about sampling the silverware that seemed to have some sort of double meaning, given the raucous laughter whenever the phrase was repeated.

"Do Marla and Hablet know each other?" Cade asked as he dismounted.

Before Rorin could answer, a tousle-haired lad of about eight or nine hurried over to them and bowed theatrically. "Mind ya mounts for ya, me lords?"

"Andry, why aren't you home in bed?" Starros asked with a frown. "It's far too late for someone your age to be out hustling the Retreat's customers."

"Boy's gotta eat, Lord Starros."

"Boy's gotta get some sleep, too," the Warlord told him. He tossed the lad a coin. "You take the horses for me and my friends 'round to the stables out back and then go home. Tell that lazy, good-for-nothing father of yours I said you weren't to be working the late shift. He wants money to drink, he can hustle his own coin."

"Yes, sir," Andry agreed with a forlorn expression. Cade and Rorin handed him their reins and he led the horses down to the lane, to what Cade assumed were the tavern's stables.

"Friend of yours?" Cade asked, a little bemused by the power this Warlord seemed to have over the citizens of Krakandar. He tried to imagine the reaction he'd get in the Citadel if he tried sending some grubby street urchin packing on the grounds that he should have been home in bed.

"His father is a member of the Thieves' Guild. We look after our own."

Still no further enlightened, Cade followed Starros and Rorin into the tavern. The Warlord was greeted by almost everyone they passed as they made their way through the crowded tavern to the only empty booth in the corner. As soon as they were seated, the tavern owner—a portly man with a fabulous mustache—hurried over to take their orders. "Evenin', Lord Starros. The usual?"

Starros nodded. "And the same for my friends." He glanced around at the crowd, adding, "Big crowd for a workday night, Phyn."

"It's the minstrel," Phyn replied, jerking his head over toward the fireplace, where the young man in question was playing a battered old lyre. The silverware song had finished. He was singing something about being far from home, and although he was barely into the second verse, there were already a few grown men dabbing at their eyes. A pretty blonde was working her way around the tables as he sang, holding out a hat for contributions. "Came in the other day looking for work. Karien lad, he is. Wish I could convince him to stay permanently. Place has never been busier. Can I get you anything to eat?"

"Just the drinks, thanks, Phyn."

Once they were alone, their conversation covered by the sweet song of the minstrel, Starros resumed their earlier discussion. "I'm sorry, what was it you were asking?"

"How often Princess Marla and King Hablet have crossed swords," Cade reminded him.

"Ah . . . that's right. Well, as far as I know they've only met the once, back when Marla was still a girl."

"But that once was enough," Rorin said, "to spark a feud that lasted more than thirty years until the demon child arranged the marriage between his daughter and Marla's son—against the wishes of both Hablet and Marla, you can be sure—which put an end to it."

Cade shook his head. *Founders, why is diplomacy never easy?* "Lord Tenragan was hoping this treaty renewal would be a formality."

"I'm sure he was," Starros agreed. "His ability to keep the peace is what keeps him in power and the Sisters of the Blade from regaining any of their former influence." Starros smiled at Cade's expression. "What? You think we don't keep abreast of Medalon's internal politics. Krakandar borders Medalon, Captain, in case you've forgotten. I remain vitally interested in the goings on in the Citadel."

"Nothing is a secret these days," Cade lamented. "That's the problem with the Harshini being back—no offense, Rorin. It's just news travels too fast and not always the news you want broadcast."

"Such is the cost of the Sisterhood failing so miserably at genocide," Starros sighed with mock sympathy. Then he turned to look at the minstrel. "That lad is really very good, isn't he?"

Cade hadn't really been paying attention, but he stopped and listened for a moment. The young man had a voice almost as pure and sweet as the Harshini who performed so regularly in the Citadel's amphitheater. "He's remarkable."

Phyn arrived with the drinks, three foaming tankards of ale. Starros stopped him as he turned to return to the bar. "When he has a break, tell the lad to come over."

"Of course, m'lord."

Phyn hurried off to deliver the message and Starros turned his attention back to Cade and Rorin.

"He reminds me of the concerts the Harshini put on in the Citadel."

"I'm hoping the Sorcerers' Collective Harshini will sing at the convocation later this year," Starros said. "It might go some way to mitigating the boredom of sitting around a large table agreeing with the High Prince for a week, when he really doesn't need the permission of the warlords to do anything he damn well pleases."

Cade frowned. "Then you've not heard . . ."

"About Damin? Marla told me as soon as she arrived. But the convocation is at the end of summer. A lot can happen by then."

"You're not worried about him?"

"Of course I'm worried," Starros said, lowering his voice a little. "But that's not something I'm going to announce in a public tavern, is it?"

"Do you have something to announce, my lord?"

Starros and Cade both jumped with surprise to find the minstrel standing beside them, his battered old lyre tucked under his arm.

"Whatever this great announcement, allow me to sing it for you so the whole world may share your joy!"

"That won't be necessary," Starros told him with a wry smile aimed at Cade. "I just wanted to compliment you on your performance. You have a remarkable voice. It's a gift from the gods, I'm sure."

The lad seemed to find that amusing. "I'm sure it must be, my lord."

"What's your name?"

"I am Mica the Marvelous."

"Well, Mica, keep up the good work. I'm sure you'll be welcome here at the Retreat as long as Phyn has a crowded taproom every night."

The minstrel bowed expansively in response to the compliment. As he leaned forward, a tiny golden lyre on a chain fell forward out of his shirt. Cade stared at it for a moment, and then when it occurred to him where he'd seen it before, he leapt to his feet. "Arrest him!"

Starros and Rorin stared up at Cade with a bemused expression. "Excuse me?"

"He's the lyre thief!"

"The what?"

Mica looked just as puzzled as Starros. "I can assure you, my lord, if I was going to steal a lyre, I'd have picked a better one than this old thing."

"Not that one; the one around your neck."

Mica reached inside his shirt and drew out the tiny golden lyre. "You mean this cheap little trinket?"

"It's the stolen lyre from the Temple of the Gods in the Citadel."

The lad shook his head. "But I've never even been to the Citadel. And this was a gift from my wife." He turned and beckoned the young woman over. "Aja! Come here! Tell the man where you bought this! He thinks I stole it from the Citadel!"

The young woman hurried to her husband's side. Mica might be acting innocent, but she looked panic stricken. She was a pretty girl with blue eyes and honey-colored blond hair that didn't really seem to fit with her olive Fardohnyan complexion. "What are you talking about?"

"This!" Mica said, holding up the chain again. "Tell them where you bought it."

"Talabar," Aja replied without hesitation. "I bought it for a wedding present when we got married three years ago. Cost me nearly ten rivets. Is there something wrong with it?"

Starros rose to his feet and placed a calming hand on Cade's shoulder. "No, my dear, just a case of mistaken identity, I fear. Sing us another song, minstrel."

The lad glared at Cade for a moment and then took his wife by the hand and made his way through the crowd back to the stool by the fireplace.

"Sit down, Captain."

"That is the missing lyre," Cade insisted. "It was solid gold. No way she bought that for ten rivets, in Talabar or anywhere else."

"And what if it is?"

"Then you need to arrest him!"

"Really? Here? In a crowded tavern? In the *Thieves'* Quarter?"

Cade glanced around at the men and women watching him warily and realized not one of them had leapt to his defense. "Founders. They're all thieves here."

"A good many of them, yes."

"And you put up with them being so blatant?"

That made Starros smile. "I don't put up with them, Captain, they are my people. I'm not saying you're wrong, but if that lad has the temple's missing lyre, we will not be addressing the issue here."

"He might get away."

"Or he might continue to entertain us and we can have a discussion with him somewhere much quieter than this, once he's done."

Cade slumped back in his seat, not able to understand why Starros wasn't marching Mica the Marvelous and his lying little hussy of a wife to the nearest dungeon.

He was still brooding about it when Mica began to sing again. Before long, Cade forgot what he was brooding about, forgot about the little golden lyre, forgot about arresting anyone.

He didn't even bat an eyelid when, at the end of the evening, Starros called for some notepaper and a quill and wrote an introduction to the High Prince so Mica could perform for Prince Damin and his family should the lad ever find himself in Greenharbour.

The minstrel accepted the letter with a bow and then turned to Cade. "I like your jacket, Captain. May I have it?"

He nodded, stood up, unbuttoned his distinct, red Medalonian officer's jacket, and handed it to Mica. The minstrel smiled as he slipped it on over his shirt.

"Excellent," he said. "This is perfect. Be well, Captain. And don't worry about losing your coat. By tomorrow you won't even remember how you lost it."

Cade smiled, feeling inordinately glad he had handed over his uniform, although by the time they walked outside and the chill of the evening hit him, he discovered he couldn't remember if he'd come here without a jacket tonight or not.

Part Five

Chapter

53

ADRINA SPOKE TO Damin every day.

Late at night, after the children were asleep and the business of ruling Hythria another day was behind her, she let herself into the room she once shared with Damin, stretched out beside his sleeping body, and told him about her day.

"I'm completely over this wedding," she said as she laid her head on his shoulder. He always seemed unnaturally warm, as if his body were battling the infection of death and refusing to give up the fight. "Rakaia's not the problem. She's proving almost suspiciously easy to please, but gods, the Branadors are killing me."

She moved his arm so she could get closer, draping it over her shoulder and snuggling in closer to his body, the way they always lay in the dark and talked about their day. "I know they're your family, darling, but surely the relationship is distant enough that we don't have to keep pandering to them?"

Damin didn't answer, of course. In fact, Adrina had no idea if he could hear anything at all. Even the Harshini healers hadn't been able to tell her that. But just in case, she continued to talk to him every single day. It would save so much catching up when he came back.

"Frederak is due tomorrow, the wedding is in a fortnight, and I still haven't worked out how I'm going to explain away your absence. I thought I had everything under control there for a while." She sighed, wishing she didn't sound so helpless. "Do you remember how clever I thought I was, spreading the rumor you weren't really in a coma, but off helping R'shiel on some dire mission to save the world? Well, now it's come back to bite me. Braun Branador heard the rumor and is expecting you back for the wedding. If you're not there, walking Rakaia down the aisle, he tells me, the whole Branador clan is going to be offended; so offended, he claims, his father might have to rethink the whole deal. Gods, I wish I thought he was bluffing. But he's not, I fear. Braun Branador is a fool and quite prepared to derail everything we fought for in this border agreement, every tiny concession we managed to drag out of my father, all for the sake of a perceived slight to his wretched—and, might I suggest, very debatable—family honor."

She fell silent. Adrina could feel herself growing angry, and she didn't want Damin worrying about her losing her temper.

Then she smiled in the darkness as another thought occurred to her. "You'll laugh when you hear me say this, but right now, I'm actually missing your mother. She grew up with Braun at Highcastle. Marla could slap him back into place with a withering look, I'm certain."

Damin did not answer her, of course, or give any indication he heard a word she said. She could hear his heart beating, however, strong and steady as a metronome, never wavering for an instant.

Before she could continue her tale of woe, there was a faint knock at the door. A moment later it opened a crack to reveal a sliver of warm yellow light from the room beyond.

"I'm sorry to disturb you, Adrina," Darvad said, poking his head through. "But you asked me to let you know when Rodja and Selena arrived."

"They're here?"

"Waiting out here in the anteroom," he confirmed.

"I'll be out in a moment."

The door closed, plunging the room back into darkness. Adrina lifted the dead weight of Damin's arm from around her shoulder and placed it gently by his side. She sat up and studied him in the darkness for a moment. He looked as if a gentle shake would wake him. He'd not changed at all since falling into this coma. He'd needed no sustenance, had expelled no bodily fluids, and he didn't need a shave. It was as if time had stopped around him.

"I have to go, my love," she explained. "Duty calls. I'll come back to-morrow. Perhaps I'll be able to share with you the gruesome details of how I disemboweled Braun in front of the whole court with my bare hands." She smiled and leaned over to kiss his warm dry lips. "I can but dream, you know."

There was no response, and in truth, Adrina wasn't expecting one. She pushed herself off the bed, smoothed down her skirts and her hair, and let herself out of the bedroom.

"Rodja!" she said with a warm smile as she emerged, blinking a little in the brighter light of the anteroom. "And Selena! Thank you so much for coming at this late hour."

Rodja Tirstone was Damin's stepbrother, the eldest son of Marla's third husband who had died in the plague that ravaged Greenharbour two decades ago. A serious but competent man, Rodja had inherited his father's spice trading business and, with the help of another of Damin's stepsiblings, Luciena Taranger—who owned a goodly portion of all the shipping in and out of Hythria and Fardohnya—had turned his father's successful business into an empire. It didn't hurt that on the death of his wife's father, he had also inherited the entire assets and resources of his main competitor.

Rodja and Selena owned a trading empire between them that stretched from the depths of southern Denika, across all three of the Trinity Isles, all the way north to the far reaches of Karien. Provided it didn't conflict with their business interests, they were usually quite happy to put their resources at the disposal of the High Prince.

It remained to be seen if those resources were available for the High Princess.

That's why Adrina had asked for this meeting here, in her private chambers, with Darvad close by. Darvad was married to Rodja's only sister, Rielle. She had a much better chance of gaining their cooperation, she figured, if Darvad was seen to be supporting her.

Rodja took her hand, kissing her palm. "Don't lament the hour, your highness. You know if there is anything we can do . . ."

Her eyes lit up with mischief. "Would you consider murdering Braun Branador for me?"

Rodja dropped her palm and smiled. "Gladly. Is he giving you trouble?"

"Of the worst kind," she agreed, kissing Selena on the cheek. "Please, have a seat, both of you. Darvad, I'll pour the wine. Would you mind fetching Rakaia for me? I don't think she'll be in bed yet."

"Of course," he said, with a bow. Darvad let himself out as Adrina sat down and leaned over the low table to pour the wine already laid out for her guests on the table. She poured five goblets, one for herself and her guests, two more for Darvad and Rakaia when they returned. For tonight—and this discussion—Darvad was family, not just a loyal servant of the crown.

Adrina turned her attention to Selena. "I was sorry to hear about your grandmother, Selena."

"Thank you, Adrina, but she was nearly ninety and ready to leave this life," Selena said. "I think she was getting quite annoyed with Death toward the end, that he was taking so long to come for her."

"Perhaps he was otherwise engaged," Rodja suggested sourly. "Making deals with the demon child."

"How is you sister liking Hythria?" Selena asked in the awkward silence that followed her husband's remark, as she accepted her wine and settled back into the cushions.

"She seems to like it well enough. But then, life as a visiting princess in the High Prince's palace in Greenharbour is a world away from being the wife of a border lord in a cold, remote place like Highcastle."

"Worth it, though," Rodja said. "Proper border controls over Highcastle are long overdue."

"Those border controls are going to cost the Branadors a large portion of their livelihood," Selena said, reminding Adrina not to underestimate this woman as being merely Rodja's wife. She had a sharp mind and an eye for the nuances of a deal her husband sometimes lacked and was an equal partner in his business. Because she was quiet and didn't say much, people were prone to forgetting that—often to their detriment. "I'm assuming that's why they demanded one of your sisters to seal the deal?"

Adrina nodded. "A vast underestimation of my father's lack of sentiment, that was," she agreed. "Damin tried to warn Braun at the time, that Hablet would gladly hand over a dozen daughters if he thought he'd profit from it, but Braun was adamant. If he was going to lose the chance to gouge every merchant crossing the border, he wanted the chance for his grandchildren to be royal. I think he believed his demand was a deal breaker, and that Hablet would never agree to marry one of his daughters to a minor Hythrun border lord."

"I'm surprised, then, that Braun didn't insist on your sister marrying his son, rather than his senile old father."

"He did," Adrina said, placing her wine on the table. A sip was enough. She needed her wits about her. "It was my idea that Rakaia marry Frederak."

Selena's eyes widened. "You were the one who arranged for your twenty-year-old sister to marry a senile old man in his eighties?"

Adrina didn't flinch from her gaze. "Have you *met* Olivah Branador?"

Selena didn't answer her for a moment, but then she nodded. "Yes. I have."

"Then you understand."

She nodded. "I understand."

"I don't," Rodja said.

"Don't worry, dear," Selena told him, winking at Adrina. "I'll explain it to you when we get home."

The door opened and Rakaia entered the room, looking a little uncertain, followed by Darvad. Rodja rose to his feet and kissed Rakaia's hand as his brother-in-law introduced them, then they settled in on the cushions. Adrina watched Rakaia out of the corner of her eye, constantly amazed at her lack of affectation.

"I invited Rodja and Selena here to help you, Rakaia," Adrina explained once they were all settled.

"Do I need help?"

"You need your own *court'esa*," she explained. "And I've been promising you for weeks that I would replace Brinnie."

"Who is Brinnie?" Rodja asked.

"A kitchen wench, best I can tell," Adrina explained, "that Braun sent along to serve as Rakaia's handmaiden."

"She does her best," Rakaia said, for some reason feeling the need to defend the girl. Adrina marveled at her younger sister, a little. She couldn't remember any of her sisters ever emerging from the Talabar harem without its taint sticking to them in some way.

"She's useless," Adrina said. "And Braun sent her here deliberately, to show us it doesn't matter who you are, or how much control he's lost over the border, he's still calling the shots in his own home. She is also reporting your every movement back to Braun, you can count on it."

"Why haven't you replaced her?" Rodja asked.

"Because Braun will see a replacement for exactly what it is," Darvad explained. "And even if he doesn't, he'll assume any personal servants assigned to Rakaia by her sister are there to spy on him. If he doesn't kill them outright as soon as they get to Highcastle, he'll find some other way of neutralizing them."

"But a wedding gift from the Tirstones is a different matter," Selena said, nodding. She got where this was going much faster than her husband.

A fraction of a second after his wife, Rodja got it, too. "Ah . . . You think if we gift your sister with the slaves she needs, he won't object."

"Braun needs you to keep your spices moving through the border at Highcastle. Even with his quota now a set percentage rather than the thinly disguised extortion racket he was running at the border before we did this deal, he still needs the revenue your caravans bring his estate. He won't risk offending you, whereas he's more than happy to thumb his nose at me, particularly with Damin not around to challenge him."

"I know this is slightly off topic," Selena said, "But that brings up an interesting point. How are you going to explain Damin's absence at the wedding, Adrina? I mean, Narvell Hawksword might do at a pinch. He's a Warlord and Damin's half-brother, but a royal wedding without the High Prince? That's a slight that won't go unremarked."

"We should have a Fardohnyan wedding," Rakaia said, so softly Adrina almost didn't hear her.

"What did you say?"

"I'm sorry . . . I shouldn't have . . ."

"No, please, say it."

"I was just wondering why we don't have a Fardohnyan wedding, rather than a Hythrun one."

"What difference would that make?" Darvad asked.

"Because the bride's family give the bride away in a Fardohnyan wedding," Adrina said, a little stunned the idea hadn't occurred to her before now.

"I thought Fardohnyan weddings were thinly disguised drunken orgies that go on for days," Selena said.

Rodja laughed. "You say that like it's a bad thing, Selly."

Adrina smiled, and not just because of Rodja's joke. He'd just referred to his wife by the name he obviously only called her in private. It was a good sign he was comfortable enough to do that here in front of the High Princess. "You're not entirely wrong, Selena. Fardohnyans worship the Goddess of Fertility above all else. Our weddings are a celebration of that, often taken to excess." She turned to Darvad. "Could we organize it in time?"

"Depends on what you want to organize."

"The ceremony would still be in the Temple of the Gods, but traditionally, there is a carnival held in the palace grounds afterward, during which the bride and groom hand out gold coins to anyone who takes their fancy, to please Jelanna and show the goddess how worthy they are of her bounty."

Darvad seemed a little aghast at the idea. "Seriously? Free food and wine laid on for anyone who can get through the gates. And gold?"

Adrina nodded. "It lasts for five days."

"And who is going to pay for this largesse to the common folk?"

"Traditionally," Adrina said, with an even wider smile. "The groom."

There was a moment of silence and then everyone else smiled, too. "Sounds like an excellent idea to me," Rodja said. He turned to Selena. "What do you think?"

She nodded, but her smile had faded. "I think our gift to Rakaia should be servants, but our gift to Frederak should be cold hard coin. You don't want him refusing this idea because he can't afford it."

"And how are you going to get Braun to agree to this, even if Rodja and Selena offset the cost?"

"I'm not," Adrina said, looking at her sister. "Rakaia is."

"Me?" Rakaia asked. She sounded horrified by the prospect. "How?"

"By asking a favor of your future husband," Adrina explained. "Frederak is due tomorrow. He's a sweet old man, Rakaia, and nothing like his son or his grandson, I promise you. You must make him promise you a Fardohnyan wedding."

"Braun will just overrule him," Rodja warned.

"He can't. However much it irks Braun, his father is still the lord of Highcastle. And besides, if she doesn't get her way, Rakaia is going to throw an epic tantrum, threaten to return to Talabar, and have our father declare war on Highcastle for the insult, aren't you, Rakaia?"

"I'm not really the tantrum-throwing kind," Rakaia said, looking very uncertain.

"Nonsense. I've seen you throw a tantrum, little sister. Remember the time our father tried to send Charisee away after you two pulled that switching identities prank on him? You almost howled the harem down for a week until they gave in and sent her back. I'm sure you remember how it it's done."

Rakaia actually blushed at the memory. "I forgot about that."

"I didn't," Adrina said, and then she smiled, not wanting to sound too harsh. "In fact when I heard Hablet was sending you, I thought *Oh no, the tantrum throwing one!*"

Selena smiled at Rakaia encouragingly. "I'm sure you can manage, my dear, considering the alternative. And I think I have exactly the right *court'esa* in mind, too. He's Fardohnyan originally, although you'd not know it to look at him. Adham bought him for us in Calavandra about ten years ago. He was both my daughters' first *court'esa* and he's been with us long enough now that I trust him implicitly. He'll look after you and not be easily corrupted by whatever Braun tries to promise him, and you'll be able to speak to him in your native tongue."

"You mean Strayan?" Rodja asked, nodding his approval. "That's an excellent idea. We were talking only the other day about what we should do with him now that both the girls are married. I'll have him sent back to town immediately. What about a handmaiden?"

"I'll have to think about that." She turned to Rakaia again. "I'll find you someone you can trust. And who knows how not to ruin silk. In fact, the Spice Traders' Ball is next week. We can present you with your wedding gifts there, in a very public place, so there is no risk of Braun trying to make you refuse it."

Darvad shook his head in amazement. "Gods. Selena, that's almost devious enough for Marla to have thought of it."

The trader's wife smiled. It seemed even her own brother-in-law underestimated her.

Rakaia seemed genuinely grateful. "You're too far kind, my lady."

"Will you give me some idea how much this wedding circus is going to cost?" Rodja asked Darvad.

"I'll send word as soon as I've worked it out."

"Then we should get home," he said, rising to his feet and offering Selena his hand to help her up. "There is much to arrange."

Adrina rose to her feet too in order to see them out. "I appreciate you coming. Both of you. And for your generous offer of help."

"There is no price to be put on helping family," Rodja promised her as he kissed her palm, adding with a grin, "which is a good thing, because this is going to cost me a fortune."

ONCE THEY WERE gone, and Darvad had retired for the evening, Adrina turned to Rakaia, who was still sitting on the cushions sipping her wine. She seemed a little pale.

"Are you unwell, Rakaia?"

The young woman shook her head. "Just a little . . . I don't know. It's suddenly becoming very real. Is Frederak Branador really arriving tomorrow?"

"I'm afraid so."

She put her wine down and climbed to her feet. "Then I should get some sleep. I need to look my best to meet my new husband."

Rakaia meant every word, which Adrina found quite astonishing. "What happened to you, Rakaia?"

"I don't know what you mean. . . ."

"I wasn't kidding, earlier. I really did think our father was sending me the tantrum terror when I learned it was you he chose to clinch this deal. But you're nothing like the little monster I remember."

"I'm not the same person I was in Talabar," Rakaia told her.

On impulse, Adrina embraced her. "I suppose we all have to grow up, eventually," she said. "Now go. Get some sleep. In the morning you can flutter your eyelids at Frederak and convince him the only way to make you happy is to give you want you want."

"Do you really think that will work?"

"Of course it will work," she assured her little sister. "I do it to Damin all the time."

54

R'SHIEL FOUND DAMIN trying to escape Sanctuary. She followed Mandah through the echoing halls in the direction of the sounds the older woman thought she'd heard periodically since waking here. When they found him, he was searching through the stacks of scrolls, littering the floor with them as he went, looking for something he clearly hadn't located yet.

"I hope you're going to clean this mess up," she said, by way of announcing herself.

Damin looked up, his eyes widening in shock. *"R'shiel?"*

"In the flesh."

"Thank the gods!" he cried, tossing aside the scroll he was holding. "It's about time." He crossed the distance between them in a few strides and crushed her in a bear hug for a moment. Then he spied Mandah standing behind her. "Mandah Tenragan? Gods, what are you doing here?"

"Same as you I suspect, your highness," she replied. "I'm sure R'shiel can explain."

Damin held R'shiel at arm's length for a moment, studying her closely. "I swear you haven't changed at all. Not since I saw you last before we lifted the siege on the Citadel. And then you just vanished."

She might not have changed, but Damin had. He was older, a little heavier, perhaps, and there were the first flecks of gray at his temples.

"Xaphista was dead," she said with a shrug. "My job was done."

"You couldn't even say goodbye? We were worried about you."

"I can kill a god, Damin. What is there that can hurt me in the mortal realm?"

"What about the immortal realm?" Mandah asked. "That's where we are, isn't it? Caught in the realm between life and death?"

"Actually, we're in Sanctuary," she told them. She looked at the scattered scrolls on the floor. "What are you doing down here anyway, Damin? A library is the last place I thought I'd find you."

"I was hoping I could find the plans to this place. I was going to try and locate a drain or a sewer I could escape through. Sanctuary, you say? I thought you destroyed it?"

She shook her head. "Brak and I threw it out of time."

"And now it's back?"

"Kalianah brought it back for me."

"Why?" Mandah asked.

R'shiel glanced over her shoulder at Mandah. "Because I asked her to."

"It doesn't matter why," Damin said, never one to question a fortuitous circumstance when it came his way. He headed for the door, satisfied he had found his escape route in R'shiel. "Let's just get out of here."

"I'm not leaving just yet, Damin. In fact, I'm headed in the other direction."

He turned to look her, frowning. "Gods, are you dead?"

"No.

"Am I? Is Mandah?"

"Not exactly."

"What in the Founders name does *not exactly* mean?" Mandah demanded.

"I came here to find Brak."

"I thought he was dead," Damin said.

"He is," she agreed. "But Death took his body and his soul . . ."

"Which means if he wanted to, Death can return Brak to a mortal life," Mandah finished for her.

R'shiel nodded. "That's right."

"Then we find Brak and get the hell out of here," Damin said. "No pun intended."

"Brak isn't here, Damin," she explained. "He's in one of the Seven Hells, and Death is not entirely convinced he wants to return to a mortal life."

"Then find him, ask him, and I repeat, let's get the hell out of here."

"That's the plan," R'shiel agreed, glad Damin was so keen.

Mandah didn't trust her, however. She never had. "What are you not telling us, R'shiel?"

"We can talk about this later," Damin urged. "Let's get this done."

"Not until she tells us why we're here," Mandah said. "If R'shiel wants to find Brak, then all power to her, but why are *we* here? What have you and I got to do with her quest to find Brak?"

Damin turned to R'shiel. "She has a point."

She knew that look. There was no getting out of an explanation. Not now. Not if she wanted Damin's help.

"There are rules surrounding bringing people back from death," R'shiel told them. "The first is that they have to want to come back. The second . . ."

"Is what?" Mandah asked impatiently.

R'shiel took a deep breath before she answered, fairly certain of Mandah's reaction, at the very least. "A life for a life. Specifically, a life of equal value. That's why Brak died in the first place. When Joyhinia ran that sword through me in Testra, Mandah, I should have died. Brak brought me here for the Harshini to heal and did a deal with Death when I wasn't getting any better. "

Damin reached out and placed his hand on her shoulder in understanding. Perhaps he hadn't figured the rest of it out yet. "He traded his life for yours, didn't he?"

She nodded. "I didn't know until Death took him after we defeated Xaphista."

Mandah wasn't nearly so sympathetic. "So what have you done, R'shiel? Traded our lives for Brak's?"

"No. It's true I will have to trade his life for a life of equal value if he wants to come back, but I believe you're here as a surety against the agreement because Death doesn't trust me not to find a way to wheedle out of the bargain."

Damin seemed to find that amusing. "Seriously? *Death* doesn't trust you?"

"He knows you well then," Mandah said, crossing her arms. "Are we dead?"

"No. Comatose probably, back in the mortal world, but not dead. Your physical bodies will come to no harm until I've found Brak."

"And then one of us dies?"

"No!" she hurried to assure them. "The life I trade is yet to be decided— assuming Brak even wants to come back—and I wouldn't trade either of your lives for his, in any case."

"I'm sure you wouldn't nominate Damin Wolfblade," Mandah agreed, not convinced at all by her assurances. "But you've always resented me, R'shiel. If I was out of the way, you could still have Tarja."

R'shiel had to fight the urge not to slap Mandah where she stood. "If Brak comes back, Mandah, why would I *want* Tarja?"

"Just because you don't want him, doesn't mean you're happy for me to have him."

R'shiel rolled her eyes in despair. "Let it go, Mandah. It's been a decade since I even saw him, and we certainly didn't part friends. Tarja despises me because he thinks I made the gods put a geas on him to love me. You know that." She threw her hands up in exasperation. "Gods, you're the mother of his children, for pity's sake. Don't you think that if I even tried to get back together with him, killing the woman who bore his children might pose something of a barrier to our happily ever after?"

"Don't you think we can have this discussion some other time?" Damin asked. "I want to get home. I'm sure you do too, Mandah. So let's find Brak and . . ."

"Get the hell out of here," Mandah finished for him. "I get it."

"Excellent." He turned to R'shiel. "What do we have to do?"

"We have to enter the Seven Hells."

"How?"

"Through the door in the cliff," Mandah said, working it out before R'shiel had a chance to explain. "That's the way in, isn't it?"

R'shiel nodded. "Probably."

"Can you come and go through the door as you please?" Damin asked.

"I'm the demon child," she said. It explained everything.

"But we're not," Mandah pointed out. "The prince and I are mortal. If we step through that door, won't it mean we've died in the mortal realm?"

"I don't know," R'shiel had to admit.

Mandah shook her head. "Then you go through it without me. I'll wait here until you get back."

R'shiel turned to Damin. "What about you? Mandah's right, you know. If you come through with me, I may not be able to bring you back out again."

Damin thought on it for a moment and then shrugged. "We all have to die of something, R'shiel, and I'd rather die doing something heroic, than rotting here in this library, looking for something that can never be found."

"You're a fool, Damin Wolfblade," Mandah said.

"Aye," he agreed, "I probably am. But at least I'll be alive, right up until the moment I die, which is better than dying a little each day for fear of taking a chance." He turned to R'shiel. "That's a nice epithet, don't you think?" he said. "Tell Adrina I want that carved on my tomb."

"You won't need a tomb if I can help it," R'shiel promised, feeling a rush of affection for the big warlord and his refusal to take anything too seriously, even death.

"I intend to hold you to that promise," he said with a grin. "Where is this wretched door?"

"Down near the amphitheater."

"Then let's go get Brak," he said. "The sooner we find him, the sooner we can all go home."

Chapter

55

IF YOU WEREN'T born with a title, then the social event of the year in Greenharbour was the Spice Traders' Ball, hosted by Rodja and Selena Tirstone. As Kiam walked up the long, curved, torch-lit drive of the Tirstone mansion, with its line of carriages waiting to unload their passengers at the front door, he marveled at the wealth on display here. Hythria was a rich country, and here in the capital, where its merchants enjoyed a large port, a healthy shipping industry, and a High Prince who encouraged trade with as many nations as they could reach by sea or land, nowhere was that wealth more evident than here.

Kiam had not had to ask for an invitation to the ball. He was invited as a matter of course, as he always was. Even though Rodja was married to Selena and had a home of his own by the time Kiam's father had married Princess Marla, the bond of the Wolfblade family was a close one. Despite his less than respectable profession, they had never treated him as anything other than one of their own.

It was a pity he was going to abuse that privilege tonight by removing Gidion Narn, but the setting was too perfect, the timing too convenient, to do anything else.

He had walked here for a reason. It gave him a chance to study the carriages, work out which one was Gidion's, and ensure the door latch was broken by the time the merchant climbed into his carriage to visit his mistress, as he always did after a social occasion where he was required to make an appearance as a loving husband. His wife and daughter—if they did what they usually did after an event like this—would stay well beyond his departure and return home in the small hours of the morning in the carriage of a friend.

Kiam had been watching Gidion for a while now. He knew where the mistress lived, and the streets surrounding her house. He knew the man's habits and his schedule. Elin was right. It rarely varied. He was so set in his ways, in fact, that Kiam wondered if his business partners had ordered him eliminated for his complete lack of imagination.

He spied the carriage he was after parked further down the curved drive, having already delivered its passengers to the ball. The horse was hobbled and munching happily on the contents of the feedbag hanging around his neck. The driver was nowhere to be seen, probably availing himself of the refreshments laid on for the drivers and coachmen in the tent set up for them on the lawn. Kiam kept walking, taking in everything as he did, knowing there was no more obvious way to look suspicious than to start looking around to see if anybody was watching.

He had deliberately entered the long, semicircular drive from the exit gate so he could walk past the parked carriages. As he neared the Narn vehicle, he did surreptitiously glance around to see if anyone was nearby, but everyone's attention was on the front entrance of the house, where Rodja and Selena were greeting their guests. The royal carriage had just pulled up, which Kiam thought a little odd, because as a rule, Damin and Adrina stayed away from this ball in order to preserve the notion it was being held for the merchants of Greenharbour and not the landed gentry. Besides, with Damin incapacitated, he couldn't imagine Adrina making a public appearance without him, which would do nothing but fuel the rumors about the High Prince's condition.

He stopped and watched as the carriage door was opened and Princess Rakaia emerged, resplendent in a dark blue traditional Fardohnyan gown, which shimmered in the firelight from scores of torches lighting the entrance, and left her midriff bare from her hips to just under her breasts. She climbed the stairs gracefully, stopped at the top to greet Selena and Rodja, and then moved inside and out of sight.

It was only then that Kiam realized he was holding his breath, not to mention wasting precious time when everyone's attention was diverted.

Annoyed at himself for being such a fool, Kiam balanced himself against the carriage, ostensibly to shake a stone out of his boot. What he shook out was actually a small sliver of metal—a broken locking pin, in fact, from a latch similar to that on Gidion Narn's carriage.

It took him only a few seconds to ease the door open, ram the sliver of metal into the workings of the lock, and close the door again, before he pulled his boot back on and made his way up the drive to greet his stepbrother and his wife on his way in to the Spice Traders' Ball.

* * *

"Do you suppose there are any ugly ones?"

Kiam hadn't realized he was staring at Rakaia until the voice jerked him back to reality. He turned to find Adham Tirstone, Rodja's younger brother, standing beside him, also admiring the Fardohnyan princess, as she did a turn around the floor with Olivah Branador while her future husband sat slumped in a wheeled wicker chair on the edge of the dance floor with a rug over his knees.

"Adham! When did you get back?"

"Yesterday," the trader replied. Adham spent most of his time in Denika these days, sourcing spices for his brother's business. He didn't return to Hythria often, and usually just long enough to plot his next exotic journey. Kiam remembered being entranced by the tales of Adham's adventures when he was younger. "Rodja sent word as soon as Damin . . . well, you know . . ."

"I do," Kiam agreed, aware this was not the place to discuss the condition of the High Prince. "Ugly what?"

"Oh! Fardohnyan princess. Never seen an ugly one yet."

"I've only met two," Kiam said. "They're both . . . passable, I suppose."

Adham laughed. "Passable, eh? Who are you trying to kid, Ky? Adrina is a veritable goddess made flesh, and I'd have made a play for her myself years ago, if I wasn't so certain Damin would tear my throat out with his bare hands if I tried. And you . . . you're standing here all but drooling over her younger sister."

"I am not."

"Of course you are. But no matter, she's certainly drool-worthy. Quite a criminal waste marrying her to old Frederak, don't you think?"

A complete travesty, Kiam thought, turning to watch her again as Rakaia smiled up at Olivah. She seemed to be having a good time. Perhaps she'd decided Olivah was a better prospect than his grandfather. The nights were long and cold in Highcastle. Maybe she'd already figured out a way to pass the time.

She did like to play games, after all.

Then she glanced over at him and for a fleeting moment their eyes met. Kiam forced himself to look away first.

"She seems happy enough," he said with a shrug.

"Really?" Adham asked in mock amazement. "You're looking at her face?"

"You're a pig, Adham."

"I know," Adham agreed with a grin. "Comes from spending all my time away from civilization. You still killing people for a living?"

"No. I quit being an assassin a while ago. I renounced my lifelong oath, left the guild, and took up needlepoint."

"Just can't keep you away from sharp objects liable to draw blood, can we?"

The music ended and Olivah led Rakaia back to his grandfather, where she knelt down beside his chair and said something to him, although Kiam had no idea what she and old Frederak had to talk about. Not far away were Gidion Narn and his family, trying to edge close enough to the princess to appear as if they were included in her party.

"Did you want to meet up for a drink later?" Adham asked. "A few of us are planning to escape this madness as soon as it's polite to leave and find some real entertainment."

Kiam really wasn't in the mood for this party, let alone another one, but it would strengthen his alibi. This kill required there be no doubt it was anything but a terrible accident. Unfortunately, any death tonight, however seemingly innocent, would still throw suspicion on him. It was no secret in Hythria that the High Prince's youngest stepbrother was an assassin, or that he regularly attended the Spice Traders' Ball as a guest. Damin traded shamelessly on his profession at times, when it suited him to make a point with an adversary. To have Adham Tirstone and his friends vouch for his whereabouts when the accident happened would remove any suspicion at all that the guild had a hand in Gidion Narn's death.

"Sure," he said, as across the dance floor Rodja Tirstone stepped up to the podium where the orchestra was ensconced. "Where will you be?"

"The Tailor's Thimble," Adham said. "Do you know it?"

Kiam nodded. It wasn't that far from Gidion's mistress's house. That was convenient. "I'll see you there."

"Excellent. We can catch up then and you can regale me with exciting tales of your . . . needlepoint." Across the floor, Rodja waved to Adham to join him on the podium. "I have to go. We have some gifts to give."

Adham left Kiam to cross the now empty dance floor. The orchestra players were taking a well-earned break, but there was clearly an announcement imminent. On the other side of the ballroom Gidion was tapping his foot impatiently.

I'm with you, Gidion, old son, he said silently. *I want out of here too, al-*

though would you be so anxious to leave, I wonder, if you knew you were going to die before you got home?

Rodja called everyone to attention and the crowd spilled onto the dance floor to hear what he had to say. Kiam lost sight of Gidion for a moment, and when he looked for him with his family, he was gone.

"Ladies and gentlemen, I'd like to thank you all for gracing our humble home tonight with your presence," Rodja began. His comment raised a laugh in his audience. There were few homes in Greenharbour less humble than this one.

Kiam looked around, and spied Gidion making his exit. His mistress was more enticing, apparently, than whatever Rodja Tirstone had to say.

"Firstly, I would like to welcome our guest of honor, Her Serene Highness, Princess Rakaia, to the ball and welcome her to Hythria."

The crowd applauded, and a moment later Rakaia, looking lovely and more than a little uncomfortable with all the attention, was helped up on to the podium beside Rodja. Kiam wanted to stay. He wanted to see her, speak to her one more time, even just hear her voice, but Gidion was getting away and there was no future in wondering . . .

Get a grip, you fool, he told himself sternly. There is work to be done.

Kiam melted back through the crowd to follow Gidion as Rodja announced that he, Selena, and his brother Adham would like to offer their wedding presents to the princess and their good friend, the lord of Highcastle tonight, in honor of the long relationship the spice traders enjoyed with the custodians of Hythria's southernmost pass into Fardohnya.

It was all a sham, he knew. Rodja considered the Branadors to be worse bandits than the poor fools who raided the Widowmaker Pass so regularly. If he was honoring them now, it was politics and not friendship or generosity at the core of it.

Kiam didn't wait around to find out what the presents were. He had a spice merchant to kill.

KIAM STAYED IN the shadows as he followed Gidion back toward his carriage. The man was weaving a little as he walked, for which Kiam was grateful. If Gidion Narn's death was going to be attributed to a drunken and unfortunate stumble, it helped matters no end if he was seen to be visibly intoxicated before he left the party.

Gidion headed first to the tent where the servants and slaves attending their masters were gathered, to call out his driver. Kiam took the opportunity to run through the darkness to the gate. Once he was out of sight of the parked carriages and their drivers, he unbuttoned his jacket, quickly turned it inside out, and put it on again, pulling up the hood concealed inside to shade his face. Then he pulled a small length of chain wrapped in cloth to silence it, out of his pocket, swinging it around a couple of times to test the weight of it. A moment later he heard the carriage coming.

Kiam waited until the vehicle slowed down so the driver could check the street beyond before he turned. As soon as the driver was past him, he trotted alongside the coach and jerked the door latch, hearing the catch jam open, thanks to the sliver of metal he'd slipped inside earlier. With one smooth movement, he swung himself into the carriage, pulled it closed, and swung the silenced chain through the open door window. The momentum swung it back around on itself, through the door and the open window, holding the door closed, temporarily.

He sat down beside Gidion, who was so inebriated it took him a moment to register that he had a passenger.

The spice trader stared myopically at Kiam for a moment, before asking, "Eh? Who are you?"

"Your guide to the afterlife," Kiam told him softly, not wanting the driver to hear.

Gidion was too drunk to understand what that meant and Kiam gave him no further opportunity for discussion. He reached across the seat, grabbed Gidion's head with both hands, and then wrenched it sideways until he heard the bones crack.

Gidion slumped in his seat. His death was instantaneous and painless and probably far less painful than what he appeared to be doing, which was drinking himself to death. Kiam glanced out of the window of the carriage. He didn't have long to stage his accident. They were almost at the corner where one of many street urchins the guild paid to be their eyes and ears was waiting with Broos.

Kiam dragged the trader's dead weight onto the floor of the carriage, turning him so he was facing the door. Once that was done, he took a sliver of wood from his other pocket and jammed it under the bottom of the door so it wouldn't open until it was jarred. Then he removed the cloth chain, satisfied the door would stay closed, and turned to the other side of the carriage. A quick look outside to confirm the street was empty and he opened the door, stepping down from the slow-moving carriage to the cobbled street. He ran along beside it for a moment to ensure the door was latched properly on the undamaged side of the vehicle, and then dropped into the shadows, confident that if he ran, he could beat the carriage to the next corner through the back alleys of the houses lining the street.

He arrived not a moment too soon. The carriage was headed toward the corner. He let out a low whistle. A moment later a young girl emerged from the shadows, barely taller than Broos, with the dog walking beside her on a rope.

"Well done, Meggie," he whispered, handing the child the coin they agreed on earlier for her to mind his dog. "You run along home now. It's late."

She bit into the coin to test its authenticity and then handed him Broos's lead. "Sure thing, Ky. See ya 'round."

Meggie melted into the shadows without another word. Kiam slipped the lead off Broos, knelt down to ruffle the dog's velvety soft ears fondly, and then whispered, "Where's the cat, boy? Is he over there?" Kiam pointed to the street corner where the carriage would appear any moment. "Is it over there? Go find the cat!"

He let go of Broos's collar and the dog bolted toward the street in search of the promised feline. As he ran after him, staying in the darkness of the alley, Kiam heard a shout and then a horse whinnying in fright. He arrived at the intersection in time to see the horse rear up, the carriage brake suddenly, and Gidion Narn tumble out of the carriage with a thud to land on the cobblestoned street as Broos vanished into the darkness, still searching for a cat.

The driver leapt from his seat and took some time to calm the horse before he noticed his passenger on the road. By then, a few lights had appeared in the windows of the houses around them, as the noise woke the sleeping inhabitants. The first one to reach the scene found the driver kneeling on the road bedside his master, trying to revive him, even though he lay there, staring into nothingness, his head at an unfortunate angle.

"There was a dog!" the driver blubbered, clearly distressed, although whether by the loss of his master or his fate if he was found to be responsible for the accident was hard to tell. "A huge dog! It came out of nowhere and spooked the horse. He must have fallen out of the carriage . . ."

Kiam didn't wait around to hear the rest of it. He moved to the other end of the lane, reversed his jacket again, and then headed off toward the Tailor's Thimble to meet Adham Tirstone and his friends.

At some point in the evening, he was sure, they would hear the terrible news that one of Rodja and Selena's guests had been killed on the way home from the ball in a tragic accident.

Chapter

56

BY THE TIME they reached Greenharbour, Rakaia was satisfied she had been able to convince Mica that trying to kill every living Wolfblade to avenge the wrongs done to him in the past was not likely to achieve anything other than get both of them killed, too.

Mica seemed to accept her logic, although she did fear he was just agreeing with her because she was turning into a nagging wife, and agreeing was the only way to shut her up. Whatever the reason, by the time they rode through the wide gates of the vast, white-walled southern city, with its crowds and smells and unbearable humidity, she was content he would do as he promised.

They were going to find a ship as soon as they could, sail away from Hythria, indeed this entire continent, and never look back.

Oh, how my life has changed from where I thought it was going.

When she'd fled Winternest, Rakaia's only thought was to find a way to her uncle's home in Lanipoor, where her mother had promised her she would be safe. Now she wasn't so sure. Returning to Fardohnya meant living in hiding. She would be welcomed into her uncle's home, of that she had no doubt, but she would be placed straight into his harem with his wives and his daughters and unlikely to ever leave it again.

She had been free long enough now to see her uncle's protection for what it was—just another form of incarceration, no matter how pleasant or safe it might seem.

Rakaia still remembered the lies she'd told Charisee about why she was running away. *Have an adventure,* she'd told her unsuspecting little sister. *Have some fun. Not die of an unfortunate accident before I reach my majority because I'm one of Hablet's wretched unwanted daughters.*

At the time she'd thought she was lying; telling Charisee whatever she needed to hear in order to play along with her ruse. Looking back, she realized she'd spoken a truth of which she wasn't even aware. She *did* want adventure. She wasn't just surviving on the road as a vagabond; she was having the time of her life. The uncertainty of her existence was thrilling. Not knowing what the next day might bring was exhilarating.

Rakaia wasn't pining for her lost life as a princess. She was sorry she hadn't escaped it sooner.

But she couldn't stay in Hythria, and Fardohnya was too dangerous. Medalon was too full of Harshini, any one of whom might casually scan her mind and learn her secret—although they swore they never abused their magical powers like that. And Karien? Well, it was full of Kariens. That was enough to keep anyone away.

That left the countries across the Trinity Straits and the Dregian Ocean. Denika, maybe, or one of the Trinity Isles.

And that's where the ship plan came in. They would find a ship sailing as soon as possible and put this land behind them.

Just to be certain Mica didn't change his mind, Rakaia had the introduction letter the warlord of Krakandar had given them tucked away in her saddlebags where it wasn't likely to tempt him. She'd wanted to toss it on the fire—along with that ridiculous red Medalonian officer's jacket he insisted on wearing, even though it was sweltering in the city—but Mica had convinced her the letter might help them secure a berth on a ship, so with some reluctance, she had confiscated the letter and tucked it away, out of sight and out of temptation's way.

She was glad of that more than she could say, when they stopped at the first likely looking inn and were informed by the tavern owner there were no beds available and they'd be lucky to find a place to sleep anywhere in the city, what with the wedding carnival going on.

"What wedding carnival?" Mica asked.

"The High Prince's sister-in-law," the man told them, without looking up from his sweeping. "Demanded a full-on Fardohnyan wedding, apparently. Don't know what it's costing poor old Branador, but given we're never normally this busy in summer with the Warlords all out of town, I find myself very kindly disposed toward the young lady."

The man went back to sweeping the taproom floor. Before Mica could decide to sing the man into evicting another guest to make room for them, Rakaia grabbed his arm and dragged him back out into the busy street.

"What's wrong with this place?" Mica asked, assuming her anxiety to be gone from the tavern was simply because she didn't like the look of it. "It's clean enough."

"We have to leave the city. Now. Let's just find a boat and be gone from here."

"Why? Didn't you hear him? There's a royal wedding about to happen. A Fardohnyan royal wedding, no less! There'll be a carnival. Every minstrel for a thousand miles will be here. They hand out gold to complete strangers at Fardohnyan royal weddings. There's a fortune to be made."

"We don't need a fortune, Mica. We can make all the money we need when we get to Calavandra, or wherever it is we find a ship to take us. We don't need to hang about here, hoping for someone to throw coins at us."

"But a royal wedding . . ."

Rakaia wanted to scream at him for not getting it. "That's right, Mica. A royal wedding. Whose *royal* wedding do you suppose it is?"

"The man said it was the High Prince's sister-in— . . . Oh."

"Oh, indeed."

Mica nodded in understanding and put his arm around her. "You're right. We shouldn't stay."

"Thank you," she said, looking around. Nobody was watching them. Nobody was looking at her oddly. No one was pointing at her, whispering, "Look, that's the real princess over there."

But they had to get out of Greenharbour. She was a fool for not realizing they should never come here in the first place. Surely there were other ports along the coast where they could have found a ship to take them away from Hythria?

"How far is it to the wharves?" she asked, untying her horse's reins from the hitching rail outside the inn. She wiped her brow with the back of her hand, surprised by the sweat beading there. Talabar was humid, but this place was ridiculous.

"A fair way," Mica said, frowning. "I was a child the last time I was here, so my memory might not be that good. This is a very big city. I remember that much."

"We'll find them," she said, swinging up into the saddle. "After all, Greenharbour is supposed to be the largest port in the whole world. I'm sure the docks are rather hard to miss."

Mica smiled at her as he mounted his own horse. "Then we will find a ship and I shall sing us a royal cabin so my lady may travel in the style to which she is accustomed."

"I'll settle for a ship sailing on tonight's tide and a clear space on deck," she said. "And let's just stop throwing around words like 'royal,' and 'my lady,' shall we?"

He bowed to her with mock gallantry. "As my royal lady commands."

"I am going to have to hit you, Mica."

He grinned at her, and then leaned over in the saddle to kiss her, whispering against her lips, "Whatever you are to the rest of the world, Rakaia, you are my queen."

Her heart clenched a little at his declaration. She wondered again if Mica had done something to her to make her feel like this, but almost reached the point where she didn't care. Mica loved her. She loved Mica. She kissed him back with a grin, saying, "In that case, I command you to take me away from this terrible place, groveling minion, so I may continue my adventure!"

Then she gathered up her reins and turned her horse south, with Mica by her side, happier than she could ever remember.

Provided, of course, she didn't let herself dwell on the fact that her happiness might well be coming at the cost of her best friend marrying an old man in her place and it would shatter into fragments in a heartbeat unless they were able to find a way out of the city before someone realized the princess at the center of this marvelous royal wedding wasn't a princess at all.

THE SHIP THEY found to take them south after a long afternoon of refusals was a smart little two-masted trader named the *Sarchlo*.

The captain, a handsome caramel-skinned young man with a ready smile, told them it meant "unsinkable" in Denikan. Rakaia spoke a smattering of Denikan and was fairly certain it meant nothing of the kind, but the ship seemed in good repair, the decks were polished, the brass work gleamed, and the captain's sister, a shy young girl of about twelve or thirteen, somehow gave the whole outfit an air of respectability.

She realized they might well be pirates, ready to toss them overboard as soon as they hit open water, but so might any other crew on the docks.

The most compelling reason for sailing with the *Sarchlo*, however, was that it was due to sail on the high tide at midnight the following day, unlike every other ship's captain they'd spoken to, who had given their crews a few days off, because that was easier than trying to fight the free food and wine on offer thanks to this wretched royal wedding.

Better yet, Captain Berin agreed to let them sleep on board tonight in the cabin they'd booked for their journey to Calavandra in the Trinity Isles.

Mica handed over almost all the remaining coin they'd earned for selling Sophany's earrings in Bordertown for their passage so they disembarked after they'd settled their passage to find a hostelry prepared to buy their horses and their saddles, and to find some dinner.

By the time the moon rose overhead, Rakaia was settled into their narrow but surprisingly comfortable bunk on the *Sarchlo*, making love to Mica as the ship rocked gently at its berth.

When they were done, and Mica collapsed on top of her with a whimper of pleasure, she sighed—not just with the euphoria of their lovemaking, but the welcome thought that in less than a day from now, she would be gone from Hythria forever.

Chapter

57

"How do I look?"

Charisee's new handmaiden eyed her mistress up and down with a critical eye, and then nodded her approval. "You are stunning."

"You're not just saying that, are you, Tazi? Because you think it's what I want to hear?"

Tazi was the slave gifted to her by Rodja and Selena Tirstone—a plain, middle-aged woman with a stern face that utterly belied her cheerful personality. She had been the handmaiden of Selena's recently deceased grandmother, she told Charisee. To go from an uncertain future as the personal slave of a dead mistress, to the security of being made handmaiden to a princess in the royal household was a stroke of fortune for the slave Charisee could well understand. She had been this woman once. And she was determined to make certain Tazi never regretted having the Princess Rakaia as her mistress.

The older woman met her eye without flinching. "Would I lie to you, your highness?"

Charisee turned to examine herself in the mirror, with just as critical an eye as her servant. "Probably. If you thought I'd punish you for the truth."

"Are you going to punish me for being honest, your highness?"

"Of course not!"

"Then I will tell you the truth. You are stunning."

Charisee smiled, prepared to concede that she did look very much the part of the traditional Fardohnyan bride. She wore her hair down, and it hung past her waist in a honey-colored fall of silken waves, as was the tradition for all Fardohnyan brides. Her dress was red, heavily embroidered in gold thread around the hips, flowing out into a glistening shimmer of skirts. The gown was in two pieces. The bodice was made of deep red lace, threaded with gold, with long narrow sleeves and a low neckline that offered a tantalizing view of her breasts and left her midriff bare. The skirt sat snugly on her hips, the same shade of red as the bodice, made up of layer upon layer of transparent silk that flowed like a waterfall against her legs and was belted with a layer of gold mesh. In her navel sat a large ruby loaned to her by Adrina.

Around her neck she wore a small fortune in rubies, garnets, and pearls, also loaned to her by her half-sister, who'd been appalled to realize Charisee had arrived without any bridal jewelry to speak of. Charisee decided it would be unwise to tell Adrina where the bridal jewelry Rakaia brought to Hythria really was—that would involve an explanation about things much better left unsaid. She turned back to the slave. "You must always tell me the truth, Tazi."

"I will, your highness. I promise."

A knock at the door saved Charisee from having to think too closely about the hypocrisy of demanding the truth from a servant when she was just one big walking lie herself. Tazi hurried to the door to admit Princess Adrina, with Julika, Marlie, and Jazrian in tow. They were all dressed for the wedding. Marlie and her cousin, Julika, were to be her attendants, and were dressed in matching red—albeit far more modest—costumes. Jaz was dressed in white pants and jacket, and with his hair combed down, a child-sized sword at his side, looking rather unhappy at the prospect of spending the day dressed so formally. Julika wore the same expression. Apparently she was no more enchanted with the idea of attending this wedding than her cousin.

"We have a present for you!" Marlie announced before anyone could say a word. She was having a ball. "Mama says all Fardohnyan brides have one."

"Thank you, Marlie," Adrina said. "I was hoping you'd spoil the surprise."

"Oh, Mama, just give it to her!"

Adrina shook her head at her daughter's impatience and smiled at Charisee. "You look lovely, Rakaia. And Marlie is right. We do have a gift for you."

She held out a small dagger in a jeweled sheath. Charisee accepted the gift, a little awed by her sister's generosity.

"It's a Fardohnyan bride's blade," Marlie explained, almost jumping up and down with excitement. "All Fardohnyan brides are supposed to carry them. You might as well have it, because Mama says Nana Marla would allow Medalon to invade Hythria before any granddaughter of hers has a Fardohnyan wedding."

"Yes, thank you, Marlie. That will be enough."

"I know what it is, Marlie," Charisee said, examining the exquisite workmanship with admiration. Centuries ago, Fardohnyan brides had carried a sword, so the story went, but it was still a tradition to carry a bride's blade. The blade was more ornamental than practical. It was sharp, though, as Charisee quickly discovered when she tested the edge with her thumb. "Thank you."

"I won't promise it will bring you luck, but it has quite a history, that little knife," Adrina explained as she helped Charisee secure it in the mesh belt she wore. "It belonged to my mother, who is your half-aunt, so it's a family heirloom of sorts, even though Hablet and my mother weren't married long, because he . . . well, beheaded her." The blade secure, she stepped back to examine her handiwork. "I carried it in both my weddings, too. One of them has worked out so far. In fact, I've only had to use it once."

"Did you use it on Uncle Damin?" Julika asked, interested now that the conversation had turned to weapons, apparently, even the ornamental kind.

"No, Julika, I used on Prince Cratyn. He slapped me. I don't take kindly to being slapped. One day, when you have a wife, Jazrian, if you slap her, you can expect the same treatment." She turned to Charisee. "You shouldn't put up with that sort of treatment either, Rakaia. Remember that."

"I will."

Adrina nodded approvingly at her sister's attire. "You've done a good job, Tazi. Selena was right to speak so highly of you."

"You sister is a delight to serve, your highness."

"Then you may go," Adrina said. "I'll help Rakaia with her veil. I want you to go downstairs and find Strayan. Selena was expecting him back last night. She said she'd send him over this morning, but he hasn't arrived yet. When you find him, you may both have the rest of the day off—as is the tradition in Fardohnyan weddings—while Rakaia is escorted to her wedding by her family."

Tazi curtseyed respectfully and let herself out of the room, closing the door behind her.

Once they were alone, Adrina took Charisee by the hands. "How are you feeling?"

"I feel so nervous I want to vomit."

Adrina laughed. "Well do it now, or after the ceremony. You'll never live it down if you do it in public. I hope you don't mind that I didn't include the twins in the wedding party today. It will be insane enough as it is, without adding a couple of excited four-year-olds to the mix."

"Of course I don't mind. Will I have time to say goodbye to them before I leave for Highcastle?"

"We'll make time," Adrina promised. "The wedding feast is back here at the palace and I promised them they could come to that. Do you know what you have to do?"

"Say yes," Julika suggested helpfully. "Not cry. Or cringe."

Adrina frowned at her niece. "Yes, thank you, Julika. That was very helpful."

"Just saying . . . ," she replied with a shrug.

Charisee got the distinct impression Julika wanted to be involved in this wedding party even less than she did.

The High Princess turned to Charisee. "We're taking a carriage to the Sorcerers' Collective," she explained, walking to the bed to pick up the long, diaphanous veil designed to cover her head and the lower half of her face. "If this was a proper Fardohnyan wedding and my husband hadn't so recently been attacked by an assassin, we'd walk. A carriage and a large honor guard will be safer."

"Can I ride on top with the driver, Mama?" Jaz asked.

"Of course not," Adrina said, without even looking at him. She kept working on the veil, making sure it was pinned in place while Julika untangled her train. The veil trailed ten paces behind, and was meant to float on the slight current of air created by her passage. "After the ceremony, we'll take a carriage back to the palace and disembark at the gate. You and your new husband will then mingle with the crowd for a time, handing out coin to anyone who takes your fancy. Darvad has checked the credentials of all the performers, and everyone permitted in the palace forecourt, so it should be safe enough."

"Does that mean we can join the carnival too, Mama?" Marlie asked, her eyes alight at the prospect.

"Yes, but only if you stay with your guards."

"We will, won't we, Jaz?"

"Of course."

A few more adjustments and Adrina was done with the veil. She stepped back to study Charisee for a moment and then nodded her approval.

"Try to make the most of today, Rakaia. It may be the last time for a while that you are the center of attention."

"I don't need to be the center of attention to be happy, Adrina."

Her sister nodded. "I'm sure you don't. But just remember this, too. Not all arranged weddings are complete disasters."

"Are you talking about your wedding to Papa?" Marlie asked. Before Adrina could answer, she turned to Charisee, bursting with the need to share everything she knew. "Mama didn't want to marry Papa. She hated him. It was the demon child who forced them to get married."

"Who told you I hated your father, Marlie?"

"Nana Marla."

Adrina rolled her eyes. "That woman will be the death of me, I swear."

"Is it true?" Julika asked. "The demon child actually *forced* you to marry Damin?"

Adrina nodded. "Sort of. I wanted to kill her at the time. Now . . . well, now I just wish I knew where to start looking for her, because until we find her, I doubt Damin is going to get any better."

The demon child saved Rakaia in the Widowmaker Pass, Charisee wanted to tell her, pained by the strain in Adrina's voice. *She was there a couple of months ago and now she's in Medalon somewhere.* Jakerlon had told her that.

But to admit she knew that would require her to admit *how* she knew.

"I wish I could tell you where she is, Adrina," she said. *The best lies of all, after all, are the stone-cold truth.*

"That's sweet of you, Rakaia, but don't let my problems get in the way of you enjoying your day. Marlie? Julika? Are you going to be all right with that veil? Like we practiced?"

"Yes, Mama," Marlie said, moving around behind her to scoop up the excess fabric.

"Then lead on, Jazrian," Adrina commanded with a smile at Charisee. "We have a wedding to attend."

Chapter

58

WHEN RAKAIA WOKE the following morning, she was alone and the sun was well up in the sky from what she could tell from the small porthole over the bunk. She stretched luxuriously for a moment, thinking this was going to be her life for the next few weeks. Sleeping late, making love to Mica, and not a care in the world.

Nobody could find her here on the *Sarchlo*. Mica had let go of his urge for vengeance.

They had nothing but the future to look forward to, whatever it might hold.

The need to relieve herself got her out of bed. Her clothes were still on the floor where she'd left them the night before, in her haste to remove them. Their few remaining belongings were packed into the saddlebags they'd carried with them since Bordertown. She was half dressed before she noticed the saddlebags had been tampered with.

There was an art to packing everything they needed in them, but someone had obviously been rifling through the bags, as if looking for valuables. Rakaia pulled on her blouse and looked around. Mica's lyre case was missing too. So was his ridiculous red Medalonian officer's jacket.

The missing lyre and the jacket might be explained by Mica's absence—after all, he rarely went anywhere without them—but not the saddlebags.

A quick inventory of the contents and she realized only one thing was missing, which also meant only one person could have taken it.

The letter the Warlord of Krakandar had written in the Pickpockets' Retreat, recommending Mica to the High Prince of Hythria, was gone.

With a muttered curse, Rakaia pulled on her shoes and hurried topside. The first person she encountered was the captain's sister, who was tipping the vegetable scraps from the galley into the harbor, much to the delight of the fish gathered below, waiting for their bounty.

"Tritinka, have you seen my husband?"

"He left a couple of hours ago, miss," the young Denikan told her. "Said he had one last performance to take care of before he left Hythria."

I will kill him. Slowly. Painfully. Over and over.

"Did he say where he was going?"

"No, miss. But I suppose he's at the palace for the carnival." She pointed to the unusually quiet docks. "That's where everyone else is today."

"Thank you," she said, and hurried to the gangplank.

"Miss!" Tritinka called as she stepped onto it.

"Yes?"

"We sail at midnight," the girl reminded her. "The tide don't wait for nobody, and neither does my brother."

"We'll be back before then, I promise," she assured the girl, and then she took the wobbly gangplank almost at a run, anger and fear for Mica lending her feet wings.

THE STREETS NEARER the palace were lined with people waiting for the royal wedding party to return from the Temple of the Gods where the High Arrion was officiating over the ceremony. The rumor had got about that the newlywed couple would be tossing gold from the carriage on their way back to the palace, so the route was packed with every hopeful in Greenharbour in need of some extra cash.

Rakaia knew the story was nonsense. The bride and groom did hand out coins at a Fardohnyan royal wedding, but it would happen in the confines of the palace grounds to the select few chosen to attend.

That's where Mica was, she knew, without a shadow of a doubt. He had taken his letter of introduction, used it to get inside the palace walls, and would take his vengeance as soon as a member of the Wolfblade family got within listening distance of him. He might not kill them outright. He might sing them into wanting to kill themselves—something he was more than capable of doing—but his song was indiscriminate. Even if she didn't care about the fate of the Wolfblades, Charisee was in there and likely to be in range of whatever dire song he chose to glamor his victims with. She didn't deserve to be caught up in Mica's vengeance, no matter how much the others may deserve it.

Rakaia took a moment to curse her sister for demanding a Fardohnyan wedding as she pushed her way through the crowd toward the palace.

What was Charisee thinking? Had she embraced being a princess so wholeheartedly that she wanted to throw her weight around, just to prove she was royal?

Why couldn't she just be content with a regular Hythrun wedding like any normal princess coming to a foreign country to marry a cousin of the High Prince would have done?

It got harder to move the closer she got to the palace. Rakaia had to elbow her way forward. Not only was the crowd denser, there were soldiers lining the streets. They wore the livery of Greenharbour, the province ruled by her half-brother Gaffen. Or rather, Adrina's half-brother. Rakaia had to constantly remind herself she was no longer a part of Hablet's extended family. She and Charisee weren't even sisters, when it got down to it, although she was related to Adrina on her mother's side. She didn't know what that made Gaffen, or if, indeed, she was related to him at all.

It didn't matter. Rakaia finally reached the gate as a roar went up from the crowd. A carriage was approaching. It was a white landau carriage, drawn by four beautifully matched golden sorcerer-bred horses. The soft folding roof lay perfectly flat so the crowd could see the lucky couple. On the raised driver's seat a guard wearing the livery of Highcastle sat, scanning the crowd for danger. Two more blatantly armed guards stood on the groom's seat, which was sprung above and behind the rear axle.

Rakaia pushed closer to the curb, but the guards held her back. As the carriage passed by, turning into the palace gates, she finally caught sight of Charisee.

She almost didn't recognize her former slave. Dressed in the full regalia of a Fardohnyan bride, she was a vision of youth and beauty, sitting opposite a wrinkled and decrepit old man who appeared to be constantly nodding off. On one side of Charisee sat a young girl, also dressed in red. Probably Princess Marlie, Adrina's daughter. The little girl was smiling, waving to the crowd, having a high old time, as many of the crowd waved back to her. Another attendant, a pretty girl of about sixteen, looked as if she would rather be anywhere else. The bride was waving too, but far less confidently than Princess Marlie. She wore an expression Rakaia knew well. It was the look she always wore when Rakaia cajoled her younger sister into doing something she didn't want to do.

Charisee wasn't enjoying herself. She was terrified.

A wave of guilt washed over Rakaia at the sight of the man she had tricked her sister into marrying, surprising her. She'd worked so hard to convince herself she had done Charisee an enormous favor by saving her from a life of slavery and hard labor. She could see the lie of her delusion writ large on Frederak Branador's face.

Thankfully, Charisee didn't see her in the crowd. As soon she was past, Rakaia pushed her way toward the gate as another carriage, this one a closed carriage bearing the royal Wolfblade escutcheon, also entered the gates, followed by several other carriages, no doubt carrying the remainder of the wedding guests invited to the official reception.

She didn't have long. Once the last of those carriages entered the gates they would be closed and she would have no chance of getting inside to stop Mica.

When she reached the gate, she hoped she'd be able to slip inside while the guards' attention was on the carriages, but they were on the lookout for people just like her, and her way was blocked before she could step a foot inside the palace forecourt.

"Off you go, lass," the guard ordered. He was an older man, probably a grandfather, if the gray in his beard was anything to judge by, but he seemed perfectly capable of wielding the sword and the baton he carried on his belt. "The show's over for you."

"My husband is Mica the Marvelous," she told him, glancing down the street to discover there were only a few more carriages left. "He's performing for the royal family."

"I'm sure he is."

"I'm not making this up!" she said, alarmed by his skeptical expression. It struck her then that Mica might have sung to the guards to prevent her following him, but perhaps he didn't have time. Perhaps he thought he'd be back at the *Sarchlo* before Rakaia discovered what he was up to. "He has a letter from the Warlord of Krakandar introducing him . . . us . . . to the High Prince. Someone here must remember letting him in! I need to find him. He can't perform without me. I'm part of his act."

The guard studied her for a moment and then walked over to the gate commander. They had a brief discussion, the commander consulted a list he was carrying and then he nodded. Filled with relief, Rakaia waited impatiently for the guard to return.

"Lucky for you the captain remembers your Mica the Marvelous." He led her to the gate and waved to the other guards to let her through as the last of the carriages passed through and they swung ponderously shut behind her. "Stay out of trouble!" he called after her.

Rakaia waved to acknowledge she'd heard him, and then turned and scanned the crowded forecourt with dismay. It was almost as congested as the street outside. But somewhere in this crowd was Mica, getting ready to wreak the vengeance he'd promised her he wouldn't take.

She hurried forward, searching at the stalls that lined the forecourt. One housed a juggler, the next was two acrobats and a contortionist. The next offered fortune telling, the one after that offered sweetmeats.

It was only as she caught a whiff of the sweetmeats that Rakaia remembered she hadn't eaten all morning. She had no coin with which to buy food, but this was a Fardohnyan wedding, so the food was probably free. Justifying putting aside her need to find Mica for a moment with the thought that she would never find him if she passed out from hunger, she pushed her way over to the food stall.

Rakaia was so intent on her purpose she didn't notice the applause or the crowd parting around the stall until she found herself face to face with the new lady of Highcastle.

There was a moment where they said nothing. Charisee's eyes were wide, but to her credit, she barely faltered before turning to her new husband, who was being wheeled along beside his bride in a wicker chair by a handsome young man with a snide expression, who didn't seem capable of taking his eyes of Charisee's bare midriff.

"Shall we gift this one, my lord?" she asked, bending down to say the words directly into the old man's ear. Apparently, besides not being able to walk unaided, he was deaf as a post, too.

"She's pretty," the old man said. He handed Charisee a single gold coin from the purse on his lap, which he clutched with skeletal fingers, as if it contained his life savings.

Charisee took the coin and turned to face Rakaia, her shocked expression replaced with the serene look of a princess doing her duty to be kind to the poor and less fortunate. "What is your name, my dear?"

"Aja, your highness," she said, remembering only then that she should probably have curtseyed to her former slave. "My husband is the minstrel, Mica the Marvelous."

Charisee smiled. "Then you're in luck. We met Mica the Marvelous almost as soon as we arrived. My husband was so impressed with his talent, he gifted him most generously."

That's unlikely, Rakaia thought, given that Frederak Branador appeared to be stone deaf, but the important thing was Charisee had seen Mica.

He'd sung for her, too, which was worrying. What had he done to her? Who else had he sung to?

Charisee pressed the coin into Rakaia's hands, gripping them tight for a moment, saying more with that brief touch than a thousand words could have done. "Be well and happy, Aja."

"I wish you the best and happiest life the gods will permit too, your highness," Rakaia said, hoping Charisee knew how much she meant it.

Charisee let go of her hands and Rakaia dropped into another low curtsey. By the time she rose to her feet, Charisee and her husband had moved on to the next peasant on whom they planned to bestow their largesse.

Rakaia wiped away an unexpected tear as she waited for a moment, but Charisee didn't look back.

As the bride and groom were lost to the crowd, Rakaia shook off her guilt, grabbed a sweetmeat from the vendor, and went back to looking for Mica before he killed someone.

Chapter

59

FOR A DAY that had such great potential for disaster, Rakaia's wedding day was progressing quite smoothly. Adrina watched over the carnival from the palace steps, her half-brother Gaffen by her side, ready to carry out her orders, should she choose to issue any.

The carnival had been an excellent idea. A Hythrun wedding involved a much more formal setting where everyone would have noted the High Prince's absence. Looking down over the crowded confusion that was the palace forecourt, Adrina was quite sure she could spread the rumor that Damin was down there somewhere, mingling with the common folk, and someone would swear they'd seen him.

She glanced up at the almost setting sun, aware it would soon be time to call the children inside. She didn't like them mixing with a crowd such as this, but she was astute enough to realize she was doing her children no favors by preventing them from ever meeting the common people of Hythria. She had controlled the situation as best she could. There was nobody in the forecourt that hadn't been vouched for by someone she trusted.

"Are you sure Wrayan checked everyone?" she asked Gaffen, frowning. She didn't want to spoil their fun, but Adrina knew she wouldn't rest until the children were safely inside. Marlie was going to be a particular problem, she was certain. As an official member of the bridal party, her daughter would consider being sent to the nursery for dinner a punishment rather than a wise move taken for her own protection.

The Warlord nodded. "I believe so. There was a minstrel who arrived after Wrayan left for the ceremony, but the guard commander said the lad had a letter from Starros introducing him to Damin, so he let him in. I doubt any threat to the Wolfblades is going to come from that direction." Gaffen leaned a little closer, adding, "I'd be more worried about the Branadors, if I were you, 'Rina. I swear that little thug, Olivah, has pilfered half the gold his grandfather was supposed to be handing out today and kept it for himself."

She allowed herself a wry smile. "You know, having spent more time in the company of that wretched family than I'd like in the past week, I am actually starting to understand why Marla is the way she is."

"Do you want me to do anything about him?"

"No," she sighed. "The money was a gift from Rodja and Selena. We have no right to dictate how it's spent." She glanced around and spied Darvad and his wife, Rielle, over by the sweet vendor's stall. They had Kimarie and Tristan with them and were plying them with treats. Darvad looked up and she waved him over.

He leaned in and said something to Rielle, then took the steps two at a time to reach Adrina.

"When you and your wife have finished plying my children with enough sweet sticky things to turn them into blobs and ensure their poor nurses will never get them to sleep tonight, could you take them back to the nursery?"

Darvad laughed. "Now? Just when they've discovered cheese custard tarts?"

"It's all the other things they've just discovered this afternoon before they got to the cheese custard tarts that worry me," she laughed. "I do appreciate you keeping an eye on them, though."

"Rielle misses her grandchildren," he said. "Any excuse to spoil yours is a bonus."

"I will have to speak to her about that," Adrina said, with mock disapproval. Then she smiled and added, almost as an afterthought, "Can you find Jaz and Marlie and send them to the nursery, too? I want them safe and sound before the evening festivities and the wine starts to flow more freely." Fardohnyan weddings honored Jelanna, the Goddess of Fertility, after all. The children were a little too young to be exposed to how some people chose to honor her when the wine was free and their inhibitions were low.

"Of course," he said, and hurried back down the steps to inform Rielle it was time for the children to retire.

Adrina thought no more of it, and turned back to Gaffen. "Do you think Damin will be angry when he hears what we did here today?"

"I think your husband is a pragmatist, 'Rina. He'll probably only be angry that he missed it."

"I hope so. I am glad Marla's not here. She'd be apoplectic at the idea of a Fardohnyan wedding in her palace, I'm sure."

"Not a dissimilar reaction to our father's, I suspect, when he realizes he has to deal with Marla during the treaty negotiations."

Adrina closed her eyes for a moment. "Gods, she must almost be at the Citadel by now. You know, I haven't spared her a thought in weeks."

Her brother laughed. "She probably hasn't slept a wink the whole time she's been on the road, worrying about you."

"You know, that's actually a comforting thought."

"Mama! Why do I have to leave?" Marlie shouted up at her from the forecourt, struggling to shake off the grip of her nurse who knew Marlie well enough not to let go.

Adrina sighed. "I knew this was going to be a problem. Excuse me, Gaff. I have a nine-year-old to tame."

She left her brother on the steps and headed down to speak to Marlie, not wishing to make any more of a scene than her daughter was already doing.

"Marlie, people are watching you," she warned in a low voice as she approached her daughter, who wore a look of unadulterated defiance. "So far today, you have conducted yourself like a princess. If you wish to start acting like a screaming shrew, then I will have to treat you like one."

"I have to stay. I'm part of the wedding party."

"The wedding is over. What is left now is a lot of foolish adults intending to get drunk. There is no need for a bridal attendant to take part in that."

"You're letting Julika stay."

"Julika is sixteen and an apprentice sorcerer. You are nine."

"You let Jaz do whatever he wants."

"Jazrian is retiring too, Marlie," Adrina assured her. "So you have nothing to complain about."

"What if Rakaia needs my help?"

"Julika's the senior attendant. She can take care of her."

Marlie's eyes brimmed with disappointed tears. "But I want to stay, Mama!"

Adrina embraced her, understanding her daughter's disappointment while being entirely unsympathetic to it. "I know you do, sweetheart, but it's not going to happen." She squatted down to meet Marlie, eye to eye. "I can promise you this, though, my darling. If you don't bow to me gracefully, right this minute, then kiss me goodnight and walk up those steps and into the palace like a lady, I will have your uncle Gaffen come down here, throw you over his shoulder, and carry you screaming to the nursery so everyone can see you being treated like a naughty child. Choose your poison, darling."

Marlie glared at her for a moment and then leaned forward and meekly kissed her mother on the cheek. "Goodnight, Mama."

Adrina rose to her feet, smiling. "Goodnight, Marlie. Sleep well."

The nurse gave Adrina a grateful look and took Marlie's hand to lead her up the steps. Adrina smiled at them, and then glanced around the crowd, wondering where Jaz was. Unlike his sister, he had probably accepted the order to retire without complaint, even if he was just as disappointed. He didn't share his sister's rebelliousness.

In fact, he might well be inside already. Jaz wouldn't think of making a scene. She made a note to check with Darvad as soon as she found him again, and then headed into the crowd to see how the new lady of Highcastle was faring.

It took Charisee quite a while to recover from finding Rakaia in the crowd. She seemed well, although the blond hair was a shock, as was the plain dress she wore. For the life of her, she couldn't imagine what Rakaia was doing here at her wedding. Had she come to see if Charisee was keeping her secret? Had she come to claim her birthright?

And yet she'd done nothing but wish her sister well.

It didn't seem to make a difference to the panic Charisee was feeling. For the rest of the day and long into the evening, Charisee searched the crowd, looking for her sister to no avail, half expecting to hear someone calling her out for a liar at any moment.

Expecting at any time for her world to come crashing down around her.

The acrobats, fortune tellers, tricksters, and fire eaters had mostly departed and the gold had all been handed out by sunset. An orchestra had taken over the entertainment for the evening and she was finally able to sit down. By then Charisee was exhausted from the gift giving, wearing an entirely insincere smile all day as she thanked a steady stream of equally insincere well-wishers, and from trying to figure out why Rakaia was here.

On top of all that, although the evening meal was about to be served, offering a moment of respite, she still had to get through her wedding night.

That was going to be no fun either. Although the promised *court'esa*—and the only hope she'd had of pretending any sort of experience—had been gifted to her more than a week ago, Charisee hadn't even met him yet. Strayan had been with Rodja and Selena's eldest daughter in Grosburn, Selena had explained apologetically. He had been sent for the day after their late-night discussion with the Tirstones in Adrina's private quarters, but it was a long way from Pentamor Province, and provided he was here in time for their departure for Highcastle tomorrow, nobody seemed to think there was any great hurry for his services.

She was still a virgin posing as a princess trained to be a satisfactory wife and she was certain everyone who looked at her could tell she was anything but.

The only thing likely to save her, Charisee thought as she took a seat at the bridal table next to her husband while the forecourt was cleared for dancing, was that she doubted he'd be able to stay awake long enough to notice if the marriage was consummated or not. Or Rakaia would expose her. That would save her from Frederak, too. But not in a good way.

"If the old boy isn't up to it," Olivah whispered in her ear, startling Charisee with his nearness, "I'd be more than happy to oblige." He slid into the seat next to her, where she had assumed Adrina, or perhaps even Gaffen would be seated, grinning at her like a cat playing with a particularly juicy mouse. "After all, one Branador cock is as good as another, don't you think . . . *Granny?*"

Charisee was aghast at the man's boldness. But Adrina had warned her well about Olivah Branador. She knew if she didn't take a stand now, she would never be rid of him.

"I'm not in a position to judge that yet," she said, forcing herself to sound far more calm and in control than she felt. "And I fear you do yourself an injustice, sir, unless you truly believe your virility to be on a par with a man sixty years your senior." She smiled at him and patted his hand on the table sympathetically. "How sad for you. Is there something you can take? My *court'esa* arrived today. Perhaps I can send him to you once we get to Highcastle, to offer some advice? I believe they learn how to deal with such . . . unfortunate circumstances . . . as part of their *court'esa* training."

Olivah's smile faded. He was not amused. "You think you're such a smart little bitch, don't you?" he said, snatching his hand from under hers.

"I am a princess of Fardohnya and your grandfather's wife," she reminded him with all the regality Rakaia would have done. "That makes me the lady of Highcastle now, and your liege lady, if I'm not mistaken. So what you really meant to say was: 'You think you're such a smart little bitch, don't you, your *highness?*' Wasn't it, Olivah?"

He apparently didn't have an answer for that, because he just grunted something that sounded very rude and left the table. Charisee sipped her wine, hiding her smile in her goblet. *I might look harmless and weak to you, Olivah Branador,* she said silently to herself, *but I grew up in the Talabar Royal Harem. I'm not as easy to torment as you think.*

The main meal was served soon after Olivah left, but the seat beside Charisee remained vacant. Nobody seemed to notice. Although the wedding party was seated, the rest of the guests were standing, either nibbling the delicate finger foods the slaves were offering around on large platters or eating their meal from bread trenchers, tapping their feet to the music. Many of the younger guests were already dancing. The noise level was quite horrendous, between the orchestra belting out a series of cheerful jigs in the hope of encouraging even more guests to dance and people trying to talk over the music.

Charisee glanced up at the sky, wondering if it would rain. It had been overcast and humid all day and a downpour would certainly put a damper on things, but the clouds had evaporated and the night was clear. There was no escape from that quarter.

"May I have this dance?"

Charisee looked up, a refusal on her lips, when she realized the man asking her to dance wasn't a man at all.

"Lord . . . Erlon? What are you doing here?"

"Asking you to dance."

"I'm not sure if my husband . . ."

"Lord Frederak! May I dance with your wife?" he leaned over and shouted into Frederak's good ear.

The old man looked up and smiled. Jakerlon had apparently woken him. "Eh? Yes . . . of course. Be my guest." He smiled at Charisee, patting her knee with his bony, arthritic hand, "No need for you to sit here watching the fun, my dear, just because I'm not up to it. Off you go. Enjoy yourself. You won't get a chance to dance much when we get to Highcastle."

With a great deal of trepidation, Charisee allowed the God of Liars to lead her out to join the rest of the dancers. She couldn't believe the sheer brazen gall of him. Or that he would risk appearing here on a night like this. But as she looked around, she realized she could shout the truth about him at the top of her voice, and not a soul would believe her.

Jakerlon said nothing as he led her beyond the dancers and the crowd and into the shadows beyond, where the now abandoned marquees of the performers stood against the white palace wall, waiting to be pulled down tomorrow once the festivities were over.

"Where are we going?" she asked, glancing back over her shoulder. Surely she would be missed if she wandered too far from the party.

"You have a problem, sugar plum," he told her. "I am helping you fix it."

"What problem? The only problem I have is you dragging me away from the wedding table. How am I going to explain . . . ?"

"Lie." He stopped and turned her to face him. "I wouldn't be here if you weren't quite exceptional at that."

"I know, but—"

"But, nothing," Jakerlon cut in. "You have bigger problems than missing dessert."

"What problems?"

"As we speak, honeycakes, the palace guard is moving quietly to lock down the palace. By midnight the whole city will be sealed, and there are more than a dozen Harshini on their way here to scan the minds of every guest at the wedding."

"Why?" she asked, shaking free of his grip. She hadn't sensed anything amiss; although the seat beside her remained empty all evening, she'd just put it down to the informality of the wedding feast.

"The *why* is not your problem, precious," Jakerlon said, lifting the closed flap of what had been the fortune teller's tent, earlier in the day. "She is."

The God of Liars gave Charisee a gentle shove in the small of her back, and pushed her inside.

A single lamp on the fortune teller's table lit the tent. There was a young woman waiting inside with her back turned. She spun around as the tent flap dropped closed and Charisee gasped with surprise.

It was Rakaia.

RAKAIA STUDIED CHARISEE in the light from the single lamp on the fortune teller's table for a moment. She was almost unrecognizable from the slave who'd balked at taking her place. Her sister was dressed in the gown Rakaia had brought to Hythria for her wedding, and no matter how glad she was not to be standing in Charisee's shoes or wearing that gown, it still irked a little to think how much better it looked on Charisee than it did on her.

"Who was that man?" she asked. "I hope you trust him, because if he tells anyone . . ."

"Lord Erlon is a friend," Charisee told her. "He won't betray me."

On impulse, Rakaia stepped forward and hugged Charisee tight, relieved she was still alive. And that she had not marched straight down from her room in Winternest all those months ago and confessed everything to Valorian Lionsclaw.

When Charisee didn't hug her back, Rakaia stepped back and smiled at her sister, wishing she could reassure Charisee she hadn't come here to spoil anything. She just wanted to find Mica and leave, but Charisee wouldn't understand that. "You look amazing, Chari."

"You look . . . different."

Rakaia smoothed down her blond hair self-consciously. "That was Mica's idea. He thought changing my hair would help my disguise."

"He knows who you are, then?" Charisee didn't sound too pleased to learn that.

She nodded. "He won't betray us, Chari. I promise."

"Why did you come here today, Rakaia?"

"I didn't come here to cause trouble for you, Chari. I was looking for Mica, actually. I was worried he might . . ." She stopped, deciding it was pointless explaining what she feared Mica might be planning. Nothing had happened all day. She hadn't found Mica in the crush, admittedly, but Charisee's wedding day had passed uneventfully. There were no killings, no guests dropping dead from strange songs . . . in fact, other than Charisee mentioning she'd seen Mica earlier in the day, she wouldn't have even known he had ever been here. "I thought he'd be here, performing. And then I saw you . . . You make a lovely bride, by the way. Red really suits you."

"You think I'm a lovely bride? Have you seen my husband?"

All Rakaia's long buried guilt came bubbling up at Charisee's question. She had escaped Hablet's wrath and convinced herself she was doing Charisee a favor, but they both knew the lie for what it was.

And yet Charisee didn't seem to be blaming her. She certainly wasn't demanding Rakaia march out of this tent and confess the truth, something she had feared was about to happen when Charisee's messenger found her in the crowd and brought her here to meet her sister.

"I'm sorry, Chari," she said.

"No, you're not," Charisee said. "You're alive and glad to be out of the way, before Hablet finds out you're not his daughter."

"How . . . how do you know that?"

"I know more than you think, Rakaia," she said.

Rakaia felt as if her head was swimming. How could Charisee know something like that? Had Sophany said something to her before they left Talabar? Rakaia's palms were sweating. The heat in the dark, closed tent was almost unbearable, made worse by the elegant stranger standing before her, who had once been her slave.

"You know, I never really thought you'd go through with this," she said, wiping her hands on her skirt. She could feel the sweat beading on her brow, while Charisee seemed as cool as snowmelt. "I really did think you'd chicken out at the last minute, throw yourself on the lord of Winternest's mercy, and set every Raider in Winternest after me."

"Then why did you suggest I pretend to be you, if you thought I wouldn't do it?"

"I figured you'd buy me some time to get away."

"You didn't need my help, Rakaia," Charisee said. "Not when you had the demon child ready to come to your rescue."

Rakaia had to grip the table. "How could you possibly know about that?"

"It doesn't matter. Do you know where she is?"

"Who? The demon child? No! Of course I don't. Who told you this?"

"The same person who told me they are about to seal the palace and scan the minds of every guest here. The Harshini are on their way."

Mica . . . what have you done?

"Has something happened?"

"I don't know," Charisee said. "And to be honest, I don't care. But you have to leave this place. You have to leave Hythria. Now. And never return."

"What about you? Aren't you afraid what they'll find if the Harshini look into your mind?"

Charisee shook her head. "I have nothing to fear," she said. "I am a princess of Fardohnya. You are the one lying when you claim to be that."

Rakaia felt she was staring at a stranger. The Charisee she had always been able to cajole or sweet-talk into doing whatever she wanted was a dim and distant memory. The quietly determined young woman standing before her was a different person. It was as if along with her regal clothes Charisee had found a regal spine to go with them.

"I'll go," she promised. "But only if you promise me something."

"What?"

"That you'll try to be happy. For me."

"For you?" Charisee asked. "You who are tripping around the countryside, free as a bird, while I live every day in fear of being exposed as a fraud. Of course I promise to be happy. Perish the thought you might feel any guilt about what you've done to me."

"You're angry at me for leaving."

"No, Rakaia, I am angry at you for coming back. You set us on this path and now you are endangering both our lives. So leave me to it. Go. Please."

There was no point in arguing about it, although what she expected Charisee to feel about what she'd done still wasn't clear even to Rakaia. Mica would have said she wanted forgiveness. If Charisee was happy, then throwing her in the path of an eighty-year-old husband and the real risk of assassination would be much easier to live with.

She shook her head. Rakaia wanted to leave, but there was one small problem. "I still haven't found Mica . . ."

"I'll speak to Lord Erlon. If Mica is still here, my . . . friend will find him. I'll have him get Mica out of here too, before they seal the gates. But you mustn't wait for your minstrel here in the palace grounds, Rakaia. You must get out of here before they try to question anyone."

Charisee turned to leave, but she stopped with her hand on the tent flap and looked back over her shoulder at her sister. "I'm glad you've found someone and I'm not happy, Rakaia, but I'm not truly unhappy, either. I have a chance, however short it might be before Hablet's assassins catch up with me, to have a good life. Please don't ruin it for me."

"I'll be gone before you're back at the bridal table. I promise."

Charisee nodded and left the tent. Filled with too many confusing emotions to sort through right now, Rakaia waited impatiently for a few minutes and then followed her. By then, there was no sign of either Charisee or her strangely compelling friend.

Rakaia hurried along in the darkness beside the empty tents to the gate, where sure enough, as Charisee had predicted, the guard was being quietly doubled. The gates were closed but as she approached one of the guards gave the signal to open them.

She moved to get a better look and realized there were more than a dozen white-robed Harshini from the Sorcerers' Collective waiting outside. In the lead was an assassin and beside him stood the High Arrion of the Sorcerers' Collective. Rakaia didn't know her on sight, but she knew what those robes and diamond-shaped pendant meant.

The gates swung open and Rakaia dashed through in the confusion of the Harshini arrival, almost shaking from fear of being called back and interrogated. But she got away clean. As soon as she was out of the palace walls, she picked up her skirts and broke into a run, certain that whatever was about to put an end to Charisee's wedding day had something to do with Mica and the revenge he wanted to take on the Wolfblades.

Her only hope now was to get back to the boat, wait for Mica, and then make him undo whatever it was he had done . . . providing of course it *could* be undone and he hadn't just murdered the entire Wolfblade family while Charisee was enjoying her wedding feast.

62

"WHAT DO YOU suppose is happening at home?" Damin asked as they waited for the door in the cliff face to open. R'shiel didn't know how long they'd been here. In the perpetual twilight of Sanctuary, time was an elusive creature that didn't like to be pinned down.

"Adrina probably hasn't even noticed you're missing, Damin."

"I probably missed the wedding." Damin didn't sound particularly upset at the prospect. He stretched his feet out and crossed his arms. "There'll be hell to pay for that. No pun intended."

"What wedding?" Mandah asked as she paced in front of Damin and the cliff door, waiting for it to open. R'shiel still wasn't sure if she was coming with them or intended to wait here until they returned—assuming, of course, they did return.

"Adrina's younger sister is marrying the man who raised my mother," Damin told her. "All for the greater glory of Hythria. I was supposed to give the bride away at the ceremony."

"Raised your *mother*? Founders, Damin, how old is the groom?"

"Eighty-something, give or take."

"That's disgusting," Mandah said.

Damin appeared amused by Mandah's righteous indignation. "You know, I've always imagined that's what Rakaia is going to say the first time she sees her husband naked."

R'shiel's turned to him, frowning. "Rakaia?"

"Her Serene Highness, the Princess Rakaia of Fardohnya. One of Adrina's countless younger sisters sent to Hythria like a brood mare off to market so her father can guarantee access to the trade routes through the Highcastle Pass."

"That's not a common name. Rakaia."

Damin shrugged. "Never really thought about it. Why?"

"It's just . . . It's odd. I met this Fardohnyan girl a few months ago named Rakaia. She wasn't on her way to Hythria, though. She was heading out of Hythria, actually, into Fardohnya through the Widowmaker Pass."

"If she wasn't surrounded by a two-hundred-strong entourage, then it wasn't our Rakaia. By all accounts, she's a holy terror. 'Rina calls her the Tantrum-Throwing One."

"Whoever the girl was that I met, she was definitely high-born. She told me she'd been sold into slavery to settle her father's debts. Or did she?" Looking back, R'shiel couldn't recall. "I might have just assumed it, now that I think about it, and she didn't bother to correct me."

"It is odd," Mandah agreed, stopping her pacing long enough to ponder the problem. "I mean, what are the chances of there being two Fardohnyan high-born girls named Rakaia in Winternest at the same time? You don't suppose . . . ?"

Damin rolled his eyes. He was sitting on a rock opposite the cliff, waiting like the rest of them for the door to open. "Gods, you two! Listen to yourselves! You see intrigue in everything!"

"How do you figure that?" R'shiel asked, wondering if she should rethink her decision to take Damin with her through the door. She'd forgotten how irritatingly sure of himself the High Prince of Hythria was.

"Two girls named Rakaia and immediately there is a plot afoot? How do you know the one you met wasn't lying to you, R'shiel? Maybe she just liked the name. Or maybe she was telling the truth and it *was* her name? The simplest reason is usually the right one, you know."

"Speaks the man who decided the woman he would eventually marry was a screaming shrew based on a great deal of third-hand gossip and the word of a man negotiating the surrender of his army."

Damin smiled, unperturbed. "Ah, but you see, my wife *is* a screaming shrew. She just chooses not to scream at me."

"I can't for the life of me imagine why not," Mandah said, resuming her pacing. "Isn't there some way you can open that door?"

R'shiel shook her head. She'd examined the door closely and tested her power against it to no avail. This was Death's realm, and her power, which in the real world was almost unlimited, was severely restricted here. "It will open when it's ready."

"Where do you think it leads?" Damin asked. "I mean, there are seven hells, right, each one of them progressively better, depending on how deserving you've been in this life?"

R'shiel turned to look at Damin, not sure where he was going with this. "I suppose."

"You *suppose*?" Mandah asked, appalled. "You're about to step into hell, R'shiel, and you *suppose*?"

Damin wasn't smiling. He seemed to be in agreement with Mandah. "My point is, some of these hells are going to be better than others. Right?"

"Of course."

"So which one is on the other side of that door? The one full of butterflies and fluffy kittens or the hell full of flesh-eating lava monsters? Do they get better or worse the further in you go? And do you even *have* a plan for getting out again?"

R'shiel really hadn't thought about any of that. Like a bride who couldn't see past the altar, all she'd dreamed of for more than a decade was finding her way here, to bring Brak back to the life Death had ended so unfairly and prematurely to save her. Somehow, she'd assumed that once Brak agreed to return, Death would let them both go.

She hadn't counted on fighting her way in and then out again.

"I don't know," she confessed.

"Will your magical powers work in hell?"

R'shiel shrugged. "I don't know that, either."

"You really haven't thought this through, have you?"

She wanted to deny the charge, even though it was patently true, when the edges of the door began to glow. Around her head, like a tiny gusts of wind, the air began to move as the gathered spirits waiting in Sanctuary were drawn to the opening. Sanctuary must be full of them, she realized. Full of the spirits of the truly dead, waiting for their chance to enter the afterlife properly, to find the hell they'd made for themselves during their mortal lives.

Turning her face up to feel their butterfly kiss on her cheeks as they clustered around the door, R'shiel wondered why she'd never noticed them before. She'd lived here for months after Joyhinia tried to kill her. Perhaps it was because only here, standing in front of this plain, inconspicuous door, was she exposed to a high enough concentration of them to notice. The Harshini had never said a word to her about this door or where it led, either, but in hindsight that didn't surprise her. The Harshini couldn't lie, but they'd never had to because she had never posed the question.

They were expert at lying by omission—the only way a people required to honor all the gods could honor the God of Liars.

She glanced at her two companions. Damin and Mandah were not dead, but captive here, which is why they were solid entities, even though they were as much a spirit as any ghost gathering for the door to the Seven Hells to open.

And that was the danger. She turned to Damin, filled with second thoughts. "You know, maybe you shouldn't come with me. Mandah was right when she said earlier that crossing into hell might actually kill you. I don't want that on my conscience."

Mandah snorted at her words.

R'shiel turned to her angrily. "You think I want you and Damin to die?"

"I was scoffing at the notion that you have a conscience."

"What happened to you, Mandah? You used to be the nicest, most forgiving soul alive."

"I grew up, R'shiel. I stopped playing at being a rebel and took some responsibility for my life. I have a family. I have a husband who relies on my counsel. I have a life I don't want to lose, and it's threatened by your selfishness."

R'shiel had no answer to that, in part because it was true. She never intended anybody else to be hurt by her quest to find Brak. She just wanted the pain of missing him to go away.

For the first time since walking out of the Citadel all those years ago, she questioned the wisdom of trying to bring Brak back.

Behind her the door had almost dissolved in a blinding light. The spirits buzzing about her head were becoming frantic.

Was it too late to turn back? Was Brak happy?

Wasn't that the whole point of an afterlife?

Admittedly, Brakandaran had done some bad things in his life—his very name struck fear into his enemies for good reason—but they were all for a noble cause. He'd saved countless Harshini lives. He'd saved her. He taught her and protected her, so that when she faced down Xaphista the Overlord, as the gods had created her to do, she was able to defeat him.

Death must have given Brak some credit for that . . .

She could feel the pull of the door. It was open now. The spirits were rushing through, stirring her hair with the haste of their passing. It was impossible to see what lay beyond because of the intensity of the light streaming from it. Mandah had stepped back from it, but Damin, ever fearless, was moving closer for a better look.

This was the moment, R'shiel realized. The point of no return. If she didn't step through, then surely the deal was off. Damin and Mandah would be returned to their bodies, and the lives held in suspension by her need to bring Brak back would be restored. Death would not require a life of equal value.

He would not require a life of any value.

All she had to do was step away.

R'shiel held out her hand to Damin, although whether to stop him coming closer or to draw him in, she couldn't really say.

All R'shiel knew is that the moment Damin grasped her hand, the door began to close, sucking everything nearby, including the loose leaves and twigs lying on the grass, into its vortex. Mandah grabbed the trunk of the nearest tree and clung to it, to prevent herself being sucked in. R'shiel staggered against the pull, appalled by the strength of it. She tried to shield herself against it with magic, but whatever magic powered this gate into hell, it was far stronger than any R'shiel could muster.

Then the door snapped closed, pulling R'shiel and Damin—who still had her by the hand—into hell.

THEY LANDED HEAVILY and skidded along the ground for a time until they came to rest against something solid. The quiet, after the rushing hiss of the door sucking souls inside, left R'shiel's ears ringing.

She looked around, climbing to her feet. As her eyes adjusted to the dim light she realized she was back in the Citadel.

"I know this place," Damin said, climbing to his feet beside her.

"It's the Citadel," R'shiel agreed. "This is the corridor outside Joyhinia's room when she was on the Quorum for the Sisterhood."

Damin shook his head. "No . . . this is the clearing where I met the God of War," he said. "I wasn't even a Warlord back then . . . I wasn't much more than a boy. Gods, that must have been more than twenty years ago now."

She looked at him curiously and then checked that he was still holding her hand. "You're standing in a forest?"

"Most definitely."

"I'm not. I'm standing in the Citadel."

He digested that information for a moment and then he smiled. "Well, then. This is going to be interesting."

R'shiel took a deep breath—although she suspected she just thought she was breathing the same way she just thought she was in the Citadel, and squeezed Damin's hand. "I'm sorry you're here, Damin. I'm sorry you got caught up in this. But I'm glad it's you that's here with me now."

"That's what friends are for, R'shiel," he assured her. "Although I think you can confidently assume the favor you're going to owe me for this is along the lines of parting the oceans to create a land bridge between Hythria and Denika."

She smiled. "Oh? For a moment there I thought you were going to ask for something impossible."

"It's early days," Damin said as he tucked his arms through hers. "And we only just got here. I'm sure I'll think of something appropriate by the time we find Brak."

R'shiel didn't really have an answer for that, because he was right. She would owe him more than she could repay if they found Brak and got out of here alive.

Without another word, she turned toward the corridor only she could see and together with the High Prince of Hythria, they took their first steps into hell.

63

CHARISEE MADE IT back to the bridal table before she found out what was going on. Now that Jakerlon had warned her something was afoot, she could see the signs of trouble everywhere she looked, from the subtle change in the number of guards to the fact that Adrina had not been seen since they sat down to eat.

Jakerlon assured her Rakaia's minstrel was long gone and then he vanished, too. He didn't want to be caught here with the Harshini any more than Rakaia did. The Harshini knew every god on sight and could probably tell when he was in the vicinity, even if they couldn't see him.

The God of Lies clearly had no intention of explaining to anybody—human or Harshini—what he was doing at her wedding.

She took her seat beside Frederak, who smiled at her as she sat down.

"Did you enjoy your dance, my dear?"

"I did," she said, smiling back at him. Adrina was right. However unpleasant Braun Branador and his son, Olivah, were, Frederak was a sweet old man. "Would you like more wine?"

"If I drink much more I'll nod right off."

He'd already nodded off more than once this evening, so she couldn't see how another cup would make much difference. Charisee poured his wine with her own hand, one eye on the wine, one eye on the crowd who were ever so gently being surrounded by a mix of Greenharbour Raiders and palace guards.

It wasn't until the High Arrion walked into their midst, with Kiam Miar and his enormous dog by her side and a dozen or more white-robed Harshini behind her, that the wedding guests noticed anything amiss.

A moment later the orchestra stopped mid-tune. Charisee glanced over to find her half-brother Gaffen, the Fardohnyan-born Warlord of Greenharbour, commanding the conductor to cease the music. Once that was done, he stepped down from the orchestra podium and walked over to join Kalan, whose appearance had drawn the attention of every man, woman, and child in the palace forecourt. Her presence alone should not have been enough to raise the alarm—she was the High Prince's sister, after all, and had officiated at the wedding ceremony earlier. But with Kiam Miar beside her, dressed not as a wedding guest but in the close-fitting black leathers everyone associated with his guild, she became someone to be wary of.

Whatever was going on, Kalan was making no secret of the fact that the Sorcerers' Collective had the support of the Assassins' Guild.

By now, an expectant silence had fallen over the crowd.

"My lords and ladies, I apologize for interrupting your festivities." The High Arrion glanced over at Charisee and Frederak. "I particularly want to apologize to the lord and lady of Highcastle."

With every eye suddenly fixed on them, Charisee bowed her head slightly in acknowledgment of the apology, although she still had no idea what Kalan was apologizing for or why the Harshini were here. For that matter, what did this have to do with the Assassins' Guild?

Although she silently willed him to look her way, Kiam didn't once glance at her. Even Broos seemed to know this was serious. He stood beside his master, his ears alert, his whole body radiating leashed power, waiting for Kiam's order.

"Some time earlier this evening, my nephew, Prince Jazrian of the House of Wolfblade, the Crown Prince of Hythria, went missing . . ."

A concerned buzz ran through the crowd. Charisee's heart skipped a beat. That's why Adrina was missing from the wedding feast, she realized. She was searching for Jaz.

"While his disappearance may simply be the result of a youthful prank, I'm sure you'll all agree the life of our young prince is not something we are prepared to gamble with. To that end, the Sorcerers' Collective has offered to assist in finding him as quickly as possible. We'll be doing this by eliminating any question that he has been the victim of foul play."

Another mutter ran through the crowd, this one much more self-serving. It had just occurred to everyone what the Harshini were here to do.

"My friends here," she continued, indicating the dozen or so white-robed Harshini who stood patiently—and smilingly—behind her, "will look into each of your minds. They are interested only in information regarding Jazrian's whereabouts and have sworn to protect any other secrets they may stumble across in the process." That raised a nervous titter from her audience, which Kalan ignored. "As you are examined and cleared by the Harshini, you will be permitted to leave. Anybody who does not wish to have their mind examined in this manner may decline. There will be no stigma or guilt assumed if you do so."

She placed her hand on Kiam's shoulder then, adding with a smile that was more threatening than anything else she had said or done this night, "In fact, our youngest brother, and Jazrian's favorite uncle, has kindly offered his expert services in the area of interrogation, to those who feel having their minds probed by the Harshini is an unwarranted invasion of their privacy."

The threat was clear and explicit. *Submit to the Harshini or summit to much harsher questioning by the Assassins' Guild.* Charisee doubted there would be many takers, although she was tempted to put her hand up. That way at least, she would be able to speak to Kiam again.

You evil, thoughtless bitch, she told herself with despair. *Jaz is missing and all you can think of is being alone with Kiam instead of worrying about what Adrina must be going through right now.*

"I didn't hear any of that," Frederak complained. "What's going on?"

She leaned in close to his ear. He smelled of old sweat and stale wine. "Prince Jazrian is missing."

"Why?"

"A very good question, my lord!" Gaffen shouted to him as he approached the table. "That's what the Harshini are here to find out!" He turned to Charisee and smiled sympathetically. "Sorry about this."

"You have nothing to apologize for, Gaffen," she assured him. "Is there anything I can do to help?"

He shook his head. "Not at this point. I'll have someone escort you and your . . . husband back to the palace."

"Shouldn't we be probed by the Harshini before we leave?" *Make it sound like the idea doesn't frighten you to death, Charisee.*

Gaffen shook his head and gave her a wan smile. "The Harshini have enough to do and I'm pretty sure you and Frederak haven't had time to kidnap anybody today, Rakaia. Although I can promise you we'll be looking very closely at your new grandson." He waved a couple of guards forward and gave instructions to have the newlyweds escorted back to the palace. As she rose to her feet, Charisee glanced around at the chaos. Her wedding day had been ruined, but it didn't matter because it really hadn't been a celebration in the first place.

She suddenly felt ill. Charisee knew in her heart of hearts that something terrible had happened to Jaz. He wasn't the prank-playing type. Marlie might think up such a scheme, but Jazrian would never be so foolish.

Had Jakerlon known? He was a god. Surely if something had happened to the child, he would know what it was?

But there was no sign of the God of Liars and even if she spotted him in the crowd, how could she explain who he was, how she knew him, or how he knew about what had happened to Jaz?

"Can you take me to Adrina?" she asked Gaffen as he turned to leave.

He thought about it for a moment and then nodded and turned to one of his men. "Escort Lord Branador to the palace and then take Lady Branador to the High Princess. She is in the Main Hall."

The Raider saluted and then bowed to Charisee as his companion maneuvered Frederak's wheeled chair from behind the table. The two of them then lifted the chair between them and carried him up the broad palace steps, leaving Charisee to follow in his wake, wishing there was something she could do to help Adrina other than tell her more lies.

Because *"Don't worry, Adrina, I'm sure Jaz will be found any moment, safe and sound"* was almost as big a lie as the one she lived every day, pretending she was Rakaia.

As she reached the top of the steps, she turned to look down over the palace forecourt, which now resembled less a wedding celebration and more a prison camp, as Gaffen's men moved in. Kiam was standing in the middle of it all, almost as tall as the calm Harshini, come to scan the guests' minds, his hand on Broos's collar as he waited for someone to be foolish enough to refuse the benign probing of the Harshini.

As if he felt her eyes on him, he looked up. For a moment their eyes met and then he looked away.

"This way, your highness."

Charisee turned to follow the guards who had reached the top of the steps with Frederak's chair. She followed him inside, glad she'd seen Kiam one last time, even if she hadn't found an opportunity to speak with him.

She closed her eyes for a moment, imprinting his face on her memory, and then followed her new husband inside, hoping the memory of Kiam was enough to see her through her wedding night.

Chapter 64

With the problem of the bastard princess taken care of now that the ludicrous price the Assassins' Guild was asking to rid the king of his embarrassment had been paid, Naveen Raveve now had time to concentrate on tying up the king's other "loose ends."

The wedding should have happened yesterday in Greenharbour, which meant soon the problem of the bastard would be taken care of and he would no longer need to fret over it.

Naveen had debated quite a few ways of taking care of the "loose ends" problem. His solutions ranged from simply walking into the Harem with an armed escort and putting all the royal women to the sword—not the slaves, of course; they could be sold for a tidy profit—to infecting them with something contagious in the hopes they all might die of disease. The former was too brutal and obvious, the latter far too difficult to control with no guarantee of success.

Poison was out of the question. The king didn't want to advertise his hand in this affair. A mass poisoning would demand an investigation and a scapegoat that Naveen simply didn't have the time to organize.

He was still pondering the problem as he entered his office after breakfast, only to find a priestess from the temple of Jelanna waiting for him, along with several members of the Talabar City Council.

Naveen sometimes regretted ever suggesting a city council. It was one of the suggestions he'd made when he became the king's chamberlain. It was part of his plans to improve efficiency. A city council, he'd argued, would reduce the number of petitioners complaining to their king about potholes in the roads, the smells coming from the meat works district, or who was supposed to deal with the backed-up sewage pipes after a storm.

For a while there, his plan had worked. But then the city elders had gotten far too enamored of their position on the council, and while the petitioners had been reduced, the problems they were complaining about hadn't. These rich merchants, upon whose good will the king often relied when he needed money, now felt as if they had a direct conduit to the king.

Naveen took a seat behind his desk, bowing first to the Goddess of Fertility's priestess—an old hag dressed in a white hooded robe who looked as if she hadn't been fertile for decades.

"My lady, gentlemen, to what do I owe this honor?"

"The king has left the city," the priestess said.

Naveen nodded slowly. "I am aware of that, my lady."

"Our understanding is that he will not return in time for the Festival of Jelanna," Master Gabynix said. He was a bloated, middle-aged man who owned several wool mills and a number of looms, mostly producing the poorer quality fabrics peasants seemed to favor. Or maybe they didn't favor the rougher fabrics so much as could not afford anything else. Either way, the man was obscenely rich. Naveen respected that.

"The king has gone to the Citadel to renegotiate the terms of the peace accord signed after the end of the Karien-Medalon war," he reminded the merchant and his council cronies. "He regrets his inability to be here for the celebrations, but will honor the goddess with the Harshini queen in the Temple of the Gods and give thanks for her bounty and, of course, his most precious gift from the goddess, the Crown Prince Alaric."

"He can honor the goddess with whomever he damn well pleases," Master Myni said, obviously annoyed there were no seats in Naveen's office for guests, forcing him to remain standing like a common petitioner. "We just want an assurance the palace will fund the celebrations. Fireworks are expensive, you know."

"And dangerous," the third councilor, Master Rifky, said, clearly in disagreement with his fellow councilors. "I'm still cleaning up the mess from last year when the wind took the sparks and landed them in the middle of my setting tanks."

Rifky was probably the richest merchant in the room. He had a virtual monopoly on the city's olive oil trade. The fire last year, caused by a stray firework landing in his compound, had taken days to extinguish and risked a large portion of the city until it was brought under control.

"I hear your concerns, gentlemen, and I can assure you, the king appreciates both the expense and the danger."

"What is he planning to do about it then?" Gabynix asked.

Not a damned thing, Naveen was tempted to reply, but this was no time for the truth. Fireworks *were* a risk. Fires were always a risk in a large city where everyone cooked over open flames. If they weren't prepared to accept that, then they shouldn't—

Fire.

Of course. Why didn't I think of that sooner?

Naveen smiled, but not for the reason his visitors thought. "The king is a devout man, as well you know," he said, bowing to the priestess again, who nodded in acknowledgment of his claim. And so she should. The king had spent a fortune on her damned temple over the years while he sired daughter after daughter, until he finally got a son—thanks not to his generosity to her order but to the direct intervention of the demon child. "He does not spare any expense demonstrating to the goddess how much he appreciates her largesse."

"That's all well and good," Myni cut in, "but—"

"But King Hablet also acknowledges the danger to your enterprises, gentlemen, and would not dream of risking your livelihoods, or those of the thousands of his subjects who depend on you for employment, by allowing the unsafe handling of such explosive substances as fireworks."

"Nice speech, Naveen," Rifky said. "What's he planning to do about it?"

"I am authorized to tell you that the king will bear the entire cost of the fireworks display this year," Naveen announced, wondering what Hablet would do when he heard about this. "Furthermore, our most generous and devout king, in order to protect your businesses, has agreed to allow the main display to be launched from the palace grounds, far away from the industrial areas of the city, rather than the docks, which I believe led to the problem last year."

That announcement left them speechless. It was the priestess who answered for the councilors after a moment of stunned silence. "The king is indeed a true and devout follower of the goddess."

"He lives only to serve Jelanna, my lady. Will that be all, gentlemen?"

They nodded, having nothing else to complain about—at least for the time being. Naveen rose to his feet and walked to the door, opening it for them himself. "I shall communicate your gratitude to the king," he assured them.

The councilors filed out of the room, with the priestess coming up last. She glared at Naveen—his status as a sterilized *court'esa* made him defective in her eyes—but she said nothing as she walked past him, satisfied her petition had been heard.

Naveen closed the door and leaned on it thoughtfully.

Fire. Tragic. Accidental. And very, *very* effective.

He had found his way to tie up those loose ends.

Now he just had to ensure that whatever stray fireworks "accidentally" landed in the harem on the night of the Festival of Jelanna hit something flammable enough to engulf the place.

All he needed to do before then was find a way to ensure that the well-trained palace fire crews couldn't get inside the harem in time to prevent any of those loose ends surviving the conflagration.

chapter

65

THE LOOK ON Princess Marla's face when she first saw the Citadel amused Caden Fletcher. He'd forgotten she had never traveled this far north into Medalon before. The princess was one of those people who seemed to know everything, have done everything, and been everywhere. It was strange to catch her in a moment where she appeared as dumbstruck at the sight of it as any young farm girl come to the big city for the first time.

The Citadel was probably the oldest city in the whole world, certainly the oldest on this continent. It was built by the Harshini when the gods first brought them into being, back in a time so long ago that most mortals still lived in tribal caves and eked out a living hunting and foraging on the vast plains that made up central Medalon. It had grown over the years, both in size and in the magnificence of its architecture, its magically infused walls dimming and brightening with each day and night for as long as anyone could remember.

According to the Harshini, the Citadel was an entity in his own right, a vast sentience that protected the Harshini from harm. Although every other city they had a hand in creating was just as white, just as elegant, and just as impressive, only the Citadel and Sanctuary—so the rumor went—had ever developed minds of their own.

Cade found himself explaining this to Marla and Rorin as they approached the city. She seemed quite taken with the notion of an aware city, although Rorin was less impressed. He'd been to the Citadel before.

The Lower Arrion of the Sorcerers' Collective was an innate sorcerer—a human with enough Harshini blood in him to wield true magic. He'd visited Medalon a number of times over the past decade or so, to meet with the Harshini in his official capacity as Kalan Hawksword's envoy, or to receive training in the arcane arts from the Harshini teachers who lived here.

Cade had just begun to tell them about the frequent entertainment on offer in the amphitheater when a rider galloped up from behind, his horse foaming at the withers.

The rider wheeled his horse around until he was in front of their column and stopped to face them, effectively blocking the road.

Cade held up his hand to halt the Raiders and reined in his own horse. With his hand resting on the hilt of his sword he stared at the young rider, who, on closer inspection, was wearing the livery of the royal house of Fardohnya.

"You're blocking our way, my friend," he said, wary of inciting some sort of diplomatic incident with the Citadel walls in sight.

"On the contrary," the rider replied in heavily accented Medalonian. "You are blocking ours. On behalf of his Royal and Most August Highness, Hablet, King of Fardohnya, Beloved of the Realm, Father of his People, Favored of the Goddess Jelanna, I demand you move aside to allow us clear passage to the Citadel."

Cade had no idea how to answer a challenge like that. He glanced over his shoulder, but there was no sign of the party in question yet. Cade had heard Hablet was sailing up the Glass River in his own ship to reach the Citadel. If he was on his way now, then he'd probably landed in Reddingdale overnight and was proceeding overland to the Citadel, sending this poor lad on ahead to clear the way.

He didn't need to answer the challenge, as it turned out. Marla answered for him. She laughed out loud at the very idea.

"Are you joking, young man?" she asked with an awe-inspiring display of regal disdain. "Do you really believe her Royal Highness, Princess Marla, Mother of Hythria, Mother of the High Prince, Beloved of Her People, Favored of *All* the Gods, not just one of them, and Mistress of a Loyal Sorcerer Ready to Smite on Her Command, is going to interrupt her journey to accommodate a minor monarch who sits a horse so poorly he doesn't know how to make it wait?"

The messenger stared at Marla in shock. "But . . . His Highness said . . ."

Poor kid, Cade thought. *His orders don't include any contingency for someone telling him to get lost.*

"You may deliver a message to his highness for me," Marla told him. "You may tell him Her Royal Highness, Princess Marla, Mother of Hythria, Mother of the High Prince, Beloved of Her People, Favored of

All the Gods, not just one of them, and Mistress of a Loyal Sorcerer Ready to Smite on Her Command, will generously permit him to travel in her wake, so that he may eat her dust and reflect on the privilege he is being afforded by being allowed to follow in her footsteps."

The young Fardohnyan stared at her in shock.

"Off you go, lad. I'm sure your king is anxious to get the message."

Without another word, the young man wheeled his horse around and galloped back the way he'd come.

Rorin turned to Marla, shaking his head. "Seriously, your highness? We've come all this way to discuss peace and that's how you're planning to deal with Hablet? *Eat my dust?*"

"Diplomacy is like a dogfight, Rorin," she informed him, gathering up her reins. "If you want to win, you have to show the other dogs in the fight which bitch is in charge."

"I fear the Lower Arrion has a point," Cade felt compelled to say. "Your message was somewhat . . . inflammatory, your highness."

"Only if Hablet runs into the back of our entourage," Marla said. "How far are we from the Citadel?"

"About four miles."

Marla turned in her saddle. "Yananara, may I speak with you a moment?"

The Harshini horse master trotted forward. Cade moved aside a little to let her ride beside Marla.

"Are the horses well rested, Yannie?"

The Harshini smiled. They always smiled. "These last few days of normally paced travel have been good for them, your highness. It was considerate of Captain Fletcher to suggest it."

Captain Fletcher wasn't being considerate at all, Cade was tempted to tell her. *He just thinks riding a magical horse that can go for days without a break at a speed likely to kill an unwary rider is an insane way to travel, and any chance he gets* not *to travel like that, he's going to jump at it.* But he said nothing, just nodded in acknowledgment of the compliment.

"Do they have a short burst left in them?" Marla asked.

"I can ask them, your highness. But I'm not sure they'll see the point. The Citadel is in sight, it is almost sundown . . ."

"And the king of Fardohnya is about to catch up with us," she explained. "If they would consider taking us forward at speed, they will be released from their duty—which they have performed flawlessly—that much sooner. I'm sure they are looking forward to a warm bed and a hearty meal as much as the rest of us."

Yananara wasn't stupid. "And we will reach the Citadel before King Hablet reaches us."

"You have a keen political eye, Yannie," Marla told her. "I should bring you to the negotiating table with me."

"I believe, your highness, that role has already been reserved for your Loyal Sorcerer Ready to Smite on Your Command."

Founders, Cade thought. *Did she just crack a joke?*

"Ah," Marla said. "You heard that."

"Yes, your highness. I did."

"You do realize her highness was just posturing for the sake of appearances, don't you, Yannie?" Rorin seemed worried the Harshini had taken Marla literally.

"I do, Rorin," she said, smiling at him. "I am not sure King Hablet will see the funny side of her suggestion, however. So I will speak to the horses and explain to them the wisdom of arriving at the Citadel before you are placed in the awkward position of having to live up to your new title."

Without waiting for an answer from Rorin or Marla, Yananara dropped back and leaned forward to whisper something to her mount. The horse shook his head and whinnied and then the other horses started doing the same thing, all along the column of riders, as they spoke to each other and discussed—Cade supposed—whether or not they wished to grant Marla's request.

After a short time, Yananara's mount began nodding his head, followed by the other horses. Cade had been through this often enough now to know what those nodding heads meant. He quickly gathered up his reins and tied them to the pommel of his saddle and then glanced over his shoulder to see Marla's escort doing the same.

Cade turned and faced forward, gripping the front edge of his saddle. The horses would be controlled by Yananara while at speed, and any attempt by a mortal rider to interfere by trying to guide his mount with a bit invariably resulted in the offending rider being tossed to the ground for his temerity. A fall from a horse at the speed a sorcerer-bred mount could travel would be fatal, he didn't doubt, so, much as it unsettled him to give up control, Cade surrendered to the beast and closed his eyes. Painful experience the first time this happened had taught him that trying to watch the scenery speed past while the horses ran a such at blinding pace was enough to unsettle his stomach to the point of vomiting.

He felt his mount move off, and then almost immediately after she started, the mare skidded to a halt. He opened his eyes to find out why they'd stopped, only to find himself looking up at the glowing white walls of the Citadel. The sorcerer-bred mounts had traveled the four miles to the Citadel in a matter of seconds.

Marla was untying her reins from her saddle, quite unperturbed by the experience. The princess glanced over her shoulder at the horse master and smiled. "Thank you, Yannie. And please, thank the horses for bringing us here safely, and for this last favor, too. It is much appreciated."

"I will pass on your thanks, your highness, but it really isn't necessary. They could feel the Citadel calling to them. I think they were glad of the excuse to get here a little quicker."

"Thank them anyway," she said, and then turned to look at the gates of the Citadel that stood open and waiting to receive them.

Almost as if they were expected, a troop of smartly dressed red-coated Defenders was riding through the gates as Marla spoke, forming an honor guard for the princess. A moment later, a tall, dark-haired Defender rode out of the city on a handsome gray gelding, his uniform adorned at the shoulders with the gold epaulettes denoting his rank.

As the Lord Defender rode forward to greet Princess Marla, Cade was struck by how tired he looked.

Lord Tenragan bowed to the princess. "Welcome to the Citadel, your highness."

"Thank you, Tarja," she said. "I hope you haven't been hanging about the gate all day in that ridiculous dress uniform, waiting for me to appear."

"Would you be impressed if I said yes?"

"I'd think you were a prize fool."

He treated her to a weary smile. "Then you'll be relieved to know your horse master informed our horse master you were on your way almost as soon as you were within sight of our walls."

Cade turned and glanced at Yananara curiously, wondering at the range of Harshini mental communications. The Harshini used the Seeing Stones to talk across vast distances. He didn't realize they could talk to one another across miles, too. Although he couldn't say why, he'd always assumed Harshini telepathy was a line-of-sight ability. He filed away the knowledge that it wasn't and turned his attention back to the Lord Defender and Princess Marla.

"Then allow me to be the bearer of similar news," Marla was saying. "Hablet is right behind us, I believe."

Tarja nodded. "We received word when he docked in Reddingdale last night."

"You've had time to lock up the silverware, then?"

"It's going to be a long negotiation, isn't it, your highness?" Tarja said with a sigh, turning his horse as Marla trotted up beside him so they entered the gates of the Citadel side by side.

Cade fell in beside Rorin, right behind them, interested in the obvious friendship between Marla and Tarja. As far as he knew, she'd only met him once before, when Tarja visited Greenharbour some years ago, but they were chatting like old friends. He glanced at Rorin, who shrugged, as if he understood what Cade was asking without having to explain it.

"This negotiation won't be nearly as long as it would be if Damin were here," the princess suggested with a laugh. "At least with me across the table there will be more negotiation, less drinking, gambling, wildly exaggerated war stories, and reminiscing about the good old days."

At the mention of Damin, Tarja lowered his voice to the point that Cade could barely hear him. "Has there been any improvement in his condition, your highness?"

Rorin leaned forward and answered for the princess. "We've not had any news to that effect."

"I feared as much," Tarja said, glancing back at the sorcerer. "I suppose I was hoping . . ."

"Is something wrong, Tarja?" Marla asked.

The Lord Defender hesitated and then he nodded, still turned to include Rorin in the conversation. "My wife, Mandah, was struck down with a similar affliction only days after Damin was attacked."

Cade was astonished. "Excuse me, sir, but are you saying someone tried to kill Lady Tenragan?"

Tarja shook his head. "She went to bed feeling poorly one night and never woke up. The Harshini cannot revive her, although she lives and seems to be merely sleeping. Queen Shananara says it has something to do with Death. And R'shiel."

"You don't happen to know where the demon child is, do you, Tarja?"

Only Marla, Cade realized, would be brave enough to pose that question to the Lord Defender in such as tactless manner.

He shook his head. "I would have her here now, your highness, if I knew where to find her," Tarja said. "And I would have sent word to the High Arrion the moment I located her."

Then Marla asked another question few people were bold enough to venture. "You know her better than any man alive, Tarja. What do you suppose she's up to?"

The Lord Defender barely hesitated before he answered. Even if nobody had asked him outright, it was obviously a puzzle to which he had given a great deal of thought. "I think she's looking for Brak."

"The Halfbreed is dead," Rorin reminded him.

Tarja frowned, his expression dark as he turned to the sorcerer. "If you knew her like I do, Lord Mariner, you'd know R'shiel would not let a minor inconvenience like death get in the way of something she wants."

And with that dire announcement, the discussion about the demon child was ended. The Lord Defender turned back to escorting Princess Marla through the Citadel, pointing out the sights as they rode.

As they passed the Temple of the Gods, Cade stared at it for a long moment, trying to recall the important information Tarja had sent him to Hythria to collect.

Something about a covenant, he thought. *Or something that was stolen?*

The memory was fleeting and he couldn't seem to pin it down.

Once they were past the temple he forgot all about it, the memory drowned out by a strange snippet of song that was suddenly stuck in his head and wouldn't go away.

Chapter

66

THE CITY BELLS were tolling midnight by the time Rakaia reached the docks. She was frantic as she ran toward the *Sarchlo*'s berth. Captain Berin had been adamant about the time he planned to sail. And she still didn't know if Mica was on board or lost somewhere in the city.

Charisee's friend had assured her Mica was no longer in the palace, but that didn't reassure her at all. He might be anywhere in the city, and there was something amiss, otherwise Charisee would not have risked tipping her off about the Harshini coming to read the minds of all the wedding guests. For that matter, whatever had happened was serious enough to get the Sorcerers' Collective involved in the first place, which didn't auger well for anyone in the city not wanting to bring themselves to the attention of the authorities.

Oh, Mica, please don't let it be something you have done.

Out of breath, a painful stitch in her side, Rakaia finally spied the *Sarchlo* getting ready to cast off.

And pacing back and forth in front of the gangplank was Mica.

Filled with relief, she called out to him. He turned and ran to her, catching her in a fierce hug, and then holding her at arm's length to check if she was all in one piece.

"What happened to you?" he asked, pale with worry. "I was frantic when I got back to the ship and found you weren't here."

"What happened to *you*?" she said. "You promised me you wouldn't go near the palace. I've been searching for you all day!"

"You two sailing with us or staying down there for a chat?" Captain Berin called down to them.

"We're coming!" Mica called back, taking her by the hand and almost dragging Rakaia with him up the perilous plank. As soon as they were aboard, two of the crew pulled the plank up after them and set about casting off.

Mica and Rakaia dodged the busy crew as they began to raise the sails and negotiate their way clear of the docks. A fresh breeze had picked up, unusual for this time of night. Not only did it offer a welcome relief from the heat, but it filled the sails quickly and pushed them away from the wharf.

Away from Greenharbour. Away from Hythria forever.

Just as I promised you, Charisee.

"I'm sorry I didn't tell you where I was going," he said, kissing her to prove how remorseful he was.

She pushed him away. "You promised you wouldn't."

"I promised I wouldn't *kill* anyone," he corrected. "And I didn't."

"Why did you go at all? Suppose someone recognized you? You didn't wear that stupid jacket into the palace did you? Everyone will remember that."

"Nobody in Hythria remembers Mikel of Kirkland," he said. "He's long dead. And I tossed the jacket in a sewer. You were right about that, too. It was silly to wear it all the time. Hot, too."

"Even so, it was an unnecessary risk," she said, not prepared to let him off quite so lightly, even if he was admitting she was right about something. "You scared the life out of me."

"I didn't mean to. It's just . . . well, it seemed like too good an opportunity to pass up. I had that letter of introduction, they were handing out gold like it was candy, we needed more coin, and . . . well, I wanted to see who you were marrying."

"You mean you wanted to see Lord Branador?"

Mica grinned. "I'm a jealous man. I thought I should check out the competition."

She hit him on the chest playfully. "You're an idiot."

"Are you sure you want to run away with me? I've seen what you're leaving behind. He's quite a catch, you know. Never seen a man drool quite so elegantly—"

"Stop it, you fool," she said, trying to stay angry with him. "It's not funny. Poor Charisee is married to that drooling old man now, thanks to me."

"Do people really think she's you? I don't think you look anything alike. I mean, she pretty enough, I suppose, but you're much prettier."

Rakaia shrugged. "People see what they want to see, I guess."

"Well, you won't have to worry about her so much now. I gave your sister a wedding present from both of us."

"What present?"

"I sang for her. Every soul who heard me sing today will never doubt that Charisee is Rakaia."

She glanced around but the crew was busy. Nobody was paying them any attention at all. "You *sang* them into believing she was me?"

He nodded, very proud of himself. "As many as I could. Whatever else befalls your sister from this day onward," he assured her, "you need not fear her being exposed as a liar will be one of them." He frowned for a moment, then, as he thought of something else. "Actually, speaking of liars, do you know something really odd? I swear, just for a moment today, I saw Jakerlon at the wedding."

That made no sense to Rakaia. "Why would the God of Lies be at Charisee's wedding?"

"Well, he wasn't at *Charisee's* wedding, was he? He was at yours. That's a pretty big lie, when you think about it. Knowing Jakerlon, he was probably just soaking up the ambience of her deception. He likes to hang around humans even more than Dacendaran. He says they lie all the time. That's why, even though he's an Incidental God and not a Primal one, he's just as old and powerful as Gimlorie and Dacendaran."

Rakaia shook her head. "I forget sometimes, until you start talking about the gods like that, what a strange life you've led."

He smiled and kissed her soundly. "Well, it is strange no more. I have you, we have a ship, and we have a whole world to explore. And I'm glad you talked me out of killing anyone to get vengeance. You were right. It wasn't going to change a thing. Do you forgive me?"

She nodded, pleased beyond words he had let go his poisonous need for revenge. He would never be truly happy while that need ate away at his soul. "Actually, I'm kind of glad you did go, Mica. Otherwise I would never have followed you and had a chance to see Charisee. I even managed to speak to her." Rakaia debated telling Mica about the circumstances of their discussion or the reason Charisee had arranged for her to flee. None it of seemed to matter now. They were safe, and in truth, she didn't know the reason anyway. Mica had kept his promise and Greenharbour was dwindling rapidly in the distance as the *Sarchlo* sailed into the night.

"Is your sister well?"

"I think she's thriving, actually," Rakaia said, now that she'd had a little more time to reflect on her discussion with Charisee. "Oh . . . and she gave me this." Rakaia dug into her pocket in her skirt and pulled out the gold coin her sister had handed her as part of the gift giving earlier in the day.

"Excellent!" Mica said. "I got one too. We're rolling in cash now. And I bought *you* a gift from the wedding, seeing as how it was like, you know . . . *your* wedding."

She laughed at that. "Gift? What gift?"

Mica grinned like a child with a secret he was bursting to tell. "A gift so precious it almost doesn't have a price. Although, at some point, we're probably going to have to name one."

"What are you taking about, Mica?"

"Wait here," he said. "I'll bring it to you." Then he kissed her again and hurried off, heading below to retrieve her gift.

Smiling at his childish enthusiasm for pleasing her, Rakaia walked across the deck to lean on the railing. The fresh wind was cool on her face, driving them on so quickly, Greenharbour was almost lost to sight already. She sighed with contentment, truly glad she was leaving the city behind. She had no real idea of where they were headed and certainly no idea of what her future might hold, but she could never remember being so happy.

Her bliss lasted for all of another minute or two before Mica returned with her gift.

"Surprise!"

Rakaia turned to see what he'd brought her.

Mica stood behind her on the deck, grinning like a fool, his hands resting on the shoulders of a tall, fair-haired lad of about eleven or twelve. "This is Little Wolf."

"I told you not to call me that," the child said. "I have a name."

"So you do, Little Wolf, so you do. Say hello to Aja."

"Hello, Aja."

"He's going to be joining our troupe. He tells me he plays the mandolin."

"*This* is your present?" she asked in shock. "Why would you buy me a slave boy?"

"I didn't buy him," Mica assured her. "He followed me home. I swear."

She glanced over her shoulder and realized they were too far out to turn back and return this child to whoever owned him. Assuming he wasn't an orphan, of course, although by the well-fed look of him and the elegant cut of his white linen shirt, he clearly had someone who looked out for him. Those hand-tooled boots he wore were not the boots of a pauper, either.

Rakaia shook her head at Mica's foolishness. He was about the same age as this lad when Brakandaran delivered him to Gimlorie. Had he found this child on the streets and decided to rescue him in some misguided attempt to save another child from the same fate?

She smiled reassuringly at the boy, who was almost as tall as she was. "Did you really follow Mica home?"

The boy nodded. "Yes, my lady."

"You don't have to call me that. Why did you follow him? Don't you have family back in Greenharbour?"

The lad shrugged. "It seemed like the right thing to do, my lady."

"You sang to him," Rakaia accused Mica, which explained the boy's unresisting demeanor. "He didn't follow you at all. You ensorcelled him."

Mica grinned at her unrepentantly. "But he's here now," he said. "And trust me, his family don't deserve him."

"How do you know that?"

"Because this is Jazrian Wolfblade," Mica told her. "And when Adrina and Damin have suffered enough with the pain of losing their precious eldest child, they can pay us handsomely for his return. So you see . . . it's just as I promised. It's a good revenge, don't you think? Maybe even *better* than killing someone. "

Her mind was suddenly blank and she felt sick to her stomach. Rakaia didn't know what to say. She glanced around, but none of the crew was taking any notice of them. It was impossible to tell if that was because they genuinely weren't interested or Mica had sung them into compliance as well.

Rakaia found herself confronted with a stark choice and little time in which to make a decision.

She could fight Mica on this or go along with it.

Fighting him would be pointless. If she tried, he would just sing to her until she agreed with him, and then she would lose more than just the argument. She would lose her free will and become a puppet dancing to Mica's enchanted song, just like all the others she'd seen him sing into submission.

Or she could play along with this insanity, and the first chance she got once they reached the Trinity Isles, she could find a way to send Jazrian home.

Assuming they made it to the Trinity Isles. The Wolfblades were a powerful family and Mica hadn't just taken vengeance on Adrina and Damin.

He'd kidnapped the crown prince of Hythria.

Surely the Hythrun would bring every resource at their disposal to bear to recover him, including the Harshini and all the magic they could bring to the search. The Harshini could call on the gods, for that matter.

How did one hide from a god?

Mica's foolishness meant they were living on borrowed time at best, so it wasn't much of a decision at all, really.

She smiled at Mica and nodded her approval. "It's better than good," she lied. "It's inspired."

He beamed at her. Relieved, happy, and trusting.

Rakaia held out her hand to Jazrian. "As for you, young man, let's find you something to wear that's a little less obvious. Then I suggest we all try to get some sleep because tomorrow is going to be the start of a whole new adventure for all of us."

The lad nodded, still under the influence of Mica's song, probably the only thing saving him from blind panic.

For his part, Mica just stood there, happier than she'd ever seen him, fingering the small golden lyre he wore on a chain around his neck, apparently oblivious to the consequences of his need to even the score against Adrina and her family—a woman he had once admired and adored.

There was a lesson in that, Rakaia realized with a small stab of fear as she headed below with Jazrian Wolfblade to find him somewhere to sleep.

She would do well to remember what Mica was capable of when he felt he had been betrayed by a woman he loved.

"NOBODY REMEMBERS SEEING anything," Kiam told Adrina in the small hours of the night, once they'd looked into the minds of every guest at the wedding. Not surprisingly, nobody had opted for being interrogated by the Assassins' Guild, so he'd had little to do but stand by, look threatening, and watch the Harshini work. "At least, they haven't found anything so far. Glenanaran said he'd send word if he found anything."

It was almost dawn. Nobody had slept. Adrina was pale and distraught, the mother in her devastated by the loss of her son. The High Princess in her was faring marginally better, and the only thing, Kiam suspected, preventing her from falling apart completely. Broos must have sensed her distress, as he padded silently to her side and laid his head in her lap. Without thinking, she smiled faintly at his audacity and began to stroke the dog.

The whole family had gathered in the main hall. Every adult member of the Wolfblade clan currently resident in Greenharbour was here—Rodja and Selena Tirstone, their son, Eyvan. Rodja's younger brother, Adham, Luciena Taranger and her husband, Xanda. Darvad Vintner, his wife Rielle and their eldest son, Andrue, Kalan Hawksword and her daughter, Julika, who'd been an attendant at Rakaia's wedding.

Every one of them ready to do whatever it took to find Jaz and bring him home.

Although it was the early hours of the morning, Kiam walked in on a discussion that had been going on for quite a while, he gathered. Everyone wanted to help and there were already maps of the city being laid out on the temporary table Darvad had arranged to be installed, in preparation for a much more detailed search of the city. Gaffen was already out, combing the streets around the palace, and he was fairly sure by now the Thieves' Guild would be looking for the missing prince, too.

The Assassins' Guild hadn't offered to help in the search directly, but Elin had released Kiam from any other guild business until the young prince was found. He also hinted that he would turn a blind eye if Kiam found the people involved and took it upon himself to undertake any un-contracted kills necessary to take care of the miscreants who dared to harm their prince.

The problem was that nobody knew where to start looking.

Rodja Tirstone rubbed his temples tiredly and looked at Adrina. "I know we discussed this already, but is there *any* chance Jaz ran off of his own accord? I mean, we used to do that sort of thing with Damin, Narvell, and Kalan all the time when we were kids in Krakandar. It was a game, giving our guards the slip."

Adrina shook her head. "Not Jazrian. Marlie would do something like that in a heartbeat, but Jaz is much more sensible."

"Then if we've ruled out a prank, someone has taken him or killed him," Luciena Taranger concluded. Her husband, Xanda, was standing behind her. He must have said something to her because she looked up at him crossly, saying, "I'm sorry you don't like me being so blunt, Xanda, but time is of the essence here. I'm sure Adrina would rather we stated the problem and started working on how to fix it than beat about the bush being diplomatic so we don't hurt her tender feelings." She turned back to Adrina. "Have you closed the port?"

Darvad answered her question. "Just after midnight," he assured her. "We're lucky, really, that a Fardohnyan wedding feast meant most of the ships' captains in port decided not to fight the inevitable and they delayed their departure until their crews sobered up."

"Most?" Xanda asked.

"I believe a couple of ships left port on last night's high tide, but there won't be many of them."

"I'll find out from the harbor master which ships they were and where they were headed," Luciena promised. "I'll contact my shipping agents by bird in whatever ports they're headed for and arrange for them to be met and searched when they arrive."

The door opened again and Wrayan Lightfinger walked in. His expression was grim. Although he wasn't strictly family, he was close enough to be included in this war council, and besides, even more than Kalan, who was High Arrion of the Sorcerers' Collective, the head of the Thieves' Guild had a direct channel to the gods.

Adrina looked up at him hopefully. "Have you spoken to Dacendaran?"

Wrayan shook his head. "I tried, but he's not answering me."

"Not surprising, really," Adham said. "And it may be a good sign."

"How can you say it's a good sign, Uncle Adham?" Andrue asked. He was just twenty and apparently not in the least awed by being included in this powerful company.

"Because it might mean Jaz has been stolen, rather than killed," Adham said. He turned to Wrayan. "That's a possibility, isn't it?"

The wraith nodded. "If Jaz has been killed, Dace would be blaming Zegarnald and bitching about it to anyone who'll listen to him. If he's not answering, it could well be that he just doesn't want to answer any awkward questions."

Adham looked at Kalan. "Have you asked the Harshini to speak to the gods?"

"Of course I did," she snapped, as if he was a fool for asking something so obvious. "It was the first thing I asked them to do."

"And?"

"They said we won't find him by looking for him."

"What did you say?" Wrayan asked with a frown.

"That's exactly what the Harshini told me, Wrayan, and I gather they were able to get at least some of the gods to answer them. *You won't find him by looking for him.*"

"That's what Dace said about the lyre missing from the Citadel. *Exactly* what he said. *You won't find it by looking for it.*"

"Do you think the two are connected?" Adrina was still unconsciously patting Broos, as if he gave her some small measure of comfort.

Kiam couldn't imagine how they might be connected, but who knew how the gods worked?

Luciena shook her head. "Gods, I hope not."

"I still don't get how they could be, " Julika said.

"One could argue," Kalan explained to her daughter, "that if Jaz has been kidnapped and this stolen token from the Citadel is important as the Medalonians would like us to believe, then right now, the God of Thieves is basking in the two greatest thefts to happen in a generation. I'm not surprised he doesn't want to talk to mere mortals like us."

"Then what do we do?" Adrina asked. "My son is out there somewhere, on his own, alone, afraid—"

"I doubt he's afraid," Kiam told her. "He's a tough little nut."

"He's eleven, Ky," Luciena reminded him. "Of course he's afraid."

Before Kiam could answer that, the door opened again and this time it was Gaffen who strode into the room, followed by the Harshini, Glenanaran, who had been leading the search of the wedding guests' thoughts. The Warlord's expression was thunderous as he walked up to the table and tossed two jackets onto it. They were filthy and reeked of shit. Even Glenanaran looked serious, which was alarming for someone who, as a rule, never stopped smiling.

One of the jackets Kiam recognized as the white embroidered jacket Jazrian had worn—under protest—to the wedding. The other was sodden and covered in grime, but it was unmistakably the distinct red jacket of a Medalonian officer.

Adrina rose to her feet, pale as Jazrian's jacket. "Where did you find them?"

"Stuffed behind a pipe in a sewer two streets from the palace. I've had men searching the tunnels since Jaz went missing."

Adrina stared at the jackets for a long time. Nobody else said a word.

"Do you have any useful information to add to this, Glenanaran?"

"Sadly not, your highness," the Harshini said. "We've scanned nearly all the guests, and other than many of them having the same tune stuck in their minds, there was nothing untoward or anything relating to Prince Jazrian in their thoughts."

"What song?" Kalan asked. "Do you mean the same song as the assassin who tried to kill Damin?"

"No, my lady. This was much less . . . influential. It was a snippet, really. Not much more than a half-forgotten memory, and certainly didn't affect any of the palace staff. Just some of the guests. I mention it only because it seemed odd, not because it offers any insight as to Prince Jazrian's whereabouts."

Adrina frowned. She seemed to have come to a decision. "Can you get a message to the Citadel for me, Glenanaran, via the Seeing Stone?"

The Harshini nodded. "Of course. I'll send it straight away, myself."

"The message is for the Princess Marla. Please inform her about what has happened to her grandson."

"As you wish, your highness." The Harshini bowed and turned for the door.

"Once you've done that," she called after him, "please ask her to inform the Lord Defender that unless the Medalonians who have taken the crown prince return him immediately, she is no longer authorized to negotiate peace."

The Harshini turned and stared at her blankly. "I'm sorry, your highness, I don't understand."

"It's quite simple, Glenanaran. If Jazrian isn't returned to us unharmed by the end of the week, I want you to tell Marla she has my full authority to declare war."

THE MEETING BROKE up around dawn. By then everyone who could do anything to help locate Jazrian was given a task to do. Kiam's task was to seek the help of the Assassins' Guild—whether officially or unofficially—and bring their considerable network of spies and informants to bear.

Kiam didn't doubt Elin Bane would offer his assistance. Keeping the guild in business was as much about politics as it was about killing. Being owed favors by powerful people in positions of real influence went a long way to securing the guild's future.

He glanced up at the sky as he let himself out of the palace doors and stepped onto the broad landing at the top of the palace steps. The morning was cool, the real heat of the day some way off. Broos bolted out of the door beside him, ran straight over to one of the large marble planters, and cocked his leg.

Kiam smiled. Poor beast had been inside for the better part of the night. Then he glanced around to make certain the palace seneschal was nowhere in sight or he'd be handing Kiam a bucket and a scrubbing brush, insisting he clean it up himself.

As soon as he was done, Broos ran to the steps and bounded down them, barking madly, the noise echoing off the palace walls in the silence of the early morning so loudly Kiam cringed. The fool dog was going to wake everyone in the palace, and Adrina had probably only just gone to bed. Kiam called him to heel, but the dog ignored him and disappeared from sight down the steps. He hurried after him, wondering if Broos had spied a cat, and that was what had riled him, but as soon as he reached the edge of the steps, he discovered why Broos was so excited.

There was a carriage parked in the forecourt. Old Lord Branador was being lifted inside by his son, Braun, as their slaves loaded Princess Rakaia's luggage onto the roof. Olivah was standing there, not helping his father at all, and beside him stood Rakaia, dressed in a dark blue gown, a fur coat in her arms, no doubt in preparation for her journey into the snowy mountains around Highcastle. She didn't look happy to be traveling. She had a resigned, almost melancholy expression on her face.

Her face lit up as soon she heard Broos. He ran up to her as she squatted down to hug him, and he slobbered all over her face.

Olivah was pushed aside in his haste. He staggered a few steps and then raised his boot to kick Broos out of the way.

"Only if you want to lose that leg, Olivah," Kiam told him. He'd moved down the steps with all the speed and silence of an assassin and his sudden appearance behind the young man made him jump with fright.

"Dear gods!" he exclaimed. "Don't sneak up on a man like that, Kiam!"

"I don't," he said, and then turned to Rakaia and bowed. "Good morning, your highness."

She stood up, unable to hide her smile. He figured she was smiling because Broos had greeted her so enthusiastically.

What other reason could there be?

"Master Miar! I missed you!" she said, and then she added, almost as an afterthought. "At the wedding, I mean."

"I was otherwise engaged, I'm afraid."

Braun had finished settling his father in the carriage. He stepped back down and turned to Kiam with a frown. "Any news?"

He shook his head. "I'm afraid not."

"It's the reason we're leaving so early," Braun explained. "We need to get back to the border. I've already sent word on ahead, but I need to be at home. It won't be across my border that someone takes Jazrian."

Kiam was sure Braun Branador meant every word. For all that he was a brute, the Branadors were family. Nobody was taking Jazrian's disappearance lightly.

Except Olivah, perhaps, who snorted impatiently, "Stupid kid's probably just run off to play with the street urchins and is going to turn up at lunchtime, covered in dirt, wondering what all the fuss is about."

"I noticed you haven't offered to stay behind and help look for Prince Jazrian, Olivah," Kiam remarked.

"I'm needed on the border."

"Sure you are," Kiam said, and then he ignored Olivah and turned back to Rakaia. "I trust you'll have a pleasant journey to Highcastle, your highness."

"I'm sure I will," she said with a vast lack of enthusiasm.

"How can she not, with me for company?" Olivah chimed in from behind. "I'm sure *Granny* and I are going to be firm friends by the time we get home."

Kiam was a trained assassin. He'd spent years learning patience, mental discipline powerful enough to resist a Harshini mind scan, and, most of all, how to keep his temper.

Right at that moment, he was prepared to ignore everything he'd ever learned for the momentary pleasure of punching Olivah Branador in the face.

He clenched his fist by his side but didn't turn around. That would be too much temptation.

Rakaia smiled faintly at him, as if she knew the internal battle he was waging. Then she bent down to kiss Broos goodbye. "I shall miss you so much," she said, although Kiam wasn't entirely certain she was talking to the dog. "You made my trip here bearable."

"Why don't you take him with you then?" Kiam said almost before he realized what he was saying.

She looked up at him in shock. "Are you serious?"

"Of course he isn't serious," Olivah said. "That thing is a beast! I hate dogs, anyway."

That decided it. Kiam nodded. "I mean it. The Raven has been at me to find him another home, and you're the only other person he's ever really taken to. I'd be honored if you'd take him."

"No! You can't! Father, tell her she can't have that beast. For one thing, it will never fit in the carriage with us!"

Braun didn't seem to care. "What's this *us* business, lad? We're riding on ahead, Ollie. In case you've forgotten, we have a border to secure. I'm not going to wait on the traveling pace of an old man and a fussy girl. Gods, lad, where do you get the idea you would be traveling with your grandfather all the way home in a carriage?"

"Yes, Ollie," Kiam asked. "Where did you get that idea?"

Olivah shot him a venomous look and then strode off to untie his mount from the back of the second wagon where Rakaia's new maid, Tazi, another much younger female slave, and a handsome, fine-boned man wearing the jeweled collar of a *loronged court'esa* sat among the other supplies and wedding gifts the Branadors had acquired since arriving in the city.

"Do you mind, Braun?" Rakaia asked her stepson. She had quickly deduced, Kiam could see, where the power lay in her new family.

"Do whatever you want," he said with a shrug. He would have been hard pressed to show less interest. "Just don't let it shit inside."

"He's house trained," Kiam promised. "Just ask the palace seneschal."

Braun grunted something and moved away, yelling at the slaves loading the carriage roof to move one of the trunks or they'd tip the damn thing over.

Rakaia smiled at Kiam. "'Thank you' seems inadequate."

"I should be thanking you for taking him."

She was looking at him with such intensity he suddenly felt the need to break away from her hypnotic gaze before he did something extremely foolish, so he squatted down and took Broos's velvety ears in his hands and looked into the dog's trusting eyes instead. "You take care of her, you hear? Don't let anybody hurt your new mistress."

Broos licked his face in reply, which make Rakaia laugh. He stood up again, wiping away the dog slobber. Whatever had happened between them a moment ago, Broos had ruined it. *Thank the gods.*

"I will take the best care of him," she promised.

"I know you will."

"You could come and visit him sometime. If you wanted to."

Kiam nodded. "As soon as Jaz is safe and sound, I'll be there."

Braun came back around the carriage before Rakaia could reply. "Come on, then, lass," he said. "The sun's almost all the way up. Get your arse aboard, and the beast, too, if he's coming."

Kiam offered her his hand and helped her up into the carriage, where Frederak was already softly snoring, his head resting on the window pillar. Broos jumped in after her as if he knew what Kiam had asked of him and was happy to obey.

With some reluctance, he let go of Rakaia's hand as she settled in beside Frederak.

"Will you give Adrina and the children my love?" she asked. "And tell her I'll pray to the gods every day that Jaz is found soon, and brought home safely?"

"I will."

He stepped back and closed the door. Almost immediately Braun gave the order to move off and the small caravan turned toward the palace gate.

Kiam watched them leave, telling himself the only reason he felt like a part of him was being ripped from him was because he'd just given away his dog.

It was a lie, but he wasn't prepared to admit the truth, even to himself, so he waited until the Branador caravan was gone from sight completely before he headed for the gate himself.

It was time to speak to Elin Bane. He needed to find out if the Raven of the Assassins' Guild had any idea who had kidnapped the crown prince of Hythria before they were plunged into war.

Epilogue

"YOU'RE LATE," ELIN said as the assassin let himself into his office. He turned from watching the empty courtyard below, already set up to test their next batch of hopefuls. It was past midnight and he wanted to get some sleep before tomorrow's recruitment began.

"Sorry," the young man said. "I'll try better next time."

"Don't you take that tone with me, lad."

"Then I'm not sorry. Why did you ask me here at this hour?"

"I have a job for you," Elin said, indicating the assassin should take a seat and he took his own seat behind the desk.

"And you couldn't tell me about it during daylight hours?"

"It's something of a . . . delicate matter," Elin said. "It requires more discretion than our normal contracts." He took a key from the chain around his neck and unlocked his desk drawer to retrieve a single, folder piece of paper. "It's a commission, actually, from the Fardohnyan guild."

"Since when do we do their dirty work?"

"As a matter of professional courtesy, we often do their dirty work, just as they will do ours when the need arises."

He slid the paper across the desk. The assassin picked it up and unfolded it, reading the name written there with no visible reaction. He considered it for a moment and then slid the paper back to Elin.

"I thought we didn't do royalty?"

"We don't," Elin agreed. "Turns out this one isn't royal at all. She's a bastard, passed off by her mother as a princess."

"And now Hablet wants his revenge."

Elin nodded. "Glad you understand."

"Are you sure you want me to do this?"

"Yes."

"Wouldn't—"

"No."

The assassin shrugged. "Where is she now?"

"On her way to Highcastle, I imagine."

The young man nodded and climbed to his feet. That was one of the things Elin liked about this man. He didn't argue or ask for reasons. He just got the job done.

He was at the door before Elin remembered the other instruction he had regarding this job. "Oh, one other thing, Arex. It has to look like an accident."

The White Fox nodded. "Of course."

And then he was gone.

Elin leaned back in his seat, relieved the job was assigned. He muttered a prayer to Zegarnald to ensure a successful kill, and then added a heartfelt plea at the end of his prayer that Kiam Miar would remain so distracted by the search for Prince Jazrian that he never found out about it.

Glossary

MEDALON

CADEN FLETCHER—Captain in the Defenders. Aide to the Lord Defender of Medalon.

GARET WARNER—Commandant of the Defenders. Head of Defender Intelligence and second most senior officer in the Defenders.

MANDAH RODAK TENRAGAN—Formerly a novice and now a pagan. Rebel from Medalon. Elder sister of Ghari. Wife of Tarja Tenragan.

TARJA TENRAGAN—Tarjanian Tenragan. Lord Defender of Medalon.

HARSHINI

BARANDANAN—Harshini healer from the Greenharbour Sorcerers' Collective.

BELENDARA—Harshini ambassador to the Fardohnyan court.

BRAK—Lord Brakandaran té Carn. Also known as the Halfbreed. Died helping the demon child in a confrontation with Xaphista the Overlord.

DRANYMIRE—Prime demon bonded to the house of té Ortyn.

KORANDELLAN TÉ ORTYN—Deceased. Last king of the Harshini. Nephew of Lorandranek and brother of Shananara.

LORANDRANEK TÉ ORTYN—Deceased. Former king of the Harshini, driven mad by the task laid on him by the gods.

R'SHIEL TÉ ORTYN—Daughter of J'nel Snowbuilder and Lorandranek, king of the Harshini. The demon child.

SHANANARA—Her Royal Highness, Shananara té Ortyn. Daughter of Rorandelan. Sister of Korandellan. Queen of the Harshini.

TELENARA—Harshini healer from the Greenharbour Sorcerers' Collective.

YANANARA—Horse master to the High Prince of Hythria.

The Gods

BREHN—God of Storms.

CHELTARAN—God of Healing.

DACENDARAN—God of Thieves.

GIMLORIE—God of Music.

JASHIA—God of Fire.

JAKERLON—God of Liars.

JELANNA—Goddess of Fertility.

JONDALUP—God of Chance.

KAELARN—God of the Oceans.

KALIANAH—Goddess of Love.

LEYLANAN—Goddess of the Ironbrook River.

MAERA—Goddess of the Glass River.

PATANAN—God of Good Fortune.

VODEN—God of Green Life.

ZEGARNALD—God of War.

Hythria

ADRINA WOLFBLADE—Princess of Fardohnya. High Princess of Hythria. Eldest legitimate daughter of King Hablet. Married to Damin Wolfblade.

DAMIN WOLFBLADE—High Prince of Hythria. Son of Princess Marla and Laran Krakenshield. Married to Adrina. Father to Jazrian, Marlie, Kimarie, and Tristan.

ELIN BANE—Raven. Head of the Hythrun Assassins' Guild.

FREDERAK BRANADOR—Lord of Highcastle.

JULIKA HAWKSWORD—Daughter of Kalan Hawksword. Apprentice at the Sorcerers' Collective.

KALAN HAWKSWORD—High Arrion of the Sorcerers' Collective in Hythria. Damin Wolfblade's half-sister, also known as Kalan of Elasapine. She has a twin brother, Narvell Hawksword.

LERNEN WOLFBLADE—Former High Prince of Hythria. Damin's uncle.

MARLA WOLFBLADE—Princess of Hythria. Sister of Lernen Wolfblade and mother of Damin. Married five times, she is also the mother of Kalan and Narvell Hawksword of Elasapine.

RORIN MARINER—Lower Arrion of the Sorcerers' Collective. Cousin of Luciena Mariner.

KARIEN

JAYMES OF KIRKLAND—Karien page attached to Lord Laetho's retinue during the Karien-Medalon war. Now a Raider in Hythria. Brother to Mikel.

MIKEL OF KIRKLAND—Karien page attached to Lord Laetho's retinue. Jaymes's younger brother. Appointed as Adrina's page following his escape from Medalon. Ordered to be executed by Damin Wolfblade for attempting to poison the demon child. Also known as Mica.

XAPHISTA—The Overlord. God of the Kariens. Destroyed by the demon child.

FARDOHNYA

ALARIC—Crown prince of Fardohnya.

HABLET—King of the Fardohnyans. Has countless illegitimate children and thirteen legitimate daughters. His heir is Alaric, his only legitimate son.

NAVEEN RAVEVE—Chamberlain of the Fardohnyan court. Naveen is a former *court'esa* who makes his fortune collecting bribes.

MEYRICK KABAR—General of the Fardohnyan army. Former captain of the harem guard in Talabar.

CHARISEE—Fardohnyan slave raised to serve Princess Rakaia. One of Hablet's illegitimate daughters.

RAKAIA—Princess of Fardohnya. One of Hablet's legitimate daughters sent to Hythria to marry Lord Frederak Branador.